The Stuff We're Made Of

The Stuff We're Made Of

Linda D. Whitlock

Library of Congress Control Number:		2011904634
ISBN:	Hardcover	978-1-4568-9178-7
	Softcover	978-1-4568-9177-0
	Ebook	978-1-4568-9179-4

To order additional copies of this book, contact:
Xlibris Corporation
1-888-795-4274
www.Xlibris.com
Orders@Xlibris.com
83539

CONTENTS

Dedication

"To God who makes all things possible."
I graciously dedicate my very first novel to my wonderful husband, Delvin, and my three beautiful sons, Delvin II, Blair, and Justice, and I thank God for all the blessings he has bestowed upon me and my family.

To my wonderful husband of twenty-six years and my best friend, Delvin, I dedicate my first novel to you. You have been the best husband and best friend that I could ever hope for and a tremendous blessing in my life. I know that I could not do any of this without your unwavering love and support. You have been there for me throughout my journey since the very first day we met, and I thank you from the bottom of my heart for everything you've done throughout the years to help me reach this point in my life. I love you, and I look forward to spending many more years together with you.

To my dearest sons, Delvin II, Blair, and Justice, you have been the absolute best sons a mother could ever hope for and a blessing. I am so truly blessed to see each of you grow and blossom into the wonderful young men we have raised you to be. You inspire me every day to be the best that I can be, and I move forward to fulfill my dreams as an example for the three of you to go forth in your lives and fulfill your own dreams as well. You give me strength and hope, and I am so proud to be your mother and to be here to see you all grow and mature into young adults. I love you all, and I look forward to sharing with you all the great things that life has in store for each of you.

PROLOGUE

TWO WEEKS AGO

*I*t was 7:00 a.m., and Helena Barnes, the president and founder of Helena Interior Designs, Inc., was about to have a private meeting with Kameron Tyndall, a senior designer with the firm, before the rest of the design staff arrived into work. Kameron was surprised Helena requested a meeting with her so early in the morning since they normally arrived for work at 9:00 a.m., but she was intrigued by what Helena had to say. She had been with Helena's for nearly three years, and she wasn't the least bit pleased about the Edwards project, the biggest account the firm had landed to date, being assigned to the newest designer, Lydia Brown. Kameron did not know of Lydia's qualifications for the job, nor did she care. All she knew was that when Helena hired her, they developed a mutual understanding. Helena would assign Kameron the huge accounts that guaranteed the huge commissions, and in turn, she would continue to receive new business opportunities through her father's business connections. Helena had lived up to her end of the bargain until the day she gave the Edwards account to Lydia. As far as Kameron was concerned, that was a mistake on Helena's part, a mistake she'd better correct quickly if she didn't want their arrangement to turn ugly. But she was pleased that Helena had requested a private meeting with her because she was about to do the same. This little situation needed to be rectified immediately because all Kameron had to do was make a little

9

call to her father, who happened to be the mayor of the city of Atlanta, and any upcoming projects for Helena would cease. *Two could play that game*, thought Kameron as she settled into her seat in Helena's office.

"Kameron, thanks for coming in so early this morning," said Helena as she poured herself a cup of freshly brewed coffee. "I have a matter I want to speak to you about privately. Would you like some coffee?"

"No thanks," said Kameron. "To tell you the truth, Helena, I have something I'd like to speak with you about. But what's on your mind?"

"I'm going to be making some changes here at Helena Designs, and since you're the senior designer, I want you to be an intricate part of the change."

"Well, in that case, we should talk about the Edwards account and why it wasn't assigned to me per our agreement about projects of that magnitude."

"I'm glad you brought that up," Helena interrupted, "because I want to talk specifically about the Edwards account. I know that you want it, and up until this time, Lydia has done a good job with it. But now it's at a point where there will be more visibility for this firm, and although Lydia can be credited for getting it off the ground and doing all the leg work, the full credit for the account should go to someone who represents the face of Helena Interior Designs and the interest of this firm, and I don't see Lydia Brown being that person."

Kameron was intrigued so far by what Helena appeared to be suggesting, but she needed some answers quickly. After all, a deal is a deal, and Helena had broken her promise with this latest account.

"Then why did you assign the account to her in the first place when we have an arrangement?"

"I'm quite aware of our arrangement, and I will continue to honor it. But Lydia has a very diverse background. She could have her pick of any design firm she wanted, so I needed leverage at the time for her to agree to come on board."

"So what are you saying? What does all of this have to do with me now?"

At this point, Helena was a little annoyed. Kameron wasn't the brightest bulb in the package, and in reality, she was nowhere near as talented or creative an interior designer as Lydia. In fact, if it wasn't for her father, Mayor Ronald Tyndall, Helena doubted very seriously if she would have even considered Kameron for employment. Her experience was limited to a few projects that had been thrown her way by her dear daddy, and since she had been with her firm, her work proved to be mediocre at best. However, Helena was willing to sacrifice a few projects to gain the type of clientele that could propel her company forward in Atlanta. Besides, Kameron had that certain look going for her that appealed to clients, and she had the right connections that Helena wanted for the firm. Where Kameron was lacking in talent and intellect, she more than made up for in physical features. She was once a runner-up in the Miss Georgia Beauty Pageant and took pride in her shoulder-length blond hair, blue eyes, and perky twenty-five-year-old breasts. Plus the fact that she was the mayor's only daughter who wanted for nothing was an added bonus. So in Helena's mind, this change had to happen. This was a business decision, and that was the name of the game, Helena told herself.

"In a couple of weeks, the Edwards account will be at phase 3 in progression, which means that we will begin the actual design phase of the project. Because of the project's size and scale, we're already receiving media attention. Imagine the attention we'll receive when the public realizes that the mayor's daughter is connected to this project. That's why I want Helena Designs to project a certain 'image' to the public, and that is why when phase 3 begins, you will become the new designer on the project."

"What about the Rhodes account? That will be starting up soon. It's nowhere near the size of the Edwards account, but still, I can't handle both projects at once."

"Nor do I expect you to, dear. The Rhodes project will be transferred to Lydia. You two will do a swap of sorts, and the change will be effective two weeks from today. Everything has been planned."

"Not that I'm questioning your decision, because I totally agree with it, but I know Lydia is not going to like this. She seems pretty attached to the Edwards project."

"Lydia won't have a choice in the matter. She may be resistant to the change at first, but I'm sure she'll go along with the program. As you are well aware, changes are inevitable in life. If Lydia hasn't learned this life lesson yet, she will soon."

Kameron smiled an almost evil grin. When Helena made the comment about how changes are inevitable in life, she knew what she was referring to. Kameron's father, Mayor Tyndall, had been in office for nine months and, during his bid for mayor, had run a very dirty and questionable campaign against the city's incumbent, Mayor Casey Fuller. Tyndall's campaign was based on mudslinging campaign ads, uncovering alleged improprieties, and erecting skeletons from Mayor Fuller's past. Damaging secrets that had been very well hidden in the past were suddenly exposed, and although Mayor Fuller tried to run a clean campaign that focused on the issues the city was facing, he couldn't overcome a very damaging fact that came to light through his opponent's obsessive digging. This fact nearly destroyed his reputation and threatened his marriage of twenty-seven years. It was uncovered that the mayor had a mistress living in one of his many upscale apartments for several years while in office. It was a revelation that rocked the city for weeks and pretty much guaranteed her father's victory. When it came to playing dirty, no one did it better than the Tyndalls. Kameron smiled to herself in deep thought; she liked Helena's thinking with this situation, not to mention the fact that the project was going to do wonders for her career. Lydia had done all the hard work and laid the groundwork. Now all she had to do was gather up Lydia's design details and put them into action. The plan was perfect as far as Kameron was concerned.

"Well, I appreciate this opportunity, and I won't let you down," said Kameron.

"That's fine, dear. Now of course, this is strictly between you and me. I want you to get acquainted with the project as much as possible. My plan is to have you transition in two weeks while Lydia walks you through phases 3 and 4 of the project. It should be a smooth transition, and I'm sure you're going to enjoy working with Kyle Edwards."

"That sounds good to me. When will you tell Lydia?" Kameron said, smiling and getting up from the chair.

"Soon. She'll find out soon enough. Don't worry about that."

*   *   *

It was now 8:45 a.m., and like every morning since Lydia started working at Helena's, she walked in like clockwork with a grande-size Starbucks cafe mocha coffee in hand. It was going to be a very busy day, Lydia thought as she sat down at her workstation to check her agenda for the day. The entire day was filled with one meeting after another, with Kyle Edwards on the Edwards account that she had been working countless hours on for several weeks. Today they had to go over some last-minute changes, and Lydia enjoyed walking the client through the entire design once more before work actually began. The work, time, and effort put into this project had been exhausting, but in two more weeks, all of her hard work was going to pay off because the actual design phase would begin. The drawings, the materials, the furniture, and all the accessories had finally been purchased, ordered, and approved by Mr. Edwards himself. Now Lydia was at the stage that really gave her a thrill, actually seeing her design proposal come to life.

Lydia took a sip of her café mocha coffee and glanced up to notice Helena and Kameron in conversation as they exited Helena's office. She wondered what those two were up to now. They always seemed to be behind closed doors about something, and that usually wasn't a good sign for the rest of the team. It was funny to Lydia how Helena didn't seem to care how her favoritism toward Kameron was so obvious to the rest of the office. Everyone was well aware that Kameron was Mayor Tyndall's daughter and how Helena threw work her way because of it. A couple of the designers complained that Kameron always received the better projects although her work did not reflect the experience those projects or clients needed. But Lydia knew those assignments were simply about Helena kissing the daughter of the mayor's ass and nothing more, although Lydia was thrilled when she assigned her the Edwards project. Maybe Helena knew real talent when she saw it after all. Lydia had been working for Helena for about a year now and had gotten her feet wet on some interesting projects involving bathroom and kitchen redesigns. But the Edwards project of redesigning an old outdated motel into a lavish luxury hotel and restaurant was right up her alley, and she thought she'd be able to showcase her talents even more. It was a beautiful project, and Lydia absolutely loved period interior design, which she considered one of her specialties. Kyle Edwards purchased and restored the exterior of an old hotel, which was built in the late 1960s, using one of Atlanta's finest restoration builders, JD Builders and Associates, and then contracted Helena Designs to design and decorate the interior of the hotel. Lydia was thrilled when Helena asked her to be the lead designer on the project and she knew that Lydia was more than capable of handling the project. After all, it was Helena who offered Lydia a job with her firm practically on the spot after seeing the total renovation of a loft she'd done for a mutual friend. Although Helena's was a small design company and Lydia had been considering some other design firms that were larger and more prestigious, she decided it was the right fit, and Helena promised to give her future projects that would diversify her portfolio. So Lydia began work almost immediately.

After thumbing through her agenda and calendar of events for the day, Lydia pulled out her notepad to get ready for her first meeting of the day. Kyle Edwards had proven to be a bit difficult to work with and to please, but Lydia had experience working with difficult people in the past. So although he tried, he didn't pose too much of a challenge, much to Lydia's relief. Lydia had learned early on with her dealings with him to always have her ducks in line, take very good notes, and to try to anticipate any questions he may have. This philosophy had saved her behind on more than one occasion, like the day he decided the color of the furniture they all agreed on previously was all wrong and that he never agreed to such a thing. Lydia calmly pulled out her notes and pointed to his initials, which indicated his concurrence with the decision. He was just that type of client, a little on the arrogant side, with selective memory.

At 10:00 a.m., Kyle Edwards walked into Helena's with his assistant, Monica, in tow, talking on her cell phone, confirming his flight to Miami later in the day. Lydia escorted them into their conference room and offered them both some coffee, for which they both declined.

"Well, thank you both for coming in this morning," said Lydia. "We're about two weeks away from the actual design, so I wanted to go over the details once more to make sure there haven't been any changes, or if there are, we can discuss them now." Lydia dimmed the lights in the conference room and turned on the overhead projector that showed each room in its entirety designed as she had proposed and with completed changes as they had all agreed. Helena peeked in just as Lydia was beginning the presentation.

"Good morning, Mr. Edwards. Monica."

"Good morning," Kyle and Monica said in unison.

"I see you're going over your design again before the work begins. This is exciting stuff."

"Yes, we are, and it certainly is," said Kyle.

"Well, I know that Lydia has it all under control, so I'll leave you to it. I just wanted to say hello."

"Thank you, Helena. We're looking forward to all of this coming together. Good to see you." Helena smiled and gave Lydia a nod to continue with the presentation.

"Lydia, there are some changes I would like to discuss with you as far as the seating area for our dining rooms and the chairs we selected for the reception area."

"Okay, that's fine. Let's take a look at what we have," Lydia said as she scrolled through the frames.

"Monica, do you have my notes?" Monica reached for her notepad and pulled out what appeared to be a laundry list of notes.

"We're looking at several changes, Lydia. There were some questions concerning the color scheme in a couple of the rooms as well as the furniture," said Monica.

"In which rooms exactly?" Lydia asked.

"All of them," said Kyle sternly.

At this point Lydia wanted to take her pointer and stick it in Kyle where the sun didn't shine, but she knew that wasn't the way to handle a client of a multimillion dollar project. She knew there would be some changes—there always were—but these suggestions sounded like several rooms would have to be changed if the color scheme and furniture were now being questioned. Lydia had a lot of patience with this client, but this was an area that they had beaten to death, and she wasn't looking forward to another round.

"What is the problem with the color? I thought everyone was in agreement," asked Lydia.

"We've changed our minds and now believe this color would be better suited." Monica pulled out a color sample from her briefcase. It was a soft green, a nice color, but would completely throw off the balance and light textures of the rest of the rooms.

"Mr. Edwards, this may require a complete change of the suites, plus we've already ordered some of the furniture."

"No, we're not going to completely change the rooms, we just want this color to be dominant."

"That's exactly what I mean. In order for it to be a dominant color, there may have to be some changes."

"Well, the changes shouldn't be anything major. I'm counting on your expertise to make this work with very little other changes. Can you do that?"

"Of course."

"Good. Now let's look at the furniture for the dining rooms. We've decided to go with something totally different, and we've brought along a catalog to give you an idea of where we're going with this." Monica pulled out a catalog that displayed all types of decorative furniture.

"We want this furniture instead. I think it will complement the entranceway more. What do you think?" Lydia took the catalog and began writing notes on the changes they wanted to be made. These next two weeks weren't going to go as smoothly as she had originally hoped, and neither was the rest of the day.

"Okay, let's look at incorporating this furniture. Maybe a change of pillows will pull in the color, or maybe we could use this new soft green to pull in the color of this furniture."

"I like that idea," said Kyle. "Now let's move on to the lighting fixtures."

Lydia resolved that this was going to be a very long day full of changes that may not even be final for the upcoming design. Kyle Edwards was notorious for making major changes just as everything was beginning to be finalized. All of a sudden, the light at the end of the tunnel for this project suddenly grew dark. It was only 10:30 a.m., and Lydia already needed Excedrin and a smooth apple martini after dealing with Mr. Edwards.

CHAPTER 1

LYDIA

Lydia was so angry she could scream, so she did as loud as she could, not caring who heard her. Never in her wildest dreams did she ever believe Helena would pull a backstabbing stunt like this. *What the hell is wrong with that woman?* Lydia wondered. Helena was actually pulling her off the Edwards account and placing that untalented, poor excuse for a designer Kameron on it. What was wrong with that picture? Lydia wasn't some wet-behind-the-ears interior designer straight out of school to take this kind of nonsense. She was Lydia Deanne Brown, a top-notch interior designer who could pretty much write her own ticket and was courted by several well-respected and reputable interior design firms. She was the same person Helena practically begged to start working at her firm, but if Lydia had known she was capable of doing something as conniving as this, she would have never accepted. Because now without any warning or explanation, she stripped Lydia of the most important account they had to date. She'd heard whispers from members of the team who also had assignments taken away after all the preliminary work was done and given to Kameron, but Lydia never dreamed it would happen to her.

She thought about her conversation with Helena earlier and became angry all over again. Lydia thought about how she wasn't even supposed to still be working for someone else. Working at Helena's was supposed to be a stepping stone while Lydia worked on creating something she could call her own. Within six months to a year, Lydia had planned to be well on her way to opening her own design firm. But somehow along the way, she became distracted and comfortable making good money and took her eyes off the prize. In the year she had been working with Helena's, she was almost ashamed to admit to herself that she hadn't done anything constructive to further her own dreams. Instead, she brought in a huge client for Helena, but what thanks did she get for everything she'd done? Just two weeks ago, during her meetings with Edwards, practically the entire plan had to be redesigned because Edwards had changed his mind on practically every detail in every room. Lydia worked long hours and came in on the weekends to remain on schedule. However, she now felt as though all the work, time, and effort had been unappreciated. Having the account stripped away from her was like being told she wasn't good enough, and Lydia wasn't about to give anyone permission to make her feel inferior. Transferring the project to Kameron, of all people, was even more a slap in the face. Helena was well aware of the capabilities of all the designers in her firm, and she knew damn well that Kameron couldn't design a room if it was painted by numbers.

To add insult to injury, the Edwards account was going to bring in a sizeable commission, a commission that Lydia deserved and earned. But instead of being rewarded for this achievement, Helena decided that it was time for Kameron to step in and reap the rewards. It was all so cliché to turn over a project as important as this to someone as untalented and unskilled as Kameron Tyndall. Lydia knew it was all about getting exposure and the right clientele. But she never believed in playing those types of games. She believed that dedication, talent, hard work, and initiative should speak for itself, and for a while, it did. Little did she know that Helena had another agenda.

After completing all the changes to the project according to Mr. Edwards's specifications, for what seemed the umpteenth time, she thought everything was back on schedule and going according to plan. But then one evening after the rest of the team had left for the day and she was straightening her work area to leave for the day, Helena called Lydia into her office to discuss what she described as a "sensitive matter." Lydia walked into her office totally unaware of what this sensitive matter could possibly be, but she would soon find out how unprepared she would be for such a turn of events. As Lydia sat down, Helena offered her some freshly brewed mocha coffee. Lydia declined, so Helena leaned back into her leather-bound chair and looked her directly in the eye.

"Lydia, I've decided to make some changes within the firm, and I'm afraid you're not going to like what I'm about to say," said Helena, shifting uncomfortably in her chair. She cleared her throat and continued as if she'd rehearsed what she was going to say in front of a mirror.

"I'm transferring the Edwards project to Kameron," she said matter-of-factly. Lydia glared at Helena in shock and disbelief at what she was hearing. The Edwards account was her baby, her client, and her work. What did she mean it was being transferred to Kameron?

"Where is this coming from?" asked Lydia. The room was suddenly becoming very warm, and her heart began to beat faster. "I've worked very hard on this project. I brought this business to you, and now you're just taking me off of it and giving it to someone else? What is this about?"

"Kameron is the senior designer in this office, and the project should have been assigned to her from the beginning since you are the most junior designer in the office."

At this point, Lydia was practically beside herself with anger, but she managed to keep her composure. Did she actually just call her a "junior" designer? *Junior my ass*, thought Lydia.

"What is this, Helena? When I first came to this firm, I came here with experience, and you assigned this project to me immediately. As a matter of fact, I made it quite clear that I would only come to work for you if I were being offered projects like the Edwards account, a huge account which I brought to you, by the way. I'm not a junior designer, and I'm certainly not junior to Kameron. I've brought in business, and I've given this firm a much-needed face-lift, and now I'm suddenly a junior designer, and you're telling me Kameron should have been assigned the project?"

Lydia stopped for a moment and stared Helena down, trying to comprehend exactly what was happening as her mind began to race. She remembered glancing up from her agenda and seeing the two of them in deep conversation about two weeks ago, and she had a feeling what they were discussing, but now she was certain that their conversation was about the Edwards account. She knew for certain this was the reason she was being replaced on the project so abruptly.

"Well, I don't know if all of that is exactly accurate," said Helena, dismissing what she had just run down. "This is how I feel, and my decision is final. The change will be made effective immediately, and you will pick up Kameron's Rhodes project," Helena said as if doing Lydia a favor, when she knew full well that the Rhodes project was much smaller in scale and less money, which meant a lot less commission. Lydia saw this action as an attack on her reputation and work, and she wasn't going to take it lying down.

"You're giving me the Rhodes account? A project that is much smaller in scale? Tell me, Helena, why exactly is Kameron being given the Edwards account?

"I've already told you."

"So it doesn't have anything to do with her being the mayor's daughter? Not to mention the fact that we all know her experience level or lack of it, I should say."

"I'm not going to dignify that question with an answer, and I don't have to explain myself to you. The bottom line is you don't make the decisions around here about who is assigned what project. I do."

"Apparently."

Helena ignored Lydia's last comment. "It's true the Rhodes project is smaller, but it's a very good project, and I want you to handle it."

This time Lydia ignored Helena's comment. "There's a meeting scheduled tomorrow with Edwards to go over his latest design changes. I'm assuming you'll want Kameron to attend in my place since this change is effective immediately," Lydia said.

"No, I need you to attend that meeting."

"What?" she asked for clarification. "Why? Isn't Kameron the 'senior designer'? She should be able to pick up where I'm leaving off. That shouldn't be too difficult for someone with her vast experience. I'll give her my notes and the changes to date, and she should be up to speed in no time."

"You're not understanding what I'm saying Lydia. You will attend that meeting with Edwards because I need you there. You're already familiar with the job. It wouldn't be fair to throw Kameron in at the last minute."

Lydia couldn't believe what she had just heard. Did Helena just express what she didn't think was fair? "No, what isn't fair is how you're taking me off the project at the last minute for no good reason after I've done all the work. How convenient for Kameron to pick up and take credit for everything I've done for the last three months. This is very unprofessional, Helena, and I don't appreciate it at all. And to make matters worse, you just implied that I haven't brought anything to the table here. That's what's not fair," she said, disgusted that she had to defend herself.

"I'm not going to argue with you about this. Edwards will be in tomorrow at 9:00 a.m., and I'll expect you here to conduct the meeting. Kameron will be there shadowing you until she gets up to speed, and I'll expect you to help get her there."

Lydia stared at Helena as if she could peel the skin off her face with a dull razor and then feed it to her. This conversation was getting more surreal by the minute. Why would the senior designer need to shadow a junior one? Lydia was too outraged to say anymore, but this was not going to be the end of it.

"I'll see you in the morning," Lydia said fuming inside.

"Nine o'clock a.m. in the conference room. I'll see you then." Lydia got up and stormed out of the office, furious by what just occurred.

As Lydia left the building, she couldn't help but wonder what had just happened. She was confused, hurt, and angry, and she didn't know what to make of any of this. But she knew one thing for sure—she sure as hell wouldn't be attending a meeting on a project she was no longer working. *She'll see me in the morning all right,* thought Lydia, *but not for a meeting.*

The next morning, at 8:45 a.m., Lydia did not arrive to work like clockwork carrying her usual Starbucks grande mocha coffee. Instead, she was carrying an envelope addressed to Helena.

Helena's office door was open, so she knocked and walked in. Helena was busy typing a memo on her computer and didn't bother to look up to acknowledge Lydia's presence.

"Shouldn't you be in the meeting with Edwards and Kameron right now?"

"I wanted to deliver this letter to you in person."

"What is it?"

"It's my letter of resignation," said Lydia.

Now Lydia had Helena's full attention. She looked up from her computer and stared at Lydia for a second as if wondering if she'd heard her right. Lydia handed her the envelope and waited for her response. Helena put on her glasses and tore the envelope open and began reading. After she read over the letter, she looked at Lydia and asked, "Are you sure you want to do this?" as if Lydia had other alternatives she should consider first.

"I think my letter states my intentions pretty clearly."

"What are you planning to do? Go to another firm? I hope you don't expect me to give you a letter of recommendation since you're leaving me high and dry at a time when you're really needed."

"I think you'll get along without me just fine, Helena. You all but told me that yesterday when you made your decision to take the Edwards account away."

Helena began to turn a flush red as anger began building up. She couldn't believe Lydia had the audacity to waltz into her office with a letter of resignation after everything she'd done for her.

"Who do you think you are? I gave you your start!" Helena said slamming her fist onto her desk. "I suggest you think about your next move very carefully because there are consequences to all actions."

"Are you threatening me?"

Helena looked surprised by the question and, after a long pause, said, "Humph. There are consequences to all actions. You need to decide right here and now if your actions are the correct response."

"Oh, I know this is the correct response. I also know that you should have thought about consequences to your actions when you arbitrarily took me off the Edwards project. Bottom line, there's no doubt in my mind that leaving here is the correct response. And I certainly don't need your permission to leave."

"Is that so? You're quite sure of yourself, are you?"

"Regardless of what you may think, I've thought this through, and *my* decision is final."

Helena stared at her for several moments, shifting the letter from one hand to the other. She leaned back into her leather-bound chair as if giving Lydia one last chance to change her mind.

"Very well then, Lydia. Have it your way."

Lydia wasn't entirely comfortable with how Helena said "have it your way," but after that, she turned to make a dramatic exit out of Helena's office, pleased with herself for throwing Helena's words back in her face and showing Helena the stuff she was made of. Lydia was pleased that Helena finally accepted her resignation because what Lydia didn't want was for Helena to suspect that she hadn't quite thought things through and just wanted out as quickly as possible. Not only would that knowledge ruin her dramatic exit, but she would also lose leverage. She wanted to get out of her office with the swiftness, but as soon as she reached for the door, Helena called out to her.

"Oh, and by the way, Lydia, if you're thinking of taking any of my clients with you, then think again. They belong to Helena Designs, including Kyle Edwards, and you will leave here the way you came. Is that clear?"

Lydia gave her a smug look that suggested "we'll see about that" and walked out of her office for the last time. As her office door closed, Helena leaned back into her leather executive chair and thought to herself, *No one leaves me this way, throwing everything I've done for them back in my face. Ungrateful little bitch. She doesn't know who she's dealing with. You're going to be sorry you didn't think this through, Lydia. I promise you.*

CHAPTER 2

CHRYSTAL

*T*he alarm clock went off at 8:00 a.m. with a fury, and Chrystal dreaded the fact that it was time to get up, but she'd already hit the snooze button twice. Rising in her bed, she was immediately engulfed by the aroma of bacon and eggs and freshly brewed coffee that filled the air. Who the heck was in her kitchen cooking? she wondered. It must have been Lydia. She remembered calling her and telling her she was too drunk to drive home, and being the absolute sweetheart that she was, she must have rushed over to the club, collected Chrystal's drunk behind, and brought her back to the safety and security of her home. Now Lydia was in the kitchen cooking up a storm. Chrystal smiled to herself about the good friends she had to look out for her in such a way. Chrystal held her head, which was throbbing like she'd banged it against a brick wall from all the partying and drinking last night. She tried very hard to remember the last events of the evening before she passed out in her bed. Serves her right for partying on a weekday when she knew she had to get up the next morning and get ready for work. But last night felt so confining in her apartment, she literally felt the walls closing in on her, so she had to get out. Now she was feeling the remnants of the half-dozen gin and Cokes on the rocks. Chrystal drank one after the other like it was going out of style. Chrystal called out to Lydia as she started to get out of bed to get some Tylenol from her medicine cabinet when a gorgeous Hispanic man with long dark curly locks appeared in her bedroom door, carrying a tray of breakfast and a long-stemmed red rose in a crystal vase. Chrystal froze where she stood. *That's not Lydia*, she thought in a panic.

"Ah, you are awake," he said in a sexy heavy Spanish accent. "I tried to surprise you with some breakfast and coffee. Are you hungry?"

Chrystal was stunned. This was a first, she thought, alarmed that a man who looked every bit of Enrique Iglesias was standing in her bedroom with a breakfast tray, and she couldn't even remember bringing him home, much less his name. He smiled at her, showing off dimpled cheeks and beautiful straight white teeth. He was wearing a sleeveless T-shirt, which revealed his perfectly toned and muscular arms. Chrystal didn't remember bringing him home, but she could tell from his considerable assets why she brought him home. He walked over to place the tray on her bed.

"Why don't you get back into bed and enjoy your breakfast, Chrystal? I have prepared for you bacon, scrambled eggs, toast, strawberries and cantaloupe, orange juice, and coffee," he said while pulling out a napkin like he'd done this many times before. "I've been told I'm a pretty good cook, so I hope you agree as well," he said smiling.

As a rule, Chrystal never visited a club, new or otherwise, without leaving with a fine man on her arm, but this was definitely one for her blog today. She looked up at him trying desperately to remember his name. Was it Carlos, Jose, Julio? She searched desperately but couldn't remember. She gave all the glory to God for looking out for her but, at the same time, gave herself kudos for selecting such an extraordinary specimen of a man instead of some psycho serial killer. She shuddered at the thought that she could have been breakfast instead of having this gorgeous hunk of manliness prepare her breakfast. Chrystal climbed back into bed, placed the tray on her lap, and then took a sip of her coffee and a bite of the scrambled eggs.

"Thank you, this is wonderful," she gushed. She hated to admit it, but she couldn't go on pretending any longer.

"I'm sorry, I seem to have forgotten your name." He smiled and sat down beside her on the bed.

"Manuel," he said. Oh, Manuel. She would have thought of that one eventually, she thought.

"You had quite a bit to drink last night. We met on the dance floor and hooked up, and you invited me to come home with you. I wanted to fix you breakfast to thank you for such a nice evening." Wow, a genuine nice guy who's considerate enough to cook after sex. That was a first for Chrystal as well. Chrystal thought it was a shame she didn't quite remember the sex, but it must have been off the chain for her to receive such special treatment. She could definitely get used to this.

"Well, thank you, Manuel. This is delicious," she said while taking a bite of the strawberries and cantaloupe. Chrystal knew she didn't have any of this food in her refrigerator since she'd neglected to go grocery shopping two weeks in a row, so she wondered where Manuel got the breakfast food.

"The fruit is very sweet and fresh," said Chrystal.

"Sweet fruit for a sweet lady," said Manuel, to which Chrystal blushed.

"Where did you get all of this? My refrigerator is bare."

"Yes, it was," he said laughing. "I just made a short trip to the market around the corner. No big deal."

Oh my god! A man who grocery shops and cooks? Chrystal was going to have a field day on her blog today, but first she needed to get something for her head, which was pounding almost out of control. Chrystal held her head back.

"You're hungover, aren't you? I'll see what you have in your medicine cabinet."

"There's some Tylenol in the cabinet," she said as Manuel headed toward the bathroom. He came back in a moment and handed the bottle to her.

"Let me get you some water," he said.

"No, that's okay, I'll drink it with the orange juice. Aren't you eating anything?"

"I had some toast and coffee. I'm good. Eat the rest of your breakfast before it gets cold," he said, dashing off toward the kitchen.

Chrystal pulled the rose out of the vase and smelled it while gleaming to herself. Manuel seemed to be a keeper, but after she finished her breakfast, he needed to roll out of here. It wasn't in her nature to get attached to any one man in particular, even one as considerate as Manuel. She wondered if she could pull off a sick day today, then she could spend the rest of the morning in bed with a cold compress pressed gently against her forehead.

As she contemplated picking up her phone to dial her office, she thought about the great time she must have had last night at that new club called Scruples. She remembered the music was on, the crowd was lively, the drinks were potent, but most importantly, the men were hot, as seen by Manuel. It's too bad her girls weren't there to partake in the smorgasbord of men she experienced last night. It wasn't for lack of trying because she did try to call them to join her. First she called Lydia but kept getting that same annoying voice message. "You've got Lydia. I can't talk to you now because I'm out living my life. Leave a message." Chrystal left several messages before she left for the club as well, but Lydia never answered any of them. So afterward, Chrystal tried to reach Elise and Sherrie, but they were both too tired to go out. *Too tired? What are they, like sixty or something?* She could understand Elise being tired because her demanding job as a marketing executive kept her traveling and on the go all the time. But what was Sherrie's excuse? *She's at home all day long in that big-ass mansion she calls a home while her live-in maid doe all the cooking, cleaning, and running all the errands. She doesn't lift a finger. In fact, if she needs to lift a finger, her maid is right there to do that for her too. She barely even picks up her own child from school either, because once I asked her to meet me at the Coffee House around three during the week, and she completely forgot that she needed to pick up Jillian from school. I called her to tell her we could meet later, but as I was dialing her number, who walks in? Sherrie. I asked her where Jillian was, and she just gave me this blank stare and said, "Oh, that's Isabella's job, that's what we pay her for." Okay!* What a life. Chrystal thought about how nice it would be to have a life like Sherrie's. *She has a gorgeous husband and daughter, a beautiful home, cars, vacations whenever she wants, and a summer home in the Hamptons. Now that's living.* Chrystal imagined herself for a moment in that kind of setting and let out a sigh just thinking about how she would be happy if she had Sherrie's ideal life. But instead, she had to work for a living, and lately, working as an assistant to a public relations representative wasn't very satisfying.

Chrystal knew she shouldn't look at Sherrie's life or anyone else's and assume the grass is greener, but damn, it sure looked that way to her. Being stuck in an assistant's position making someone's coffee and running their errands wasn't exactly the way she pictured her life would be. Chrystal was sick and tired of answering phones, taking messages, scheduling meetings, and making travel arrangements for someone else. It was times like this that she wished she'd listened to her mother and finished school. Chrystal never liked school and dreaded the idea of attending four more years after she graduated from high school. But her mother gave her a long spill about the advantages of having a college education and the opportunities it would open up for her, and she finally convinced her to attend. So in the fall, after she graduated from high school, like thousands of other rising freshmen around the country, Chrystal entered college at her selected college, Granby University. However, once there, instead of studying and making the most of her academics, she fell into the syndrome that many young freshmen succumb to when they get a taste of freedom away from their parents. She attended every campus and fraternity party imaginable, started skipping classes regularly, was unprepared for classes when she did attend, and rarely turned in assignments on time, if at all. When she ended up on academic probation with her school standing in jeopardy, instead of getting focused on her studies and buckling down, she dropped out of school altogether without her parent's knowledge. When her parents finally found out she was no longer attending college, they were furious and gave Chrystal six months to find a job and a place of her own or else. Now, with an ultimatum hanging over her head and very little time to fulfill it, she hopped from one minimum wage job to another until finally landing a position with Goldman and Associates, a public relations firm, as Dana Little's associate public relations assistant. It was an entry-level position with very little potential for growth, but it was employment, and Chrystal didn't have the luxury or the time to be choosy. One day before her six-month cut-off was due, Chrystal moved into her own apartment and began work the following day with her parent's blessings.

The job itself wasn't too bad, but Chrystal didn't enjoy what she considered menial tasks, like the other day when Dana asked her to pick up lunch for her and several clients at this Thai food restaurant clear across town. She had to dash over to the restaurant, stop at a client's office and pick up some paperwork, and then double time it back to the office so that lunch was served promptly at 12:00 noon. In Dana's mind, lunch began at 12:00 sharp, not 12:01, and certainly not 12:02. If Chrystal dare be late or, God forbid, have Dana and the clients waiting in the conference for their lunch a mere minute after 12:00, there would be hell to pay, and Chrystal wasn't about to deal with Dana's mood swings. That was just one of the tasks Chrystal looked at as beneath her, not to mention she had to make sure the coffee was ready and brewing before Dana arrived at work around 9:15 every morning. Chrystal knew she was more than an errand girl, and she needed to find a field that she enjoyed where even if she woke up in the morning with a hangover, she would still want to go in to work because she loved what she did that much. Those were the types of careers Lydia and Elise enjoyed. Lydia was very passionate about interior design, and Elise lived and breathed marketing. Chrystal smiled when she thought about her girls Lydia, Elise, and Sherrie. They were all fierce in their own individual ways, and even though not one of those heifers was available to go out with her last night, she loved them all to death.

Breaking out of her momentary trance, Chrystal glanced at the clock on her nightstand. It was almost 8:45 a.m., and her regular work hours began at 9:00 a.m. If she was going to fain illness, now would be a good time to call in although she knew Dana wouldn't be in yet. That was fine with Chrystal because she really didn't want to speak to her anyway. The first thing Dana did even before she sat down was listen to her messages, although walking in and seeing Chrystal's desk, which was located right outside her office, should clue her in. Chrystal thought about all the things she could get done today around the house if she took some personal time off to justify the call she was about to make. Then she took a deep breath and dialed her supervisor's work number, 878-2559. The phone rang a couple of times and then clicked on to her supervisor's voice mail. "You have reached the voice mail of Dana Little. I'm either away from my desk or on another line. Please leave your name and a brief message after the beep, and I'll get back with you as soon as possible. Have a nice day." Chrystal cleared her throat and waited for the beep before she began her message. *Beep!* In the huskiest, throatiest voice Chrystal could conjure, she began. "Uh, Dana, it's me, Chrystal. Listen, I'm not feeling too well this morning. My throat is very sore, and I have a terrible migraine, so I won't be in today. If you need anything, please give me a call at home. Thanks, good-bye." Chrystal hurriedly hung up the phone. She knew Dana wouldn't be happy about her being out of the office unexpectedly today, but she wanted to take a personal day off, and that was all to it.

Now that the call had been made, Chrystal felt free to do whatever she pleased. She picked up the TV remote and turned on the TV to *The Tyra Banks Show*, which would be starting in a few minutes. She hit the guide button on the remote to see a synopsis of what the show would be about today. "Tyra talks to teenage girls who want to have plastic surgery." *Ewwww*, thought Chrystal. Her girl Tyra really hit on some very important topics out there. Just as Chrystal was about to see what else was on right now, her telephone rang. It startled her because she immediately thought that it could be Dana calling as she was driving in to work. *What does she need me to pick up now?* Chrystal wondered. *Bagels and cream cheese? Doughnuts? Or her personal favorite, her dry cleaning.* She glanced at the caller ID on the phone and was relieved to see that it was Elise's number.

"Hello," Chrystal answered.

"Hey, girl!" said Elise in a voice that was a little too chipper for Chrystal right now. "What's going on?"

"Nothing's going on right now other than my splitting headache. What about you?"

"You know I just got back from Phoenix last night. It was a week of presentations, marathon meetings, and meetings with new clients. I didn't get a chance to do anything fun outside of work. Sorry I couldn't come with you last night, but I was dead tired."

Elise was a top-notch marketing executive working for Omnibus Inc. She was doing quite well for herself and, at the age of twenty-nine, was already the head of her division in charge of product sales. Her position in the company kept her traveling constantly between the East and West Coasts. Chrystal always thought her job sounded glamorous and only wished that when she was preparing travel arrangements for Dana, she would be asked to attend as well.

"Don't worry about it. At least you get to travel. I haven't been anywhere on my job since I started there two years ago."

"Sounds like you need a vacation."

"Yes, that and a better-paying job. One that's going to make me want to go to work."

"Why aren't you at work, by the way? I just called thinking I'd leave you a message because I didn't think you'd be in."

"I'm taking a personal day today. My head is killing me from all the drinking and partying last night. I knew I should've waited until Friday to party, but I had to get out last night."

"Well, although you're paying for it now, it sounds like you had a good time. So did you meet any cute guys?"

"Apparently I did. He's in my kitchen now making himself some breakfast. He just brought me a tray of bacon and eggs, and guess what the best part is? I don't remember bringing him home with me last night, I was that wasted," Chrystal whispered into the phone.

"What? You are so scandalous Chrystal! Is he okay? He's not a mass murderer or anything? Are you okay?" Elise loved Chrystal to death, but her dating antics scared her sometimes. Last month she met a guy in the club, talked with him for about twenty minutes, and literally left with him for the night, and now this.

"He's gorgeous Elise, and he's considerate. He made me breakfast in bed, and he makes some mean scrambled eggs. I mean seriously, I don't know what he put in these eggs but they're off the chain! And he looks like Enrique Iglesias. Did I miss anything?" Chrystal said as if having a strange man in her home cooking breakfast was a normal event, and perhaps for Chrystal, it was as normal as anything could be.

"Yes. Do you know his name?"

"His name is Manuel," she said in her best Spanish accent. "Do you hear how that rolls off my tongue?" Just then, Manuel poked his head into the bedroom.

"Did you call me? Do you need anything?" said Manuel holding a spatula in one hand and an egg in the other.

"No, sweetie, I'm great. Thank you."

He smiled and winked at her and went back into the kitchen.

"Did you hear that Elise?"

"Yes, I did. Very sexy. Get a picture for me before he leaves," she said, smiling to herself. "Hey, we need to call Lydia and Sherrie and get together for dinner tonight. What do you think?" asked Elise.

"That sounds good. But have you heard from Lydia lately? I've been calling her, and she hasn't returned any of my calls."

"I haven't talked to her since I left for Phoenix, but I'll give her a call so we can go out and catch up."

Just then, Chrystal heard a beep on her phone. It was her call-waiting. "Elise, hold on for a second, another call is coming through. I sure hope it's not Dana," she said with a laugh.

"Okay, I'll hold."

Chrystal pressed the button to answer the call. "Hello," she said, hoping like hell Dana's voice wouldn't answer.

"Hey there!" said Lydia.

"Girl! Where in the world have you been? I have Elise on the other line, and we were just saying we hadn't heard from you."

"It's a long story, Chrys, but I've been going through something on my job . . . well, my former job."

"Your former job? What happened, Lydia?"

"We all need to get together, and I'll tell you all at once so I won't have to repeat it three times. Can you meet for dinner tonight?"

"Hey, hold on, let me pull Elise into this conversation."

"Okay," said Lydia.

Chrystal was dumbfounded but, oddly enough, a little relieved to hear that all wasn't well for Lydia. Lydia quit her job? *Helena must have done something really foul for Lydia to take a step like this one*, Chrystal thought. She pressed the button again to get Elise back on the line. "Elise?" she said.

"Yes, I'm still here."

"It's Lydia on the line. Let me pull her in too." Chrystal pressed the button twice to pull Lydia into the conversation.

"Lydia?"

"Yeah, I'm here."

"I've got Elise on the line."

"Girl, don't you know how to return phone calls?" Elise asked Lydia.

"Well, hello to you too, Ms. Elise! Like I was telling Chrystal, it's been a long week, and we need to go out so I can tell you about the BS I had to handle on my job. I quit, Elise. I gave the heifer my resignation, I was so ticked off."

"What?" said Elise. "What do you mean you quit . . . as in your job? Lydia, what in the world happened?"

"It's a long story," said Chrystal, repeating Lydia's vague explanation. "But I can't wait to hear it."

"Okay, we need to get Sherrie on the line as well," said Lydia.

"You're right about that," said Elise. "Can you do that on your phone, Chrys?"

"Girl, this phone can act as a vibrator if I need it to, and there have been some nights that I definitely needed it." All three ladies laughed at the comment. "You guys hold on for a second." Chrystal hit the button twice and started dialing Sherrie's cell number because she knew she was either getting her hair done or doing Pilates. The telephone rang, and Sherrie answered on the second ring.

"Hello, girl," Sherrie answered sounding out of breath.

"Is it safe to ask you what you're doing right now?" Chrystal asked laughing.

"I'm on my Stairmaster. Just two more laps to go and I'm done! You can stick a fork in me." Sherrie laughed. "What's up?"

"I've got Lydia and Elise on the line, so I'm going to pull you into our little conference call."

"Oh good. I haven't spoken to those heifers in a minute."

"Hold on."

"Okay."

After another moment, Chrystal was able to have a four-way conversation going on the phone. "Okay, everyone should be here. Roll call. Lydia, Elise, Sherrie." They all answered in unison and were elated to hear one another's voices.

"What's up my, girls?" Sherrie said in a high-pitched voice. It was obvious she was still on the Stairmaster working it out.

"Can you come to dinner tonight?" asked Lydia. "We all need to catch up, and I miss my girls."

You could almost hear the ladies smile over the phone. It had been a while since they'd all gotten together because lately, everyone seemed to be so busy. But they always made an effort to slow down and catch up on what's going on in one another's lives.

"Absolutely! Where are we going?"

"What does everyone have a taste for?"

"Let's go to Ruth's Chris Steak House. I can use a nice thick steak right now," said Sherrie, sounding as if she wanted to smack her lips.

"Sounds good to me," said Lydia. Lydia, Chrystal, and Elise all agreed they had a taste for Ruth's Chris as well.

"Let's meet there about 7:00 p.m. Is that good for everyone?"

Everyone agreed that seven would be perfect to meet for dinner. They each promised to talk more at dinner to catch up before hanging up. Somehow hearing the girl's voices gave Chrystal the energy boost she desperately needed, in particular Lydia's news. She was suddenly feeling a lot better. She knew it wasn't right, but somehow hearing Lydia's news about her job made her feel better about herself. Here she was complaining about her job, and now Lydia didn't have one. Chrystal felt a little guilty that Lydia's bad news made her feel better, but she knew Lydia would land on her feet. Chrystal leaped from the bed and headed to the bathroom to take a shower. Suddenly, she felt like going in to work after all.

CHAPTER 3

ELISE

After hanging up with the girls, Elise decided to make herself some tea with honey and a couple slices of toast with her favorite raspberry preserve. It was so good to be home after her weeklong trip to Arizona, where she spent the majority of her time in one marathon meeting after another. But as she looked around her condo, it was a reminder that what she wasn't looking forward to constantly picking up behind her boyfriend, Quinton. She was so tired of getting up in the morning, walking into her bathroom, and finding his nasty, funky drawers lying in the middle of the floor and the toilet seat up—again. *There's going to be some changes around here*, Elise thought to herself.

What is it about men and their bathroom behavior and leaving their underwear in full view? Do they really think it's attractive or even sexy to see their Fruit of the Looms sprawled on the floor? Elise thought to herself. She had broken her own golden rule of not allowing any man to stay with her. Elise was independent and really needed her space, so she wondered at what point Quinton felt it was okay to practically move in with her. And since they'd been spending so much time together except when she's traveling, just about everything he did got on her damn nerves. Like the other day when they went out to this seafood joint for dinner and he ordered crab legs. Elise just sat there watching him break open those crab legs while slipping and slurping the meat out like it was going out of style. It was enough to drive her up the wall, not to mention that he smacked his food all the time when he ate. *Smack, smack, smack!* Why couldn't he eat with his damn mouth closed and quietly like he had some sense? And although the man was fine as hell, he could certainly have been less than courteous at times. Last weekend, Elise and Quinton were walking through the mall to find a gift for her niece's fifth birthday when they ran into one of Elise's old high school friends, Tonya Jenkins, whom she had hadn't seen in at least ten years. Elise barely recognized her because it didn't look like the last ten years had been kind to Tonya. Her once shapely, curvy seventeen-year-old body was now about fifty pounds overweight, and her stomach was bulging and hanging over a pair of jeans that were so tight they looked as though the seams were about to break free, along with her breasts out of that blouse. They hugged and kissed each other and laughed about old times while Elise pretended not to notice how much weight she'd gained. But instead of Quinton following Elise's lead and just letting the obvious go, he jumped off and asked Tonya when her baby was due. Needless to say, Tonya went all sista' on him and started twisting her neck and swinging her hands while asking him what the hell he meant by that question. Elise was so embarrassed by the entire scene, she could have fallen down and crawled away while pretending she didn't know Quinton. And although she and Tonya promised to keep in touch and call each other for lunch, she knew that it would probably be another ten years before she ever saw her again, thanks to Quinton and his big mouth. Later, after they walked away, she hit him upside his head and told him to never ask a woman if she's pregnant unless she volunteered the information. He just stood there dumbfounded and said, "Well, maybe instead of calling her for lunch, you should call her to meet you at the gym because she looked preggers to me." Elise just rolled her eyes and kept walking.

Elise didn't quite know when Quinton started becoming more of a pain in the behind, but she thought maybe their relationship was getting a little too settled and predictable for her taste. Elise hoped the thrill wasn't gone, but she knew for certain things were still hot in the bedroom because Quinton knew how to lay the pipe and work it out. Elise was thinking maybe they needed some time apart. When they first met at a new club called Secrets that Chrystal dragged her to one night, he was this fine brown-cinnamon young man who was clean cut and had a great sense of humor. Quinton was looking too good in his black jeans and a form-fitting black T-shirt with printing that read Protect Yourself from Hollywood. Elise asked him what his T-shirt meant, and he said that you had to protect yourself from the pitfalls that fame and money could bring. He wanted to stay clear of those trappings since he was an investment banker and doing quite well for himself. Elise was very impressed. She had managed to meet a fine brother, with a great job, hopefully single, and not on the down low. So they sat at the bar ordering drinks, and they laughed all night about everybody and everything. They nearly closed down the club at 3:00 a.m., and they still weren't ready to go home. Elise could not remember the last time she had so much fun with a man. So after their first evening together, they started dating regularly, and Elise thought it was strange how Quinton never took her to his place for "coffee" or anything else. At first she thought Quinton was married after all; not that it would have been a problem for Elise, because she figured if a wife couldn't keep her man happy and at home, he's fair game for those who could. So she asked him point blank if he had a wife just to know what she was dealing with, but he denied it and said he was single and that he just didn't want her to see his home right now because he was the middle of a remodel and his home was a disaster. That didn't matter to Elise, and she offered to have her good friend Lydia, who she explained was an excellent interior designer, to hook him up after he finished with the renovations. He declined the offer, and then before Elise realized it, her condo had become their little sexcapades hideaway, and now he was there more than in his own damn house. Elise wasn't happy with this current arrangement because she didn't sign up for a live-in boyfriend, especially one who wasn't paying any rent, utilities, or picking up his dirty drawers.

She peered at Quinton's nude sculpted body lying across the bed on top of her new down comforter and smiled to herself. Now she remembered why she allowed him to unofficially move into her place. His 6'2" 190-pound frame of pure muscle was delicious. And although she was a little annoyed that he had all of his nude manhood laying on top of her $500 duvet, just looking at him made her want to wake him up for another round of head-banging sex. She walked over to the bed and started to curl under him and caress his muscular back to wake him up when suddenly he broke wind.

"Damn, Quinton, was that necessary?" she said, fanning swiftly and lurching back to get rid of the stench.

"Sorry, baby," he said, startled by his own eruption.

"You know, Quinton, it's almost eleven o'clock in the morning. Too late for anyone who's still alive and kicking to be lying around in bed, and since you've ruined any thought of what I was about to do to you, you need to get up."

"Ah, come on, baby, don't be like that. We can still make it happen. Besides, I had a hard day at work yesterday. I didn't get in until 10:00 p.m., right after you came in."

"And your point is?"

"My point is, I just want to relax for a moment with my baby if you would just stop with the complaining and bring your sweet, sexy, bootylicious body over here," said Quinton as he licked his lips and reached over to pull Elise into bed with him. Elise giggled and landed on top of him.

"You're nasty." she says with a broad smile.

"Yeah, but you like me that way, don't you?" She couldn't lie to herself or to him. Although there was a lot about his little habits that did annoy her, his blatant, sensual sexiness always got the best of her, and she couldn't deny him even if she truly wanted.

"I plead the fifth," she said, not wanting to reveal how much she liked his raw and downright nastiness when it came to his bedroom antics.

"You know, if you're going to take advantage of me, I better call in to say I'll be out for a few hours. I want to have plenty of time to recover."

"You do that because it's about to be on."

"You're beautiful, do you know that? You're like a blossoming flower on a spring morning just waiting for the world to notice the brilliance of your stunning beauty. I want to pick you, inhale your fragrance, and take in all that is you," he said while caressing her back.

Damn him, thought Elise. Every time she got upset with him, he always managed to do or say something really sweet to make it all right again. Elise looked into Quinton's beautiful light brown eyes. He looked like an Adonis with his smooth, silky, creamy brown skin. Quinton was the product of a black father from Alabama and a white English mother, although he was born and raised in New York City. His parents divorced when he was very young, and he was raised by his mother while his father was a distant memory, never really being a substantial part of his life. He was an only child that learned early on the significance of being independent, although he seemed to gravitate toward Elise as if there were cosmic forces that brought them together.

She gazed into his piercing eyes and knew she could have her way with him the rest of the day if she so desired, and she intended to have her way. She was full of desire or more like lust. She loved the new bald look he'd been sporting for a couple of weeks now. There was something about a bald muscular man that made her weak in the knees and a little moist between her legs. Quinton began smiling, showing off his pearly whites, as if he could read what was going through her mind. He then began squeezing her ample behind with his huge hands before giving it a gentle slap.

"Oh, don't spank me like that," she said teasingly, "Okay, spank me again, daddy," she purred in his ear while he began rocking his body against hers. He pulled the bedsheet off his body, revealing his aroused manhood. Elise kissed him deeply on his mouth and started down his chest, kissing gently and intentionally in the right areas. When she reached his erection and kissed the tip of his penis as a prelude to what was about to happen, he let out a little moan of approval. She smiled at him, opened her mouth, and devoured him whole. Quinton moaned with pleasure as she took him into her mouth deeply and ate him like his penis was made of pure milk chocolate as he lay back to enjoy every stroke. She slid her mouth in and out, up and down his manhood, licking it like a lollipop and kissing the tip as she pulled it all the way out.

"Baby!" he yelled out, his body beginning to quiver and gyrate from the motions of her mouth clasped around his penis. "Oh, baby . . . do that shit," he moaned as he was nearing climax, but before he could, Elise pulled up and slipped off her pajama bottoms, revealing her sexy, well-toned body and her ripe breasts. Quinton grabbed her tiny waistline and then put his mouth around the areola of her breasts as Elise stroked his head gently.

"It's your turn," he whispered gently in her ear, and then he turned her over on her back, pressed her legs back against her chest, and started licking the inside of her thighs. He kissed it and then pushed his tongue into her gently and began moving it in and out before placing his entire mouth around her most sensitive spot. Elise cried out and started moving her hips, pushing her clitoris into his tongue and then his mouth. She sat up and reached into the top drawer of the nightstand and pulled out a Trojan extrasensitive condom, opened the wrapper, and placed it seductively on Quinton's awaiting erection. She climbed on top of Quinton and pushed his manhood inside of her as she began to slowly rock her pelvis back and forth, up and down. The headboard began hitting the wall to the beat of their rhythm. Elise moaned loudly, and their lovemaking intensified as their motions became quicker as their bodies moved together as one. Elise gazed down into Quinton's contorted face and smiled as she rode him into ecstasy, into that place where nothing or no one in the universe existed except the two of them. It was hypnotic, and she felt a sense of euphoria at the thought of having him exactly where she wanted him. She lifted her body and straddled him back and forth, up and down, and then suddenly, their motions were quickened as their bodies moved in unison. Elise could feel the intenseness welling up inside of her until she couldn't take it any longer. And just as she felt she'd lose herself in the passion, her body exploded while she and Quinton yelled out in pure pleasure. The headboard hit harder into the wall, and the sounds of raw sexual energy filled the air. Their sweaty bodies glistened and then became limp as Elise collapsed onto Quinton's broad chest. Their breathing was heavy at first and then began to subside. Elise could hear Quinton's racing heartbeat calming into a more relaxed beat. They lay there quietly in each other's arms, slowly coming down from their euphoria. They embraced and kissed each other gently.

"That was incredible," said Quinton.

"You rocked it out as always, baby," said Elise, smiling at Quinton as she gave him a gentle kiss on the lips.

"We're really good together . . . you and I, and you know I love you," he said. "Even when you're being all mean and catty." He kissed Elise on the mouth deeply, and she returned his kisses as they held each other tightly.

"I love you too," she said. And at that very moment, she really believed that she did love him.

CHAPTER 4

SHERRIE

Sherrie stepped out of the shower and patted herself dry. She felt very good about getting up early to exercise to keep her figure tight. She pulled her white silk robe over her body and stepped out onto her balcony outside of her bedroom to take in some fresh air. It was a beautiful sunny morning with a light, cool breeze blowing in the air. She took in the air with a deep breath and released it as she gazed below at her award-winning rose garden. Last year she had taken first place in the Garden Club's annual rose competition, a feat she had been working toward for the past three years after placing second each year. The Marshalls had a very capable gardener to care for their lawn and grounds, but Sherrie insisted on taking care of her roses personally. She breathed in and out the fresh air with the sweet aroma of her new rose blooms. As she enjoyed the sereneness of the moment, her attention diverted for a second as she suddenly wondered if her husband was truly working a double shift at the hospital like he claimed. Brad was a neurosurgeon at Sentara Careplex Hospital, and she was not accustomed to him being home at this time of the morning, especially lately since he'd been working two shifts back to back. But lately something was tugging at her. For some reason, she felt that Brad volunteered to work doubles to avoid coming home to her. In the past few months, they seemed to be drifting further and further apart, and she didn't know why, and when she tried to talk to Brad about it, he refused to listen. Desperate to get some type of dialogue going with her husband, she suggested that they seek counseling to help their marriage and their communication. Brad suggested that she seek psychiatric counseling if she was delusional enough to think he was going to spend $300 an hour for any psychiatrist to tell them what they already knew. Sherrie was at a loss. She wanted so desperately to try to rekindle their relationship and get things back on track. She just wished that Brad would tell her what she needed to do to fix whatever was wrong because she wanted things to be the way they were before all the long hours and late nights interfered with their marriage.

They always say the grass is always greener, and from the outside looking in, it appeared the Marshalls were the epitome of a perfect family. Financially, the Marshalls were very secure, and Sherrie wanted for nothing because Brad was a wonderful provider. They had a huge 9,500-square-foot home set on a golf course, complete with every modern amenity imaginable, including an authentic movie theater, indoor lap pool, and an outside pool. They owned several expensive cars. Sherrie usually drove an S550, metallic diamond-white Mercedes Benz, a birthday gift from her husband last year, while Brad drove a black 911 Carrera soft-top convertible Porsche. The Marshalls have a vacation home in the Hamptons and in Maui, and Brad regularly showered Sherrie with expensive jewelry. Brad was the love of her life, but lately, it just seemed like he was slipping through her fingers, and Sherrie felt she was losing her connection with him.

It wasn't always this way Sherrie remembered. She and Brad were once madly in love and couldn't bear to spend any time apart. This proved to be difficult for an intern who regularly put in over one hundred hours per week. Sherrie thought it was important for her to be at home supporting her husband's career, taking care of their home, and caring for their four-year-old-daughter, Jillian, for which Brad agreed wholeheartedly. No wife of his would be in the workforce when he could provide for her, and he did not want his daughter to be raised by a nanny or a day care center. He wanted a wife at home caring for their home and their child. And so Sherrie became the dutiful wife cooking, cleaning, running errands, and attending to their daughter's needs, while Brad continued to advance in his career. It seemed the only thing that gave her a real sense of accomplishment was being a wife and mother. Sherrie loved being a mother to their daughter, and she wanted all the best for Jillian, which included a stable home with two parents who really loved and cared for each other.

Sherrie wondered a few times if another woman was getting between her and Brad but decided that her husband would never do anything like that to hurt their relationship. However, she couldn't quite put her finger on it, but she knew there had to be a reason why he seemed so distant lately. Sherrie went back into her bedroom and closed the French doors. She glanced at the clock and thought to herself that she had a few more hours to run a couple of errands before meeting the girls for dinner. She opened her custom-built walk-in closet and scanned the large assortment of designer clothes and shoes. Her closet looked more like a Sax Fifth Avenue department and shoe store than a personal wardrobe closet. Sherrie chose a pair of jeans and a T-shirt shirt along with some boots to run out for a few minutes.

After getting dressed, Sherrie began combing her hair and applying a little makeup when the telephone rang. The caller ID said the phone number belonged to Brad. Sherrie picked up, anxious to hear that he was on his way home; that way they could spend a little time alone before she left for dinner, and she would put off her errands until tomorrow.

"Hi, honey," she answered anxiously.

"Hi. Listen, I'll probably be here at the hospital for a while, so don't worry about waiting up for me. It's going to be a long night."

"Brad, it's barely noon, and you're already calling to say you won't be home in time for dinner?"

"Yes, I know, but it's been a very busy morning, and the rest of the day doesn't look good."

"But I asked Isabella to fix your favorite rib eye steak tonight with all the trimmings. I thought we could have a late dinner together with a little candlelight, a little music, and maybe run a bath afterward." Sherrie spoke seductively into the receiver in an attempt to change Brad's plans to work late. "I just feel that we haven't spent any quality time together lately, so I wanted to make tonight a little special for us."

"I'm sorry, darling, but I'm going to have to ask for a rain check on this evening, although it sounds great." Brad spoke as if he were busy focusing on another task like writing out a report on a patient. "I'll make it up to you, okay? We'll do it another night."

Sherrie sighed at the thought of another well-planned evening not coming to fruition. She'd planned to eat lightly with the girls this evening and then have a late night rendezvous with her husband, but clearly that wasn't going to happen. Everything would have been perfect except the one major detail flaw, which was Brad's schedule getting in the way. She knew discussing the issue any further would lead nowhere, so she decided to leave well enough alone.

"Do you want Isabella to set a plate aside for you for dinner? I'm going out to meet the girls for dinner tonight. I guess I'll order the rib eye instead of the house Salad," she said, sounding disappointed that her plans for their evening were being postponed.

"Oh, that sounds great, and don't bother Isabella about dinner. I'll just grab something here at the hospital," Brad said ignoring the tone in her voice. "Listen, I have to go, but enjoy your dinner this evening with the ladies."

"Okay, Brad. I love you." But before she could get a reciprocal "I love you" back, Brad had hung up the phone on the other end. Sherrie stared at the telephone for a moment as if waiting for Brad to pick the phone back up and tell her he loved her back, but after a few seconds, she placed it back on the receiver.

A couple of hours later, Sherrie emerged from her bedroom wearing a silk robe. She'd been so preoccupied thinking about Brad and his having another late evening at the hospital that she hadn't bother to go out to run any errands. She went downstairs into the living room, where Isabella had just finished vacuuming and was now polishing the furniture. Sherrie insisted that her home have that barely lived-in look at all times. She took much pride in her home, the lavish but comfortable decor that her girl Lydia assisted her in pulling together. The Marshall home always looked camera ready and certainly ready to entertain at a moment's notice, which was a good thing since there had been occasions when Brad brought home a visiting colleague after barely a half hour's notice. Isabella had been working for the Marshalls for five years now, and Sherrie didn't know how they ever got along without her before that time. Isabella was humming one of her favorite songs as she polished the furniture and noticed Sherrie standing near her.

"Hello, Ms. Sherrie, how's your morning going? Do you want any breakfast?"

"Good morning, Isabella. I'll just have some toast and coffee. Is Jillian awake?"

"I checked on her a few moments ago, and she's still fast asleep. I'll get your toast and coffee."

"Thank you, Isabella."

Isabella walked into the kitchen to pour Sherrie a cup of coffee with whole wheat toast with a light spread of I Can't Believe It's Not Butter! and some strawberry preserves. She placed the toast and coffee in front of Sherrie along with some half-and-half and sweetener for her coffee.

"I took the rib eyes out of the freezer for your special dinner tonight with Mr. Brad. I'm going to make all his favorites. I can make that dump cake he loves for dessert if you like."

"Oh, don't bother," Sherrie said, waving her hand as if signaling that her plans for the evening with her husband were a bust. "Brad will be working late, and I'll be going out with the girls tonight. We'll save the rib eyes for another night," said Sherrie dryly as she took a sip of her coffee. "I was looking forward to this evening, but oh well, right?" Sherrie took a bite of her toast and sulked at the thought of another evening going by without Brad, without passion, without foreplay, and without sex. She didn't want to think about how long it had been since the last time they'd actually had sex. Something had to give and fast.

"I'm sorry, Ms. Sherrie, I'll put the rib eyes back in the freezer for another time." Sherrie seemed to be somewhere else thinking to herself. "You know Mr. Brad is a very busy man. He's doing important work at the hospital."

Sherrie snapped out of her daze and stared at Isabella. "Brad needs to balance the importance of his work against the importance of his family. One is suffering while the other is thriving, and I'm getting a little tired of trying to get him to see it. He needs to figure out what is more important to him. By the amount of time he spends at the hospital, it seems to be his job."

Isabella didn't want to get into a debate about Mr. Brad. She'd heard some of their late night and early morning discussions all centering around his lack of quality time with Sherrie and Jillian, and she was a believer that disagreements between spouses should remain between spouses.

"Isabella, what would you do if your husband were constantly away?"

"I don't have a husband, so I can't answer that question."

"Think about how you would feel if you had a husband, but he was never at home. How would you handle it?"

"Ms. Sherrie, I think you need to be patient with your husband. What Mr. Brad does is not just a job to him. He is completely dedicated to his work. A wife should be supportive of her husband."

"You don't think I'm supportive? I'm almost too supportive, Isabella. I've been behind him every step of the way. I just don't think it's too much to ask for him to make me and Jillian a priority in his life for a change."

"You asked me what I would do in this situation. Well, if I had a husband, I would be supportive of him, that's what I would do. Especially if I had the luxury of owning a fine home such as this one. You are very fortunate to have a man who wants to provide for you and your daughter in such a way. It is very rare. You are very blessed, and you should count your blessings and give praise to God for the lifestyle you live." Isabella stopped for a moment to notice if Sherrie was taking in anything she had just said. "I need to finish in the living room, unless you need something else for your breakfast."

"No, I'm fine. Go finish up. Thanks, Isabella."

Isabella headed back for the living room while Sherrie sipped the last of her coffee and thought about her words. Although she'd asked for Isabella's opinion, she didn't like the answer. How could she possibly know what she would do in her shoes? After all, she wasn't even married and never had been as far as Sherrie knew. It's quite easy to look around and see all of their material possessions and then conclude that it's all worth it. Isabella had no idea how many of her friends were living the same lifestyle but were unhappy with their circumstances. She could never know unless she'd experienced the loneliness and the distance between two people who claimed to be in love with each other. Why should she be the one to compromise in the relationship all the time? Wasn't it enough that she gave up her own dreams to support his? But now when Sherrie was asking for a little understanding and time, she must continue to compromise and be supportive? There was something not quite right with that type of logic, and Sherrie wasn't about to succumb to it.

It was now 5:00 p.m., and Sherrie was supposed to meet the girls at 7:30 p.m., so she decided there was a little time to run a couple of errands beforehand. Brad probably wouldn't be back in before she returned from dinner with the girls, so she finished getting dressed and decided to take one of her Louis Vuitton handbags from her closet. As she started to walk out of the bedroom, she remembered Brad needed some things taken to the cleaners. She turned on the light to Brad's walk-in closet and found the clothes set aside on the floor in the room. She began checking the pockets of the pants to make sure there wasn't anything of value in his pockets like money or his wedding band. On more than one occasion, Brad had carelessly left his wedding band in his pants pocket, although she knew he couldn't wear jewelry into surgery. Or at least she hoped that was the reason he left his ring behind. As Sherrie cleared out the pockets, she pulled out receipts for Starbucks, Catalina Restaurant—where she knew Brad loved the brisket—and some sort of business card. Sherrie started to discard the card when the title of the agency on the card caught her eye. Sherrie looked at the name, address, and telephone number, and suddenly her heart began racing to the point she had to sit down for moment.

The Simmons Private Detective Agency? Why would Brad need the services of a private detective? Sherrie wondered nervously.

CHAPTER 5

LYDIA

*I*t was a busy night as usual at Ruth's Chris Steak House restaurant with all the hustle and bustle of the hostesses and waiters seating awaiting guests and taking orders. The atmosphere was casual elegance, the tables were each adorned with white linen table cloths, and the decor was reminiscent of Louisiana home style. The aroma of fine cuisine filled the air while customers sipped on fine wine that accompanied their entrées. Lydia had called ahead earlier and reserved a table for four. When she entered the corridor, she was greeted by a pretty dark-skinned woman with midlength micro-minibraids and an infectious smile. The hostess informed Lydia that she was the first from her party to arrive and escorted her to their table for the evening. The table was perfectly placed in a corner off to the side where the ladies could talk and catch up on their individual lives. Once Lydia was seated comfortably, the hostess handed her a menu to peruse for her dinner selection while she waited for the others to arrive.

"Your waiter will be with you shortly. Enjoy your meal and evening."

"Thank you," said Lydia, glancing at the menu. She knew what she wanted but decided to check out the menu for anything new that may look good, which everything did. The lobster ravioli—which was described as tomato, tarragon, and shellfish bisque and mascarpone cheese—sounded divine, and the Thai spiced wings sounded great to start as an appetizer. As Lydia continued reading the menu, their waiter appeared, a handsome young dark-chocolate brother who immediately reminded Lydia of the model-turned-actor Tyrese.

"Good evening, my name is Darius, and I'll be your waiter for this evening," he said with a smile that could challenge Tyrese's. "Can I get you started with something to drink?"

"Yes, please," said Lydia. "I'm expecting three friends to join me as well."

"Great, I'll get their orders when they arrive. What can I get for you?"

"I'll have an apple cinnamon martini," she said.

"Excellent. I'll be right back with your drink," he said as he turned quickly to place the order. *What a yummy distraction he would be for some lucky woman,* Lydia thought to herself as she watched him walk away. She was really looking forward to having a nice evening out with her girls after the week she'd had; this was a welcome break. Her mind flashed back a moment to her last conversation with Helena. The sting of the entire encounter was still with her, and she still couldn't believe Helena would pull such a scandalous stunt. As she began to go over the events that led to her resignation in her mind, Elise walked up to the table, escorted by the same pretty hostess. Her arms were extended to give Lydia a big hug. Lydia stood up as they hugged and gave each other air kisses.

"Girl, look at you, you look fabulous!" Elise squealed. She was looking rather aglow herself, Lydia observed, and she had an idea why but thought she'd leave that discussion for later when the other ladies arrived.

"What's going on, Elise? It's so good to see you, girl," Lydia said as they grabbed each other's hand, giddy as girlfriends. Just then, Darius came back with Lydia's drink.

"Ah, we have another one to show up. Can I get you something to drink?"

"That apple martini looks right on time. I'll have the same." Darius nodded and, with a broad smile, was off again to place the order. Elise and Lydia looked at each other and laughed.

"He's a cutie," said Elise.

"Isn't he?" said Lydia, taking a sip of her drink. Lydia's eyes widened as she watched Chrystal and Sherrie walk in together and be escorted to the table by the lovely hostess. Lydia and Elise jumped to their feet and hugged the remaining ladies, gave air kisses, and exchanged grins.

"Okay, Chrystal is in the house, so now this party can get started," said Chrystal, doing a little shimmy in her chair. Chrystal looked as if she already had a couple of drinks, or perhaps the remnants of the evening before.

"Ooooh, what looks good? I'm actually starving," said Sherrie, glancing through the menu.

"Our waiter," said Elise as she observed him walking toward their table with her martini in one hand and a basket of freshly baked rolls in the other. Darius walked over to the table and placed the martini in front of Elise and the basket of bread in the center of the table.

"Here you are," he said. "Well, do we have everyone now?" he said, looking at the ladies with his Tyrese smile. "What can I get for you two ladies?"

"I'll have a glass of white wine," said Sherrie, which happened to be her signature drink.

"I'll have a margarita," said Chrystal with a little wink of the eye to Darius.

"Very good," he said. "Would you ladies care for an appetizer with your drinks?"

"The Thai spiced wings are really good, ladies," said Lydia.

"Yes, they are, in fact, they're my favorite appetizer," said Darius.

"Great. Thai wings it is. We'll have two orders," said Chrystal.

"Very good. I'll give you ladies a moment to look over the menu, and then I'll come back and take your dinner selection. Good?" All the ladies nodded in agreement as Darius turned and walked away from the table.

"Yum!" said Chrystal, practically licking her lips. The ladies all laughed in agreement. They all began chatting about their day and the past week since the last time they'd gotten together for brunch. Chrystal complained about the monotony of her job, Sherrie talked about how much Brad was working, and Elise talked about how Quinton was now practically a live-in lover much to her dissatisfaction.

"Girl, I don't know how you could be dissatisfied with a man that fine living with you," said Chrystal as she reached for a roll and the cinnamon butter.

"You don't understand, Chrystal. You know how I am. I need my space. I don't know why Quinton decided it was time to move in together."

Lydia laughed. "Maybe he wants to spend every waking moment with you Elise. I'm sure he had something to do with your skin looking particularly clear and that glow that you're wearing."

"I know he did too," said Sherrie as she slapped hands with Lydia.

"Okay, nosey heifers, if you must know. Yes. Quinton put it on me, or shall I say, I put it on him, twice this morning and right before I came here," she said with a grin. "Our problem ain't in the bedroom, okay?" The ladies all howled in laughter because they knew Elise loved talking about the mind-blowing sex she was having with Quinton, but she didn't want to admit she cared a lot more for him than she was letting on.

"Well, at least you're having sex," said Sherrie. "Brad called me this morning before noon to tell me he wouldn't be home until after midnight. How do you know twelve hours beforehand that you're going to be late? Shucks, we can't even be in the same room long enough to have sex. Isabella said I need to count my blessings for having a man like him, but what does she know?"

"Girl, leave that man alone, and Isabella is right," said Chrystal. "You should count your blessings because you could be out here struggling like me. Brad is out there making all that money so you and Jillian can live the life of luxury in that big-ass house to even have an Isabella to tell you what you should already know. Not to mention the newest Mercedes Benz SL550 Roadster in your driveway, in my favorite color, red."

"Actually, it's Mars red," said Sherrie.

"Oh, excuse me," said Chrystal in a rough English accent and rolling her eyes. "It's Mars red! My point is, your highness . . . you're spoiled. At least you know where your husband is, so stop complaining."

"Money and material possessions aren't everything you know," said Sherrie in an uncharacteristically serious tone. All the ladies looked at one another and burst out laughing.

"Money isn't everything? Now I've heard it all," said Elise.

"Yeah, what do you mean by that, Ms. I'll-drop-eight-hundred-dollars-on-a-pair-of-Christian-Louboutin-without-giving-it-a-second-thought?" asked Chrystal.

Lydia was laughing and swinging her hands back and forth in the air in agreement. The ladies were all well aware of Sherrie's legendary shopping sprees. Lydia herself had witnessed Sherrie spend no less than $3,000 in clothing in one store alone on several occasions. If Sherrie purchased an outfit, all of the accessories had to be purchased as well. The shopping sprees extended to little Jillian as well, who was the best dressed four-year-old any of the ladies have ever seen.

"Sherrie, sweetie, you may not like what Brad has to do to make that money, the long hours at the hospital and such, but you have to admit you sure love spending it," said Lydia with a chuckle.

"You guys just don't get it. Yeah, I shop . . . a lot." The ladies burst out laughing because Sherrie's comment was such an understatement. "But what else do I have to do when my husband is never around? Shopping gives me an outlet, a hobby, a way to bide my time until Brad gets home. I would rather take a nice long romantic walk in the park with Brad instead of shoe shopping anytime."

"Well, I'm sure Sax Fifth Avenue would be sorry to hear that," said Elise. "Their sales would drop dramatically if that ever happened."

"Very funny, Elise," said Sherrie.

Chrystal smiled. "I'm just finding it a little hard to feel sorry for you, girl. You're married to a world-class surgeon. He has responsibilities at work, and he's taking care of his family. What more do you want? Also, the next time you need an outlet to bide your time, why don't you give your girl a holla', okay?" Chrystal said laughing, slapping Elise and Lydia's hands, to which Sherrie just rolled her eyes.

"Anyway, I woke up this morning to a man I didn't even remember bringing home last night from the club," said Chrystal suddenly changing the subject.

The ladies all stared at one another and burst out laughing again. They could always count on Chrystal to trump any conversation they happened to be having with stories of her wild nightlife.

"It's true. When I was talking to her on the telephone this morning, her mystery man asked if she needed anything else to go with the scrumptious eggs and bacon he prepared for her," Elise said, amused by the thought of a strange, although apparently hot, Latin man cooking Chrystal breakfast.

"Oh, I have no doubt. So, Chrystal, when did you realize that your Latin one-nighter was in your house?" asked Lydia.

"I realized it when I discovered it wasn't you in the kitchen whipping up breakfast."

"What?" asked Lydia, confused by her answer.

"Yeah, it was Manuel, and he looks very much like Enrique Iglesias by the way."

"Manuel, huh? Chrystal, you picked up a man from the club and didn't remember him?" asked Sherrie.

"Yup, but luckily for me, he was a very good cook."

"And hopefully even better in bed," added Elise. "Not that you remember that either, right?"

"Oh, be quiet, Elise. Not every romp is going to be memorable whether you're drunk or sober," Chrystal said as if stating a statistical fact.

"You are really something else," said Sherrie in amazement, looking at Lydia, who could only manage to sit there with her mouth wide open. Lydia wasn't quite sure why she was so shocked. They all knew Chrystal enjoyed living on the edge when it came to gorgeous men, sex, and partying, and not necessarily in that order.

"Well, let's get off of Chrystal's scandalous mystery man and Sherrie's shopping woes and talk about you, Lydia. Girl, what in the world is happening with you?" said Elise, turning the conversation to a more serious matter. The ladies all stared at Lydia, who announced to them just that morning that she had quit her job, and they were anxious to hear how it all came about. Lydia took a deep breath and sighed. She and the ladies were so busy up talking about everything else that it had taken her mind off her own problems for just a moment.

"Helena was straight up tripping last week and pulled me off of the Edwards account I've been working on for months. In fact, that was the account she told me I would be handling exclusively when she hired me. It was one of the reasons why I agreed to come and work for her."

"You mean that huge account you've been working on so hard all this time?" asked Chrystal.

"Yup! And the funny part is, she gave it to Kameron of all people," added Lydia.

"Kameron?" said Chrystal in disbelief. "You mean Ms. I'm-the-mayor's-daughter Kameron?"

"That's ridiculous, Lydia. Did she give you a reason, and did you know she was going to do this?" asked Elise.

"No, she didn't give me a reason other than she felt Kameron was the senior designer of the office and should have been given the project all along."

"That's lot of bull," said Sherrie. "Well, you know what that's about. It's the old classic 'let me get the black girl to do all the hard work to get the project up to speed, then I'll slide it over to the white girl and pretend she's performed all these miracles.'"

"That's exactly what that's about because Kameron isn't senior to Lydia or anyone else in her office, isn't that right, Lydia?" said Elise.

"Yes, that's right. Her skills are so limited it's pathetic, and for Helena to even utter such nonsense to me was insulting to me, my experience as a designer, and to my intelligence."

"Well, you know they think they can say anything they want to you and you'll just accept it as gospel. I bet she was shocked as hell when you quit wasn't she?" asked Chrystal.

"She never saw it coming, although I don't know why not," said Lydia. "She should have known I wasn't going to accept that bull."

"So what happened next?," asked Sherrie.

"Well, the next morning, she expected me to be in the office in a meeting with Kyle Edwards with Kameron shadowing me, which still confuses me since she's the so-called senior designer in the office, but instead, I gave her my letter of resignation. Helena actually wanted me to hold Kameron's hand throughout the remainder of the project while she got all the credit. I told her it wasn't going to happen."

"Good for you, Lyd!" said Chrystal.

"How did she react to you giving her your resignation?" asked Elise.

"She was shocked and then angry that I had the nerve. Imagine that. She takes away the biggest project we've had to date in the firm, and she's shocked that I quit."

"That woman is a hot mess," said Chrystal.

"She's crazy as hell!" Sherrie added. "Do you know how many design companies would kill for my girl Lydia's skills? Girl, you did an awesome job on our bedroom and family room. People are always giving me compliments on the way it looks, and I tell them it was Lydia Brown's concept and design. I love it, and so does Brad," Sherrie said proudly.

Lydia smiled at Sherrie. "Thanks, girl."

Darius came back to the table with Sherrie's white wine and Chrystal's margarita and their double order of Thai chicken wings and sat the plate in front of them. Chrystal gave him a flirtatious smile and took a drink of her margarita as he walked away.

"Lydia, what are you planning to do now?" asked Chrystal. This was the moment Lydia was waiting for, a chance to unveil her plan of action.

"Well, you guys know how I've been talking about opening up my own place? It's really weird how all of this came about because while I was working with Helena, I kind of put my own aspirations aside. But now they're back on the table in full force. I'm going to start my own design firm," she announced proudly.

"Oh, Lydia, that's a wonderful idea," said Sherrie excitedly.

"Absolutely. Lydia, you can definitely do this. You're smart, you're educated, and you have the skills and the drive. I have no doubt you can do this at all," said Elise.

"Yeah, she has all of that, but does she have the startup money?" Chrystal asked, looking at Lydia while taking a large gulp of her margarita.

"I have some money saved. In fact, I have a good bit of what I think I'll need. I've put together a business plan, and beginning Monday, I will be looking at getting a loan together for the rest. I did some really wise investing thanks to the advice of my broker and our resident financial expert, Elise." Lydia and Sherrie snapped their fingers to Elise, both of whom had benefitted from her advice in the past.

"I'm going to do just fine," beamed Lydia.

"I'm so proud of you, Lydia. It sounds like you've thought all of this through and you're taking action. That's the stuff!" Elise almost shouted.

"That's my girl," said Sherrie. "One thing I've always loved about you is how you handle your money. I want to be like Lydia when I grow up," said Sherrie with a grin.

"So where are you going to set up your little business?" Chrystal asked with a hint of skepticism in her voice.

"Well, I'm going to start from my home office until I find a nice space to occupy, and I'll be on the lookout for that too real soon," said Lydia, tasting a Thai wing and sipping on her apple martini. Chrystal's tone and lack of enthusiasm had not gone unnoticed by Lydia, but she dismissed it for now, choosing instead to focus on the positive steps she was taking.

"Oh, you know, the other day, I saw a space on the corner of Pleasance and Hyde Street that was available for rent. It's a cute little space that used to be a beauty-supply shop. Do you guys remember that place? I think it was called Lola's Beauty Supplies," said Sherrie.

"Yeah, I remember. Lydia, do you think that would be a good location for your business?" asked Elise.

"I don't know, I'd have to check it out. Are you ladies available next week to maybe go with me to check it out?"

"Sure, I will definitely make myself available," said Elise

"You know I'll be there. Whatever you need," said Sherrie. Everyone looked at Chrystal, who was now playing with her empty margarita glass, for a response, but she just shrugged.

"I don't know yet. You know Dana is always on my ass about things. I don't know if I can get away."

"You get a lunch break, don't you? And just today, you were talking about not going in at all. I'm sure you can find the time to break away, even if it's after work," said Elise. Everyone looked at Chrystal for a response, but she still didn't give one right away.

"Well, just let us know when you can get away, Chrystal. We'll try to set it up for after work one day next week," Lydia said, trying to overlook the fact the she obviously wasn't interested in joining them.

"Oh, this is going to be exciting, right, Lydia?" Sherrie said full of excitement.

"I am excited, but it's going to be a lot of hard work. I have so many things to do."

"Nothing worth having comes easy. Take it day by day, and it'll all come together. You're going to do this, and we're going to be right there for you, right, ladies?"

Everyone joined in agreement. Just then, Darius came back to the table to take their orders for dinner. They were all very hungry by now after the long discussions. Lydia decided on the lobster ravioli, Chrystal the slow-roasted ribs, Sherrie the filet mignon with cabernet mashed potatoes and greens, and Elise the Southern-style fried chicken. Darius took down all of their meal selections and headed for the kitchen to place their orders. In the meantime, they each ordered another round of drinks. Lydia smiled and laughed with each of her girls, all of them very much their own person and yet they all seemed to click. She was happy that she had them to talk to about everything including quitting her job. She felt very fortunate to have each of them as friends. She glanced at her girls, Elise with her jovial yet always insightful advice, Sherrie who was always positive and tried to look for the best in everyone and every situation, and then there was Chrystal.

She and Chrystal had been friends the longest out of the group, and they'd had their share of ups and downs, including a difficult period a couple years ago involving a man Chrystal was dating at the time. However, they got through it like they'd gotten through a few other times in the past. For the most part, the girls were all very encouraging, uplifting, and in many ways spiritual women who could always count on one another. But on this journey Lydia was about to embark, the jury was still out on Chrystal, and Lydia didn't know what to do about it.

CHAPTER 6

HELENA

*I*t was 8:30 a.m., and Helena was already in her office with a throbbing headache, and there was too much going on for pain. When Helena came in and checked her voice messages, there were several messages on her telephone from agitated clients and, at the top of the list, Kyle Edwards. She knew this was going to be one hell of a day with several meetings scheduled, and she wasn't particularly looking forward to the meeting later today with Kyle. After Lydia just up and left without warning, Kameron chose this crucial time when they were trying to wrap things up on the Edwards account to become creative and alter the designs instead of just going with the plan Lydia had already laid out like they had agreed. Now Kyle wasn't pleased with the layout changes of the dining areas, the flooring, or the lighting fixtures, just about anything Kameron touched, and he wanted it all to be redone. Since Lydia bolted on her, several of her clients had been reassigned to Kameron, and none of them were pleased with the progression of their projects, and to be quite honest, neither was Helena. When Helena placed Kameron in charge of the Edwards account along with the Barons account and the Sheldon account, she didn't foresee having to hold her hand throughout the entire process or redo just about every drawing or presentation because it was just plain garbage. She was beginning to regret her decision to give anything substantial to Kameron, but there was still the matter of dealing with Lydia's disloyalty.

No one left her in the lurch with a client as important as Kyle Edwards. She underestimated Lydia and didn't plan for her to trump her move by leaving. But now she had a plan of her own set in motion that would teach Lydia that she couldn't play with the big dogs and not expect to get bitten.

Helena reached in her desk drawer and pulled out a bottle of Extra Strength Tylenol, opened the bottle, and popped two in her mouth. Then she swallowed them with a big gulp of her bottled water. She threw her head back against her leather-bound chair and ran her fingers through her shoulder-length salt-and-pepper hair and let out a heavy sigh when her assistant, Bernard, buzzed her on her speaker phone.

"Yes, what is it, Bernard?"

"It's a Jasper Pearsall on the line. Do you want me to put him through?"

"Yes, put him through, and hold any other calls."

"Certainly," said Bernard, and a after a few moments, Helena heard the voice of Jasper on her speaker phone.

"Helena, Jasper here," he said in a slightly feminine tone of voice.

"Hold on for a second while I take you off speaker," said Helena as she grabbed the telephone off the receiver. "Are you there?"

"Yes, I am. Long time no hear from my old friend. I got your message to give you a holla', so here I am, sweetheart. What can Jasper do for you?" he said with almost wink in his voice.

Helena and Jasper went way back. She and his mother, Eartha, who was now deceased, were very close friends and came up in interior design school together. They were even partners in business together once until about eight years ago when she became ill with an acute case of leukemia and died shortly after her diagnosis. Jasper was her only child, and Helena had always been like a second mother to him, although in the last couple of years, they hadn't spoken as often as Helena would have liked. Eartha had done very well for herself and invested well with the money she made through their business in interior design and real estate. After she passed away, she left her only son a sizeable inheritance, and Jasper, in turn, took great pleasure in spending his inheritance freely, traveling throughout Europe and the United States, purchasing the latest in fast cars, partying, and just living the good life. Eartha left this earth not having a clue about her little boy who didn't want her to know all the details of his bachelor life, but Helena wasn't as naive and trusting as her dear friend and was fully aware of the type of lifestyle Jasper was leading.

"Jasper, where have you been? Bernard had a heck of a time trying to locate you this time around, and you never answer that silly BlackBerry of yours. How have you been?"

"Oh, Auntie Helena, where has Jasper not been?" he said giggling. "Jasper has been in San Francisco for the past month, doing well. I'm working on a couple of projects here that are about to blow completely up. Kaboom!" he yelled in laughter. "You know Jasper always has a couple of irons in the fire."

Helena loved the way Jasper always referred to himself in the third person and was all too familiar with the irons in the fire he called projects. One year he was in New York producing an Off-Broadway show that didn't last through two showings, and another time he was investing in real estate in Arizona that never came to fruition, and then there was the time when he decided he wanted to be a music-video director in LA, supposedly working with big names like Beyoncé, Usher, Justin Bieber, and Rihanna. Needless to say, all of his little projects were all failures, leaving him to once again regroup and figure out where he belonged in this world before sinking more of his inheritance into the next huge bomb. Helena always felt he was an extremely gifted and talented interior designer like his mother, but he lacked focus and never pursued the field to carry on his mother's legacy. Helena would have even considered allowing Jasper to take over his mother's partnership in the business, but he had no discipline or dedication about himself. So instead of concentrating on an area where his talents lay, he simply drifted from one failed project to the next. Helena shook her head and wondered if she should even ask about his latest venture but decided against it.

"Jasper, darling, if you're not too busy at the moment, I have a little proposition for you here I'd like you to think about."

"Proposition? Sounds intriguing. What do you have in mind?"

"Well, I have an issue that I need taken care of, but it's going to take a little time. Are you interested? I'll make it worth your while."

"You know Jasper is always there for you, Auntie Helena. Jasper will be on the next plane out there."

"Good boy. Now let me fill you in."

As Helena explained the details of what she needed him to do, she gleamed at the thought of having Jasper on board. Obviously, whatever he had going on in San Francisco wasn't going to blow up anytime soon since he practically leaped at her offer before even knowing the details. Now with Jasper in, she could fully set her plan into motion.

*   *   *

Kyle Edwards was closely examining the latest design drawings with a scowl on his face, his eyeglasses tilted on his nose, and his pen tapping the table. He didn't look pleased. Helena and Kameron sat across the table from him in silence, practically holding their breath for his reaction. Kameron had just completed the presentation for the third time since Lydia's departure, and he still wasn't satisfied with the outcome. He took off his eyeglasses and glared directly at Helena.

"These designs are nowhere near what we talked about," he said sounding very annoyed.

Helena and Kameron were a bit shocked at his comment, and Kameron stepped in to defend her work.

"What's the problem this time? I thought we had all agreed on what you're seeing here and this meeting was to give the go-ahead to proceed further."

Kyle totally ignored Kameron's comments and again stared directly at Helena.

"Can we talk privately?" he said, indicating that he didn't want Kameron in the room.

Helena stared back at him for a second while Kameron let out a loud sigh of exasperation.

"Kameron, why don't you go grab yourself a cup of coffee, and I'll finish up here."

Kameron rolled her eyes, pushed the chair back from the table, hurriedly grabbed her pad and drawings, and stormed out of the room, practically slamming the door behind her. Helena watched Kameron's abrupt exit and then turned her attention to Kyle, who was giving her a look of displeasure with the entire scene.

"Helena, what's going on here? I'm spending a lot of money on this project, and the best you can do is give me a designer who's prone to temper tantrums? This is a very complex project, and I was assured I would get your best designers to work it. I feel like I'm wasting my time and money here, and I don't like wasting either. Please tell me I'm wrong. Please tell me that this isn't the best you have to offer."

"Kyle calm down. I've had to make some changes recently. Kameron is an experienced designer, she just—"

"Experienced? Is that what you call experienced? Where's Lydia, and why has my project been reassigned to someone who's obviously not up to the challenge or the magnitude of this project?"

"Lydia is no longer with us. I had to reassign your project, but I assure you everything we talked about will be done . . . and more. We're still on schedule, and we can make the deadlines we've set. Just give us a day to redo the designs as you requested."

Kyle glared at Helena, not quite sure if he believed that she could actually deliver on her promises, but at this stage of the project, he'd already put too much money into it to back out and start all over with another firm. He began gathering his papers and drawings together to place in his briefcase as Helena stood up to walk him to the door. He walked over to the door and then turned to look at Helena before leaving.

"You have twenty-four hours to convince me that I should continue doing business with Helena Designs. I have a lot riding on this project, but I'm not totally against taking my money elsewhere."

"We'll be in touch," said Helena not appreciating the threat but trying to appear accommodating.

Kyle opened the conference room door but turned back to Helena before he exited.

"Twenty-four hours, Helena. I won't waste a second more."

He stared at her an extra second to let her know he meant business and then walked swiftly out of the office and out of the building. Kameron, who was in the lounge drinking a second cup of coffee, saw Kyle leave and ducked out to find Helena and see what was happening. When she went into the conference room, she found Helena still there looking over the drawings.

"So what did the big bad wolf have to say?"

Helena slung the drawings down and looked at Kameron. "He said we have twenty-four hours to clean up our act or he walks."

"Humph. So what? Let him. We have other clients," said Kameron.

"You just don't get it, do you, Kameron? This is business. My business. And the Edwards account is going to bring in a huge commission that Helena Designs will not lose out on. We'll be ready for him in twenty-four hours, you can bank on it."

"Whatever. It's five o'clock, and I have a date in a couple of hours, so I'll be leaving in a few minutes."

"I think you better cancel your date. We have twenty-four hours to get these designs ready, and I've assured Kyle that they will be ready, so roll up your sleeves. It's going to be a late night."

"What? Helena, I have plans this evening."

"I don't give a damn about your social life, Kameron. I put you in charge of this project, and you will work it to my satisfaction as well as the client's. Right now the client isn't satisfied, and I can't say that I blame him. Don't make me regret giving you this opportunity. It's time for you to earn the recognition I've already given you." Helena gathered her things and walked out of the office, leaving Kameron in the room alone to think about her next move. Kameron picked up the conference room telephone and reluctantly dialed a telephone number. The phone rang twice, and then a raspy voice answered.

"Hello."

"Hey, it's me. I hate to do this, but I'm going to have to ask for a rain check for tonight. I'm working late on a project. I'm sorry. I was really looking forward to this evening." As Kameron listened to the voice on the receiver, who sounded disappointed but replied he would call a buddy and go out anyway and catch her another time, she wondered if she wasn't going to be the one with regrets about Helena's decision.

*   *   *

The Starbucks located just a couple of blocks down from Helena's on the corner of Concord and Blanding was alive with the hustle and bustle of customers rushing in for their morning coffee, espresso, or Danish, and Lydia was right in the mix. There were customers sitting on the outside of the store sipping their coffee while working on their laptops and friends and acquaintances having a quick morning coffee together before dashing off to their respective jobs. Lydia loved the smell of this place. If she wasn't an interior designer, she would surely be an owner of a Starbucks franchise; in fact, she thought she'd look into investing into one anyway. She was next in line and already knew what she wanted to order.

"I'll help the person next in line," said a young woman with black frizzy hair and red pimples on her face. The name on her name tag said Ashley, but Lydia thought to herself that she looked more like a Debbie than an Ashley. Lydia walked up to the counter to order her coffee.

"I'll have a grande-size mocha café with whipped cream to go. That's all."

"That will be $4.35," said the young woman as she rang up the order in the cash register.

"I've got that, Ashley. Can you also add an espresso on that order as well?" said a voice coming directly behind Lydia. Lydia turned around and was surprised to see Kyle Edwards, who was pleasantly surprised to see her as well.

"Mr. Edwards. What are you doing here?" said Lydia with a smile.

"I like my coffee strong, flavorful, and hot. Starbucks is the place for all of that," he said. "Fancy meeting you here."

Lydia smiled to herself, thinking that was exactly the way she liked her men—strong, flavorful, and hot. "I should buy stock in Starbucks, I'm here so much." She grinned. "So how is everything going?" Lydia asked, indirectly referring to his project.

Kyle Edwards gave out a sigh of frustration. "Not too well. You didn't ask me if you could leave Helena's. Why did you leave me like that, and what are you doing now?"

"It's a long story, and believe me it wasn't a decision I came to lightly. I'm in the process of opening my own place. In fact, I found a spot that I think will be perfect for it. So what's going on with the project?"

"That's great, Lydia. You're a very talented designer. You should have your own place. As far as what's going on, the designs just aren't right, and they can't seem to get them right. I'm not happy with how this woman, Kameron, changed everything around. We had an agreement on the rooms before you left, and I haven't seen any of that since."

"I'm sorry to hear that. I actually thought your project would be close to being finished by now. I left it in good shape."

"Well, it's supposed to be almost finished, but we keep running into snags. I've got a lot of money invested in this, and I don't want it to be for nothing. I've given them one more shot to get it together, and if they don't, we'll be looking for another designer."

The wheels in Lydia's head were turning at the thought of a commission like the one Helena Designs stood to receive if they got a designer on the project that knew what he or she was doing, but luckily, she had her newly printed business cards in her wallet. So she reached into her purse and pulled out her wallet to hand him one of her new business cards.

"Here's my business card if you ever need anything. I'm just getting set up, but you know my work, and you know what I can do for you. Let me know if I can be of any help."

Kyle willingly took the business card and thanked Lydia. Ashley was back with the mocha café and the espresso. Lydia picked up her drink and smiled at Kyle.

"I've got to run, but give me a call. I'll buy you a cup of coffee next time. Have a good day."

"You have a good day too, Lydia, and thanks for the offer."

As Lydia walked out of the door wearing a form-fitting black-and-red lightweight jogging suit, Kyle couldn't help but think that not only was she a talented designer, but she was also a very intelligent, vibrant, and extraordinarily beautiful woman. "Lydia's Loft," he read on the card. "True beauty comes from within." *Very clever and certainly true*, he thought. He would definitely give Lydia a call. Suddenly, Kyle felt as if he had real options with his project and possibly a new option in his social life as well.

CHAPTER 7

CHRYSTAL

Monday mornings at Goldman and Associates was like the bull pit on Wall Street—pure chaos. Telephones began ringing at 7:30 a.m. sharp and did not slow down until around 3:00 p.m. Clients, potential clients, parents of clients, attorneys, publicists, and managers were all on the horn bright and early, attempting to reach their most valued expert when damage control was needed for some scandalous event that happened over the weekend. Goldman and Associates had a reputation for being one of the most sought after public relations firms in the city, and this made for a very busy office, so much so that Chrystal dreaded Mondays more than anything. As soon as she walked through the double glass doors that led to her desk, which was located directly outside of Dana's plush office, there were no less than twenty to thirty messages left on her voice mail and a tasking list from Dana as long as the day is long. There was barely enough time to utter "good morning" greetings before she had to hit the ground running. Chrystal was answering several lines at once, a task she'd become very proficient at performing without losing one single call, and this morning was no different.

"Good morning, Goldman and Associates, Dana Little's office, please hold."

"Good morning, Goldman and Associates, Dana Little's office, please hold." As she placed the third call in a row on hold, Dana was preparing for her Monday 9:00 a.m. meeting and didn't want to be distracted by calls. Chrystal was putting the finishing touches on the minutes from last week's meeting in between answering calls, and there were meeting dates and times that needed to be confirmed for Dana.

"Chrystal, I need Jeff McKenna on the line now!" shouted Dana through her office door. Chrystal rolled her eyes and began dialing the number. *Jeff McKenna should have a direct line to Dana as much as they talk,* she thought, *but whatever.* After two rings, a young voice answered and spoke distinctly into the receiver.

"Good Morning. Mr. McKenna's office. Can I help you?"

"Yes, I'm calling on behalf of Dana Little for Mr. McKenna."

"Certainly. Please hold." After a short pause, a heavy voice was heard on the other end of the receiver.

"Jeff McKenna."

"Yes, Mr. McKenna, I'm calling on behalf of Dana Little. Please hold." Chrystal promptly placed the call on hold to begin transferring it onto Dana's line. "Dana. I have Jeff McKenna on the line."

"Thank you," said Dana as she took the call and began talking. "Jeff! Dana Little. I have some exciting news for you . . ." Chrystal hung up the line although she was tempted to stay on for a few more seconds to hear the great news. She gave out a loud sigh and stood up to go get another cup of coffee from the break room. It was only 8:30 a.m., and she already felt the day should be over. After she got her coffee, she sat back down at her desk and began taking a sip when the telephone rang again.

"Good morning, Goldman and Associates, Dana Little's office."

"Good morning, sexy," the voice said in a heavy Spanish accent. "How is your morning going so far?"

For a second, Chrystal sat in silence scanning her mind for voice recognition. The voice was sexy and sounded vaguely familiar, but she couldn't place it.

"I'm sorry, who am I speaking with?"

"Oh, you're hurting my feelings, sweet pea. We shared a beautiful evening together, and in the morning, I made you breakfast, and you don't remember me. It's me, Manuel."

"Manuel," Chrystal said in a low voice. "How are you?" she asked, wondering how he found her place of business and this number.

"I'm well. Did you get the flowers I sent to your home the other day?"

"Yes, I did. Roses. That was very sweet and thoughtful of you."

"I was hoping you'd like them, although I wasn't sure about your favorite flowers. I didn't think I could go wrong with roses."

"No, you're right. Roses are always on point." Speaking of point, Chrystal was wondering what was the point of Manuel sending her flowers or making this telephone call. Yes, they'd shared an evening together, which she barely remembered because she was too drunk and hungover. But he was what she'd characterize as a one-night stand, and one-nighters did not send flowers or call after the night was over. That's in the player's handbook, and Chrystal subscribed to it and even agreed with it.

"How did you know where I work, Manuel?" Chrystal asked out of curiosity since she never mentioned to him where she worked or what she did for a living.

"Ah, I have my sources, and I'm afraid I can't reveal them to you," he said teasingly.

"Well, you're very resourceful. So what can I do for you? I have a busy morning ahead of me," Chrystal asked, trying to get to the point of his call.

As if reading Chrystal's mind, Manuel began explaining the purpose of his call.

"I was wondering when we can get together again. Maybe go out for dinner and get to know each other better. You know, have a real date this time around. The night at the club was great, and I was happy to meet such a beautiful woman, but I would definitely like to know more about you."

Chrystal wasn't happy with the direction of this conversation. Yes, he was fine and she appreciated the breakfast, the flowers, and maybe even the sex, but she wasn't interested in making a love connection. She decided it would be best to avoid the situation, and maybe he'd get the hint and move on.

"You know, Manuel, I'm going to have to get back to you on that. I have so much going on right now. In fact, I have a meeting to go into in just a few minutes, and a client just walked in," said Chrystal in an attempt to rush him off the telephone.

"Okay, I understand. Let's talk later tonight."

"Unfortunately, tonight isn't good for me. My schedule is a bit hectic right now because I have a lot on my plate, but we'll talk soon. I'm sorry I have to go. I have calls waiting."

There was a long silent pause on the telephone, which made Chrystal wonder if Manuel had hung up the line, until he finally commented, "Of course. I didn't mean to bother you at work. You have a good day, okay?"

"I will, and you too. Take care." *Have a nice life is more like it*, Chrystal thought to herself as she hung up the receiver. She hoped Manuel wasn't one of those really dense guys who couldn't take a hint or know a brush-off if it smacked him in the face. She didn't have a problem using the same basic principles that men used on women they no longer had use for once they'd gotten what they wanted: be brief, be vague, and be inaccessible. Manuel seemed to be a nice enough guy, but she wasn't looking to get into anything remotely serious or permanent with anyone. She hoped for his sake he understood.

*   *   *

The 9:00 meeting had turned into the inevitable debating match with the partners bickering over minor details about a prospective client's product. Every Monday meeting became a lesson in the art of beating a dead horse to death. Chrystal absolutely hated when they got into these sessions because Dana was obsessively detail oriented and made it Chrystal's responsibility to take accurate minutes right down to the person who ate the last lemon-filled doughnut. Because of this, Chrystal had resorted to recording the meetings and transcribing them later at her desk. This appeared to work very well for her and kept Dana off her back. After the meeting had finally concluded and the partners each disbursed into their respective offices, Chrystal began gathering up the remaining doughnuts, pastries, fruit, and orange juice and put them away to be eaten later in the day. She was grateful that the phones had calmed down for a while so she could concentrate on making Dana's travel arrangements for her upcoming trip to San Diego. There were several meetings that needed to be rearranged due to her schedule, and she needed to confirm her hotel reservations at the Regency Hyatt Hotel and reserve a rental car with Budget for her stay. Just as Chrystal was checking her e-mail, Dana appeared in front of her desk with a handful of files to be placed back in the filing cabinets.

"Chrystal, make sure these files are placed back in the cabinets, and get me Jeff McKenna on the line. I'll take the call in the conference room," said Dana hurriedly. She'd been behaving even more high strung than usual, racing around the building all morning, like the caffeine was truly kicking in.

Chrystal made a mental note to herself to place Jeff McKenna's office number on speed dial and then dialed his office, getting on the line the same young voice as earlier. After going through the same steps and after a brief pause, Jeff McKenna was on the line. Chrystal transferred the call into the conference room and beeped Dana to notify her of the call, for which she promptly picked up. Chrystal pushed the button and picked up another line to contact their travel agent to make plane reservations to San Diego for Dana. After that task was complete, she decided to begin transcribing the minutes for next week's meeting when she discovered her tape recorder was missing. She noticed Dana coming out of the conference room and figured she'd finished her call with Jeff McKenna and was now headed into another meeting with a new client.

"Chrystal, I'm expecting another call from Jeff and Susan McKenna, but I'll be in a meeting for at least an hour. Buzz me when it comes through."

"Okay, I will," said Chrystal.

"Thank you," said Dana as she scurried away into a smaller conference room where the new clients had been escorted and waiting. Chrystal wondered if she'd left her tape recorder in the conference room after their nine o'clock meeting and headed there to look for it. After searching for a few minutes, she found that it had fallen between the cushions in the chair where she was sitting. She picked up the recorder and noticed that it hadn't been turned off when the meeting had concluded. Great, thought Chrystal. Now she'd have to wade through the garbage to get the main ideas from the meeting. She turned the tape recorder off and headed back to her desk, placed on her headphones, and rewound the tape a little to make sure it had recorded. She pressed the start button and immediately heard Dana's voice on the recording, speaking in a rather unusual manner, in an almost seductive tone. *What the hell?* thought Chrystal, realizing that her conversation was definitely not from the meeting. Although confused by Dana's tone of voice, curiosity got the best of her as she listened intently to what was being said.

"Jeff, baby, are you ready for our little San Diego getaway? . . . I know, baby, but we'll be together for three romance-filled days, and I can't wait . . . No, Chrystal will be making my arrangements today, so I'll give you my agenda so you can get on the same flight, but we'll be in our usual hotel . . . [laughs] . . . I know it's been a while, but I can't do this too often without Paul getting suspicious, and you need to be careful of Susan [laughs]. You're a naughty boy, but I'll take care of you when we get there. I have all kinds of plans for you big boy . . . I know. I can't wait either. I'll talk to you later, I have another meeting . . . Of course I'll wear that cute little thong you bought me. I've been saving it [laughs] . . . Okay, talk to you later [kisses]."

Chrystal's mouth dropped completely open. Damn! Dana and Jeff were having an affair! Chrystal couldn't believe how she'd missed the signs that now seemed so obvious. This explains the excessive phone calls, the unscheduled lunch meetings, the supposed unaccompanied trips to San Diego, and the reason she had never been asked to go with her to San Diego. So many odd things about their relationship now made sense with this explosive bit of information. Who would guess that frumpy Dana Little was actually stepping out on her husband and smiling in Susan McKenna's face during their face-to-face meetings every week while she's secretly screwing her husband? Scandalous skank! Dana wasn't as dull and lifeless as she'd thought, getting her freak on regularly. Chrystal laughed to herself. Now the question in Chrystal's mind was how she could use this damaging evidence to her advantage. Maybe she'd use it as leverage for a nice raise or, better yet, a promotion with a nice raise. She'd always thought of her job as dead-end with no possibility for upward mobility, but not anymore. Suddenly, the possibilities were limitless, and her dead-end job now had a lot more potential.

CHAPTER 8

ELISE

*I*t had been a long tedious day at the office, and Elise was grateful it was Friday because all she wanted to do now was take off her clothes and relax in a nice hot bubble bath with scented candles and a glass of Chablis. She didn't want to think about anything or talk to anyone because her entire day consisted of talking to clients or brainstorming about the next promotion for their client's products. After entering her spacious condo in which she purchased two units and that Lydia helped her design, she headed toward her bedroom and then placed her briefcase beside the bed. *Thank goodness Quinton isn't home yet so I could take a bath in peace*, thought Elise. She began peeling off her silk Prada blouse and suit, kicked off her Roberto Cavalli pumps, and carefully removed her stockings. Elise loved her bathroom and tub. Lydia had remodeled the bathroom for her and replaced her old ceramic tub with a beautiful Victorian claw-foot tub, and she absolutely loved it. She turned on the hot and cold water, gave it a feel to gauge the temperature, and began running her bath. She poured in some bath oil, which began to make bubbles, and then headed back toward the bedroom where she decided to turn on some smooth jazz. She went into the kitchen for a wineglass and poured herself some Chablis and then headed back into the bedroom where she removed her red laced bra and matching panties. As she walked into the bathroom nude to check the water, she began humming the sweet sounds of Kenny G. His music was soothing to her soul. She lit the candles that were around the tub, placed the wineglass where she could reach it, and then climbed into the tub slowly, allowing her body to adjust to the temperature of the welcoming water. Once her body was submerged, she let out a deep sigh of relief, closed her eyes, and allowed the warmth of the water and the feeling of the bath oil take over her body as she released the excess stress from the day. As Elise opened her eyes and reached for her wineglass, she was startled by Quinton's image standing in the doorway and let out a loud and long shriek.

"Dammit, Quinton!" she yelled. "Where did you come from? I didn't even hear your ass come in!"

Quinton laughed heartily. "Sorry, baby, I didn't mean to scare you. I just walked in, but it looks like a few minutes too late since I didn't catch that sexy, sensual body getting into the tub."

"Well, I'm trying to relax. It was one hell of a day at work. Can I have a moment?"

"Yeah, baby. Take as long as you like, and when you get out, I'll have dinner all prepared." He came over to the tub and gave Elise a deep kiss in her mouth and smiled and then turned to walk out the door. Elise took a huge gulp of her wine as she tried to slow down her racing heart. Elise closed her eyes and concentrated on breathing deeply in and out, focusing on the warmth of the bath and the soothing music in the background. She picked up the wineglass again, this time only taking a sip of wine, and allowed her body to become completely relaxed. This was exactly what she needed.

After a forty-five-minute bath and another half hour to pamper herself with body oils, lotions, and perfume, Elise emerged from her bedroom feeling refreshed and hungry. The aroma of beef tips braised in red wine sauce filled the air as she walked into the kitchen. As she looked around, she saw Caesar salad had been prepared, and Quinton's muscular physique was leaning over the oven, taking out freshly baked dinner rolls. Quinton was a fantastic cook, much better than Elise would ever be since her specialty dish was scrambled eggs and toast, although the toast was normally burned to a crisp. So Quinton prepared most of their meals because he realized

Elise's limitations in the kitchen, and he really enjoyed cooking. Quinton and Sherrie traded recipes on occasion and even started an annual chili cook-off for the group to enjoy and judge. Elise walked over to Quinton and wrapped her arms around his thirty-two-inch waistline.

"It smells good in here, and look, you have my favorite scallops with beef tips," she cooed. "My bath was so relaxing and just what I needed. Now I'm starving," said Elise as she turned and reached for the wine to pour herself another glass.

"I'm glad you're hungry. Dinner will be ready in just a minute."

Quinton had already set the dining room table with lighted candles. He took the baked potatoes out of the oven and placed them on each of the plates along with the beef tips. He then filled the salad bowls with Caesar salad and placed them on the table. Elise sat down at the dining room table and waited for her main course to be served. She poured Quinton a glass of wine and then, with the remote control, turned on the stereo to some soothing jazz. Quinton headed into the dining room with both plates in hand.

"Here you are, baby. Medium rare, just like you like it." He sat down, Elise said grace, and then they began enjoying the delicious meal Quinton had prepared.

"So you enjoyed your bath, right? Soaked those beautiful muscles and released some stress?"

"Yes, I did," she said, smiling and taking a bite of her scallops. "It took me to my happy place and got rid of all the tension I was still carrying when I came home."

"Good, I'm glad you enjoyed it. You know, there is another more pleasurable way to get rid of tension and burn calories at the same time." Quinton grinned as he took a bite of his salad.

"Yeah, we'll explore that later on tonight," said Elise as she poured Caesar dressing over her salad. Quinton watched Elise intently and then asked.

"How is everything?" he asked referring to the dinner.

"Great as usual. I would ask you to teach me to cook, but you and I both know that I don't have any desire to cook, and I'm not ashamed to admit it." She grinned.

"Well, in that case, it's a good thing you have me around to feed you."

"Yes, it is," said Elise as she and Quinton clicked their wineglasses together in agreement.

Quinton wondered if this was a good time to bring up the possibility of him and Elise living together permanently now that she was relaxed and being fed. He decided that this was as good a time as any and went for it.

"Speaking of me being around, I wanted to talk to you about making our living arrangement a little more official."

"What do you mean?"

"I mean moving in with you permanently and making a real commitment to being together, maybe adding my name to the town house. What do you think?" Quinton waited for a reaction, but Elise continued eating her beef tips and mixing the baked potato with sour cream without skipping a beat.

"Did you hear what I just said to you, Elise?"

"Yes, I heard you."

"So what do you think?"

"Quinton, I think we both need to take some time to think about this before we jump into it. Living together is a big step, and I think right now we both need our own space on occasion. I mean, don't get me wrong, I love having you here and being with you, but we have our own places, and maybe we should just think about keeping it that way." Quinton was disappointed with her response but not totally surprised. Elise had been on her own for a long time, and making a commitment like this would be huge for her, but he couldn't let the idea drop like this.

"Elise, just think about this. I'm here most of the time anyway, and I love waking up with you every morning. You and I are good together, and for me, you're the one. Don't you think that way about me?"

"Yes, but that has nothing to do with it. It's a big step. Maybe we should take some time to think about it."

"What's there to think about? We love each other, and we should want to be together."

"I don't think this is a decision we should take lightly. This is a major decision, and we should both be ready for it."

"Are you saying you're not ready to take that step?"

"I'm saying that I think we should both think this through. What would you do with your apartment and your things? All of your things can't fit in here."

"What would anyone do when they decide to move? You give your notice and then you move. As far as my things, we'll work that out. I'll put some things in storage. I'm not worried about any of that. I just want us to be together on a more permanent basis. I thought our relationship had grown enough to think about taking it to the next level."

Elise was beginning to think she would need another hot soothing bath and a shot of vodka after this conversation. The last thing she wanted to discuss with Quinton was him formally moving into her condo, invading her space. She didn't want to hurt his feelings, but moving in with her permanently was not on her agenda. In fact, it wasn't even a real consideration. She enjoyed her independence and needed her space, although lately his junk was beginning to take up more room than her own. In any case, she wasn't going to be forced to give up her independence. Not now, not ever. She would simply put him off as long as possible with an empty promise to think long and hard about changing their living arrangements. Maybe he'll just drop the whole thing, and they could get back to doing what they do best, which were cooking, eating, going to work, and having mind-blowing sex. Elise didn't see anything wrong with their current arrangement. Why fix it if it's not broken?

"Okay, you've given me something to think about, so why don't we take some time to digest it? We don't have to make any decisions tonight, right?"

"Elise, I know you. I don't want this to just drop. If we take some time to think about it, I want you to seriously consider what I've said. Baby, I want you. I want us to be together. Let's do this."

"I'm not going to be forced into a decision I'm not ready to make."

"Well, I'm not going to let you string me along without an answer."

Elise was a little annoyed yet impressed that he actually called her out on her plan. But at this point, she was getting angry. Who did he think he was anyway, and why the sudden rush to move into her condo? Why wasn't he asking her to move into his apartment like a real man? However, she didn't want to go down that road with him.

"Well, are you going to really think about this, or are you blowing smoke?"

"If you insist on an answer at this very moment, it will have to be no, so your best bet is to give me some time. I said I would think about it, and I will. What more do you want?"

Quinton looked at her with distrust. He knew Elise would use avoidance to handle any situation she didn't want to deal with or talk about, and he really wanted her to seriously consider his moving in with her. Quinton also knew that if he pushed too hard, she would just shut down and refuse to talk about anything. So he decided to concede this round and let her play her little game for now.

"Okay. I know this is a big step, and I don't want us to jump into anything without thinking it through. We need to be on the same page with this, so take some time to think about it. But I'm telling you, Elise, this is important to me, so don't think for a second that I'm going to drop it because that's not going to happen."

"Fair enough. That's all I can ask. Now can we have dessert?" asked Elise as she got up to walk over to him.

"I didn't make any," he said, still a little put off from the discussion. Elise stood in front of him, untied her robe, and allowed it to drop to the floor, revealing a sexy short black laced nightie.

"No matter because dessert is served," she said suggestively. He snapped out of his funk instantaneously, grabbed her, and pulled her onto his lap.

"I see you've thought of everything. You look delicious," he said as he kissed her on the mouth and then along her breasts, which were bulging out of the nightie.

"And the good thing is, I'm low fat, so there's no guilt. And I'm *very* satisfying."

"That you are. I'll get the low-fat whip cream," he said as he stood up, scooped her up into his arms, and carried her into the bedroom. Elise was pleased with herself. A night of passionate animalistic sex would buy her some time or at least get his mind off this moving in business for a day or two. She would just make sure to put it on him every chance she got as always anytime the subject came up. She didn't know what brought on this conversation, although she'd felt it coming for quite some time. He just couldn't leave it well enough alone. *Why are relationships so difficult,* she asked herself, *and why must we recreate the wheel when what's working for us now is tried and true?*

CHAPTER 9

SHERRIE

*I*t was Saturday morning and almost 10:00 a.m., and it was Sherrie's turn to host the ladies' monthly brunch, and they were due to arrive at 11:00 a.m. Each month the brunch alternated among the four ladies, and last month, the brunch was hosted at Lydia's fabulous home. Isabella was already in full swing downstairs, making waffles and frying chicken for Sherrie's famous chicken-and-waffles brunch with fresh fruit, muffins, and Isabella's famous scrambled eggs. Isabella would never reveal exactly what she put in her eggs, citing that it was a family secret recipe, but they were to die for. Jillian had been up for an hour watching her favorite cartoons and playing with her dolls. Sherrie came downstairs in a comfortable light-blue-and-white sweat suit with her long black hair pulled back into a neat ponytail. She leaned over and gave Jillian a big kiss on the cheek.

"Sweetie, run upstairs and wash your face and hands with soap so you can get ready to eat soon. Then when you come back down, Mommy will do your hair and get you dressed before your aunties Lydia, Elise, and Chrystal come over, okay?"

"Okay, Mommy!" said Jillian as she got up and ran upstairs with her doll. She was an absolutely gorgeous little girl who would be celebrating her fifth birthday in a couple of months. Sherrie and Brad had talked about having another child, but lately that subject had not come up. Sherrie always thought their family would be complete with a little girl and a little boy. Now she wasn't sure where Brad's head was in their marriage, and she was concerned about the card she found in his pocket for a private detective agency. She couldn't help but wonder why he would need their services. Sherrie walked into the kitchen, where Isabella was busy placing the last secret ingredients of her scrambled eggs. The food looked wonderful. She'd outdone herself as usual. The table was decorated festively with beautiful spring colors and dinnerware and napkins of bright yellow, light blue, pink rose, and lavender. Sherrie enjoyed having a theme for her brunches. This month's theme was spring is in the air. She checked each setting, making sure everything was perfect. Nothing was too good for her girls.

"Isabella, everything looks absolutely wonderful."

"I'm glad you like it, Ms. Sherrie. All of the food will be ready to serve once the ladies all arrive."

"Great," said Sherrie while placing some gardenias in a vase to place on the kitchen counter. Jillian returned from upstairs with a little soap still on her face and in her hair.

"Mommy, I finished washing my face and hands. Can I eat now?"

"Oh, look at you, niña. How pretty is your face, eh?" said Isabella while placing the last of the fried chicken in a decorative basket.

"Come here sweet pea. Look at you. You still have soap on your face, and what's this in your hair?" asked Sherrie, rolling her fingers through Jillian's hair. "Come here and let me get you all dolled up." Sherrie smiled. She took Jillian's hand and headed into the half bath downstairs to wash her face. Afterward, they headed into the family room where Sherrie changed her into a cute pink Baby Phat top and ankle jeans. She loosened her long wavy hair and began brushing it.

"Mommy, make my hair really pretty. I want two ponytails with ribbons on both sides."

"You've got it, sweet pea." Sherrie parted her hair straight down the middle and brushed through both sides while placing an elastic band on each ponytail along with pretty pink ribbons. When she finished, she gave Jillian a mirror to check out her new do.

"So do you like it, pretty girl?"

"It's beautiful!" gushed Jillian as she hugged her mother tightly. Just then, Sherrie heard the front door open and then close. She got up and took Jillian's hand to see if one of the girls had arrived a little early, but instead she found Brad standing in the foyer, taking off his jacket to reveal his surgical scrubs.

"Daddy! Daddy!" Jillian shouted as she ran down the stairs toward him. Brad knelt down and threw his arms open wide awaiting his little girl's big hug. He scooped her up when she arrived and gave her a big kiss on the cheek.

"Hey there, cupcake! How's my girl? Look how pretty you look."

"Mommy just fixed my hair because aunties Chrystal, Lydia, and Elise are coming over."

"Is that so? Well, you look beautiful and ready to entertain."

"Thank you, Daddy."

"Yes, so why don't you go help Isabella finish up before your aunties get here?" he said, giving her another big kiss.

"Okay, Daddy." He put her down, and she ran into the kitchen, where Isabella gave her a small tray to take over to the table. Brad gazed at Sherrie, who was silently watching him with their daughter. She wasn't sure about how Brad felt about her and their marriage, but he certainly loved his little girl, no doubt about that.

"Hey, honey," said Brad, stepping over to her to give her a quick kiss on the lips.

"Hi. I wasn't expecting you so soon. I thought you were working late today."

"I was going to work late, but someone took my shift."

"Oh, Brad, that's great, and right on time. Isabella has brunch all ready, so you can join me and the ladies," Sherrie said excitedly.

"I don't want to crash your ladies' brunch. Besides, I need to go upstairs and pack. I have a flight out for Colorado this evening. There's a fascinating case at the University of Colorado that they need an opinion on, so Dr. Bowers and I will be flying out there together to act as consultants."

Sherrie was flabbergasted. On the one day that Brad was actually home on a Saturday, he had the nerve to be headed out of town.

"Brad, how long have you known about this?"

"I just found out a couple of hours ago. I won't be gone long, just a few days." He kissed Sherrie on the forehead. "I need to get cleaned up and start packing."

He turned and rushed upstairs, leaving Sherrie with her mouth hung open and a little numb, trying to figure out what had just happened. She glanced at the clock sitting on a stand in the sitting room. It was now a few minutes before 11:00 a.m., and she knew Lydia and Elise would be right on time, so there was no time to debate the issue with Brad. But their conversation was not over by any means. Sherrie would make sure of that. Just as she was thinking of how she would express her disappointment to Brad, she saw two fierce lean figures strutting up her walkway and onto the front porch through her stained-glass front door. It was Lydia and Elise on time as usual, and they both looked amazing. Sherrie pulled herself together and walked over to the door to let the girls in.

"Look at you two! Right on time," she squealed as she gave them both a hug at the same time.

"Yes, we're here and we're starving. What does Isabella have for us today?" said Elise, tiptoeing daintily into the foyer entrance.

"It sure smells good in here. I can use some coffee," said Lydia as she took off toward the kitchen. One of the things Sherrie loved about her girls was they always made themselves right at home no matter who happened to be hosting. They were like family. As Sherrie and Elise walked into the kitchen, Lydia was holding Jillian on her hip and giving her a big kiss while saying hello to Isabella. Jillian was giggling uncontrollably because Lydia was tickling Jillian in her side.

"Look how big she's getting, Elise. If we don't see this little munchkin every day, she's going to be all grown up before our eyes." Elise walked over while Lydia handed Jillian over to her. Jillian gave Elise a big hug and a kiss on the cheek. They absolutely adored Jillian since so far, she was the only offspring from their foursome, and they all made a point of treating her just like the little princess she was and spoiling her to death. Jillian was a very lucky little girl to have three honorary aunties who loved her to no end. Among her parents, relatives, and the three aunties, birthdays, Christmas, Easter, and Halloween were occasions fit for a princess, and they were always extra special with the aunties all involved. They were all gathered around the kitchen counter laughing and talking about their week while Isabella poured coffee and put out the last few brunch items. Elise had a tall glass of orange juice while Sherrie took a sip of her cranberry juice. Jillian was now sitting at the counter eating her brunch and enjoying a glass of milk. Just then, the doorbell rang.

"That's Chrystal," said Lydia, heading for the front door to let her in.

"Hey, girl," screamed Chrystal and giving Lydia a big hug. "Is everyone here?"

"The gang's all here, and we're about to throw down."

"Good because I didn't have anything to eat this morning, not even a dry piece of toast, so I'm ready." They walked back into the kitchen where Elise, Sherrie, Jillian, and Isabella were all smiles to see Ms. Chrystal. Isabella handed her a cup of coffee because she knew that was Chrystal's specialty request.

"Brunch is served," said Isabella. The table was gorgeous as usual, and the ladies all sat down in their usual seats, passing the bacon, Isabella's famous eggs, hash browns, fruit, chicken, and waffles. It was like a smorgasbord with all the trimmings.

"Okay, so what's been up with everyone? I know there's something going on," said Sherrie. "Who wants to go first?"

Elise poured some blueberry syrup over her waffles and started to dig in. "Quinton wants to officially move in with me. He says he wants to take our relationship to the next level," she said dryly.

"And I take from your tone that's not exactly working for you," said Chrystal as she took a bite of a chicken leg.

"It kind of caught me off guard. I knew something was brewing in that shiny head of his, but I didn't think it would come up so soon."

"So what's the big deal? You guys are practically living together anyway, right? Just give him his own drawer and closet space and call it a day," said Lydia.

"Yeah, Elise. Quinton is fine! So why the reservations?" said Sherrie.

"Are you people just meeting me?" said Elise, reaching for another waffle. "You know how I am. I need my own space and a little privacy once in a while. My home is my haven, and I want to keep it that way. Quinton moving in is just going to make things all weird."

"So what did you tell him?" asked Lydia. 'I know you didn't hurt that man's heart and say no."

Elise was looking a little sheepish and let out a grin that asked for understanding. "I didn't tell him anything. I just put him off and told him I would think about it. But you know what? There's nothing to think about. I don't want us to move in together officially, and that's just all to it."

"You know, you're crazy Elise," said Chrystal. "It sounds like Quinton is the sweetest man you've ever dated. He cooks, he's always fussing over your ass, and all you do is complain. Damn, hand him over if you don't want him. He can move in with me today if he wants."

Elise shoved Chrystal's head.

"Okay now, heifer, hold up. We're not going there. Besides, you're talking about a man who cooks and fusses over you. What happened with Manuel? As I recall, he called you at work, something a real dog would never do, and you got rid of him so fast his head is probably still spinning."

"That was different. I didn't know who the hell Manuel was. You've been with Quinton a couple of years now."

"So when are you going to have this discussion with Quinton?" asked Lydia. "If you're not ready to move in together, then you should tell him you're not ready. That is a big step."

"That's exactly what I told him. Uh-huh, that moving in together is a big step and we shouldn't take it lightly, but he's all gung ho about it."

"Well, you both have to be on the same page. Lord knows I know a little something about what it's like to be on different pages," said Sherrie.

"I told him that too Sherrie . . . that we need to both be on the same page, and I asked him not to push me on it. So to get his mind off the subject, I put it on him, and I'll keep putting it down on him until it's a nonissue."

Chrystal laughed. "Only you would think giving a man sex would keep his mind off being with you. Girl, you need to come up with another strategy." All the ladies burst out laughing when they noticed little Jillian drinking her milk and listening to their conversation. They'd forgotten she was still in the room, and Elise's sexcapades wasn't exactly talk for small children.

"Ah, Isabella, can you take Jillian upstairs? Let her play with her computer games," asked Sherrie.

"Of course, Ms. Sherrie. Come, little one," said Isabella, beckoning Jillian to her side. "We'll have some fun upstairs with your games and toys."

"Okay!" said Jillian as she leaped off the kitchen stool and ran over to Isabella. When they disappeared upstairs, Sherrie turned back to the ladies.

"You were saying?" She laughed.

"I don't know what to do. I don't want to hurt his little feelings or anything, but I'm not ready for this. I mean, we're doing just fine the way things are right now. Why can't he be happy with the way things are right now?"

"Maybe he's ready for more, Elise," said Lydia as if she'd just had a revelation. "You know, we're always talking about men not being able to commit, but when they are, we're not willing to accept it. Sometimes I think women are noncommittal too, not just men."

"Hell, I know I'm noncommittal because there are too many fine men out there that I haven't explored, and they're just waiting for me out there," said Chyrstal.

"I guess I'm just not in that place yet either. I care about Quinton a lot, and Lord knows the man rocks my world in bed, but I just don't want this right now. I don't know when I'll be ready, I just know it isn't now."

"Well, then you have your answer. You just have to break the news to him gently, like maybe during sex or something." Sherrie giggled while getting more fruit.

"Not just during sex," said Chrystal. "Do it during orgasm. Men will agree to do anything during orgasm. I once made a man agree to pay my rent for six months while he was climaxing."

"I can always count on you for the good tips. I'll keep that in mind," said Elise, taking a bite of the last bit of waffle on her plate.

"Well, what other exciting news do we have?" asked Lydia.

"You mean besides my boss having a torrid affair with one of our married clients?" said Chrystal, drinking the last of her coffee.

"What? Are you kidding?" asked Lydia. "Dana is having an affair?"

"Yes, that little Ms. Prim-and-proper is screwing Mr. McKenna's brains out. I can't believe I didn't pick up on it sooner," said Chrystal.

"Wow, nothing scandalous like that happens in my office!" said Elise, looking around for agreement from the other ladies.

"How do you know she's sleeping with him? Did you see them together, or did you hear something?" asked Sherrie.

"Well, that's the thing. I record our Monday morning meetings to make sure I get every little detail because you guys know how anal Dana can be. Well, after the meeting, I made a mistake and left the tape recorder in the conference room, so I went back in there to get it. When I found it, it was still on and it recorded a conversation she had with him on the telephone just a few minutes before. She was talking about how she couldn't wait to go on her trip to San Diego because he's coming with her. Talking about taking care of him and wearing some damn thong he bought for her for the occasion."

"Dang! I wonder how long this has been going on?" said Lydia.

"Me too. I made travel arrangements for her to go to San Diego on Friday. So they'll be together for the weekend. His wife is gorgeous. I really don't know what he sees in humdrum Dana."

"Some men are just looking for a side piece that's willing to spread their legs anytime they want. It doesn't matter what they look like," said Elise.

"What does his wife look like?" asked Sherrie.

"She's Hispanic and resembles Salma Hayek with long black wavy hair and curves. Girlfriend has a little booty too. Hell, I would date her if I went that way because she has it going on. But Dana, I don't know what that's about."

"It's about the booty, girl. That's all," said Elise, snapping her fingers.

"What are you going to do with this information, Chrystal?" asked Lydia, knowing how Chrystal's mind works.

"I think I'll sit on this juicy piece of information for now. But I'm sure it will be useful to me when the time is right," said Chrystal with a mischievous tone.

"What does that mean?" asked Sherrie.

"You're not thinking of doing anything crazy, are you, because you need your job," said Lydia.

"Damn right," said Elise. You still owe me five hundred dollars you know, so don't think I forgot about it," she said pointing at Chrystal.

"Well . . . you know I could use a raise," said Chrystal.

"Girl, don't even go there. That's her mess. Don't make it yours. Dana is going to have to deal with that mess with her husband and his wife. She's playing with fire, so you should stay out of it before you get burned," said Lydia.

"She may have to deal with it with me first," said Chrystal, laughing.

"Okay, think about that, Chrystal. You need to leave that alone. Dana will trip herself up soon enough, and you don't want to have anything to do with it when it happens," said Sherrie.

"I'm not saying I'll mess with her, but she owes me. Maybe this is my way to get what I want. Lighten up. I'm not going to do anything with her. Dana can screw him 'til the cows come home for all I care."

"Good. But keep us informed, and don't leave out any details." Elise laughed.

Chrystal got up from the table to get another cup of coffee. This was exactly why she couldn't tell her girlfriends everything because all they did was get all uptight about nothing, but it didn't matter because she had already made up her mind. Chrystal was going to keep an eye on Dana and Jeff no matter what her girlfriends thought about it. The last time Chrystal spoke to Dana about a raise, Dana brushed her off, but that wouldn't be the case this time around. Dana was going to give Chrystal what she deserved for working as hard as she did and for putting up with all her crap. For once, Chrystal was going to be on top. She gazed over her shoulder to watch her friends all laughing and having a good time. Elise was telling Lydia about a possible space she'd found for her interior design company, and Sherrie was talking about Brad leaving for Denver that afternoon. They all seemed to have so much going for themselves. What was wrong with Chrystal wanting the same things? Didn't she deserve to be happy and have nice things too? *Look at this big-ass house,* thought Chrystal as she scanned the downstairs living space that was twice the size of her entire apartment. It was much too big for Sherrie, a little girl, and a husband who's barely home. Chrystal wanted her piece of the pie, and if knowing this little bit of information about her boss was her path to getting it, she was going to take it. All she had to do was sit back and wait for the right moment.

CHAPTER 10

LYDIA

*I*t had been weeks since Lydia walked out of Helena's office for good, but it felt more like months. The time had brought about a calmness and self-assuredness that Lydia hadn't felt in a long time, and she was happy to be in control of her career and her life once again. It was a glorious feeling. Having the Edwards accounts stripped away from her was a professional and personal setback, but Lydia was always one to see the brighter side of any situation. If that hadn't happened, Lydia would still be working for Helena instead of pursuing her own dream of opening her own interior design firm. *Everything happens for a reason,* Lydia thought to herself. *It's not easy for African-American women to establish themselves and receive the respect and recognition they so richly deserve in the workplace. We have to remember that sometimes God takes us through something to position us for something better, something wonderful.*

Lydia reached over and picked up the latest issue of *Essence* magazine from her nightstand. The first family, the Obamas, graced the cover, and she thought about what it had taken for this black man to get where he was today and the sacrifices he'd made along with the people before him. She remembered during the Democratic National Convention, Michelle Obama gave a riveting, emotion-filled speech to explain to the nation and to the world that her husband and family were no different than any other family in America and why Mr. Obama should be the next president of the United States. Like all people in America, they wanted to be given opportunities to improve themselves and their lives. They wanted bright futures for their children and their future grandchildren. Lydia could not recall ever seeing a presidential candidate's wife address the nation to give such explanations about who they were and what they stood for. However, these were the situations that African-American women had to deal with to make it in this world, constantly having to prove themselves and show the stuff they're made of. Lydia remembered how proud she was to see a beautiful, intelligent sista' from the South—as Michelle Obama called herself—deliver and knock it out of the park. Lydia thumbed through the magazine to begin reading the article about the Obamas when her telephone rang. She glanced at the caller ID and recognized the telephone number right away.

"What's up, girl?" she said, answering almost immediately.

"Hey, girl, I've got some great news for you!" said Elise excitedly. "The owner of that space we looked at together the other day wants to accept your offer. He wants to meet today to sign the paperwork for the deed! Congratulations, Lyd!"

"No! Oh my goodness, I can't believe this, Elise! My very own place! This is almost surreal," said Lydia, overcome with the excitement of everything that was happening. "You really hooked me up, and I'm so grateful."

"You deserve it, Lydia, and I'm proud of you. So when do you want to go to his office?"

"As soon as I get my clothes on, I'll be ready. Give me about thirty minutes."

"Okay, I'll swing around in about thirty minutes, and we'll go do this, see you in a bit."

"Okay, great." Lydia closed her cell phone, leaped in the air, and did a Mary Tyler Moore twirl around her living room floor. She was elated at the news and knew this was a big step toward opening her own place. She ran into her bedroom to change into a pair of slacks and a nice top, combed her naturally curly locks, put on just enough CoverGirl eye shadow and lip gloss for the occasion, and grabbed her cell phone off her nightstand and her Gucci purse that was sitting on the chaise chair. Lydia took one last glance in the mirror to make sure her makeup and hair were perfect and patiently awaited Elise's arrival.

*   *   *

Elise glided up into Lydia's driveway in her fierce new black 2011 Lexus GX 460 that she bought as a gift to herself after closing her last big deal for her firm, Catalina Marketing Inc. Elise was a tough negotiator that was highly respected and viewed as a valued member of her marketing team, a reputation she worked very long and hard for to attain. Elise stopped and started to blow the horn when she noticed Lydia walking out of her house talking on her cell phone. She unlocked the passenger door so that Lydia could climb in.

"Yes, we're leaving now. Elise just drove up. When are you going to be finished with your hair appointment? Maybe we can meet for lunch afterwards and have a mini celebration." Lydia was talking as she slipped into the SUV and gave Elise two air kisses. "It's Sherrie," Lydia whispered to Elise. Elise nodded and then set the SUV in motion out of the driveway, heading down the street, outside of the neighborhood, and into the flow of traffic in the direction of the freeway.

"If you're going to be done with your hair in about an hour or so, why don't we all meet at Paschal's Restaurant for lunch? Do you want to do that Elise?" Lydia asked, turning to Elise.

"Sounds like a plan to me," said Elise, smiling.

"Okay, Sherrie, we'll meet you at Paschal's about noon. I'll call Chrystal to see if she can be there too. Okay, we'll see you later, sweetie." Lydia hung up her cell and turned to Elise.

"So Sherrie's getting her hair done? You know how long her hairdresser takes. It'll be a miracle if she does meet us on time," Elise laughed.

"I know. But she says she was in the chair about to get curled now, so she should be done. Let me call Chrystal and see what she's doing." Lydia dialed Chrystal's cell phone, but it went straight to voice mail, so Lydia decided to leave a message. "Hey, girl, Elise, Sherrie, and I are going to lunch today at Paschal's around noon, so meet us there if you can. Call me."

"There was no answer," she mentioned to Elise. "So tell me what happened with Mr. Thompson," asked Lydia.

"Girl, he just called and said he discussed the offer with his wife, and they both decided it was a good offer, so he wanted to do the paperwork. That's one of the quickest deals I've ever closed." She laughed.

"Elise, I can't thank you enough for finding this location. It's going to be perfect, right downtown near several little shops and restaurants. I'm so excited, I can't wait."

"I'm excited for you. I know you're going to hook your space up and get all your clients going. You should steal some back from that backstabbing Helena."

"Speaking of old clients, did I tell you I ran into Kyle Edwards at Starbucks the other day?"

"No! Really? So what's up with him?"

"He's not happy with how his project is going. He's really not pleased with Kameron, and he's upset that Helena handed his project over to her. I don't blame him because she just doesn't have the experience."

"So did you give him your card? Tell me you did."

"I did! And I told him to call me if I could help in any way. I think he will be calling me because he said he was giving them one last chance to pull their act together, and you know even Helena can't pull that rabbit out of her hat, not with Kameron anyway."

"That's how you do it, Lyd. You have to start establishing your own clients, and if Helena isn't cutting it, he's fair game. I hope he calls you. That would be a really nice commission, wouldn't it?"

"It would be a very nice commission, and I can definitely use it."

"So let's pray on it, and I know that the work will come back to where it should have been all along, right?"

"Right on!"

They had been so engrossed in conversation that before they knew it, they'd arrived at the location. Elise was thrilled to actually find a parking space right in front of the building. She parked, and they both got out of the car and headed toward the entryway and into the building. Mr. Thompson was standing in the middle of the room talking to a young woman who looked like she could be his daughter. When he saw Lydia and Elise enter, he stopped talking to greet them.

"Hello, Ms. Brown and Ms. Dixon. So good to see you both again," said Mr. Brown.

"Mr. Thompson, thanks for calling," said Lydia.

"Let's go into my office and we'll conclude our business, eh?"

"Yes, of course," said Lydia.

"I'll wait out here, Lydia. Holler if you need me," said Elise as she sat down in one of the chairs in the waiting area.

"Would you like some coffee or tea while you wait, Ms. Dixon? Anna, get Ms. Dixon something to drink," said Mr. Thompson to the young woman who was now sitting behind a counter looking through an appointment book. There was a flat-screen TV on the wall of the waiting area with news on the station for clients to watch while they waited.

"Yes, thank you. I'll have a cup of coffee if it's no trouble," said Elise to Mr. Thompson and Anna.

"No trouble at all," said Anna as she scurried away into another room to get the coffee. Lydia and Mr. Thompson made their way into his office, and he closed the door behind them.

In the waiting area, Elise looked around the room and could just imagine how Lydia would redecorate it and make it her own. A few seconds later, Anna returned from the room with a cup of coffee, sugar, and creamers and set them on the coffee table in front of Elise.

"Thank you," said Elise as she began to pour cream in her coffee. She glanced up at the TV and noticed the news now showed a picture of a Victorian home and then a picture of Helena Barnes. Elise put down her coffee. "Can you turn that up please?" she asked Anna, who in turn picked up the remote control and turned up the volume. The newscaster was announcing that Kyle Edwards had decided to pull out of a deal with his current designer, Helena Designs.

"In a statement from highly successful businessman Kyle Edwards just this morning, the Edwards Group Inc. has decided to discontinue services with Helena Designs on their highly anticipated renovated luxury hotel project. Mr. Edwards purchased the property and restored the exterior and then contracted Helena Designs for the interior redesign. Mr. Edwards intends to open a luxury hotel and a restaurant within this renovation, which was previously scheduled to open two months from now. The group has estimated that the entire project is at about 4.5 million dollars. When asked why he was currently looking for a new designer for the project, Mr. Edwards declined to answer. However, sources close to him cite that the group has not been pleased with the progression or the direction of the project, citing several delays and disagreements over the design and drawings as one of the main causes for the disassociation. At the center of the controversy is the designer for the project, Kameron Tyndall, Mayor Tyndall's daughter. Neither the mayor's office nor Helena Designs owner, Helena Barnes, could be reached for comment prior to our broadcast. We'll keep you updated on this story as we find out more. Back to you, Ted."

"Oh my goodness, this is the break that Lydia has been waiting for," said Elise, who couldn't believe her ears. She felt Lydia had just been vindicated because when you did ugly, it always came back on you. Elise couldn't wait for Lydia to finish up so they could talk about this latest development and what that could mean for her new business.

*   *   *

Inside Mr. Thompson's office, Lydia was just finishing signing the last of the paperwork. She was pleased with the arrangement and the terms of the agreement, and everything was set for her to move into the building in two weeks. Mr. Thompson assured her that he could be moved out within that time frame. As she placed her signature on the last of the paperwork, Lydia thanked Mr. Thompson for the deal.

"Mr. Thompson, thank you."

"I think you will be very pleased here. We've done quite well in this area, but now it's time for me to retire and spend more time with my wife. She wants to travel and visit our grandchildren more."

"That's exactly what you should do because you've worked hard and you deserve it," said Lydia as she got up from the table. She then extended her hand for a handshake, for which Mr. Thompson reciprocated.

"Best of luck, Lydia, and I'll be in touch. Just two weeks from today and it's all yours."

"Thank you so much, and good luck to you. Enjoy your retirement," she said walking to the door as he escorted her out."

"We certainly will. You have a good day."

Lydia walked outside of the office as Elise was rising from her seat in the waiting area. She gave her a look to say "all done." "Thank you, Mr. Thompson," said Elise.

"Likewise. You both have a good day."

Elise and Lydia walked out of the building, and Lydia squealed with excitement.

"It's all mine, Elise! All mine!" Lydia screamed, giving Elise a high five.

"That is wonderful, Lydia. But I have even more wonderful news. I'll tell you in the car," said Elise as they approached her vehicle. She unlocked the doors with her keys, and they both climbed into the vehicle. Just as they were driving away and Elise was about to explode about the news, Lydia's cell phone went off. She glanced at the caller ID, which said "Kyle." Lydia immediately opened the cell.

"Hello."

"Well hello, Lydia. It's Kyle Edwards. Did you see the news this morning?"

"Mr. Edwards, so nice to hear from you. No, I haven't seen the news. I just came out of a meeting. Is there something I should have seen?"

"I've dissolved my association with Helena Designs. They just aren't cutting the mustard. Now I see who was really doing all the great work. I'd like to set up an appointment with you to talk. When is a good time for you?" Lydia was stunned. She couldn't believe all of this was happening on the same day.

"Well, what about tomorrow morning? My office is in my home until I can move into my new space in a couple of weeks. So how about we meet at the Starbucks at about 10:00 a.m.?"

"Sounds good. I'll meet you at 10:00 a.m. See you then."

"Okay, thank you," Lydia said smiling as she hung up her cell. She was practically glowing with excitement and then looked at Elise. "That was Kyle Edwards . . ."

"Girl, that was the news I wanted to tell you. While you were in the office with Mr. Thompson, there was a news broadcast that Kyle Edwards had fired Helena Designs! It was amazing!"

"What?" said Lydia. "Helena is probably beside herself right now. Wow, this is really turning out to be some kind of day. I can't believe it. I have my own space, and now I have my client back. God is good."

"All the time," said Elise.

"And all the time."

"God is good! You got that right, girl." Elise laughed.

Lydia was raising her hands in praise as they were making their way to Paschal's for lunch. Just then, Lydia's phone rang again. She was hoping it was Chrystal since they hadn't heard from her about lunch yet, but instead, it was Sherrie. Lydia opened her phone and said hello.

"Hey, girl. I'm finished and I'm on my way to Paschal's. I'll get a table if I get there first. Are you guys on your way?"

"Yes we are, and I have some more fabulous news!"

"Girl, I saw it on the news about Kyle Edwards and Helena in the beauty shop. I had all the ladies buzzing about it. Serves that old wench right!"

Lydia started laughing. "We will definitely talk at lunch. Have you heard from Chrystal? She hasn't returned my phone call."

"No, I haven't heard from her either. Maybe she'll show up, but I'll try to call her. I'll see you guys there. Go, Lyd! Go, Lyd!." Sherrie shouted.

Lydia just couldn't stop smiling. She felt like everything was starting to fall into place. Lydia had her own place and she had begun contacting old clients, but of course, getting Kyle Edwards back was going to make victory seem so much sweeter. There was still so much to do in moving in the building in a couple of weeks, not to mention the fact that she was going to need an assistant. She made a mental note to place a notice in the paper the next day. She just couldn't believe all of this was happening, and in a way she wanted to thank Helena. Her mother always told her that God placed people in your life for a reason, and maybe Helena's purpose was to get her back on track with her dream, and for that she certainly couldn't continue to hold a grudge. God was good, and she was going to bask in this blessing.

CHAPTER 11

CHRYSTAL

"**D**amn phone!" Chrystal yelled as she tried to dial but discovered her battery was dead. She pulled out her charger to get it charged back up because her cell phone was like her lifeline. Without it, she couldn't get in touch with her girls and find out what was going on in their little circle. She plugged her phone into the charger and then the charger into the socket on the wall of her kitchen counter. She was happy to have the day off after getting Dana off on her skank weekend with her part-time lover, Jeff McKenna. Dana thought she was so slick carrying on a torrid affair with a client right in the office. Did she actually think no one would ever find out? Since discovering this bit of information about her boss, Chrystal had been thinking of all types of scenarios to bust her with it. She knew her midyear review was coming up next week, which was when she would normally ask for a raise or a promotion, whichever provided the biggest increase in salary. In the last couple of reviews, Dana had denied her either, citing funding issues and all types of bull when Chrystal knew the bottom line was she just didn't want to give her any more money. Well, this year was going to be different unless she wanted her little affair to blow up in her face. Chrystal smiled when thinking about the reaction Dana would have when she broke the news to her that her little secret was no longer a secret, and if Dana wanted to keep it that way, she better come off the money. *It will be perfect*, thought

Chrystal. She opened her refrigerator door to get a cold Diet Coke, snapped it open, and took a long drink before swallowing. *Soft drinks just aren't what they used to be,* she thought. A few years ago, if she had drank a soft drink down like that, it would have burned her insides to bits. Chrystal threw herself down onto her leather chair in the living room and turned on the TV to the local news station. Chrystal wasn't one to watch the news, but the headline about Kyle Edwards dumping Helena Designs caught her eye as she turned up the volume and listened intently.

"Damn!" she shouted. "I wonder if Lydia and the girls know about this?"

She grabbed her cell phone off the charger and noticed there were enough bars to place a call, but beforehand, she checked her messages. *One missed call from Lydia, Chrystal, Elise, and dammit, Dana too.* She decided not to return Dana's call right away but listened to Lydia's message:

"Hey girl, Elise, Sherrie, and I are going to lunch today at Paschal's around noon, so meet us there if you can. Call me."

It was almost 4:30 p.m., so she'd missed out on lunch. She immediately hit redial, and Lydia's phone rang twice before she picked up.

"Hello."

"Hey, Lydia. Sorry I missed your call, girl. My phone was out."

"Yeah, we were hoping you would join us for lunch. We did a little mini-celebration because I closed on my new place today. I also got a call from Kyle Edwards. He wants me to finish up his project since he dumped Helena. We have a meeting in the morning."

"Yeah, I just saw that shit on TV just now. I was wondering if you knew about it. Hey, why don't we all go out tonight to a club to celebrate? You know, get our dance and drink on. What do you think?"

"I like that idea!" said Lydia with a gleam. "Let's round up Elise and Sherrie. Where did you want to go? How about the Apache Café? We haven't been there in a minute."

"Yeah, we haven't," said Chrystal, suddenly remembering her last visit to the establishment. "How about around 8:00 p.m.? That way we can grab something to eat there and just relax."

"Okay, I'll call Sherrie and Elise. See you there, girl."

They both hung up the line, and Chrystal immediately thought about what she was going to wear. And although, as she recalled, her last visit to the Apache left a lot to be desired, this was going to be a good night; she could just feel it.

*   *   *

The Apache was one of the ladies' favorite hot spots in the city. They loved it for its diverse atmosphere, the intimate café style, the artwork, not to mention that they served all types of food from southwestern to Latin to Caribbean delights. The artwork displayed on the walls were magnificent, and being lovers of local talent, the Apache always delivered. One night, about six months ago, Chrystal dragged Elise out to the Apache on a weeknight, and she met a guy who happened to be performing that evening. He was very handsome, just like Chrystal liked her men, and noticed her and Elise sitting at a table off to the right of the stage, sipping on apple martinis and enjoying the music. His name was Elijah, and his singing style was a cross between Luther Vandross and Babyface, so of course, all the ladies in the audience were swooning to the sweet, soulful sounds of his music and calling out his name. But it was Chrystal and Elise's table that he visited after his set. Chrystal remembered watching him in awe as he glided over to her table with a smoothness that only a brother like himself could command. He was sporting a low fade, a form-fitting T-shirt revealing his muscular chest and powerful arms, and jeans. His hazel eyes were piercing and almost looked right through Chrystal as he approached. She remembered how Elise was nudging her under the table as he drew closer to the two of them. They were both giddy with anticipation of his arrival.

"Good evening, ladies. Are you enjoying the show?" he said in a low voice that could pass for Dennis Haysbert from *The Unit*.

"We're doing well," Chrystal and Elise replied almost in unison. Chrystal giggled.

"You sound good up there. I like your vibe," she said.

"Well, thank you. It's always good to know that beautiful ladies like yourselves are enjoying what I'm doing. May I join you ladies?" he asked while waiting for a positive response.

"Yes, you may!" Elise answered almost too soon, but Chrystal agreed, and he pulled over an empty chair from the next table and sat down.

"I'm Elijah," he said extending his hand to Chrystal and then Elise, "and you are?"

"I'm Chrystal, and this is my friend Elise," Chrystal said with a sly smile as she shook his hand and then took another sip of her apple cinnamon martini.

"Nice to meet you both. So are you ladies from here? I know a lot of people come in here from out of town."

"No, we're from the ATL. This is one of our favorite spots because of the atmosphere, the food, and of course, the excellent music," said Chrystal.

"Yeah, this is a hot little spot. A friend of mine owns it, and he was kind enough to allow me to play here and showcase my music," offered Elijah.

"Your music is amazing," said Elise. "I hope you'll showcase it more often." He smiled at Elise, but it was obvious to Chrystal that he was into her, and they all knew it. So Chrystal decided to take a little ladies' room break with Elise to explain the situation to her.

"Would you excuse us for a moment, we're going to go to the little girl's room," said Chrystal, nudging Elise up from her chair.

"Of course. I'll be waiting," he said smiling. Chrystal smiled back at him and grabbed Elise's arm to head toward the ladies' room. Once they were in there, Chrystal made sure no one else was in the bathroom.

"Elise, he's into me, so I need you to politely excuse yourself and leave."

Elise looked at her and rolled her eyes. "This is so like you. We come out together, and as soon as someone with a swinging dick between his legs comes sniffing around, you wanna drop your girl. What's up?"

"Girl, you know what's up. You got a man. Let your girl get a little somethin', somethin'. I'll pay your cab fare if you like. Just make up an excuse and go, okay? I'll catch up with you in the morning."

"You are such a ho." Elise smiled.

"Yeah, but I'm your ho, so get going."

"Okay, okay. But be careful. I'll call you tomorrow."

They gave each other air kisses, and instead of Elise going back to the table to make an excuse, she just headed for the front door while Chrystal rejoined Elijah who was now waiting at the table with a glass of red wine.

"I'm back," she smiled as she sat down closer to him, crossing her legs to reveal her sexy thighs in her thigh-high form-fitting dress.

"Yes, you are. Where's Elise?"

"Oh, she has an early morning tomorrow. You know, she's a big-time marketing executive, and she has to get ready for a huge presentation early. My girl's always on the job."

"Oh, really?" he said, obviously disappointed. "Wow, I wish I'd known she had to leave so soon because I was hoping to get to know her a little better." Chrystal was stunned. *What did he just say? Is this fool saying he is really into Elise?* thought Chrystal.

"Chrystal, I have another set coming up in a few minutes. Can I offer you another drink before I leave?"

Well, I'll be damned, he was interested in Elise! She couldn't believe this shit.

"No, I'm fine," Chrystal answered, a little embarrassed and feeling her face burning.

"It was nice meeting you. Enjoy the rest of the show."

Chrystal watched Elijah get up from the table and walk across the room to whisper something into another young lady's ear who was sitting at the bar. They both laughed out loud, and he gave her a kiss on the cheek and then walked over to a guy, slapped hands with him as a greeting, and then headed back on stage for his next set. Chrystal was humiliated. She couldn't believe she'd read him so wrong. This didn't normally happen to her. It was all she could do to slink out of the club quietly and unnoticed.

The next morning, when Elise called to make sure Chrystal had arrived home safely, Chrystal made up a story about a night of passionate sex with Elijah because said she didn't think she'd see him again. Elise laughed about it, called her a scandalous ho, and asked her over for dinner with Quinton that evening. Chrystal accepted the invitation. She'd always considered herself the ultimate player of their group, so she wasn't about to tell Elise what really went down, and she hadn't set foot in the Apache since.

CHAPTER 12

LADIES' NIGHT OUT

*T*he ladies were all looking beautiful and tight in their night gear and were all ready to celebrate Lydia's victory. It was good to get away and go out to be with the girls. The Apache was lively as usual, and the ladies were all seated at their table with their drinks while munching on their appetizers, jerk glazed chicken wings and barbecue skewers. The aroma of Latin and Caribbean cuisine filled the air, the music was on point, and there were quite a few good-looking men roaming around. Chrystal who had all but forgotten about the incident during her last visit to the Apache had already set her sights on two good-looking men for a little later. In the meantime, all the ladies raised their glasses for a toast.

"To our girl Lydia who knows how to kick butt like nobody's business," said Sherrie. Everyone clinked their glasses together.

"Yeah, girl," hollered Chrystal.

"You go, girl!" said Elise. Lydia was ecstatic with all the kudos and praise from her girls.

"You know, I couldn't do any of this without the love and support of my girls. So for that, I thank all of you. You're all invited to the opening of Lydia's Loft. In fact, you're all invited to help me clean the place up in a couple of weeks. So bring your buckets, brooms, and mops because we're going to be some cleaning fools."

"Yeah, sounds like fun as always, Lyd," said Chrystal flatly.

"Right, so make sure you're there because I know you hate to miss out on fun."

"Don't worry, she'll be there. We'll all be there," assured Sherrie.

"Hell to the yes," hollered Elise as she took another sip of her winter-white cosmopolitan.

"So, Lydia, what do you think is going on in Helena's camp right now? What a blow this must be for her, right, although she surely deserves it," said Sherrie.

"I'm sure she's feeling the sting of it all to have all this blow up in her face, but now she knows how it feels. She gave Kameron the project to gain a little media attention, but I'm sure she didn't want this kind of media attention," said Lydia.

"Wow, if I could have been a fly on the wall when Kyle Edwards lowered the boom on her ass. I bet that was classic," said Elise. "I bet she's really regretting what she did about now."

"If she's not, she should be. You can't do hateful things to people and not have that karma come back on you. You have to be careful how you treat people," said Sherrie.

"I wonder how Kameron is taking all of this? Did you guys hear the news? They said, 'In the center of all the controversy is Kameron Tyndall, the mayor's daughter.' I don't think Kyle Edwards or the media cares that she's the mayor's daughter," said Chrystal.

"My meeting with him tomorrow is going to be interesting, but I'll have to see how much damage has been done and how much of their mess I'll have to repair."

"Well, Lydia, if anyone can do it, you can, so don't even sweat it," said Elise, taking another bite of her wing.

"Exactly. Lydia, whatever he throws at you, you can handle it. You did before. That's why he's coming back to you," said Sherrie.

"All men, no matter what they want from you, know a good thing when they see it. Kyle ain't no fool. So do your thing, Lydia." Chrystal grinned, taking a big sip of her Chardonnay when suddenly she began choking and coughing.

"Are you okay?" asked Sherrie, patting her gently on her back.

"Yeah, I'm okay," she said looking toward the front door and regaining her composure.

"What's wrong with you?" asked Elise, noticing her looking in the direction of the front entrance. "Do you see someone?"

All of the ladies turned around to see what was going on at the entryway when they noticed a gorgeous Hispanic man arm in arm with a pretty blond woman waiting to be seated. The couple was all over each other and laughing, obviously enjoying each other's company.

"Whoa, I didn't know Enrique Iglesias was going to be here tonight performing," said Lydia. "He's gorgeous!"

All the ladies agreed, but Chrystal started slumping down in her chair and then grabbed a menu to place in front of her face.

"What's the matter with you?" asked Sherrie.

"It's him," said Chrystal under her breath.

"It's who?" asked Lydia and Elise at the same time.

"It's him . . . Manuel!" Chrystal said, straining under her breath.

"Oh, it's Manuel. No wonder you're trippin'." Elise laughed. "Damn, girl. You should have thought twice about throwing that fish back into the sea."

"No way, that's Manuel?" asked Sherrie. "Chrystal, you are crazy as hell. He was definitely worth a second and third date. Or maybe you should have just dated him for a while. Now look who's got him," she said laughing.

"Well, maybe men know a good thing when they see it, but some women sure don't." Lydia laughed.

"Okay, y'all got jokes, but I met him under strange circumstances, okay?"

"You met him the same way you meet most men, heifer. You need to stop it," said Elise.

They all howled in laughter when Chrystal sank deeper into her seat as the hostess escorted Manuel and his date right past their table. They all turned to see the hostess seating them at an intimate table for two near the stage. The hostess gave them each a menu to look over, and they smiled at each other as she left them to make a decision about their drinks and appetizers.

"I can't believe this," said Chrystal. "Of all the establishments he could walk into, he walks in here."

"Are we in a scene from *Casablanca* now?" Elise laughed. "It's just a coincidence he's here, with a pretty date!" Elise laughed. "Maybe he won't remember you."

"Now you're trippin' because once a man takes a ride on Chrystal Delight, he never forgets."

"Well, maybe he's just weighing his options," Sherrie laughed as she watched him and the blonde feed each other the breadsticks the waiter placed on their table. "Yeah, it really looks like you're on his mind," said Sherrie.

Lydia and Elise were dying laughing.

"The hell with all of you!" yelled Chrystal. "I need another Chardonnay. Where's our waiter? I can see that I'll need to get blasted tonight."

"It's a good thing you rode with Elise then because we wouldn't want Enrique over there to have to take you home again tonight," said Lydia, to which Elise and Sherrie fell out laughing.

"Very funny, Lyd. Where's that waiter," said Chrystal, looking around.

Just then, the host of the show came on stage to announce the next act.

"How y'all doing out there tonight? Are you enjoying yourselves?"

"Yes!" yelled the crowd with screams and whistles.

"Well, we're gonna keep tonight rocking for you. Tonight we have a very special young man here to perform for us. He's a homeboy from right here in the ATL. He's been here on several occasions, but the ladies keep the requests in for him, so we keep bringing him back. Give it up for my man, ELIJAH EVERS!"

There was thunderous applause from the audience, and the ladies were all screaming at the sound of his name. Chrystal could not believe this was happening and turned to look at Elise, who was equally surprised but amused at the same time.

"Wow, Chrystal. All of your men are coming out to play tonight." She giggled.

"What's going on now?" asked Lydia.

"Elijah up there and our little Chrystal."

"Dang, girl! I guess you threw him back too, huh?" said Sherrie.

Elijah grabbed the microphone. "I want to dedicate this song to all the lovely ladies in the house tonight. You're all looking so beautiful. Can I sing for you?"

"Yes!" yelled a dark-skinned sista' sitting directly in front of the stage.

"I wrote this song especially for the beautiful ladies, and I hope you all enjoy it."

The music began to play, and Elijah started singing.

"Hmmmm, hmmmm. Girl, you are the one for me, girl, you are the one I'd love to see, every day, every way. And, girl, you are my most desire, girl, you set my heart on fire, I need you, I'm ready to receive you . . . Oh, you are the girl I've been searching for. I'll give everything you desire and so much more. You are everything to me. You are everything to me . . . hmmmmm."

Chrystal couldn't believe this. First there was Manuel sitting across the room playing kissy face with the blond bombshell, and now Elijah, although technically she and Elijah never got together, but Elise knew a different story.

"I'm going to the ladies' room," Chrystal announced.

"Now? But he's singing and it's beautiful," said Sherrie.

"Well, enjoy it. I gotta pee." Chrystal swooped up her purse and headed in the direction of the ladies' room while Elise, Lydia, and Sherrie were completely enthralled with Elijah's song. She pushed open the door and headed to the sink. Chrystal looked in the mirror and admired her reflection, touched up her makeup, gently powdered the slight shine on her forehead, refreshed her lipstick, and then washed and dried her hands. As she headed back out the door, she practically ran right into Manuel.

"Oh, excuse me," he said in a sexy heavy Spanish accent. Chrystal could smell his cologne, and she loved the intoxicating aroma. "That's okay," she said as she tried to scurry away before he recognized her, but it was too late.

"Chrystal?" he said as her name rolled off his tongue.

"Manuel, is that you? How are you? Taking in a little music?"

"Yes, I am. How are you?"

"I'm fine," said Chrystal, a little uncomfortable with the entire scene.

"Are you here with a date?" asked Manuel.

"No, I'm here with my girlfriends. We're celebrating that my friend Lydia purchased her own space for her new interior design firm."

"Excellent. So is your schedule still too tight to fit me in?" he asked looking at Chrystal in a way she knew he shouldn't since he was there with another woman.

"Manuel, you're here with someone."

"She's just a friend, nothing more."

"That's not what it looks like to me," Chrystal snapped.

"What?" Manuel began to smile as he realized Chrystal had obviously spotted him earlier than she was letting on. "Are you spying on me, Chrystal?" he said with a little tease.

"Don't be ridiculous. I just happened to see you come in, that's all. I have to get back to my friends, and I'm sure you need to get back to your date," said Chrystal almost accusingly.

Manuel laughed heartily. "You are jealous. Strange response from someone who tried to put me off, but I like it." He smiled. "Let me call you and take you out."

Chrystal stared at him for a moment, annoyed with herself for showing such an obvious emotion. But she reached in her purse and handed him her card.

"Call me, and we'll go out," she said.

"Count on it," said Manuel, taking the card and placing it inside his jacket.

Chrystal turned and tried to walk away, swinging her hips from side to side, but the heel of her shoe got caught in the carpet, and she stumbled a little but recovered before it was too noticeable to anyone who happened to be watching. She turned slightly to see if Manuel saw her little stumble, and he appeared to be amused, so she figured he was watching. She pulled herself together and continued walking toward the table to rejoin her friends but was shocked to find that Elijah had finished his song and was now at their table laughing and talking with Elise and the others. She stopped dead in her tracks and wondered if this night could get any weirder. She didn't know if she should continue to the table or head back for the ladies' room. She looked behind her to find that Manuel had returned to his seat with his date but was checking her out on the sly. Then she looked forward to see Elise looking at her as if to ask what's wrong with her now. Sherrie turned around to see Chrystal frozen in the middle of the floor and waved to her to come over. Chrystal inched over to the table like she was walking to the guillotine. As she stepped over to the table, Sherrie took it upon herself to introduce Elijah to Chrystal, unaware of their alleged night together.

"Elijah, this is another friend of ours, Chrystal. Chrystal, this is Elijah. Wasn't he wonderful just now?" Elijah turned and looked at Chrystal.

"Haven't I met you before? You were with your beautiful friend here, Elise, that night you came in the club when I was performing."

"Yes, that's right. We met a while back. It's nice to see you again."

Chrystal took her seat and avoided looking at Elise, who didn't know if they were both pretending not to really know each other or if Chrystal's alleged passionate evening with Elijah was a figment of her imagination.

Chrystal was careful not to look directly at Elise, who was busy trying to put this little puzzle together.

"Well, ladies, it was nice talking to you, and Elise, I'm sorry you're already taken. I wanted to ask you out that night, but you left before I could talk to you a little more."

Damn, thought Chrystal. The jig was up and now Elise knew everything.

"Well, maybe another time and another place. But you keep singing that beautiful music, and we'll keep enjoying it," said Elise.

"I will." He reached over to take Elise's hand in his and gave it a kiss as Lydia and Sherrie swooned. Chrystal was off to the side, livid at the entire scene.

"Ladies, have a good evening," said Elijah was a big, beautiful smile.

"You too, and nice to meet you," they all chimed in. As he walked away to the back of the room, Elise glared at Chrystal, who was now busy playing with her napkin. Elise kicked her under the table.

"Ouch! Girl, what's wrong with you?" said Chrystal, trying to be coy.

"You straight up lied to me, Chrystal! You are a trip!"

"What are you two talking about?" asked Lydia.

"I'll fill you in later," said Elise, shaking her head at Chrystal, who was now rolling her eyes up in her head at being placed on blast in front of the group. She then looked up and noticed Manuel leaving with his date, but not before he looked over at her with a devilish little smile on his face. Chrystal didn't like the thought of Manuel thinking she was hung up over him. This night had been a serious bust for her.

"No, tell us what's going on now," said Sherrie.

"Oh, what a tangled web Chrystal weaves is all I have to say," Elise laughed.

"So I guess that means there's more to the story with Mr. Elijah, huh?" asked Lydia.

"Oh, so Chrystal would have you believe." Elise laughed.

"You know, when I said earlier that all of you could go to hell, I meant it," said Chrystal in a snappy little tone, to which they all laughed.

"Yeah, fill us in later, Elise. I know this is going to be good," said Lydia as Sherrie was still laughing.

Luckily, Elise, Lydia, and Sherrie never took any of Chrystal's antics to heart. They knew Chrystal was confused and thought she was all that, so it wouldn't be in Chrystal's nature to admit that a man was more interested in someone other than her. One thing about all of the ladies was that they all accepted and loved each other for who they were without passing judgment and without trying to change their friend into someone else. They had all had a great time at the club just being together and joking with one another. They were always there for one another, and although Chrystal was the most self-absorbed of the entire group, they loved her just the same. But Elise was going to joke the hell out of Chrystal on this one later. Chrystal could count on it.

CHAPTER 13

HELENA

elena was sitting in her office in complete darkness, with the exception of the flickering light coming from her engraved cigarette lighter. As she flicked the lighter continuously on and off, she thought about what a total disaster the Edwards account had turned out to be and the public relations nightmare that followed. After Kyle Edwards left their meeting, giving them a mere twenty-four hours to come up with a design plan that suited him, she and Kameron worked well into the next morning preparing and revamping the drawings. However, Kyle had grown tired and impatient with what he assumed was incompetence, walked into the meeting, took a quick glance at their efforts, and then politely informed Helena that he'd decided to go with another design firm. Helena was furious but attempted to persuade Kyle to stay with them, but he had already made up his mind to go elsewhere. Helena assured him that her design firm could do much better than any other he'd decided to go to and asked where that might be, but he declined to give up that information. So not only did Kyle Edwards pull his account, but someone also leaked the story to the damn media, who promptly broadcast the story for the entire city to see, all in the same day. This was not the outcome she'd hoped for with this venture. Helena Designs would now be known for losing a very lucrative account, and she was certain that her reputation would suffer as a result. She blamed Lydia. She blamed Kameron. She blamed Kyle Edwards. She blamed everyone but herself for this failure, and she was determined to set everything right.

The thought of Lydia leaving her at such a crucial time made her blood boil. She still couldn't believe the audacity of that ungrateful little bitch. Who did Lydia think she was, leaving the way she did, and to make matters worse, Helena heard through her inner circle that Lydia was opening her own store. Did she really think she could create competition against Helena Designs? As Helena flicked open the cigarette lighter again, she opened her desk drawer and pulled out a single cigarette she'd left there for emergency situations only. She lit the cigarette and began puffing, smoke rapidly filling the air. Helena had given up smoking some time ago, but this situation made her revert to her old habits. As she blew a couple of smoke rings into the air, she heard a light tapping at her office door. She knew it had to be Bernard and didn't want to be disturbed, but she yelled for him to come in anyway. He opened the door slightly, noticing Helena sitting alone in the dark and smoking, a habit he'd hoped would never return.

"Helena?"

"Yes, what is it, Bernard?"

"Why are you sitting in the dark?" He opened the door further and then reached in to turn on the light.

"You're smoking again. This can't be good."

Helena was annoyed with his observation but took another puff of the cigarette and waved at him to come in.

"Come in, Bernard, and close the door behind you," she said.

Bernard walked in as he was told, closed the door, and sat in a chair in front of Helena's desk facing her. *She looks terrible*, he thought to himself and wondered if she'd been at the office all night.

"We're going to have to do some damage control," said Helena as she put out her cigarette in an ash tray on her desk.

"What kind of damage control?"

Helena peered at him as if he'd suddenly grown an extra head. *Are all of my employees this dense?* she wondered.

"Unless you've been living under a rock for the past forty-eight hours, you know damn well that we lost the Edwards account, and as my assistant, you should be on top of this instead of me having to break it down for you!" she yelled. "You should also be aware that our business was broadcast on the news just last night, if you actually watch or read the news. Do you watch the news, Bernard?" she snapped.

"Yes, Helena." He jumped, a little shaken by her sudden change in demeanor. "I meant what do you want me to do?"

Helena leaned back in her chair now that Bernard understood the gravity of the situation.

"I want you to cancel all of my meetings and any calls for today and get all of our current clients on the line. We need to reassure them that we have everything under control here and the Edwards account in no way affects their projects."

"Yes, ma'am." He nodded. "Is there anything else?"

"Yes. I'm not answering any questions or taking any calls from the media. If they call, we simply have no comment," she barked. "I also need you to do a little digging on which design firm Kyle Edwards is taking my commission to, is that clear?"

"Of course," nodded Bernard. "Can I do or get you anything?"

"Yes. You can get me a large coffee and an apple crump Danish from the bakery around the corner," she said as she waved at him, dismissing him to carry out her commands.

Bernard got up from the chair to begin carrying out his instructions when Helena stopped him before he reached the door.

"Oh, and, Bernard, when Kameron finally gets her ass in here, tell her that I want to see her right away."

"Yes, ma'am, I will." And Bernard turned and quickly exited.

Helena opened her desk drawer and took out another cigarette, lit it, and began smoking. She truly missed the taste of nicotine in her mouth, and it soothed her tension for the moment. She closed her eyes, trying to calm her nerves from the events of the last couple of days, when suddenly her cell phone rang. She picked it up from her desk and noticed she had a new text message. She pressed the text and began reading:

"On my way. Wish me luck."

She quickly replied back, "Good luck and keep me posted."

Helena took another puff of her cigarette and allowed the smoke to slowly fill her lungs. Her mind was once again turned to Lydia's betrayal and desertion. If it wasn't for her, none of this would have been happening. In fact, instead of drawing negative media attention, she would be receiving praises and congratulations from the mayor himself for a successful multimillion dollar project. Lydia was going to pay dearly for everything she'd put Helena through since she just up and left. Helena didn't take being made a fool of lightly, and if Lydia didn't know that about her by now, she soon would.

CHAPTER 14

LYDIA

*I*t was Saturday and a perfect spring morning. The sun was shining brightly just over the horizon, the air was crisp with just the right amount of wind blowing softly, and the flowers were brilliant in bright yellows, pinks, and purples. The birds were chirping as they began their day searching for food for their young, and Lydia was happy too because today was the day that she'd worked so long and hard for in the last several months. She was moving into her new office space, and she couldn't be more pleased with her accomplishment. Lydia's Loft was officially open for business. It was hard to believe how quickly all of this came about because she took a leap of faith and did what she was truly meant to do when just a few months ago, she was working for someone who didn't appreciate her talents or hard work. But that was all behind Lydia now, and she had emerged stronger and more determined than ever to make her dream come true.

The movers were busy bringing in Lydia's newly purchased furniture and office equipment as she directed them to each of the spaces where she laid out in her mind and on paper where every piece of furniture would be placed. She used some of her connections with retailers and manufacturers to get quality name brand furniture at great prices. Sherrie and Elise had shopped with her to pick out beautiful artwork to frame her walls, and

Lydia was very pleased with the coloring of the room, which she'd designed herself. Elise helped her with designing her logo and the sign placed above the front entryway, which turned out beautifully. Lydia stepped outside the building and took a look at her new space. She then took a picture because she wanted to always remember the moment she was bursting with pride at the thought that she'd done it herself with the blessings of God and her best friends in the world.

"Ms. Brown, where would you like the second desk to go?" asked one of the movers. He was a huge guy wearing a sleeveless shirt that revealed a tattoo of a rattlesnake, and his hair was pulled back into a long ponytail.

"Oh, that desk is going to be for my future assistant, and it's going right over here," said Lydia as she pointed to an area facing the front door, where clients and potential clients would be greeted. Lydia knew she was going to need an assistant to help her keep things organized and in order, like her appointments, jobs, and other assignments. She had already placed an ad in several local papers and was hoping to get some bites real soon.

"Okay, sure," said the mover as he signaled two other movers to bring in the desk and place it where Lydia had motioned. Lydia had selected beautifully crafted furniture because she wanted to attract a certain type of clientele and give off a certain feel.

"This desk is heavy, so be careful," said the mover to his assistants sharply. They were also bringing in a couple of huge statues that Lydia had purchased during an auction she attended last year but, until now, never had a place to put them. Lydia happily watched the hustle and bustle of the movers bringing in items steadily when her cell phone rang.

"Hello."

"Hey, Lyd! How's it going? Are the movers there?" asked Elise.

"Elise, they're here, and they're actually almost done. It's so exciting! I can't believe this is actually happening."

"Lydia's Loft is officially open, girl. Congratulations!"

"Thanks so much for all of your help and support, Elise. You are just an angel, and I love you so much."

"Awwww, you're just saying that because it's true," teased Elise. "You know I'm always here for you girl, for whatever you need. So what time do we need to be there tonight for the grand opening event?"

"Can you be here around 6:00 p.m.? I'm expecting other guests around 7:30 p.m., so that will give us a little time to set up the hors d'oeurves and wine."

"I will be there with bells on, and I'm bringing Sherrie with me. Chrystal said she'll be there whenever you need her too."

"Great."

"You know, I am in the area, so why don't I come over now and help you get things arranged," offered Elise. "I'll bring some cleaning supplies and furniture polish. You still have some boxes to unpack."

"That would be great, Elise."

"Okay, I'll be there in a few." Just as Lydia was hanging up with Elise, she turned around and found Sherrie with little Jillian in hand. Sherrie was carrying a huge bouquet of yellow roses, Lydia's favorite flowers.

"What in the world!" screamed Lydia as she gave Sherrie a big hug and kissed little Jillian.

"This is for your opening day. We were out doing a few errands and we wanted to stop by to see if you needed any help before tonight. We're all ready to jump in, right, Jillian?" said Sherrie to Jillian, who nodded her head in agreement. "These are for you," she said, handing Lydia the flowers.

"Oh my goodness, they're beautiful. Wow, Elise just called too, and she's on her way over. I can definitely use a hand."

"Look at this place, Lydia, it's gorgeous! I see the movers have all the furniture in place."

"Yes, I just need to get the paintings n the walls and tidy up a bit."

"No problem, let's pull up our sleeves and hit it," said Sherrie, taking off her jacket and placing it on one of the new chairs. Just then, the movers came up to Lydia.

"Ms. Brown, we're done. You have a good day."

"Thanks so much for your help."

"Certainly," he said, glancing at Sherrie and leaving out the front door.

About twenty minutes later, Elise walked through the door carrying a box filled with all types of cleaning supplies.

"I'm here!" she announced. "Hey there, Sherrie, hi, sweetheart," she said looking at Jillian as she and Sherrie air kissed. "Looks like you're getting your cleaning crew together, Lyd."

"I know, you guys are so great. We can start dusting and getting pictures on the walls over here."

Lydia pointed to the empty walls and dust on the furniture and floor left from moving furniture and boxes around. She headed toward a closet and pulled out a vacuum cleaner to use later when her cell phone rang on the desk.

"It's your cell, Lyd," said Sherrie as she picked it up and saw it was Chrystal calling. "It's Chrystal," she said as she hit Talk to answer. "Chrystal, you better be on your way over here to help out. We're all here. And bring some snacks on your way. I'm hungry." Sherrie laughed.

She listened intently to Chrystal on the other end of the phone and then said, "We're helping clean up to get this place ready for tonight. You should see it, Chrystal, it's beautiful. I can't wait for Lyd to get everything in place. Why don't you bring us some sandwiches from Arties, and hold the pickles on mine. Bring Jillian a kid's meal. Right, heifer, I'll give you the money when you get here, just come on and be here in an hour or less. We'll save some cleaning for you." Sherrie laughed as she hung up the phone.

"That was Chrystal. She's coming over too, and she's going to grab some sandwiches on the way."

"Great. I was wondering if she was bringing her lazy ass over. You know Chrystal," said Elise.

All the ladies laughed because Chrystal was notorious for getting out of anything that resembled work, even her own job. Elise and Sherrie grabbed a couple of dust rags out of the box along with some furniture polish and started getting to work while Lydia decided where she wanted to hang the paintings. They were all consumed with pulling everything together that they didn't even notice a tall young man had walked into the office. He was wearing a pin-striped black-and-white shirt, black slacks, and a solid light-pink tie. His hair was curly and cut close, and he wore glasses. He had stepped into the office and was looking around when Lydia and Elise looked up and spotted him.

"Hello. I'm sorry to interrupt, but I'm looking for Lydia Brown," he said while scanning the room and the ladies to see who would reveal themselves as Lydia. Lydia walked over to the young man. "Yes, I'm Lydia Brown, can I help you?"

"Hello, Ms. Brown. I ran across your ad for an assistant, and I'm very interested in the position if you haven't filled it yet. I see you're moving in. This is a beautiful space," he said, looking around the room.

Lydia smiled broadly and looked at Elise and Sherrie, who were now aware of his presence. Lydia couldn't believe how great this day was shaping up to be.

"Yes, and thanks to my friends and the movers that left not long ago, it's coming along pretty well so far." Lydia looked at him and said, "I haven't filled the position yet, so I'm happy you came in."

"Great," said the young man as he reached into his briefcase to hand Lydia a copy of his résumé. "Here's my résumé. I've worked with several interior design agencies as an assistant, and I've taken some classes in interior design myself. I've always been interested in it. It's my passion. In fact, I love the way you've decorated this place. You've done a great job." Lydia glanced at his resume and noticed a couple of very well-known firms.

"Why don't you step into my office for a moment . . . Mr. Pearsall? Did I pronounce that right?" she said, motioning him to the door directly across where they were standing.

"Yes, Jasper Pearsall, and you pronounced it perfectly," he said, smiling and walking in the direction of the office where she pointed. Lydia looked at the ladies and beamed as Elise gave her a thumbs-up. She turned and followed him into the office and closed the door only halfway.

"Sorry about the mess," said Lydia while moving a small box from her desk. "We're trying to get ready for my grand opening this evening."

"It's tonight? Wow, congratulations, this must be very exciting for you."

"It is. This is my first time out of the gate, so I'm looking forward to it. So I see you worked for Diane Lehman Designs. She's a very talented designer. What did you do for her?"

"Oh yes, Diane was a sweetheart. I loved working with her. I handled everything with Diane from her appointments, bookings, travel arrangements, to her accounts and invoices. I even scheduled her manicures and pedicures, honey. I did it all. I only left after she no longer needed an assistant. I guess I was too efficient and put myself out of a job but left her pretty well off. I'm a very hard worker, and I take my duties very seriously. Jasper is no slouch, honey," he said, leaning back into the chair while crossing his legs.

Lydia was trying to remain objective and not make a decision too quickly, but she couldn't help but like him already. He appeared to be very professional, and his résumé was pretty impressive. She was thinking he was exactly what she needed for Lydia's Loft.

"Well, Jasper, I'm looking for someone who can help me get organized and keep my appointments, clients, and bookings in order for me. I have so much to do to get started, and this evening is going to be the beginning of all of it. In fact, excuse me for a moment while I contact the caterer. I'm sorry, but I need to make sure they're going to be on time."

Jasper gave her a serious look and asked, "Do you have the caterer's telephone or cell number?"

"Yes, it's right here. Why do you ask?"

"You're busy. Why don't you let Jasper contact the caterer? In fact, give Jasper a list of people that will be making deliveries this evening, and I'll confirm with them. Then, I can run out and purchase anything we'll need for this evening."

Lydia was impressed by his initiative and take-charge attitude. She did need to get the place together along with the girls, but she also needed to check with the caterer for the food, the Cake Lady who was bringing the cake, the champagne, and the glassware. It was now 11:30 a.m., and there wasn't a moment to spare.

"Jasper, if you can pull all of this together for me, you're hired," said Lydia, pleased with her first executive decision. She handed him a few business cards with contact information and food and beverage items for the various businesses. Jasper smiled broadly, winked at her, pulled out his cell phone, and immediately began making the calls.

"Hello, yes, I'm Lydia Brown's assistant, Jasper Pearsall, honey, and I'm calling to confirm that you'll be delivering the caviar and stuffed shrimp for our grand opening tonight. Yes, that's Lydia's Loft at 204 Wellesley Place." Jasper pulled out his notebook and began writing down notes as he confirmed their arrival. Lydia was pleased with his jump-right-in attitude and left him to it.

When she entered the main area again, Chrystal had arrived bearing food and drinks along with cleaning items like Windex to get started.

"Hey, girl," said Chrystal in a very high-pitched voice.

"Lydia, what's going on with what's his name in your office?" asked Elise.

"You mean my new assistant, Jasper? I just hired him and look, he's already on the job. I like his drive," said Lydia, raising her hand to receive a high five. "He's making calls and confirming the food and refreshments for this evening. He just jumped right in."

"Wow, that was fast. Are you sure he's okay?" asked Sherrie.

"He's going to be great. I can feel it," beamed Lydia.

"So you have an assistant already, and he's a man? Where is he?" asked Chrystal, fixing her blouse that revealed her ample breasts and primping her hair.

"Hold your horses, hot stuff. I'm pretty sure he's playing for the other team," said Elise.

"Shhhhh!" said Lydia. "He's right in the next room." Just then, Jasper walked in like he couldn't wait to deliver some great news.

"Lydia, the caterer will be here at 6:00 p.m. with the food and the champagne. Also, lady, my cousin Latifah works with that caterer, so I was able to get you an even better discount. Plus I can tell you that their food is off the chain!" he said laughing.

Lydia turned and looked at all her girls with a pleasing grin.

"A discount? See, he's on the job for ten minutes and he's already saving me money. Ladies, meet my new assistant, Jasper. Jasper, these are my BFFs in the world, Chrystal, Elise, and Sherrie. And that little sweetheart over there is Jillian, Sherrie's daughter."

"So nice to meet all of you, ladies. Oh, I'm so excited! Thank you for this opportunity, Lydia. You won't be sorry."

"Welcome aboard, Jasper," said Sherrie. "You know this place is a labor of love for all of us, and we're so proud of our girl Lydia, so you have to take good care of her."

"I sure will, Ms. Sherrie, don't you worry yourself about that. Girl, I love those shoes. You're working those," he said, referring to Sherrie's new Jimmy Choo shoes. Sherrie smiled. "I just picked these up. They just came in," she said proudly.

"Well, you are working them, girl. Now let Jasper get a list of items we'll need for this evening, and I'll make a little trip to the store. Do we have glassware, or do I need to go downtown and pick up some champagne glasses? I know a place where I can get some fabulous stemware dirt cheap."

"I can definitely use some more stemware," said Lydia as she pulled him away to her office to put together a list of items. The ladies all looked at each other and smiled about everything seeming to come together. Chrystal began distributing the delicious sandwiches she brought in from Arties. They were all glad that they were here to see things come together for Lydia so nicely.

Elise took a bite of her roast-beef sandwich while watching Jasper with Lydia as they discussed everything from decorations to flatware for the evening's event. It was strange because something about him seemed very familiar. Elise couldn't quite put her finger on it, but she could swear she'd seen him somewhere before.

*   *   *

Lydia took one last look at herself in the floor-length mirror in her office. She looked gorgeous in her black one-shoulder floor-length Elizabeth and James dress. It was show time, and Lydia's Loft was bursting at the seams with invited guests who were impressed at how absolutely beautiful the place looked. Lydia and the girls, along with Jasper, worked diligently to get everything in order before the arrival of the guests. Now the store was bustling with family, friends, colleagues, neighbors, and a couple of Chrystal's ex-boyfriends. Lydia was excited and nervous at the same time as she sipped a glass of white wine. She scanned the crowd to make sure everyone was having a good time. The champagne was flowing as guests dined on caviar, stuffed shrimp and mushrooms, shrimp cocktail, along with chicken, assorted fruits, cheeses, and wine. The place looked fabulous, and Lydia had plenty of business cards to give out. Jasper was busying himself making sure everything was running smoothly and in its place. Lydia's hair was fabulous too, and her girls Chrystal, Elise and Sherrie were equally as beautiful.

"Can you believe this crowd?" asked Sherrie. "Girl, you have a great turnout, and everyone seems to be enjoying themselves," she said, holding a glass of burgundy.

"Jasper is working the crowd like you're paying him triple overtime, Lyd. Check him out," said Elise.

"I know. Isn't he something? He just jumped right in and started handling things like an old pro. I love it!" Just then, Chrystal came over with a small plate of shrimp cocktail.

"Your grand opening is a hit, Lydia. I mean, look at all these people. Can you feel the love or what?" said Chrystal.

"I'm blessed to have such great friends to come out and support me," she smiled. Just then Jasper whisked over to Lydia from across the room.

"Hello, ladies, isn't this a fabulous party? Are you enjoying yourselves?"

"Yes we are. We're so proud of Lydia."

"It's time," he said, motioning Lydia to go to the front of the room and greet her guests. Lydia handed him her wineglass, smiled at her girls, and headed to the front facing everyone. Jasper placed her drink on a table and picked up an empty wineglass and began tapping it to get the crowd's attention.

"Good evening everyone, and welcome to Lydia's Loft!" Lydia said excitedly. The crowd responded in a thunderous applause. "First of all, I would like to thank each and every one of you for taking the time to come out and support a sista' in her new endeavor!" she shouted, raising her hands in praise as everyone chuckled.

"This has truly been a dream come true and a labor of love, and it wouldn't have come about if it weren't for God above and my friends who believed in me and stood by me and my new assistant, Jasper. So I thank all of them from the bottom of my heart. There's plenty of food, champagne, and wine, so please eat, drink, and have a good time. Thank you again!" Everyone applauded, and members from the group began coming up to Lydia and congratulating her on her success. Many of them were leaving housewarming gifts on a table Jasper put together for the occasion.

"Congratulations, Lydia!" said Carla, one of her dear neighbors. "I am so proud of you. I always knew you needed your own place after the job you did on my living room. People are still raving about it," she said proudly.

"Thank you so much, Carla, and thank you for coming. I really appreciate it." She hugged her back. "Enjoy yourself, and make sure you get plenty to eat," she motioned back toward the food. A few more neighbors and old colleagues also congratulated her, and Lydia was so overwhelmed by the flood of people. She had just finished greeting one of the last guests in line when she heard a familiar voice directly behind her.

"Congratulations, Lydia," said a woman in a rather husky voice. Lydia recognized the voice immediately but thought she must have been mistaken until she turned around to see that she was right. Standing before her eyes was Helena Barnes. Lydia's first thought was to call security, if she'd actually had security. Helena was blatantly crashing her grand opening because she sure as hell didn't invite her. She decided to remain cool as to not give Helena the satisfaction in knowing how much her presence annoyed her.

"Helena?" said Lydia regaining her composure. "What a surprise."

"Hello, Lydia. You know I've always been good at surprises."

Yes, you have, you old cow, thought Lydia as she smiled at Helena.

"I just thought I'd drop by to congratulate a talented colleague and give you my best," said Helena as Lydia stared at her in disbelief.

"So when I heard you were having this little affair, well, I thought it would be just downright rude not to come by and wish you well. After all, we're all decorators, and we should support one another, right?"

"That's very thoughtful of you," said Lydia, wondering how the hell Helena found out about her opening and making a mental note to have her next event strictly by invitation only.

"My, my, you've done a marvelous job transforming this space," she said taking in the view. "I remember what it used to look like. It was an absolute wreck. But of course, you've always been good at turning something dreadful into something fabulous, haven't you?" she said, turning to Lydia.

I couldn't have said it better, you witch, thought Lydia while consciously thinking of the best response to that obvious question.

"That's very nice of you to say, Helena. Well, thanks so much for stopping by to help me celebrate my success. Help yourself to some champagne and food," said Lydia, removing herself from her presence to continue greeting invited guests. Helena watched as Lydia slinked off, stopping to get a glass of champagne and greeting more guests. Lydia was furious with the entire grand affair. She didn't know why Helena decided to drop in uninvited, but she wasn't about to let her presence bring her down from her high. Lydia walked over to where Chrystal, Elise, and Sherrie were standing. They were all watching from the other side of the room in amazement.

"I can't believe that bitch would show up like this. Let me kick her ass, Lydia!" said Chrystal.

"Unbelievable!" said Elise. "How did she know about your opening?"

"I don't know because invitations were sent to specific people, but it won't happen again, believe me," said Lydia.

"Lydia, don't let her ruin your night. That's what she wants to do. This is your night to shine, girl. Enjoy it. Let her see you strut your successful ass all over the room," said Sherrie.

"Damn right," said Elise as they all lifted and clinked their glasses together.

"Let's get some more champagne and keep this party going!" Chrystal yelled, and all the ladies followed her lead over to the waiter pouring the champagne. They laughed and hugged each other to show a united front.

On the opposite side of the room, Jasper was busy making sure the food was plentiful when his cell began to buzz. He pulled his cell out of its holder and flipped it open to see he had a new text message. He clicked on the message and read, "Nice party. We'll celebrate too when this is all over." He immediately texted back saying, "Will contact you later," when Lydia walked up and startled him.

"Whew, girl, you about scared the crap outta me! 'Bout gave Jasper a heart attack," he said while holding his chest with his left hand and slyly flipping down his cell with his right.

"Oh, I'm sorry," said Lydia, laughing. "Are you okay?" she asked, patting him on the back. "I just wanted to thank you again for all of your help today. You came in at just the right moment, it's just unbelievable. I think everything came together perfectly, and I couldn't have done it without you and the girls jumping in the way you did."

"No problem, girl. That's what I do. Jasper just jumps right in and gets things done," he said, flashing his eyes. "You know, I think we're going to make a good team. The dynamic duo, L and J."

"I think you're right, Jasper. I think you're right," she said, suddenly giving him a big hug.

"Congratulations, sweetheart. You did it," he said, hugging her back and glancing up just in time to see Helena's devilish eyes staring them down. She leaned her head back, throwing a glass of champagne down her throat. Helena glared at them again, sat the champagne glass down on a nearby table, and then left as quietly as she'd appeared.

CHAPTER 15

CHRYSTAL

*I*t was the usual crazy Monday morning at the office. The phones were ringing off the hook like something bizarre was about to happen. There were several voice messages to return, and another trip to San Francisco for Dana was scheduled. Chrystal had thought long and hard about what she wanted to do with the information she'd discovered about Dana and decided that she was tired of the position she was in with no raises and no chance for advancement. It was time for her to move on up like her girls, who were all doing well. Lydia opening her own place, Elise heading a huge department at her marketing firm, and Sherrie living the life of luxury were all things she wanted in her future, and she didn't see why her plan couldn't get her there. Dana was in her office going over some documents and said she didn't want to be disturbed by anyone. She had been unusually quiet and behind closed doors all morning, and Chrystal knew she didn't have any important meetings or presentations on her schedule. She'd also been on the telephone with her husband several times this morning, which was also unusual, and there had not been any calls from Jeff McKenna. Chrystal played the tape she'd heard of the two of them planning their trip back in her mind again and again and wondered what would make a man like Jeff McKenna stray for someone like Dana. His wife was beautiful, and they had two adorable little boys whom he adored because he was always bragging about them whenever he came in for an appointment. So what was it? Chrystal remembered the other day watching an episode of *Oprah*, who had a panel of men on stage with their wives, and all of them had extramarital affairs. When Oprah asked what it was all about, just about all of them and the guest expert who'd written a book on the subject said it wasn't about the sex but about how the other woman made them feel. Chrystal wondered if Dana made Jeff McKenna feel differently than his wife did and if that was why he was in this affair. She thought about what their meetings to San Francisco must be like, and she was both disgusted and intrigued. What would an average person do with this kind of information? Would they ignore it and move on? Make an anonymous call to each of their spouses? Confront their boss? Or would they use this information to their advantage like Chrystal was planning to do? The average person would probably ignore the situation and mind his or her business. But Chrystal never considered herself average by any standards. The buzzer from Dana's office awakened her from her momentary trance.

"Chrystal, bring me the McKenna file please," she said impatiently. Chrystal sighed and pulled out the file from the filing cabinet behind her desk. She walked in Dana's office to hand her the file when Dana asked her to close the door. She took off her glasses, and Chrystal could see that she'd been crying and her eyes were bloodshot.

"Is there something wrong?" asked Chrystal.

"I'm going to take a personal day the rest of today and tomorrow, and I need you to cancel my trip to San Francisco and my hotel reservations," she said.

"Okay. Do you want me to reschedule for another day, or—"

"No, I won't be going to San Francisco for a while. Maybe not ever again!" she snapped.

"Dana, what's wrong?" asked Chrystal, again puzzled by her disposition.

"Jeff McKenna's wife is demanding that he no longer be a client with our firm," she said dryly, taking a tissue from her tissue box and wiping her eyes.

"What happened?" Chrystal's mind began to race about how this all came about. Did Jeff's wife know? Did she confront Dana? Did she tell the front office?

"It's complicated," said Dana, blowing her nose and glaring at Chrystal. "It's a personal matter," she said slowly.

"I'm sorry to hear this. They were a huge account and I—"

"I don't need you to remind me of that!" yelled Dana, cutting Chrystal off. "I already have to explain this to Mr. Sanders somehow as delicately as I can. I don't want this to go any further than it already has."

"What do you want me to do?" asked Chrystal, annoyed that Dana was taking her frustrations out on her.

"Just do as I ask and cancel my reservations. I'm leaving for the day in a few minutes, and I'll be out of the office tomorrow. I'll call you if I need anything. I'll have my laptop and my PDA with me."

"Okay. Let me know if you need anything. I'll be here." Chrystal got up and started to leave when Dana called her again.

"Chrystal, please keep this quiet. I don't want people in the office to start any unnecessary gossip."

"Okay, I will," said Chrystal as she exited the office.

Yeah, like that's going to happen, thought Chrystal. There was a lot more to this story than Dana was letting on, and Chrystal was determined to find out what really happened, and she knew just the person to ask. She sat down at her desk and responded to a couple of e-mails and then decided to head down to the break room to get some coffee and a Danish. When she walked into the room, Mr. Sanders's secretary, Jill, and Mr. Jonasen's secretary, Myra, were huddled in conversation, and they stopped as soon as Chrystal walked into the room. Jill always had the latest scoop on what was happening with anyone and anything in the firm, and Chrystal knew she was the go-to person for what was going on with Dana. Chrystal walked in cautiously, knowing that she'd stumbled upon a conversation that they didn't want overheard.

"Good morning, ladies," said Chrystal.

"Hi," said Myra as she quickly exited the room. Chrystal watched her in amusement as she scurried out the door. Myra was a timid little thing who looked like she'd be frightened by her own shadow.

"Hi, Chrystal," chimed Jill. "How's everything over in your section?" she said, itching to spill the beans. Chrystal looked around and walked over to her. They'd done this dance before when Mr. Sanders was about to fire one of his associates. Jill always had the latest gossip.

"You tell me how things are going in my section. I just had an interesting conversation with Dana about one of our biggest accounts. I sure would like to know what that's all about," she said in a whisper.

"What did Dana tell you?" asked Jill.

"She just said that Jeff McKenna's wife insisted he no longer be a client and that she was taking a personal day," Chrystal said as if she didn't have a clue on what to make of all of this.

"Well, between you and me," said Jill whispering, "Mrs. McKenna called Mr. Sanders's office last night outraged. Apparently, Dana and Jeff have been having an affair. Mrs. McKenna found receipts in his pocket for expensive gifts that he didn't buy for her, and she found a very compromising text message on his cell phone from Dana."

Damn, thought Chrystal. The jig was up.

"Wow, I had no idea. How long has this been going on?"

"I don't know exactly, but it sounds like maybe a few months at least. I don't know what Mr. Sanders is going to do. But he's angry that he's lost a huge account over an affair between one of his employees and a client. Dana may be taking more than a few personal days off. Well, I better get back to my desk before Mr. Sanders sends out a search party. Keep this closed lip," said Jill, grabbing a glazed donut and dashing out the door.

One thing Chrystal loved about Jill was her inability to keep anything confidential. She would give up her mama just for the thrill of being in the know. *How could Dana and Jeff be so careless?* thought Chrystal. Now she was in possession of useless information since the firm was now well aware of the situation. Damn! How was she going to get her raise now? Then a devilish grin came across Chrystal's face as she wondered if Dana's husband knew what was going on. Her plan was still in motion until she knew for sure.

CHAPTER 16

ELISE

Quinton walked in the house from his early morning jog with his bulldog, Cain, resting comfortably on a leash. He was winded and sweating, wearing a lightweight Sean John jogging suit, with Cain decked out in a cute blue shirt. Quinton thought clothing for animals was ridiculous if not downright humiliating. But Elise purchased the shirt along with several other gifts for Cain whom she adored, so he decided to let him wear them for her sake. He was invigorated from his run. Exercising was a huge part of Quinton's daily regimen. He loved keeping himself in shape for himself, his health, and his woman, and getting in a hard run of at least six miles three or four times a week in the morning got his blood flowing and freed his mind of stress from work and the ongoing situation with Elise. Since the day he asked Elise about moving in together, she'd conveniently put him off anytime he wanted to discuss the issue further. Either she was working on a presentation for work or she was heading out the door to meet up with her girls or she was having her period or she was just too tired to get into it. There was always an excuse, and Quinton was beginning to get tired of it. The only thing about their relationship that he could count on lately was their sex life. If nothing else, Elise was a bona fide freak, and he completely enjoyed being with her in that way, but he was ready for their relation to go to another level, and he couldn't help but think she didn't feel the same way.

He stretched his arms out and took off his jacket and threw it across the couch, revealing a sleeveless shirt and his rippling arms. Elise was in the kitchen cooking breakfast that smelled like bacon, pancakes, and eggs, and she was humming a little tune to herself, unaware that Quinton was watching her from the living room. He was very much in love with Elise. More than he wanted to admit even to himself. To him, she was simply amazing and everything he'd ever wanted in a woman. She was smart, educated, sexy, and beautiful, and she took great care of her body. She was very physical, opinionated, caring, loving, and not afraid to tell you her thoughts or debate you on any assortment of topics. She was well-informed about the issues of the day and passionate about the things that were important to her. She was also very protective of her girlfriends. In a lot of ways, Quinton felt that he was lucky to come in maybe fourth in her life after her three lifelong girlfriends, and he learned very early in their relationship that he had to be fine with that because no one was coming between her and her girls. She turned around and noticed Quinton standing there watching her while Cain entered the kitchen to drink water from his bowl.

"Hey, there. How was your run?" she asked as she cracked another egg into a mixing bowl and began stirring.

"It was good. Me and my boy Cain did about six miles, and we even made it up to the parkway this time around. That food smells good, girl," he said, grabbing Elise and putting her in a bear hug. He gave her a gentle kiss on the lips.

"Breakfast is almost ready. Whew! You're gonna take a shower first, right?"

"What you tryin' to say?" he said smiling.

"I'm just saying that when you lifted your arms, my sinuses cleared. That's all I'm saying," she said grinning.

"Oh, see, you got jokes. But that's okay, girl. I'll let you have that one. I'm going to grab a shower, and then I'll be back to partake of this delicious breakfast my beautiful woman has prepared. Right, boy?" he said as Cain looked up and him and then sat down flat on his stomach. "Be right back, girl!" Quinton rushed off to the bedroom and closed the door behind him.

Later after they finished breakfast, Quinton suggested that he and Elise take Cain for a walk around the park and maybe get some ice cream later on from their favorite place, Cold Stone. It was a beautiful Sunday afternoon with perfect weather for a nice leisurely walk. Lakewood Park was very serene and a great place to take a nice long stroll. There were couples walking hand in hand around the water fountain, sitting on the grass eating ice cream, or sitting on benches having conversations. While he and Elise were walking together with Cain, they walked pass a couple that appeared to be in a very heated conversation with each other. It was interesting seeing the dynamics of the different couples and trying to picture what their relationships were like. Quinton wanted to take this time to talk seriously about moving in together, but he had to wait for the right moment. He and Elise walked around the park a few times and then decided to get some Cold Stone ice cream and have a seat on one of the benches outside. Elise ordered Birthday Remix and Quinton had Chocolate Surprise. As they were enjoying their ice cream and each other, Quinton felt the time was now to make his plea.

"This is all right?" he said, looking at Elise and nodding his head.

"Yes, it is. I'm glad you thought of it. It's so relaxing out here."

"So how did the opening go the other night at Lydia's?"

"It was great, Quinton. I'm so proud of Lydia. You should see the place. In fact, I'll take you by there so you can see what she's done with it. You won't recognize it from the time you first helped moved stuff out of there."

"Wow, that's good. I'm happy for her. She deserves it because she really knows her stuff."

"She does, but you know what? Remember when I was telling you about what she went through with that Helena chick? Well she had the nerve to crash the party. She just showed up uninvited like it was nothing but a thing. She had a lot of damn nerve!"

"What? You're joking, right? She just walked up in there like she was invited, huh? Maybe she's not playing with a full deck or something."

"Oh, she knew exactly what she was doing. She was trying to ruin Lydia's night, but we all ignored her and moved on, and after a little while, she just left."

"Good for y'all. You can't let people steal your joy, right?"

"That's right!" said Elise, taking another lick of her ice cream cone.

Quinton felt that now was the right time to bring up their living arrangement, but he hesitated for a moment when he noticed the same couple on the opposite side of the park that they'd observed earlier now in a full-blown argument. The woman was waving her hands around, and the guy was now looking extremely distressed. Then suddenly, the woman jumped up to her feet and walked off while the man sat there looking surprised that she would just walk away. Quinton turned and looked at Elise to see if she had observed the same scene, but she had now finished her ice cream and was playing with Cain when she looked up at him.

"He needs a pedicure. Do you see these claws on him?"

"Baby, we need to talk," said Quinton, disregarding Cain's grooming needs.

"About?" said Elise as if there were certain subjects she didn't want to talk about.

"When are you going to give me an answer about us living together? I asked you a while ago, and every time I bring it up, you change the subject or you're too busy to talk about it."

"Oh, is that why you brought me out here?" she said sounding bitter. "I guess you thought you would just take me out for a nice little stroll in public to talk about this," she said as if Quinton had deliberately trapped her.

"No, actually, I wanted to go for a walk and spend some quality time with you. But what's wrong with talking about it? You can't put me off forever."

"Who said I'm putting you off? I'm not putting you off about anything. If I wanted to put you off, you would know it. I don't have to put you off about this or anything else." Elise was shaking her head from side to side and pointing her fingers as she spoke.

"Okay, maybe that was a bad choice of words, but you have to admit that you haven't exactly been open to us discussing it."

"I don't know what you're talking about, Quinton. If you want to talk about it, we can talk about it. I really don't know why you're acting like I'm the one that doesn't want to talk to you about things. We're always talking about things," she said defensively.

"Okay, well then, let's talk about moving in together. I want to. Where are you on this?" Elise began fidgeting in her seat and clearing her throat uncomfortably while Quinton waited for an answer.

"Well?" he asked again, looking at his watch. "If you want, we can sit here all day while you think about it, although you've had more than enough time to think about it."

She cleared her throat again and twisted in her seat with her arms now folded.

"I don't want to live with anyone until I'm married," she said finally. Quinton was stunned. Marriage? He never thought Elise was ready for anything like marriage. That's why he wanted to take baby steps and try living together first.

"I didn't think you were ready for marriage. And what would be the difference anyway?"

"There's a difference, and you know it. So now you have my answer. I don't really believe in living together. I just didn't know how to tell you, but since you've backed me in a corner, that's my answer," she said, sounding almost relieved to get it out.

"Okay, baby, I guess I have to respect your thoughts on that. I wish you would have told me sooner, but hey, now it's out there and I know where you stand on it."

They both sat there quietly for a moment, Quinton taking in this new bit of information and Elise relieved that she no longer had the subject hanging over her head.

"I hope you're not disappointed," she said finally. "I just really feel strongly about this. I hope you understand."

"I do understand, and I'm happy you finally told me what's been bothering you about all of this."

Elise smiled at him, happy to hear that he wasn't angry or disappointed with her answer and also happy that now things could get back to normal.

"Do you wanna go see an early movie? The Tyler Perry movie, *For Colored Girls*, is playing at the Cinema Café. We can catch the matinee and grab some dinner there before 4:00 p.m."

"Sure, I'm up for a movie. Let's go," he said, getting up and tugging on Cain's leash. They walked out of the park together, and Elise casually placed her hand inside of his. She felt like a huge weight had been lifted from her shoulders and knew everything would be fine now. For her, living together wasn't an option, and she knew marriage wasn't an option for either of them. He would just have to be satisfied with the relationship as it was now, and Elise didn't see any reason to change it.

*   *   *

It was now 7:00 p.m., and Elise was stepping out of the shower, patting her face and hair dry. She and Quinton returned from the movie about six thirty and then he left to run an errand while Elise decided to take a quick shower. She was very happy about how everything had turned out with the living arrangements subject. She was an independent woman and wanted to keep it that way at least for a while. As she was about to blow-dry her hair, she heard her cell phone go off. She picked it up from the nightstand and noticed an unfamiliar number, so she didn't bother to answer it. She began to blow-dry her hair out and then brushed it back into a ponytail. She then placed Victoria's Secret lotion all over her body and put on her comfortable Baby Phat PJs. There on the nightstand was the latest edition of Oprah's *O* magazine, and she began thumbing through it when she heard Quinton come in.

"Quinton, is that you?" she yelled to the living room.

"Yeah baby, I'm back."

Elise started reading one of the articles in the magazine about recognizing the signs when your man is stepping out on you. She laughed to herself after reading the first sign is if your man constantly leaves for no reason and then returns later since Quinton had just ducked out.

"What are you doing?" she yelled again.

"Nothing, I'm just getting some water," he said. A moment later, he was standing in front of her in the bedroom getting undressed and doing a little striptease while talking about how much he enjoyed the movie.

"I think Tyler did a great job on the movie. What do you think, baby?"

"I liked it, but for me, he hasn't done anything as good as *Diary of a Mad Black Woman*. I just loved the intimacy between Shemar Moore and Kimberly Elise's characters. They had so much chemistry together."

"Yeah, right. You just like that movie because of cutie pie Shemar Moore," he said, teasing her. "Tell me, what does Shemar have that I don't have?" he said flexing his muscles and pumping his arms. Elise smiled at him.

"He doesn't have anything on you, baby. Come over here," she said as he jumped on the bed and pulled her into his arms.

"You know, we have a lot of chemistry together too. We can make our own movie."

"I thought we did. In fact, several times," she laughed.

"Yeah, you're right," he said as he began kissing her on her lips. They locked lips for several moments before coming back up for air.

"Hold on, I need to go tinkle real quick. I'll be right back," she said as she bounced out of bed and ran into the bathroom.

"Don't be long. I'm waiting." He smiled. A few moments later, Elise emerged out of the bathroom and was shocked to see Quinton standing near the door with a little black box revealing a beautiful two-carat diamond ring. Her eyes became huge as he lowered himself to one knee.

"I know that *Diary* is your favorite movie, and I know your favorite part of the movie is when Orlando proposes to Helen. I know you're an independent woman, Elise, and I know you're afraid of losing your independence. How about if you let me be your knight in shining armor and an asset in your life, not a liability? We complement each other and we're right for each other and I love you so much. Will you marry me?"

Elise imagined the floor literally opening up so she could fall through it. This was just too much for her to take in, and now the thought of them just living together didn't seem very intrusive at all. All of a sudden, she was beginning to feel a little light-headed and nauseous to her stomach at the same time. She put her hand over her mouth and darted back into the bathroom, where she vomited all over the floor and fell to her knees. Quinton rushed inside to help her up, only for her to vomit again, this time in the toilet. He held her head over the toilet for a second to make sure she'd finished. He had never proposed to a woman before, but it didn't take a rocket scientist to know this wasn't a good response.

CHAPTER 17

SHERRIE

There was a loud bang coming from downstairs in the kitchen that startled Sherrie out of her sleep. She turned over to find Brad lying next to her sleeping silently. She had pretended to be asleep when he got in from the hospital around midnight because she didn't want him to know that she stayed up regularly waiting for him to come home. She sat up in bed being careful not to disturb him, reached for her robe at the foot of the bed, slipped out of the bed quietly, and headed downstairs to the kitchen. There she found Isabella rolling dough for her famous homemade biscuits and putting the finishing touches on breakfast. There was a skillet sitting on the edge of the counter, and Sherrie assumed that was the banging noise she'd heard earlier.

"Good morning, Isabella," said Sherrie, smiling.

"Buenos dias, Ms. Sherrie. I'm sorry if I woke you with the noise. The pot slipped out of my hand. My arthritis seems to be flaring up more nowadays."

"Don't worry about it. I needed to get up anyway to get Jillian ready for her dance class," said Sherrie as she poured herself a glass of water from the faucet.

Isabella had been with the Marshalls for nearly five years, and they loved her like a member of their family. She took care of everything from cooking, cleaning, running errands, and even picking up Jillian from school on occasion. She loved spending time with Jillian. Ironically, Sherrie never really thought much about having a live-in housekeeper, and hiring Isabella was Brad's idea. Brad wanted Sherrie to spend every waking moment just being available to attend functions for the hospital, to host dinner parties for his colleagues, or to participate in charity events along with the other surgeons' wives. Sherrie enjoyed these events, and she was proud to be his wife. But she was more than Mrs. Bradley Marshall, and she sometimes thought Brad didn't quite see it that way. Sherrie was an excellent cook and had even thought about starting her own catering business before they were married. But once she became Mrs. Bradley Marshall, she placed her dreams aside, making Brad's career the priority. Now, with his career in full swing and the little time they spent together, Sherrie wondered if it she shouldn't revisit her dream of starting a catering business.

"Would you like some coffee or orange juice, Ms. Sherrie?" asked Isabella.

"Coffee would be wonderful, Isabella. Thank you."

Isabella poured Sherrie a cup of freshly brewed coffee and set the creamer and sugar dish on the table. Sherrie placed a teaspoon of creamer and Sweet'N Low in her coffee and took a sip.

"Isabella, those biscuits smell wonderful as usual. I wish you would show me how you make them so flaky and fluffy."

"Oh, it's my mother's recipe. She flours the dough just so. There's no real recipe or formula to it. It's just the feel of the dough itself."

"I know how to bring together just the right ingredients. My mother never measured anything, and it was always perfect," said Sherrie.

"It must be where you get your talent, Ms. Sherrie."

"It's where we both get our talents, from our mothers." They both laughed at the coincidence of having mothers that passed on the art of cooking.

"Will Mr. Brad be down shortly? Breakfast will be ready in about ten minutes."

"I'll see if he wants breakfast downstairs or in bed," she said, standing up to head upstairs.

Just then, Jillian rushed into the kitchen wearing a little Barbie nightgown with two long ponytails on either side of her head.

"Mommy, mommy!"

"Oh, good morning, sweetness." Sherrie swooped up Jillian in her arms.

"Good morning, Ms. Jillian," said Isabella, smiling at the sight of the child.

"Good morning," said Jillian. "Can I have biscuits and bacon this morning, Mommy?"

"Yes, let's see what Isabella has in store for us. Let's go wash our hands and face and brush our teeth. When we come back downstairs, breakfast will be ready."

Sherrie took Jillian's hand to lead her back upstairs as they smiled and sang "Step by Step" to each step. At the top of the stairs was Brad dressed in a jogging outfit ready for his morning run. He swooped up Jillian as she reached the top step and gave her a big kiss on the cheek.

"Brad, I didn't know you were awake," said Sherrie.

"I wanted to get in a short run before breakfast, but it smells like it's already prepared."

"Yes, Isabella says in about ten minutes, breakfast will be ready."

"Okay then, I'll have a little breakfast and go for a short run afterwards." Sherrie looked at Brad with eyes that told him there was something pressing on her mind.

"What is it, Sherrie?"

"It's us Brad. We really need to talk about us."

"Sherrie, today is my day off. The only day I get the entire week, and sometimes I'm even called in. I just want to relax and enjoy the day. Can I do that?"

Sherrie started walking to the bedroom, and Brad put Jillian down so she could wash her face and hands in her bathroom. Sherrie followed behind him into their bedroom.

"Why don't you ever want to talk about what's going on between us, Brad? Isn't it important to you?"

"Sherrie, you're exaggerating as usual. What's so wrong with us that we need to talk about all the time?"

"We don't talk to each other anymore. It seems that you never want to be around me anymore. We don't spend any time together."

"You're being ridiculous."

"I'm not being ridiculous. I'm trying to tell you how I feel. We're not intimate anymore. When is the last time we made love?"

Brad stared at her and then finally said, "In case you haven't noticed, I work long hours. When I get home, you're asleep, and the next morning I have to get up early to go back to work and start it all over again. I'm sorry that my schedule is interfering with our sex life, but my schedule is what keeps you and Jillian in this big house, not to mention the vacations, the shopping sprees, and a live-in maid. I want to spend more time with you, but that's just the way it is right now."

"I never asked for any of this, Brad. I never wanted a live-in maid. In fact, that was your decision. I would be just as happy living in a smaller home if that meant you spending fewer hours at work and more at home. So please don't make material things sound so important that you're willing to sacrifice our marriage for it."

"I never said anything like that."

"So it doesn't bother you that we don't even spend enough time together to make love? Brad, I need you. I need you to want me like I want you."

"You know that I want you. It's just that my schedule is crazy right now. Maybe in another month or so when we finally hire the position that was left open by Dr. Grier, I can stop working all the doubles and get back to a more normal schedule. We'll have more time together then," said Brad, pulling another T-shirt out of his dresser drawer.

"Another month or so?" Sherrie looked at Brad in disbelief. She couldn't believe he thought they could hold out another month or so before they made love or spent any real time together to talk about their marriage. Sherrie never thought another woman was involved until now. That must be the answer.

"Are you seeing someone?"

"What?"

"Are you seeing someone on the side? Are you stepping out on me and screwing some little whore like that little big-breasted intern of yours? That would explain why you don't want to be with me."

"No! See, this is exactly why I didn't want to get into this discussion with you. It always ends with me having to prove my fidelity when I have never cheated on you . . . not that I haven't had the opportunity."

Sherrie eyed Brad as he spoke. She didn't like the thought that he's had opportunities to cheat or that the opportunity had presented itself. She wondered if he had been tempted to cheat even a little, and that possibility made her uneasy.

"And exactly what does that mean? Have you thought of cheating, Brad? What exactly is going on with you . . . with us?"

"I don't want to argue with you, and I don't want to talk about this anymore. All I want to do is go downstairs, have some breakfast, go for a run, and enjoy my day off. Is that possible, Sherrie? Can you just drop this so I can enjoy the day?"

"Brad, we have to get a handle on our situation before things get out of hand, and waiting a month or so to do it doesn't work for me, and it shouldn't work for you either."

"Sherrie, we can go around and around on this same subject, but we always end up in the same place. I'm a doctor, I work long hours, there's nothing more to read into this other than that. Now can we please go downstairs and get some breakfast? I'm starved."

Sherrie threw up her hands in defeat. She knew that she wasn't going to gain any more ground in this discussion, not with Brad being so closed minded to talking about their situation rationally. She was very hurt that he didn't understand how important this was to her and should have been to him. Why couldn't Brad see that they were becoming more and more disconnected? Why didn't it seem to matter to him? Brad turned to go downstairs for breakfast where Isabella already had the table set with her delicious baked biscuits, eggs, bacon, grits, and Danishes. There was freshly squeezed orange juice and roasted brewed coffee. Sherrie decided to join her husband and daughter downstairs for breakfast and put off the conversation for later. At least they would have today to enjoy, and she would try to make the most of it. Sherrie smiled when she saw the sight of Brad and Jillian together eating breakfast. They were sharing eggs and biscuits with each other.

"Drink your orange juice, baby cakes," he said to Jillian as she smiled back at him.

"Isabella, your breakfast is on point as usual. It was just what I needed before my run," said Brad.

"Thank you, Mr. Brad, I'm glad you enjoyed it. But make sure you don't overdo it with your run since you have just eaten." Isabella was always very protective of all of them.

"Ah, don't worry. I'll take it easy, although I need to run at least three miles today, so I better get started." Brad reached over to Jillian and kissed her on the forehead and then gave Sherrie a quick peck on the lips.

"I'll be back before you know it. There's nothing better to get the blood flowing than a nice jog. Luckily, it's beautiful out too," he said while grabbing his IP player and heading out the door. Sherrie got up from the table and peered through the glass pane of the front entryway door. Brad was waving at the neighbors next door and had begun his run. She suddenly thought of the card from the detective agency she'd found in his pocket and thought now would be a good time to start searching for clues while he was out on his run.

"Isabel, I'll be upstairs for a few minutes, please look after Jillian."

"Yes, I will," said Isabella, pinching Jillian's cheeks while Jillian sipped her orange juice. With that, Sherrie dashed upstairs as quickly as she could, headed for her bedroom, and then closed and locked the door behind her. She walked over to the nightstand where she had placed the card she found in Brad's pocket. She didn't know what she was looking for, but she knew if Brad had contacted an agency, he would have a report of some kind. She walked over to his walk-in closet and began going through his drawers, files, boxes, and clothing. Nothing. She searched the bottom drawers and the boxes on the shelves only to come up empty. Sherrie knew something had to be around there somewhere, but where? She stopped for a moment and then remembered the safe that he had installed in the wall behind a picture last year. Sherrie glanced up at the picture and walked over to it, took the picture from the wall, and thought about the combination, which happened to be Jillian's birthday—6-26-06. She turned the dial, and it opened without any problems. Inside were a couple of stacks of money, not unusual, but under a file, she found a manila envelope addressed to Brad from the detective agency. She could feel that there was something inside, and the envelope had been opened and sealed back up. She opened the broken seal again and reached inside. There was a letter addressed to Brad:

Mr. Marshall, as we discussed on Tuesday, May 18, enclosed you will find my report and the results of the subject you contracted me to follow. If there are any other questions, please feel free to contact me.

Sherrie thumbed through the remaining pages and let out a loud gasp. Her heart started beating rapidly as she clasped her hand over her mouth at what she was reading while thumbing through the remaining pages of the report. When she got to the last page, her body went limp, and the pages of the report slipped through her fingers and fell onto the floor. Sherrie's knees became weak, and her body fell back onto a wall as her knees began to collapse underneath her. Suddenly she understood why Brad was so distant. Suddenly, it all made sense.

CHAPTER 18

LYDIA

"**T**he phone has been blowing up all morning! That was another potential client on the line," yelled Jasper from his black glass desk that held his flat-screen computer and office cell phone. Lydia had decided on a sleek, contemporary, and stylish look for Lydia's Loft with the entire decor in elegant simplicity, with black glass desks and colorful couches and chairs in the waiting area. Jasper added an espresso machine and an area to serve bite-size sandwiches or delicious Danishes from the bakery around the corner called The Sweet Tooth.

"We're moving right along," said Lydia as she walked out of her office to give Jasper a high five. "How many does that make this morning so far?"

"That's about six new possible clients, lady. At this rate, you're going to have to hire a full staff real soon."

"Well, I'll need to see some commissions generated first before I can think about anything like that, but you're right. We're doing pretty well so far, aren't we?"

"We're doing great, Lydia, and I hear ya'. Don't worry, the money is going to start rolling in real soon, and Jasper has your back all the way."

Lydia looked at him and smiled. She was so proud of her decision to hire him. He was definitely a godsend, almost too good to be true, which in a way made her wonder how she stumbled upon someone so perfect for her new venture. However, she decided instead to think about the blessing that God had given her. A few months ago, she walked away from a satisfying and lucrative position at an established designer firm into the unknown. But with the help of her friends and the blessings of God, she was now in her own place with old and new clients contacting her every day for services. Jasper had proven to be quite an expert in getting her organized and helping pull in clients and advertising. He had even shared with her some drawings he did for a bathroom renovation. He was very talented, and Lydia wasn't sure why he hadn't been designing on his own, but she felt very fortunate to have him behind her. He was even working on a website for Lydia's Loft, which he expected to be completed very soon.

"You've been such a great help, Jasper, and I really appreciate it. We're making a great team."

"I just love seeing a sista' doing her thing, so if I can be a part of that, you know Jasper is on board, honey," he said with his signature wide smile.

"What time is Kyle Edwards coming in tomorrow?" asked Lydia as she poured herself a cup of espresso. Jasper quickly checked his calendar on his computer to confirm the time.

"He will be in at 2:30 p.m. His project is huge. I was looking at his file when I was inputting it in the new database. That's going to be a sizeable commission, darling."

"Yes, it is. Actually, getting this project back is like sweet revenge. I was actually working with him before I left my last position."

"Really?" said Jasper, intrigued on what seemed to be a juicy little story.

"Yup. He wasn't pleased with the direction they were taking with his project after I left, so he left as well and looked me up," Lydia said, smiling almost in vindication. "I guess what goes around really does come around."

"Lydia, this story sounds too good. You've got to tell me what happened."

"Ugh, it's a long story, but I'll fill you in later. Right now I need to look over the presentation for the Taylor account. Where did we save that in the database?" After hitting a couple of keys on the keyboard, Jasper brought up the particular file Lydia was looking for to show her how to access it.

"All new accounts will be located here, and I've placed your other accounts that you brought over with you in a separate file. They're filed alphabetically as well, so it should be simple to find if I'm not here."

"Great! Thanks, Jasper. I'll be in my office pulling this together for next week and getting ready for Kyle Edwards tomorrow. It's eleven o'clock, do you think we should order some lunch for later? That Thai restaurant about a block up is really good, and they deliver."

"Sounds good to me," said Jasper, getting up to stretch his legs. "I'll call and order some food and let you know when it's ready."

"Okay, great." Lydia went into her office and closed the door behind her. Whenever she was working on a presentation and needed to concentrate, she would close the door to get completely focused. Jasper had already seen a couple of her presentations for new clients, and he was very impressed by how talented a designer she was, and he loved her signature contemporary elegance style with a touch of classic design. She already had three confirmed projects after giving her showstopper presentation. He sat back down at his desk and checked out the new client list with the estimates Lydia had drawn up. The Taylor account was going to bring in about $65,000 for a complete kitchen renovation. The Mitchell account about $45,000 for a master bedroom and bath, and the Kyle Edwards account was astronomical.

Just as he was about to look up the Thai restaurant's number to place an order, a text message came in on his cell. "How's business?" the text stated.

Jasper texted back. "Business is booming. Will contact you later." And then he clicked off just as Lydia opened her office door and peeked out.

"Hey, Jasper, order that chicken I like and sauce without onions. I hate onions!" she said with a frown. "I'm getting hungry too."

"Me too. I'm ordering now," said Jasper as he began dialing. Lydia closed the door to her office again, and Jasper looked at the closed door with a crooked smile on his face.

*   *   *

"I can't believe the day is just about over," said Jasper while inputting the last account. It was now almost 6:00 p.m., and they'd been at it for hours making calls, returning calls, setting up dates for presentations, and finishing up the website. It had been a full, productive day, and Lydia was pleased with what they'd accomplished.

"We did awesome today, Jasper. Why don't you wrap it up for the day and head on out? I'm right behind you, and I'll see you in the morning."

"Oh no, I know you, girl. You'll say you're right behind me, and then you'll be here another three hours just plugging away. Let me stay and help you with whatever you want to get done tonight. I don't have anything real pressing this evening, and I can always finish up on these inputs and put the finishing touches on the website, which looks beautiful by the way."

Lydia laughed. "Yeah, you're right, normally, I would be here a little longer, but actually, I have plans tonight, so I will be leaving in a few minutes. So don't worry about me, I am right on your heels. So get going. I'll close up."

"Okay then, I'm going to pack up and maybe meet a friend for drinks before I head on home. Are you sure you don't need me for anything else today?"

"Nope. Take off. You did a great job today, and I thank you," said Lydia, waving her hand to usher him off on his way.

"Well, you have a good evening then," said Jasper, picking up his briefcase and shades. "I will see you bright and early in the morning, and don't forget that you have the Chandler account at 9:00 a.m."

"I won't. Have a good evening, Jasper." Jasper began walking to the front of the door and then threw up his left hand, waving good-bye before disappearing into the openness of the street. Lydia started gathering her things together and shutting off the espresso machine, turning off the lights and then finally arming the alarm. She was worried about the message she received from Quinton earlier about Elise, so she wanted to go over and see how she was doing. She took one last look at Lydia's Loft and beamed with pride and excitement. *God is good*, she thought to herself, and *so is life.*

Meanwhile, Jasper was driving downtown to his favorite hot spot bar, Rick's, to unwind for the night when he received a text message on his cell. "Well? How about it?" the text stated.

Damn, thought Jasper. *Whatever happened to being patient? Whatever.* He then answered the text: "Ms. Justine Taylor, kitchen renovation, $65,000 . . . Ms Thomasina Mitchell, master bedroom and bath, $45,000 . . . for starters."

A text came back in. "Good deal!" Jasper closed his phone and felt a little twinge of guilt come over him. He quickly shrugged it off as he arrived at his destination, parked and got out of his car, and headed into the bar. He spotted his friend, a handsome, well-dressed tall caramel-complexioned gentleman sitting at the bar and gleaming at the sight of him.

CHAPTER 19

CHRYSTAL

*I*t was almost 6:30 p.m., Friday evening, and Chrystal couldn't believe that she was still at her desk typing yet another revised memorandum for the same client file. Since Dana had been suspended from her position for two weeks without pay, Chrystal was now answering directly to Dana's supervisor, Mr. Sanders. Chrystal couldn't believe she was having these thoughts, but compared with the demands of Mr. Sanders, Dana was an angel, and she couldn't wait for her to get back to work on Monday morning.

"Chrystal, how about we wrap-up for the evening?" said Mr. Sanders, suddenly appearing in front of Chrystal's desk with his overcoat draped across his arm and a briefcase in the other hand. "You've done excellent work, and I appreciate your efforts. Now get out of here and have a good weekend."

"Thanks, Mr. Sanders. You have a good weekend too." He smiled and nodded at her and then headed toward the front door before stopping for one more comment.

"Uh, Chrystal, as you know, Dana will be back in on Monday, and your duties with her will resume. Thanks again for all of your hard work."

Chrystal nodded as he opened the door and swiftly walked out. *Dana, Dana,* thought Chrystal. She'll be back on Monday as if nothing happened. Chrystal wondered what Dana told her husband about being at home for two weeks. She also thought about how Dana's husband would react to the news of her little indiscretion if Chrystal decided to drop a dime on her.

Chrystal finished the last line of the memorandum before saving the document and shutting down her computer for the evening. She grabbed her Coach purse from her desk, pulled out her car keys, turned out the lamplight on her desk, and headed out the front door. It was Friday night, and the girls were planning to meet at Lydia's house for drinks, a little dinner, and a little girl talk. Lydia was still celebrating the opening of her new shop, Lydia's Loft, and her new assistant, Jasper, who appeared to have superhuman abilities in the world of interior design.

Chrystal headed out the front door into the cool, crisp air of the evening. She walked swiftly through the parking lot to get to her 1998 Toyota Corolla and hopped in without missing a beat. As she began driving out of the parking lot, her cell phone rang. She checked for the number and noticed it was Lydia calling.

"What's up, girl?" she answered almost immediately.

"Hey, where are you?" asked Lydia in a hurried voice.

"I'm pulling out of the parking lot at work, and I'm on my way to your house."

"Okay, good I caught you in time because I need you to swing by and pick up another bottle of wine."

"Dang, I always get last-minute pick-up duty."

"That's because you're always the last one to show up. So be a sweetheart and pick up *two* more bottles of wine."

"I thought you said one?"

"Yeah, but I think we're going to need at least two more bottles. I don't know if you've heard, but Elise has some kind of news for us."

"She does? About what?"

"Just hurry up and get here and you'll find out."

"Okay, I'm on my way." Just as Chrystal was about to pull out of the parking lot, a Mercedes Benz convertible swung into the parking lot and pulled up alongside her. Chrystal glanced over to see that it was Dana's husband, Paul.

"Chrystal!" he yelled, motioning for her to not pull off just yet. Chrystal was surprised to see him and rolled down her window and greeted him.

"Oh hi, Paul, how are you?"

"I'm fine, thanks. Listen, I've been trying to reach Dana, is she still in her office?"

Chrystal was confused. Didn't Paul know that Dana had been suspended without pay for two weeks and wasn't due back into work until Monday? This was awkward, but Chrystal had always been quick on her feet.

"Uh, no, she's not here. Did you try her on her cell?"

"I did, but there's no answer. Do you know what time she left for the day? We have an important meeting this evening, and I think she may have forgotten about it."

"I'm sorry, Paul, I don't know," said Chrystal, hating the fact that she was being forced to lie for the likes of Dana.

"Okay, I don't want to hold you up. I'm sure she'll give me a call back. Have a good weekend, Chrystal."

"You do the same."

As he pulled away, Chrystal wondered what Dana had been doing for the last couple of weeks. She was obviously pretending to go to work, but where was she actually going? Dana was a little more intriguing than Chrystal had ever imagined. Chrystal put her car in drive and pulled out of the parking lot. It looked like Elise wouldn't be the only one with a story to tell tonight.

CHAPTER 20

ELISE

*E*lise pulled into Lydia's spacious driveway, turned off the ignition, and sat there silently for a moment. She was still trying to understand what happened with Quinton the other day and how a marriage proposal came out of her refusal to live with him right now. How was she going to answer Quinton's question, or did he already have her answer? Things had been a little tense at home since she responded to his question by regurgitating her lunch into the toilet. Elise didn't know how Quinton was supposed to interpret that when she didn't quite know what to make of it herself. She looked to her right and noticed that Chrystal's car was in the driveway along with Sherrie's Benz parked further up. So she decided to go inside and get the girl's opinions on what she should do next. Elise didn't have any answers since she wasn't ready for Quinton to move in with her, so she certainly wasn't ready to become a wife. She sure hoped the girls had an answer.

*   *   *

"What's going on with you and Sherrie tonight?" asked Chrystal. "You've been really quiet, and we all know that both of you have the biggest mouths in town."

"Yeah, are you guys feeling okay? Because there is a bug going around," said Lydia, sipping her margarita.

Sherrie sipped her margarita and looked at Elise who in turn looked at her. "You want to go first?." asked Sherrie. Elise just nodded her head yes and took a sip of her drink.

"I don't know how to say this, so I'll just say it."

"Okay, just say it," said Lydia, looking concerned about what Elise was about to say.

"Okay, here's the deal." Elise gave out a huge sigh. "Quinton asked me to marry him."

"What?" yelled Lydia and Chrystal at the same time. Even Sherrie was awakened from her funk with the news.

"That's great news Elise! Congratulations!" squealed Lydia, hugging her.

"I thought something had happened the way you were acting, girl. But this is great, isn't it?" asked Chrystal.

"No! This isn't great. This isn't great news at all, guys. I don't want to get married. I don't even want to live together with anyone, why would I want to get married?"

"Okay, back up, so you're saying that you don't want to get married? What's wrong with you?" asked Chrystal. Sherrie was silently watching this all unfold. Elise could be getting married while her marriage could be possibly ending.

"No, Chrystal. I don't want to get married," said Elise. "You know, sometimes you guys don't get me at all."

"That's because your ass is weird Elise. Any other woman would be screaming for joy, but you, you walk in here acting like someone just gave you thirty days to live."

"Whatever, Chrystal," said Elise, rolling her eyes.

"Okay, so you don't want to get married. So what did you say to him?" asked Lydia.

"I didn't exactly say anything."

"What do you mean you didn't say anything?" asked Sherrie, now intrigued with the conversation.

"Well, I just kind of ran in the bathroom and threw up all over the floor." The girls looked at one another and then at Elise.

"So my guess is that's not the answer he was looking for," said Chrystal, shaking her head.

"You think!" said Elise. She put her head in her hands. "Oh, it's been so weird in the house since it happened. We haven't talked about it, and I think I may have hurt his feelings. I don't know what to do now."

"Well, sweetie, you're going to have to talk to him and let him know how you feel," said Lydia, rubbing Elise's hair. "If you're not ready for marriage, then he needs to know you're not ready."

"I don't want to lose him. I just want a little time and my own space for now. Is that so wrong?"

"No, of course that isn't wrong. But you have to talk to him and let him know what you're thinking," said Lydia.

"I agree," said Sherrie. "You have to be honest with him."

"How did this come about?" asked Chrystal.

"We were still going back and forth about living together, so finally I told him the reason I didn't want to live together was because we weren't married and I didn't want to live with anyone unless I was married to him. The next thing I know, he's reciting a scene from *Diary* on one knee."

"Oh," said Lydia. "Why did you tell him that knowing you weren't ready for marriage?"

"Because I thought he wasn't ready either!"

"Oh, so the reverse psychology backfired on your ass." Chrystal laughed.

"Shut up, heifer. You know, you can really be an ass sometimes."

"Sorry," said Chrystal leaning back into her chair.

"Well, the only thing you can do now is tell him that you're not ready for marriage because that's the truth. You don't want to dig yourself deeper into this than you already are, right?" asked Sherrie.

"You're right. You're all right. I just don't know how I'm going to tell him."

"Just do it gently. Tell him you love him but you want some time to think about marriage," said Lydia.

"Oh, I'm gonna need a lot more to drink tonight," said Elise.

"More margaritas coming up!" yelled Chrystal as she ran into the kitchen to mix some more drinks. A few minutes later, Chrystal emerged from the kitchen with a pitcher of freshly mixed margaritas to top everyone off. All of the ladies were relaxing on either the couch or the floor with their drinks, just ready to spend the evening sharing, when Chrystal made an announcement about Dana.

"I have some news about Dana," she said teasingly.

"Really? What's she been up to now?" asked Elise as she took a bite of the sushi Lydia laid out.

"I thought she was on suspension for bumping and grinding with your client," said Lydia.

"See, that's the interesting part," said Chrystal, slurping her Margarita. "As I was about to leave the parking lot to come here tonight, Dana's husband swings by and asks if Dana is still working because she hadn't been answering her cell all day," she said with a wink.

"So her husband doesn't know she hasn't been at work?" asked Sherrie.

"Apparently not, and it put me in a position to have to cover for her ass, and I didn't really like it."

"The plot thickens, right?" said Elise.

"If her husband finds out that bit of information, it will be like, 'Lucy, you have some 'splainin' to do," said Chrystal in her best Ricky Ricardo accent.

"She is really something else. Not quite the humdrum person you've always talked about, Chrystal," said Lydia.

"Yes, she is," said Chrystal, thinking to herself that this information could also be used to her benefit.

"Where do you think she's been going these past two weeks? Do you think she's still hooking up with your former client?" asked Elise.

"That's what I'd like to know, and believe me, I will find out. The bloodhound in me is alive and well." Chrystal snickered.

Now the attention was turned to Sherrie, who had still been unusually quiet especially for girl's night of sharing.

"Sherrie, is everything okay?" asked Lydia. "Do you want to talk about anything? Because you know you can talk to us about anything and we'll always be there for you. What's wrong?" asked Lydia.

Sherrie took a deep breath and looked at her friends when tears suddenly began to run down her cheeks. She put her head in her hands and began to sob.

"Sherrie, what's the matter?" said Chrystal as Lydia and Elise both began to rub her back to comfort her. Sherrie had always been the rock of the group, and they had never really seen her break down in tears like this before. They knew she was having some issues with Brad, but they thought it was something they would eventually work out together. But now they were all wondering if something more serious was happening in her marriage. Sherrie looked up and wiped her eyes and started to pull herself together.

"This is very hard for me. I don't know how to begin," she said in a low voice.

"Just start at the beginning. Take your time," said Lydia while Chrystal and Elise looked on with encouragement. Sherrie took a deep breath and then started to cry again.

"I'm afraid you won't look at me the same."

"Sherrie, whatever it is, we can talk about it. We can work through it. Just tell us so we can help you," said Lydia. Sherrie let out a deep sigh and another deep breath as if bracing herself for the judgment she assumed she'd get from her friends, but she decided to tell them because she needed to talk to someone about it, and who better than her girls?

"You won't judge me?"

"No, we're here for you, Sherrie. No judgment, only love, okay? So what's bothering you?"

"You won't look at me differently?"

"No. Please tell us what is going on," said Lydia.

"You promise? All of you have to promise that you will still love me no matter what."

They all huddled together and gave a huge group hug to encourage Sherrie to trust them with the information she was about to reveal. Sherrie took another deep breath and let it out at last.

"Jillian is not Brad's daughter, and he found out!" she blurted out and then began to cry uncontrollably as Lydia, Elise, and Chrystal stood paralyzed by the news. They all stared at one another, shocked by this revelation.

Chrystal reached over to comfort Sherrie as tears filled all the girls' eyes. *Damn*, thought Chrystal. She thought that out of all of them, Sherrie was the only one who had gotten the relationship puzzle right.

CHAPTER 21

JASPER

*E*arly Sunday morning and all was still and quiet at Lydia's Loft. Only the faint remnants of the grand opening several days before could be felt in the air while quick flashes of light came through the front entryway from passing cars. Suddenly, there was a click at the front door and the sound of a lock unhinging, and a tall lean figure stepped in and quickly closed the door behind him. A beeping sound rang out, signaling the APX security system had been activated. The lean figure walked over to the security keypad and punched in the security code—1286. The beeping stopped, and the figure walked over to Jasper's desk to access the computer. The figure turned the computer on, revealing a password-protect block to gain access. Slowly, the figure punched in the password and within seconds was in. There were several files on the computer's desktop but one in particular, Clients, was clicked on, and several subfolders popped up on the screen. The figure clicked on the Thomasina Mitchell and Justine Taylor files, and all of the information for the project including, drawings, sketch work, floor and material samples, and the estimates were uploaded onto a thumb drive. Once the information was uploaded, the figure logged off the computer and shut it down and then placed the thumb drive into his jacket pocket. He then walked over to the security pad and reset the alarm system, and within seconds, the figure was gone as silently and quickly as he had arrived.

*   *   *

Monday morning

Jasper pulled up the last of the information on the Thomasina Mitchell project and copied it onto a thumb drive for Lydia's presentation this morning. He also printed out hard copies just in case there were any technical difficulties with her laptop. Jasper always believed in having a contingency plan, and he didn't want anything to go wrong with this presentation. Lydia's appointment with Mrs. Mitchell was scheduled for 10:00 a.m., and he could tell that she was a little nervous. She had a preliminary meeting with Mrs. Mitchell, who explained what she'd like done to her master bedroom and bathroom. The house had been built in the 1960s and still had much of the original design, which by today's standards were totally outdated. Jasper had seen pictures of the bedroom with its wood-paneled walls and outdated floor tiling on the bathroom's walls and floors. It was a total disaster, but Lydia was about to wow them with her vision of what a master bedroom and bath should look like today. The sketches and drawings for this presentation were breathtaking, and Jasper knew that they would be blown away by her concept. He was just finishing placing all the information together when Lydia came out of her office with laptop in hand.

"Well, how do I look?" she twirled around excitedly. She was wearing a beautiful black-and-white form-fitting dress with black Jimmy Choo sling backs.

"You look like you're about to close this deal, lady," said Jasper, giving her a once-over. "You look fantastic! How do you feel?"

"A little nervous," said Lydia, gritting her teeth and revealing her beautiful straight white teeth.

"Nothing to be worried about, girl. You got this. We went over your presentation several times, and I have to tell you. I've worked with a lot of designers, in fact, my mother, God rest her soul, was a designer, but, Lydia, you are brilliant! I mean your concepts and the way you pull together colors and textures is really impressive."

Lydia was so touched by his words and compliments, and she walked over to him to give him a hug.

"Thank you, Jasper. I needed that, I really did." She smiled at him confidently and said, "I can do this!"

"Yes, ma'am, you certainly can, and not only that, you will!" shouted Jasper, handing her the information he'd just compiled. "Now here is your thumb drive that has everything here for your presentation, and I've made hard copies just in case they want something to look at and think over."

"Got it," said Lydia, smiling. "Thanks so much, Jasper. Well, I better get out of here. I don't want to be late. Wish me luck," she said, walking quickly toward the front entrance.

"Much love, lady. Knock 'em dead," said Jasper, blowing kisses her way. Lydia disappeared through the door, leaving Jasper alone to catch up on some on his e-filing and updates on their new website. He clicked on the website's URL, LydiasLoft.com, and began making some additions to the main page when the telephone rang.

"Good morning, Lydia's Loft, this is Jasper, can I help you?"

"Hey, you," said a male voice on the other end.

"Hey back at you," said Jasper in a seductive tone.

"What are you up to?"

"Just doing some updates to our website. Lydia just took off for a presentation, and she'll probably be gone for a few hours, so I have a little quiet time. What are you up to?"

"Nothing much. I was thinking of you, so I thought I'd call," said the voice.

"Well, aren't you so sweet to be thinking about me? By the way, I meant to ask you, where did you go last night? I woke up and turned over to maybe get a little more of what you put on me last night, and you weren't there. I thought you went home, but when I got up this morning, you were there fast asleep," said Jasper inquisitively.

"Oh, I, uh, just couldn't sleep, so I got up and went to get some ice cream from around the corner. You know me and ice cream, always have to have it."

"That better be all you're getting up in the middle of the night to get because you just have to have it. But seriously, is that where you were?"

"Of course, where else? I'll make it up to you tonight, is that a deal?"

"You better," said Jasper suggestively as another telephone line lit up and started to ring. "I have to go, but you stay sweet, and I'll see you this evening."

"Cool," said the voice. "Can't wait."

Jasper clicked off the line and picked up the other line. "Lydia's Loft, this is Jasper, can I help you?"

"Is this Lydia's Loft?" said a woman on the line.

"Yes, it is. Can I help you?" asked Jasper.

"I'm looking for someone to redo my guest bedroom. My name is Sarah McDonald, and I was referred by one of Lydia's previous clients. Can I speak with Lydia?"

"Ms. Brown is out of the office doing a presentation, but you've called the right place, Ms. McDonald. Let me get your information, and I'll have her contact you when she gets back," said Jasper as he grabbed a sticky pad from his desk.

"Okay, she can reach me at home at 668-5540, that's Sarah McDonald."

"Yes, ma'am, Sarah McDonald, guest-bedroom renovation," Jasper repeated. "Got it. You have a great day, and she will contact you as soon as possible."

"Thank you, good-bye," said Ms. McDonald, and Jasper heard a click at the other end of the line.

He wrote down the message and placed it in her message inbox to get once she returned. He sat there for a moment wondering if Lydia had arrived at Mitchell home yet. Lydia had a great reputation, so he knew everything would go well. Jasper got up from his desk and walked over to the espresso machine to get a cup when he thought that he should run an update on his and Lydia's computers. He'd always made a routine of running updates on his system to make sure there were no viruses and to keep information protected, and since Lydia would be out for a few hours, this would be a great time to do it. There was a lot of sensitive information on his and Lydia's systems, so he wanted to ensure they were safe.

Jasper took a sip of his espresso, which was rich, a little tart, but strong, just like he liked his companions, he smiled to himself. He clicked on a virus-protection icon, and the program began to run an update on his files. Jasper was taking another sip of his espresso when he noticed something strange about the time and date of the last access into a couple of the client files. Sunday, 3:00 a.m., the Mitchell and Taylor files were accessed.

"What the hell?" thought Jasper out loud.

CHAPTER 22

SHERRIE

*I*t was an unusually warm spring afternoon, and Sherrie wanted to take advantage of the nice weather by lying in a lounge chair next to their luxurious swimming pool. She wore sunglasses, a low top revealing her size 36DD cleavage, and tan capri pants. Jillian was nearby playing happily with her Barbie dolls and a small stroller. Sherrie gazed at her little girl and thought about the secret she revealed to her friends just a few days before. She'd never told anyone about Jillian's real father because she would then have to admit that she had an affair, and she'd done a good job at burying that secret until she discovered the manila envelope in the safe. Brad was away attending a seminar in Houston, Texas, so it gave her time to think about what she was going to do and why Brad hadn't confronted her since he knew the truth. Was he planning to catch her in a lie, or was he secretly planning to divorce her, leaving her with nothing? All types of scenarios were running through Sherrie's mind as she tried desperately to think about how to handle the situation and save her marriage at the same time.

She was fearful that her girlfriends would think less of her knowing that she'd had an affair that produced a child, especially since she had always been rock solid about marriage and she actually suspected Brad of cheating at one time. But she was even more afraid that Brad no longer loved her.

And what of Jillian? How will Brad behave toward her knowing that she wasn't his biological daughter? From everything she'd seen so far, he was still acting like the loving and adoring father, but would this all change because of her actions? She was going crazy with questions that she had no answers to. She sipped on her lemonade and laid her head back into the lounge chair. Jillian was now rolling her dolls around in a circle in her play stroller when she walked over to Sherrie.

"Mommy, can I have a peanut butter and jelly sandwich?" she asked.

"Yes, you can, sweetie. Come with me," said Sherrie, getting up from the chair and extending her hand out for Jillian to take it. They walked in the house together, Jillian holding her mother's hand and skipping away. It was Isabella's day off, so once inside, Sherrie pulled out the bread, peanut butter, and jelly and made the sandwich to give her daughter. She poured her a glass of milk and sat her up in a bar chair at the kitchen counter.

"Eat up, sweetie, this will make you nice and strong," she said, giving Jillian a kiss on her little cheek. Jillian began eating the sandwich while bobbing her head up and down. She loved peanut butter and jelly sandwiches with milk, so she was happy her mother made her favorite dish. Sherrie smiled at her for a moment when then telephone rang. She checked the caller ID before picking it up and noticed it was Elise.

"Hi there," she greeted Elise.

"Hi, Sherrie. How are you doing?" asked Elise.

"I've been better, Elise. I've been sitting here thinking about how I'm going to save my marriage. I just don't know what to do. What's worse is that Brad knows, but he hasn't said a thing. He's just going about business as usual. I don't know what that means, Elise, or what he's thinking."

"What exactly did you see in the envelope, Sherrie, and do you know for sure that Brad knows?"

"Yes, he definitely knows. The envelope was from a lab to determine paternity, and the names on the form were Jillian Marshall and Bradford

Marshall. The results of the test said that it was a 0 percent chance that he was the father," said Sherrie as tears began to well up in her eyes again.

"Wow, Sherrie, I don't know what to say sweetheart," said Elise, who was uncharacteristically at a loss for words. "Sherrie, if Brad isn't the father, then who is? Who did you have an affair with, and when did it happen? Also, why are we just finding out about this?" asked Elise, wondering how something this explosive was hidden from even her closest friends.

Sherrie took a deep breath and wiped her eyes. This was something from her past that was very painful, and she'd never spoken about it to anyone. It was about 1:30 p.m., and Jillian was now finished with her sandwich, and Sherrie wanted to put her down for a nap.

"Elise, can we meet somewhere and talk about this? I don't want to talk about it over the phone, and it's time for Jillian's nap."

"Yes, sweetie, sure. Where do you want to meet?"

"Let me get a sitter for Jillian, and I'll meet you in about an hour at One for a drink and dessert."

"Sounds good, I'll see you there," said Elise. Sherrie hung up the telephone and immediately called Kady, a sixteen-year-old who lived a couple of doors down from them, for an unscheduled sit. Kady was always reliable, and Jillian loved her, so she didn't think there'd be a problem with the last-minute notice. She picked Jillian up and informed her it was time for her nap for which she resisted, but Sherrie was well aware of her timetable and knew she'd be asleep within minutes. As they reached Jillian's bedroom, Kady answered the telephone.

"Kady, it's Mrs. Marshall. Listen, I wonder if you can sit with Jillian for me now for a couple of hours."

*　　*　　*

The One was one of Sherrie's favorite dining spots in Atlanta. It offered a chic ambiance, perfect for any occasion. The food was wonderful, especially the dessert, which Sherrie had a weakness for. It also had a nice atmosphere to sit and talk with friends or just have a nice gathering, which was why Sherrie suggested it.

Both Sherrie and Elise arrived promptly, each ordering delicious desserts and a drink to start off. Sherrie ordered the parsnip spice cake with cream cheese frosting and pear sorbet, while Elise ordered the Kit Kat bar peanut butter ice cream. They ordered and were sipping white wine with their desserts. Elise watched Sherrie as she slowly ate her cake and allowed her to begin talking when she felt comfortable. Sherrie felt Elise's eyes upon her and looked up with a half smile, which Elise returned. Elise put her hand on Sherrie's hand.

"I know it's hard, so just start when you're ready," said Elise.

Sherrie put down her fork and wiped her lips with her white cloth napkin.

"You know that Brad and I have been having problems because he isn't at home very often. I know it's the nature of his job, and I'm his wife and I want us to spend more time together with him without the constant ringing of his cell or beeper," said Sherrie.

"I understand, that's just natural," said Elise.

"I didn't intend for any of this to happen, it just did. A few years ago, I met one of Brad's colleagues at a fundraiser for multiple sclerosis. At the time, I was the chair of the event. Brad was working as usual, so he wasn't able to attend. So out of nowhere walks this gorgeous man. He introduced himself, and at the time, I had no idea that he and Brad even knew each other, much less worked together. Well, he was very charming, and he gave a huge donation for the cause. He also gave me his telephone number. I don't know why, other than I was lonely, but I took the number and didn't bother to mention that I was married, and he didn't ask. For about two weeks, we met at different places for lunch and dinner, and he took me out on his boat. It was magical. I felt alive, and I felt like someone was paying attention to me and found me attractive. I knew it was wrong, but we started having sex. At first it was the one time and I told him it could only be once, but I was weak and lonely, and Brad was away a lot or working late, and this gentleman was available. He always seemed to be available for me, and in turn, I made myself available to him. Well, this went on for about six months, and Brad didn't have a clue, which made me angry because I was spending quite a bit of time with this gentleman and Brad was so busy that he didn't even notice." Sherrie paused and took a sip of her wine.

"So, what happened next, and how did it end?" asked Elise, intrigued by all of the details.

"One night, Brad came home early from work totally unexpected with flowers, a bottle of wine, and a little black box. He told me that he realized that he'd been working hard and we hadn't spent a lot of time together, and then he gave me this." Sherrie lifted her right hand to reveal a stunning five-carat perfectly cut diamond ring.

"It wasn't for anything special," she continued. "He just wanted to say he loved me. I was so happy and touched, and we made love that night for the first time in months. That was the year that we went to Paris, do you remember?"

"Yes, I do remember," said Elise, listening intently. "We didn't even know you were out of the country until we each received separate postcards from Paris and you brought us back that wonderful candy and cheeses," said Elise, recalling the time.

"Yeah," said Sherrie reminiscing. "That's when I decided that I could no longer see his colleague again. I felt like our marriage had been renewed and that Brad really did care about me. So I broke it off with his colleague. He wasn't happy about it, but he said he understood, and we went our separate ways. The day after I broke it off with him, I had my annual Pap smear, and that's when I found out I was three months pregnant. I didn't even know," said Sherrie, shaking her head. "I knew it couldn't be Brad's because before the night he gave me this ring, we hadn't had sex in months. I was devastated, but all I could do was go along and pretend that it was Brad's. What else could I do? I couldn't tell him," said Sherrie regretfully.

"But, Sherrie, Brad's a doctor. If you figured out the baby couldn't be his, couldn't he?"

"I thought about that too, so when I told him, I pretended not to be as far along as I was, and prayed to God that he wouldn't give it a second thought. So after Paris and the news about the baby, things were good for a while, and we were spending more time together, but then Brad was promoted to chief of the surgery unit, and his work began to pick up again. I attended most of my prenatal appointments alone, so he became so busy again that he didn't notice that I was further along than I said."

"What about his colleague, did you ever tell him?"

"No. I've only seen him once or twice since at charity events."

"So how do you think Brad became suspicious and got a paternity test?"

"I don't know. Maybe he started putting two and two together."

"Why didn't you tell his coworker? Did you think he would demand to see his daughter?"

"It's complicated," said Sherrie as she took a long gulp from her wineglass.

"I know it's messy, but don't you think he should know?"

"No!" said Sherrie, almost agitated.

"Okay, I'm sorry, but why?" asked Elise, curious of how she'd answer. Sherrie took the last sip of her wine and took a deep breath.

"Because he's married too," she said.

Elise could not believe her ears. She had always thought of Sherrie and Brad as the ultimate power couple with money, a beautiful home, and a gorgeous little daughter. She couldn't believe the stress Sherrie had been under all this time keeping this bombshell of a secret. But now she totally understood that Sherrie wasn't joking when she said it was complicated.

CHAPTER 23

LYDIA

Lydia was smiling to herself as she drove back to her office after giving a superb presentation to Mrs. Mitchell. She had a good feeling about the outcome because Mrs. Mitchell said that she'd totally nailed what she was looking for in a renovation. Lydia didn't want to start celebrating yet since Mrs. Mitchell also mentioned that she was seeing a couple more designers before she made her final decision, but Lydia was confident that she was pretty much sold on her concept. *This is going to be a good day—no, it is going to be a good year*, thought Lydia as she pulled her red 328i BMW convertible into her own reserved parking space directly in front of Lydia's Loft. She let up the hard top and stepped out with laptop in hand. She couldn't wait to tell Jasper the good news.

Jasper was taking another telephone message when Lydia walked into the office. He saw her come in and hung up the phone, anxious to hear how the presentation had gone.

"So how did it go?" asked Jasper, coming from behind his desk, ready to hear the news.

"It was fantastic, Jasper!" squealed Lydia. "In fact, it went a lot better than I expected. She loved the concept. I mean, she really loved it. I don't want to say it before we know for sure, but I think we got it, Jasper. I just have a good feeling about it," she said smiling.

"Oh, girl, that is wonderful! See, I knew you could do it, so let's just sit back and wait for the confirmation, and then we'll go out and celebrate your first job with Lydia's Loft."

"Right on, you got it," said Lydia as they gave each other high fives.

"In the meantime, lady, you have like a gazillion messages here that you need to return. Oh, and you got a call from Elise. She wants you to call her as soon as possible," he said, handing her all of the messages that had come in.

"Oh, Elise called? She probably tried to reach me on my cell, but I had it on vibrate during the presentation. Thanks, Jasper, I'll get right on these. So did anything else go on while I was out?" she asked while walking into her office and setting down her laptop.

"No, not really," he said, following behind her to the office. "I finished up the changes on the website, so when you get a chance, you can take a peek at it, and I have your package together for your presentation for tomorrow with Mrs. Taylor."

"Yes, that's going to be an exciting presentation too. Oh, I hope we get them both," said Lydia, who was now behind her desk and going through her messages.

"Don't worry, we'll do fine," said Jasper. "Do you want me to do anything else right now?"

"Yes, I need a dinner reservation for Paschal's for Friday night around 7:00 p.m. for four. Can you make those?"

"Is sugar sweet? You got it, girl, I'll do it right away."

As Jasper returned to his desk to start on reservations, his cell began to ring, and when he picked it up, there was a new text message.

"So how did the presentation go?"

He clicked on Reply and answered immediately. "The presentation was marvelous. What about yours?"

There was another buzz on his cell. "We got the job."

"Congrats! Will talk later."

Jasper closed his cell and picked up the office phone to make reservations, "Yes, this is Jasper Pearsall, and I need a reservation for four on Friday under the name Lydia Brown. Yes, that's right, four for this Friday at 7:00 p.m." There was a pause. "Wonderful! Thanks, sugar!" He hung up the phone and began to place the dinner date on Lydia's appointment calendar in his computer. *If all goes as planned, there will be lots to celebrate by Friday*, thought Jasper, and he knew exactly how he'd do it.

CHAPTER 24

CHRYSTAL

*T*he bitch is back, thought Chrystal while typing the last paragraph of a memorandum Dana needed done as soon as possible. Chrystal was expecting Dana to walk in the office this morning in shame with a jacket practically thrown over her head to cover her face, similar to the handcuffed suspects you saw on TV attempting to avoid the media. Instead, she waltzed in like she owned the place, like she was returning from a relaxing spa treatment instead of an ordered unpaid suspension. Chrystal was pissed. Dana's indiscretion put everyone in a difficult position, and Chrystal didn't appreciate the fact that she was forced to cover for her ass with Paul. Chrystal had a plan for her cheating ass, though, all laid out and the evidence to back it up. All she needed now was the right opportunity to present Dana with her proposition.

Chrystal finished the memo and took it in to Dana for her signature. When she walked into her office, Dana was just finishing up a telephone call, and she motioned Chrystal to come in. Chrystal stepped in the office and placed the memo in front of her to sign. Dana quickly scribbled a couple of letters under the signature block and handed the memo back to Chrystal.

"Thanks, Chrystal, that was quick work," she said, looking at her over her glasses.

"No problem," said Chrystal, getting ready to turn and walk out of the office when Dana asked her to close the door.

"Chrystal, close the door and have a seat," she said. Chrystal turned and looked at her and then did as she was asked. She took a seat in one of the customer chairs near Dana's desk.

"Paul told me that he ran into you here in the parking lot the other day," she said.

"Yes, he came by looking for you."

"I . . . appreciate you not letting on that I wasn't at work." Chrystal thought that maybe this was a good time to bring up how she could repay her, when there was a tap on the door. Dana looked at Chrystal and then yelled for the person to enter. When the door opened, Dana and Chrystal were surprised to see that it was Paul.

"Hi, Chrystal, hi, honey," he said, greeting them both.

"Hello, Paul, nice to see you again," said Chrystal.

"Chrystal, she's not working too hard, is she? The last couple of weeks have been tough on her. It got so bad I didn't know when to expect her home."

Whatever she was doing in the last two weeks had nothing to do with work, but you might want to check with Jeff McKenna, thought Chrystal, but instead she just smiled and gave the politically correct response.

"I'll try to make sure she doesn't overdo it, Paul. You know Dana is such a hard worker, and she keeps me pretty busy too, so we look out for each other," said Chrystal, turning and smiling at Dana.

"Honey, what are you doing here?" asked Dana.

"Oh, I just stopped by to see if you're available for lunch. You can take a break for lunch, can't you?" smiled Paul.

"Sure, where would you like to go?"

"Your choice, I'm open to anything," he said.

"Would you like me to make reservations for the two of you somewhere?" asked Chrystal.

"No, that won't be necessary, we'll just stop in somewhere. Paul, give me a moment, and I'll meet you outside."

"Sure, hon, I'll see you in a minute," said Paul. He turned and started to walk out when there was another tap on the door. He opened the door to see an unfamiliar face. It was Tina, a new employee who started only a month ago and was hired as a temporary administrative help for any of the associates that needed her.

"Oh, I'm sorry to interrupt," she apologized. "I just saw you come in the morning, Dana, and I wanted to say welcome back," she said sweetly. Chrystal looked at Dana, who was beginning to turn red, and Paul looked totally confused. "Okay, I better get back to work now, but welcome back again."

"Thanks Tina," said Dana, looking almost like her cover had been blown. Chrystal closed the door after Tina left.

"What did she mean by that, Dana? Why is she welcoming you back?" asked Paul.

Dana was a loss for words. She fiddled with her pencil, and Chrystal could see little beads of perspiration sprouting on her forehead.

"She's new, Paul, so she probably hasn't seen Dana for a couple of days. Dana's been in and out of the office so much that I've barely seen her myself," Chrystal offered.

"Well, make sure she slows down, Chrystal, I'm counting on you," said Paul, patting her on the back.

"I will, don't worry about that," said Chrystal.

"I'll see you outside. Have a nice day, Chrystal," he said as he walked out of the office.

"You too, Paul," said Chrystal as she closed the door behind him. Once she was sure he was out of earshot, Chrystal turned to Dana and smiled.

"You and I need to have a long productive talk when you get back from lunch."

"What about?" asked Dana.

"About something that will interest you a great deal," said Chrystal. Dana stared at her over her glasses and responded in an almost dismissive tone.

"I have a lot of work to catch up on, Chrystal, so I'll give you about five minutes for whatever it is."

"You will give me as much time as I need," said a determined Chrystal. Dana couldn't believe that her assistant was speaking to her in such a way.

"I don't think I like your tone."

"I'll see you after your lunch with your husband, unless you'd rather him find out the real reason Tina was welcoming you back." Dana jumped up from her desk, grabbed her purse, and began to walk out.

"After lunch, Dana, or things could get very interesting for you," said Chrystal, smiling.

Dana rolled her eyes and headed out the door to meet her husband waiting patiently outside smiling, as giddy and clueless as ever.

*   *   *

Chrystal watched the door, intently awaiting Dana's return. This was the moment she was waiting for to slam Dana with the evidence she had against her involving Jeff McKenna. She had no idea that Chrystal knew everything that was going on between them and the reason their firm lost the McKenna account and why Mr. Sanders ordered her on two weeks' suspension. *The things a girl has to do to get a raise*, thought Chrystal. Suddenly, Dana walked in from her lunch, once again strutting like she owned the place. She cut her eyes at Chrystal and walked right past her without saying a word. Chrystal got up from her desk and followed her into her office and closed the door.

"I'm not ready for you yet," she said, putting her purse away and then primping her hair.

"I'll wait. Like I said, you'll give me as much time as I need," said Chrystal. Dana began rearranging the folders on her desk, checked her mail, and even retouched her lipstick before acknowledging Chrystal's request for a discussion. After stalling for what Chrystal considered the inevitable, Dana sat back in her chair and stared at Chrystal.

"I see you're not taking this seriously," said Chrystal.

"You haven't given me any reason to take you seriously, Chrystal. And let me say that I've told Paul everything about the suspension, so save your breath and your threats because we're squared away on that subject," she said, feeling a sense of victory.

"Is that so? You told him everything?"

"That's right. He knows that I lost the McKenna account and was on two weeks' suspension because of it. I told him I was too embarrassed to tell him. My husband is very understanding and supportive. Maybe you'll find a husband as wonderful one of these days," she said, almost smirking at the thought of Chrystal finding a husband.

Chrystal began laughing. "Dana, you know you always keep it interesting, don't you? But the one thing that's constant with you is that you're a flat-out liar. I know exactly why you were suspended. It's funny how you conveniently left out the real reason for your suspension."

"The real reason? I've told you the reason."

"You haven't told the whole story."

"Which is?" asked Dana, sure that she had the upper hand.

"You want me to say it out loud?"

"Look, I don't know what you're talking about, and I have a lot of work to do this afternoon, so I suggest you stop wasting my time."

Chrystal was angry with Dana's dismissive and superior attitude, and she was tired of her lies. It was time to call the bitch out.

"Okay, here it is. You were bangin' Jeff McKenna, and that's why your trifling ass was suspended. Don't try to deny it because I have evidence," said Chrystal.

"How dare you!" shouted Dana. "I could have you fired and thrown out of here for that kind of accusation," said Dana angrily.

"Oh, I wouldn't do that unless you want a copy of this mailed to your husband." Chrystal pulled out the tape recorder and pressed play as Dana's recorded conversation with Jeff McKenna began to play throughout her office.

"Jeff, baby, are you ready for our little San Diego getaway? . . . I know, baby, but we'll be together for three romance-filled days, and I can't wait . . . No, Chrystal will be making my arrangements today, so I'll give you my agenda so you can get on the same flight, but we'll be in our usual hotel . . . [laughs]"

Chrystal turned the recording off. "Sound familiar? I wonder how 'understanding and supportive' your husband will be after hearing how you've been screwing another man," said Chrystal sarcastically.

Dana was in shock. She couldn't believe her ears, and she couldn't believe that she was now in this position. She had to find out what Chrystal wanted to make this go away.

"Where did you get that?" said Dana

"It fell in my lap . . . literally, but it was bound to happen because you're sloppy, Dana."

"What do you want?"

Chrystal smiled. Now that was the question she'd been waiting for Dana to ask.

"What do I want? That's a very good question since you've never given a damn about what I wanted before. But now you're in a compromising position, aren't you?"

"Just tell me what you want, Chrystal," said Dana, irritated with the entire situation.

"I'll tell you what I want. I'm tired of being your lapdog, getting your coffee, and picking up your damn dry cleaning. I'm tired of making reservations for you to go places I've never even set foot in. In fact, I'm just tired of you!" said Chrystal as Dana glared at her.

"There's another assistant position in Erin's section with a raise. I can recommend you for that position," said Dana.

"You're not hearing me. I don't want to be an assistant. I don't want to pick up anyone's dry cleaning but my own."

"Well, what do you want?" said Dana, once again annoyed. Chrystal leaned forward toward Dana to get her undivided attention.

"There's an intern position posted with a huge raise. I want you to not only recommend me for the position, I want you to make sure that I get it," said Chrystal decisively.

"I can't do that. The position requires a bachelor's degree, and I know you don't have one—"

"Bullshit," said Chrystal. "You can and you will get me that position, or you can explain to your husband and Jeff's wife that your business trips with Jeff involved a hell of a lot more than business," Chrystal warned.

Dana sat still for a moment as if weighing her options. She couldn't believe that this little tart was blackmailing her for a promotion of all things. Getting her the job would be easy enough; the next question was how she could get that tape.

"Okay, I will arrange for you to get the intern position, effective next week. But I want the tape in return, and I don't want to hear about any of this again. Do we have a deal?"

"Not yet," said Chrystal. "I want a huge bonus in my check in the next pay period."

"How much are we talking?"

Chrystal pulled a sticky off Dana's desk, wrote down a number, and handed it to Dana.

"You have to be joking!" said Dana.

"That's what I thought when I saw the amount of your last bonus. What did you do to get it? Maybe services rendered to Jeff McKenna?" said Chrystal. "Okay, never mind, maybe Paul will think this tape is a joke," said Chrystal, picking up the tape recorder and getting up from the chair.

"Okay, okay. In your next check you will have that amount extra. I'll arrange a cash bonus for all your *hard* work," she said sarcastically.

"Damn right," said Chrystal.

"I want that tape and all the copies," said Dana.

"You'll get them after I receive the money and the position, not a moment before," said Chrystal, getting up to leave. "I'm glad we had this talk, Dana. I feel it was long overdue," she said smiling and leaving the office, closing the door behind her. Dana let out a controlled scream and slammed her hand on the desk. This was the last thing she needed on her first day back to work, but it looked like Chrystal had all the cards, at least for now.

CHAPTER 25

ELISE

The meeting with Sherrie at the One was enlightening to say the very least. Elise couldn't believe the situation Sherrie was in and she felt for her dear friend and her family. She could only hope that things would work out for the best. When she left Sherrie, she seemed to be okay, and she promised to call Elise, Lydia, or Chrystal if she needed to talk. It was nothing for them to all meet at Lydia's or one of their favorite restaurants to talk about anything going on in their lives, and Elise definitely wanted to be there for Sherrie now. Elise was so engrossed in thinking about the conversation she had with Sherrie that when she entered her condo, she barely noticed a suitcase sitting in the living room and Quinton sitting on the couch, waiting for her return. Elise stopped in her tracks and looked at the suitcase and then at Quinton. She began to think quickly about what this meant.

"Quinton, what's going on? Why is your suitcase packed?" asked Elise, genuinely taken by surprise.

"I was just waiting for you to come home because I didn't think it would be fair to leave you a note," he said, getting up and walking toward the suitcase. "I'm moving out," he said. "I think under the circumstances, it's for the best."

"You think it's for the best? What circumstances are you talking about, and why are you leaving?" said Elise. Her heart was beginning to beat rapidly, and she felt a panic attack coming on.

"It's clear to me that we're not in the same place in this relationship, Elise. I ask you about living together, and you put me off and give me some bullshit about not wanting to live together because we're not married. Then like a damn fool, I ask you to marry me and you answer that question by throwing up all over the damn floor. I'm not stupid, Elise. I'm a man, and as a man, I need to leave before I do or say something we'll both regret."

Elise was stunned although she didn't quite know why. With the way she'd been treating him, any other man would have walked out on her long ago, but Quinton had a good heart, and Elise had to admit to herself that she sometimes used his good nature to her advantage.

"Quinton, please, let's talk about this," said Elise, practically pleading.

"Oh, now you want to talk. You mean you don't want to play mind games with me or string me along like your little puppet? You think I'm a fool, don't you, Elise? You think you can do or say anything to me and I'm so damn stupid, I won't know when I'm being played!" he said so angrily he was shaking.

"Okay, I understand you're upset, but please don't leave. I want us to discuss this for real this time."

Quinton stared at her and shook his head. It was the same tired song with Elise all the time, but this time he wasn't falling for it.

"You want everything to be on your terms. You say you want me here, but we both know that's not what you really want. You say you want me, but you want me when it's convenient for you. You want to be attached to someone but still be single. You want it both ways, and I'm sorry, baby, but that's just not how it works." He stopped for a moment to wait for some kind of rebuttal from Elise, but she couldn't offer one.

"You know what, Elise? I'm going to leave you to think about what you really want, because for the life of me, I don't know what it is and I'm tired of trying to figure it out. I'll be at my apartment if you want to really talk. Until then, I don't want to hear from you." He grabbed his suitcase, opened the door, and slammed it behind him, leaving Elise standing in the middle of the floor, wondering what had just happened.

She fell to the floor and began sobbing. She didn't want to lose Quinton, and she knew she'd been playing with his emotions and ego for a long time, and it was clear that he was fed up and now the ball was in her court. She wiped her eyes as tears continued to stream down her face, and then suddenly she became nauseous to her stomach. She pulled herself up, rushed into the bathroom, and pulled the toilet seat up just in time to vomit. She allowed her head to hang over the toilet to make sure she was done when another wave of nausea came over her, allowing her to relieve herself once again. She flushed the toilet and walked over to the sink and poured some mouthwash into a glass to rinse her mouth. She looked into the huge mirror at her reflection and began to speak to herself. *Do you even know what you want?* she thought. After staring at herself for a few seconds, she realized that if she didn't know what she wanted out of life, from Quinton, or even herself, how could she possibly expect anyone else to know?

CHAPTER 26

LYDIA

*I*t had taken long hard hours during the week and a couple of full Saturdays, but the Kyle Edwards's drawings and sketches were now finalized, and she was sure he would be pleased with the results. Jasper was a huge help giving suggestions on accessories for each of the rooms for the Edward Luxury Hotel, and now Lydia was ready to present Kyle with her ideas. Lydia couldn't believe how much Kameron and Helena had screwed up her original designs, attempting to place their own signatures on her work. When Kyle gave her the last drawings Helena presented to him that solidified his decision to walk, Lydia could definitely understand his decision. The drawings were laughable. They weren't even up to Helena's standards, so Lydia knew the presentation was based solely on Kameron's vision, and that proved to be a huge mistake on Helena's part, one of the many huge mistakes she'd made in the past year. But luckily for Lydia, their incompetence led the Edwards account right back where it belonged with Lydia's Loft. Lydia began to scroll through the drawings on her laptop once again before Kyle and his assistant, Monica, arrived, going over each detail in her mind. Kyle Edwards was very detail oriented and liked to hear specifics about his projects. She began to laugh to herself as she recalled the first time she'd met Kyle and the relationship they'd built while working closely together on the project.

Helena and Kyle had several small meetings to discuss his project before Lydia actually met him and before the project had been assigned to her. Helena had made Kyle a lot of big promises. Promises she knew she couldn't deliver on her own, so one day, when he came in for the preliminary meeting, out of the blue, Helena asked Lydia to join them. She pulled out some drawings, which were actually very good. There were a lot of things Lydia didn't like about Helena, but she did respect her as a designer. As they all looked through the designs, Lydia could tell that Kyle was interested but not completely sold on the concept, and although Helena didn't ask, she offered some opinions about the sketches. Lydia suggested larger furniture in the massive reception area with textures and colors indicative to the period he wanted to display. Kyle was impressed. He liked Lydia's foresight and asked her to continue. Lydia pointed out that the accessories would play a huge part in pulling the theme together and that the dining area and the guest rooms should reflect a sense of comfort while still emphasizing that visitors were on vacation. Kyle was sold, and Helena, knowing that Lydia had just convinced him to give Helena Designs the project, made her the lead.

"Great, I like her style," said Kyle to Helena agreeing with the decision.

"Lydia's a wonderful designer, and you'll be very pleased with what we can do for you." They shook hands and the deal was done. During the course of the project, Lydia found Kyle to be difficult to please, but she was always ready with new ideas that impressed him, and he liked that about her. Lydia felt that he was almost challenging her, pushing her to come up with even more impressive work, and she kind of liked that about him, although at times he could really be a pain in the ass. As the weeks went by, the design was finalized, and he was pleased with the direction of the project. Then out of nowhere, Helena pulled her little stunt. But now, several months later, Lydia was once again presenting Kyle with a finalized design. It was so odd to her how things had worked out, and now here she was in her own design firm doing what she loved. Life was good. Suddenly she thought of the presentation she'd given to Mrs. Mitchell the other day and wondered why she hadn't heard back from her yet. She made a mental note to herself to have Jasper follow up on it and find out if Mrs. Mitchell had made a decision. The Taylor presentation went well too, so that was two follow-up calls Jasper needed to make. There was so much to do, and there never seemed to be enough time, but everything was going to work out; she knew it.

*   *   *

"Lydia, everything looks absolutely fabulous," said Kyle Edwards, looking at the drawings on the computer screen. "You've done a great job as usual. When can we get started?"

"Well, we can start selecting and purchasing the furniture, and Jasper and I will select the fabric for the window treatments and the accessories right away."

"That sounds good, I like it," said Kyle, smiling at Lydia and looking at the designs again. He was very pleased. Lydia watched as he scrolled through the drawings on the screen. She hadn't quite noticed before, but Kyle was a very handsome man, and as far as she knew, he was single. He'd never mentioned a wife or even kids, not that that necessarily meant he didn't have a wife and family. *He is an interesting man*, she thought. He was very successful, rich, and focused. He was about ten years older than Lydia, but he didn't look it since he obviously kept himself in great shape. Lydia was naturally drawn to older men but, because she was so focused on her career, hadn't been involved with one for longer than she cared to remember. Her last relationship was with a man named Richard, who was fifteen years her senior and a successful broker on Wall Street. They dated for almost a year when one day he announced that he'd taken a position in Italy, which was due to last at least three years. This, of course, came as a complete surprise to Lydia since he'd never mentioned applying for another job, especially one that would take him outside of the United States. So he left for Italy, and for a while they kept in touch on Facebook, occasional calls, and text messages, and Lydia received a few postcards from Rome, Venice, and even Sicily. But Lydia knew it was over between them as soon as he accepted the job abroad. Lydia knew Kyle was very driven by his career, and she didn't want to get involved with another man who could possibly put his career before their relationship. Besides, Kyle was a client, and she never mixed business with pleasure, but still . . .

"Lydia," said Kyle, interrupting her daydream, "Why don't we take a ride out to the site? You game?"

"That's a great idea," said Lydia. "Let me grab my purse and let Jasper know where we're headed."

"Good deal. I'll see you out front," he said as he and Monica walked out the door, saying their good-byes to Jasper as they left.

Jasper walked in afterward with a couple of messages in his hand.

"Here are a few messages, and one of them is from Mrs. Mitchell. She wants you to give her a call right away," he said with a wink.

"Okay, this could be it," said Lydia excitedly. "Let me call her now. Stay here, Jasper, so we can celebrate together," she said as she dialed the number on her cell. The number rang twice before a woman answered.

"Hello, Mrs. Mitchell? This is Lydia Brown returning your call," she said, looking at Jasper smiling. There was a pause. "Uh-huh, uh-huh, okay," said Lydia as her smile suddenly turned into a look of disappointment. Jasper looked on, a little confused by the change in her expression. "Well, can you tell me who you decided to go with?" she asked. There was a pause, and then suddenly, Lydia's left eyebrow raised as if surprised by the response. "Oh right, she is a very good designer. Well, I thank you for the opportunity. Maybe we can help you in the future," said Lydia. Okay, bye now." Lydia closed the top on her cell and looked up at Jasper.

"We didn't get it," she said.

"Lydia, I'm sorry. We'll get 'em next time. Who did she go with?"

"Helena Designs," said Lydia.

Jasper was shocked and didn't know what to say. He wondered why Auntie Helena never mentioned that she was up for the same job. Something wasn't right about this, and Jasper was going to get to the bottom of it.

CHAPTER 27

HELENA

*H*elena and Kameron clinked their champagne glasses together, celebrating their newly acquired project from Thomasina Mitchell, a master bedroom and bath they priced at $60,000, just under their competition. After the loss of the Edwards account, Helena Designs needed a boost in earnings as well as a boost in Helena's ego. Kameron knew that Lydia's Loft, Lydia's new design firm, was also up for the job, and it gave her great pleasure to know that they got it over her. She also knew that Helena was up to something involving Lydia and was frustrated that Helena refused to share the details. Since Lydia's departure, Helena had become totally focused on destroying her, which meant going after the same accounts she bid on and ensuring that Lydia didn't get them. Kameron was pleased with Helena's dedication to this new cause, although she was almost obsessed with Lydia. Just the other day, she'd overheard a conversation between Helena and someone over the phone in her office discussing Lydia's Loft. She tried to pick up the line, but the conversation had ended, and she didn't get to find out who Helena was talking to. Kameron thought it was brilliant the way Helena crashed her opening night, and she had an idea that Helena was getting inside information about Lydia's business endeavors. Whatever she was up to, Kameron wanted to make sure they crushed Lydia. She was the reason why Kyle Edwards pulled his business. Kameron had always suspected that Kyle had more interest in Lydia than business, and she found the whole thing disgusting since Kyle was an old man. He was at least thirty-eight years, and being that Lydia would be twenty-eight in a few months, the thought of it seemed vile to Kameron.

"Congratulations, Helena, you did it!" said Kameron as she sipped some more champagne.

"This is just the beginning," she said, lifting her champagne glass toward Kameron. "I guarantee you that when I'm finished with Lydia, she'll wish she never left here. Imagine her leaving and starting her own business. Who does she think she is?"

"Exactly! We'll show her who's on top of the design game here in Atlanta," said Kameron. "By the way, Helena, a little birdie told me that your play nephew, Jasper, is playing her little assistant over at that pseudodesign company. Is that true?"

"Yes, it is true. I asked him to come and do me a little favor, so in the meantime, I guess Lydia is his newest project. You know he's had so many," said Helena snidely.

"Well, I'm sure this one won't fair any differently than his past projects."

"Not if I have anything to do with it, it won't," said Helena as she took a seat in her leather-bound chair.

"So what's next on the agenda?"

"What's next is the Taylor account that Lydia also made a presentation for. Sadly, she won't be getting that job either," said Helena with an almost wicked laugh.

Kameron was intrigued and needed to know the details of Helena's plan, but more importantly, who was the mole?

"How are you getting this information? Do you have someone on the inside feeding it to you, Helena? Is it Jasper?"

"Kameron, dear, the less you know about any of this, the better," said Helena, shifting her ample behind from side to side in the chair. "Just know that Lydia's Loft is going to fail, and so is Lydia," she said smiling, pleased that her plan was coming together.

Helena watched Kameron as she was visibly annoyed with the lack of details about her plans, but she knew what she was doing. *Kameron is a sweet girl*, she thought, *but not the type I'd dare trust with this type of information.* It was best that she left the heavy lifting for herself and allowed Kameron to enjoy the ride. Besides, more than likely, Kameron wouldn't understand the concept anyway.

"Maybe I can help you, that's why I asked," said Kameron

"I have everything under control. Just wait until Lydia finds out that Mrs. Taylor has decided on Helena Designs. She'll lose her mind at the thought," smiled Helena. Just as she was about to pour herself another glass of champagne, she received a text message on her cell.

"Meet me in 30 minutes at the usual place. Have some new information."

"On my way," Helena replied quickly.

"Kameron, I have an errand I need to run. I'll be back shortly," said Helena, grabbing her purse and heading for the door.

"Where are you going?" asked Kameron, wondering if the text she'd just received had anything to do with her plans for Lydia.

"Be back soon!" Helena shouted at the door, ignoring Kameron's question. She leaped into her Lexus and hurriedly pulled away. Kameron hated secrets, unless they were her own, of course. She wanted desperately to know what Helena was up to and with whom. Maybe it was time for her to plan her own reconnaissance mission. She grabbed a bag of dried apples from the snack bar without paying and walked back over to her desk. *Why should Helena have all the fun?* she thought.

*   *   *

Meanwhile, Helena arrived at coffee shop where she and her accomplice had decided would be their meeting place to exchange information.

"Is this everything?" she asked him.

"These are the drawings and estimates for two more jobs that she'll be presenting in the next two weeks."

"Good, I'll get the jump on her," said Helena, quickly glancing at the drawings and placing them back into the manila envelope. She then pulled out a white envelope from her purse and pushed it over to her accomplice. "Count it if you like," she said.

"I'm sure it's all there," he said, quickly placing it into the inner pocket of his jacket. "By the way, you wanted information on where Kyle Edwards took his business. None other than Lydia's Loft," he said.

Helena's eyes widened, and a feeling of fury rose over her at the thought of Lydia receiving all that commission.

"Son of a bitch!" she snapped and then regained her composure. "Thanks for the information," she said. "Could you get anything on his project?"

"Wherever she's keeping his information, it's not on the computers in the office. She must be guarding it with her life."

"Well, see if a little pillow talk will reveal its location, will you?"

"Sure. I'll be in touch. How long are you going to keep this up?" he asked.

"As long as Lydia's Loft is in business, I'm going to make it my business to see that it folds," she said. She took a drink of her coffee and looked at her accomplice. "Keep me informed."

He nodded, threw a tip on the table for his coffee, and walked out of the shop slowly, attempting to be unnoticed. Helena watched him leave and did the same after a few moments. She opened her car door, stepped in, and then put on her seat belt before pulling away from the coffee shop.

*   *   *

On the other end of the coffee shop, Jasper sat silently in his black Range Rover, observing Helena as she pulled away. Earlier he had stopped by Helena Designs to speak with her about the Thomasina Mitchell account that she got over Lydia's Loft, but before he could get out of his car, he saw her rush out of the shop, get into her car, and quickly drive away. So he followed her to the coffee shop and was surprised to see a familiar tall slender man pull up shortly after. After they both walked in, Jasper quietly slipped into the coffee shop and observed the two of them sitting together and exchange envelopes. He immediately left before being detected and waited in his SUV for them to come out. First, the tall slender man came out of the coffee shop, and then Helena. What business did they have together and why? Jasper was determined to find out.

CHAPTER 28

CHRYSTAL

*T*he five associates of Goldman and Associates and their assistants were all gathered around the conference table for their regular 9:00 a.m. Monday meeting. Chrystal sat directly across from Dana with a notepad and was tingling with anticipation about the announcement that was going to be made. Dana sat perched in her chair, avoiding eye contact with Chrystal and looking defeated after Chrystal presented her with an ultimatum: either make sure the internship was hers or bank on her husband receiving the tape revealing her sordid affair with Jeff McKenna. To Chrystal, the decision was for Dana, and now that the deal had been struck and honored, Chrystal turned over the original tapes and the copies to Dana right after confirming with her bank, First Advantage, that $2,500 had been deposited into her checking account and after being told in private by Mr. Sanders that she had been selected for the internship. Chrystal wanted more but knew that $2,500 was the limit if she didn't want to arouse any suspicion with the associates. So after Dana presented a very compelling and convincing argument to the committee about why Chrystal deserved the internship instead of the other candidates that were being considered, the unanimous decision was made in Chrystal's favor. Now all she had to do was sit back and enjoy the official public announcement and the accolades to follow.

"Morning, everyone," said Mr. Sanders. "We have quite a few items to go over this morning, but I'd like to start off with the good stuff. We have a few recognitions and announcements to make before we begin."

Chrystal's heart was beginning to beat fast. This was the moment she'd been waiting for since her discussion and agreement with Dana. *Here it comes*, she thought, smiling inside.

"As you all know, each year we select a new intern here at Goldman and Associates to begin training under one or several of our associate PRs. This individual may be selected from outside of our firm, or we may choose some talented person right here already working with us. I'm proud to announce that we've made a selection, and this young lady is here with us today. Everyone, please join me in congratulating our newest intern, Ms. Chrystal Meyers!"

Everyone at the table gave out a surprised gasp, and a welcoming and thunderous applause followed. Chrystal began smiling and blushing at the recognition as her coworkers patted her on the back and congratulated her together and individually. Dana was smiling and clapping as well, playing the game by acting pleased with Chrystal's promotion.

"Chrystal has been working with Dana here for how long?"

"Two years," Dana interjected.

"And in those two years, she's shown drive, initiative, and true professionalism. I've personally seen her work, and she's very dynamic, so although it's a great opportunity, I know Dana is going to miss you, Chrystal," he said, looking at Chrystal and then Dana.

"Yes, I definitely will," said Dana.

"Do you have anything to say, Chrystal?," asked Mr. Sanders.

Chrystal stood up to make her speech like she was accepting an Oscar. "Yes, Mr. Sanders, I'd like to thank you, Dana, and the committee for this opportunity. It's been my dream to move into an associate PR position, and this internship is going to help me accomplish that dream. So thanks again for the opportunity," she said and then sat down to more applause.

Dana sat across the table from her, smiling, clapping, and joining in on the celebration, but inside she was brewing with anger. Chrystal had crossed the line, and to get a mere promotion, she was messing with her life. Chrystal kept her word about giving Dana the tapes and copies after the money had been deposited and the position solidified. Dana smiled a phony and contrived smile. She would let Chrystal enjoy her moment, the bonus she didn't earn, and the promotion she extorted, but the celebration would be short-lived. Dana would see to it.

*   *   *

When Chrystal got home from work, she couldn't wait to call all of her girls to get together for a celebration tonight. For the first time in a long time, it would be Chrystal who had good news about work. She wouldn't bother to tell the ladies exactly how the promotion came about; those minor details weren't important. What was important was that Chrystal's powers of persuasion was landing her a $35,000 increase in salary just this year, not including the bonus she'd just received in her paycheck this week. She couldn't believe how easy it was for Dana to get her the promotion. All she did was waltz her narrow ass into Mr. Sanders's office and tell him that Chrystal should have the job, and because he'd seen her work while Dana was on suspension, he didn't even question it. It was just that simple. That's all the heifer had to do in the first place, and then all the blackmailing and deceit wouldn't have been necessary. But no, Dana wanted to keep a sista' down, so Chrystal did what she had to do. She loved that quote from the movie *The Great Debaters* when that fine ass Denzel Washington tells one of his students to "do what you have to do so you can do what you want to do." That's exactly what Chrystal did with Dana. At least that's how she convinced herself that what she did was the only way to get ahead.

She pulled the last copy of the recorded conversation out of her purse and locked it away in her dresser drawer. It was insurance. Insurance that she hoped she wouldn't need. Unbeknownst to Dana, there were actually five copies of the tape instead of just the original and four copies she'd given her. If Dana thought Chrystal was going to hand over all of the copies and all of her leverage, she had another thing coming. She didn't trust Dana, and she knew she needed to keep the upper hand just in case she came up with some bullshit later about the promotion.

Chrystal pulled off her shoes and clothes and then put on a silk robe to get comfortable. Then she picked up her cell to text the girls to invite them out for drinks, and within seconds, she got positive responses from all of them. She texted them all back to meet her at Benihana's for sushi and drinks at 7:00 p.m.

This was going to be a celebration to remember, and tonight she'd do something special for her girls. Tonight she'd actually pick up the check.

"We haven't been to Benihana's in a minute, have we?" asked Lydia as she took a bite of her California spring roll.

"It's been a little bit," agreed Elise.

"Well, we're all dying here, Chrystal, what is this great news you had to tell us?" asked Sherrie.

Chrystal took a sip of her Manhattan and then readied herself for her announcement.

"Okay, ladies, you are looking at the newest Goldman and Associates intern! Give it up!" she said.

"What? Chrystal, that is wonderful!" said Lydia.

"OMG, our girl is growing up," said Elise.

"Congratulations, Chrystal, that is wonderful," said Sherrie.

"Thank you, thank you," said Chrystal, taking a bow sitting down. "I am very, very happy because you know if I had to pick up Dana's dry cleaning one more time, I was going to lose my mind!" she laughed. "But it's so exciting, I can't wait to start the training."

"So how did this come about? Did you apply for the job? What? Spill, spill," said Elise.

Chrystal was prepared for the question, so she continued with the answer she devised just for the girls.

"You know I was just tired of doing the same ole boring-ass stuff day in and day out, so I had a nice heart-to-heart with Dana again and told her why she should recommend me for the position. Not to mention how I picked up the slack while she was on her forced vacation and how I covered for her with her husband. She finally agreed with me and told me she'd do what she could. So the next thing I knew, Mr. Sanders called me in his office, and you know, I was wondering what kind of shit I'd gotten myself into now, because that man don't call you in his office for anything good. But when I got in there, there was Dana and the other associates congratulating me for being their selection for this year's internship. I was shocked but so happy it happened," said Chrystal, smiling.

"Wow, so Dana had a change of heart because you were saying she wouldn't promote you," said Lydia.

"I persuaded her that it was in her and the firm's best interest to promote me," said Chrystal, giving an ominous smile.

"Okay, what does that mean?" said Elise picking up on the tone.

"Nothing, Elise. Hell, I work hard at that firm. I'm a great choice, so it's in their best interest to give me the job, that's all," said Chrystal, who was secretly annoyed with Elise's perceptiveness.

"Well, Chrystal, we're very proud of you, and this is cause for another round of drinks on me," said Sherrie.

"Oh no, none of your money is any good tonight. Tonight is on me," said Chrystal, proud that she was able to pick up the check without praying to God that her credit card wouldn't be denied.

"A promotion and you're picking up the check? I think we're seeing a brand-new Chrystal, ladies. Let's drink to that," said Elise, for which they all lifted their glasses.

"So is this a huge promotion, and when do you start?" asked Lydia.

"Hell yeah, girl. It's going to be a real big promotion for me, and I start this week under another associate, so I'm no longer working for Dana."

"Hear, hear!" said Sherrie sipping her piña colada.

"That's a good deal, I'm really proud of you, Chrystal. I knew you could do it," said Lydia.

"So what's going on with all of you?" said Chrystal.

They all looked at one another and did not want to spoil the occasion.

"What?" asked Chrystal.

"Well, I don't want to be the one to bring us all down, but Quinton packed his bags and left the other night, and I haven't heard from him since," said Elise. All the ladies were looking at her with concern and wanted to encourage her that everything would be okay. Lydia went next.

"I didn't get a job that we pretty much thought was in the bag. Who did get it? Helena Designs."

"Get the hell out of here," said Elise.

"That hag is still in the design business after that embarrassing fiasco with Kyle Edwards?" said Sherrie.

"Wow, I'm sorry, Lydia. I don't know what that client was thinking because you design rings around that has-been," said Chrystal. Lydia thanked them all for their thoughts and support and then told them about several new projects she was hopeful in getting. Afterward, their attention was turned to Sherrie. They were all still trying to digest her announcement from just the other day that little Jillian wasn't Brad's daughter.

"Well, you guys know my situation right now. Brad is still in Houston, and he's been calling to speak with Jillian every night before she goes to bed, but that's about it. I don't know what I'm going to say to him when he gets home," said Sherrie. She shook her head, not knowing quite what to say or do next.

It all seemed so surreal, and Sherrie was definitely hurting from it, although they weren't quite sure if she was upset because Jillian wasn't Brad's daughter or if she was upset because he found out. In any case, they all knew the crap was about to hit the fan, so they knew they would have to brace themselves for the next wave of drama as soon as Brad returned home from Houston.

All the ladies sat in silence for a moment, thinking of their separate ordeals, when suddenly Lydia snapped out of her funk and reminded everyone that they were there to celebrate Chrystal's promotion.

"Hey, what are we doing? This isn't supposed to be a night for us to be feeling sorry for ourselves. This is Chrystal's night, right? Let's celebrate!" said Lydia as she turned her attention back to Chrystal.

"Chrystal, I just want you to know that I've always known that you had it in you to move forward and do something special with your life. And I know that this is something you've wanted for a long time, and I'm so proud of you for going after it. Do you see what hard work and determination can do for you?" said Lydia, giving Chrystal a huge pat on the back and smiling at her so proudly. Sherrie and Elise both chimed in telling Chrystal how proud they were of her for going after what she wanted. Chrystal smiled at them, but inside there was a tiny bit of guilt, almost like when a child did something wrong and didn't tell his or her parents because they believed in him or her so much. But she decided to shrug it off and enjoy the moment. Everyone made sacrifices to get the things they wanted in life, and if getting a promotion she deserved meant Dana had to sacrifice a little dignity, then so be it. Maybe next time she'd think about sleeping with her own husband instead of someone else's.

Chrystal watched her girls as they enjoyed their sushi and drinks and talked about pleasant things, including their next get-together. Lydia suggested going over Elise's house for a movie marathon just to help lift Elise's and Sherrie's spirits that weekend, and they all agreed that would be a good idea. Chrystal loved being out with her girls because she knew that no matter what craziness might have been happening in their individual lives, they could always count on one another to be uplifting and positive even if they didn't agree with one another. What she really liked about being with her girls was that she could be herself and not worry about anyone judging or pointing fingers. Everyone in the group had their own special qualities about them that she loved. Lydia was the strong one and the glue of the group. She always made sure that they kept in touch with one another no matter what was going on. Elise was the independent one who always made time for each one of them whenever she was needed, and Sherrie was the one they all wanted to grow up to be one day, which was married with a home and a family. None of the ladies were perfect, and none of them expected perfection from one another. They expected only love, mutual respect, support, and sisterhood, and for all of these things, Chrystal was grateful.

CHAPTER 29

ELISE

*I*t had been over a week since Quinton packed his bags and left, and other than a couple of texts that he finally decided to answer, Elise hadn't heard a peep from him. Quinton was obviously very serious about what he said to her the other day, and unless Elise intended to have a meaningful discussion about their future, he didn't want to hear it, plain and simple. She tried calling him and leaving messages, but he didn't bother to return them, and when he did, they always seemed to be when she was conveniently not at home. *I know that trick*, she thought. Quinton knew damn well that she wasn't at home at 2:30 p.m., so why the hell would he call her home at that time instead of calling her back on her cell? Elise went over the scene of him leaving over and over in her head. She was very hurt by what he did, but somewhere along the line, her hurt turned into anger, and it was really pissing her off that he wouldn't return her phone calls. She thought about showing up at his apartment unannounced, but Chrystal talked her out of doing that. "You don't know if he'll have someone else there, girl. You better drop a dime and call first," she said. Elise shuddered at the thought that Quinton could have moved on so quickly; didn't he love her? Didn't he want to work things out? She wasn't really sure anymore since he refused to return her calls. And then Lydia suggested that she give him some time to cool off. "You know men," she said. "Give him a minute to miss you, so when you do call, he'll be ready to hear you out," she said so optimistically. Elise loved Lydia for always being so positive even when sometimes there wasn't a damn thing to be positive about. But how could she let him just "cool off" for a minute? *How long is that going to take?* she thought to herself.

She went into her luxurious bathroom that Lydia designed for her to throw some water on her face. When Quinton was there with her, she longed for some alone time. Now that she was there alone, she longed for his touch, his smile, and his body. Oh, how she missed that body. It was very unusual for Elise and Quinton to go longer than a day without making love, and her body was going through withdrawal from the lack of intimacy. Something had to give. She and Quinton would have to come to some kind of agreement about their relationship that they could both live with, but Elise was still not willing to talk about what she wanted from him, especially since she still didn't know. She wanted to throw all caution to the wind and march over to his apartment right now to demand that he talk to her but decided that maybe she would do that as the last resort. Her cell phone was on her nightstand in the bedroom, so she quickly walked out of the bathroom and picked it up to dial his number. The number rang several times and, after the fourth ring, went straight to his voice mail.

"Quinton, baby, it's me again. I really need to talk to you, please call me back. I miss you," she said and then closed the lid to her cell. She sat the phone back down on the nightstand and sat on the edge of her bed waiting to see if the phone would ring immediately. Several minutes went by and still nothing. Another ten minutes went by while Elise sat there watching and waiting for the phone to ring, but still nothing. She started to become angry again and was about to call him and tell him about himself when suddenly the phone rang. She picked up so quickly that she didn't even notice the number on caller ID.

"Hello, Quinton!" she said, almost sounding desperate.

"No, girl, it's me, Chrystal."

"Oh," said Elise, sounding disappointed.

"Damn girl. You picked up that phone so fast, I was thinking for a second, maybe I was Quinton."

"I've been calling him and still no answer," said Elise.

"Girl, you are so sprung. You need to cool it like Lydia said and give the man some time. You've left enough messages, so now the ball is in his court. He'll call when he's ready. In the meantime, you need to get on with your life."

"I'm hearing you guys, but I'm thinking the longer I don't hear from him, then maybe things aren't right," said Elise

"Things aren't right, Elise, which is why he left. But calling him every five seconds isn't going to convince him that you're really ready to talk. Just chill, and he'll call you when he's ready to talk."

Elise couldn't believe how much sense Chrystal was making, and maybe she was right. She had left like a billion messages on his phone already, so the ball was in his court. Maybe she should calm down like the girls were telling her and see what he would do next.

"You're right. I'm acting like a bitch, aren't I?"

"Uh, just a little." Chrystal laughed. "But I understand. We've all been there. Well, not me exactly, because you know I don't roll like that. Men call *me* begging, not the other way around."

"Shut the hell up," said Elise, letting out a laugh. She hadn't laughed in a while, and it felt good. "So why are you calling anyway?"

"Just to check up on you and to remind you that we'll be over tonight for a movie marathon, so which movies do you want me to pick up?" said Chrystal.

"I don't want any touchy-feely crap. You know, no chick flicks. I want to see action, suspense, and drama."

"Like any of us need more of that, right?" Chrystal laughed. "We have more than enough drama going on between the four of us."

"I know that's right," said Elise. "Well, get whatever you want to see. It doesn't really matter to me as long as my girls are here," she said with a smile in her voice.

"Okay, we will see you around 4:00 p.m., okay? You got the popcorn, right?

"Butter and kettle corn is waiting," she laughed.

"See ya in a few then. Talk to you later," said Chrystal, and Elise clicked off her cell. She went into the bathroom to take a nice hot shower to get ready for the girls to come over. A movie night with them would be just what she needed to get Quinton off her mind, at least for a few hours anyway. She turned on the four shower heads and stepped into the shower, allowing the water to stream down her body as she began caressing herself with Dove body wash. The water felt good, and she was beginning to get a feeling of relaxation as the muscles in her neck and shoulders began to loosen. After several minutes, she stepped out of the shower and toweled herself off. She reached for her Victoria's Secret lotion and rubbed her entire body in it. After putting on laced black underwear with matching bra and panties, she reached into her closet and pulled out a chocolate brown Baby Phat jogging suit, with a white low cut tee to wear underneath. Movies, drinks, the girls—Elise couldn't think of anything else more she needed right at this very moment.

*   *   *

Tears were streaming down Lydia's and Sherrie's faces at the ending of the movie *Imitation of Life*, starring Lana Turner. Elise loved old movies, especially anything with Cary Grant, Elizabeth Taylor, or Lana Turner and any Alfred Hitchcock movie. She loved the way the characters talked and dressed during the '30s, '40s, and even '50s. *Imitation of Life*, which was about two women raising two girls that couldn't be more different from each other, was one of her all-time favorite movies, and no matter how many times she watched it, she always cried at the end just like Lydia and Sherrie, especially during the funeral procession scene. Elise observed that Chrystal was also a little misty eyed, but she wiped her eyes quickly because she didn't want the girls to know how sensitive she was watching these movies.

"What?" said Chrystal, trying to hide her tearstained eyes as the girls were looking at her, amused because she was so emotional.

"You're crying too, Chrystal, so don't even try it," laughed Elise.

"I know. This movie is really good," said Chrystal, getting up to freshen up her margarita.

"What's next?" said Lydia, munching on some sweet kettle corn popcorn.

"Let me see, we have *North by Northwest, All About Eve, Notorious,* or *A Letter to Three Wives,*" said Sherrie, flipping through the remaining movies.

"Oh, put on *All About Eve,*" said Chrystal. "That is some scandalous retro shit." She laughed. "I love the part where the young actress learns everything from Bette Davis and then does what it takes to get ahead herself," said Chrystal, thinking of how ironic it was that she'd just done something similar with Dana to get ahead.

"Great choice," said Lydia, who was now pouring more margarita in her glass. "This movie will show you how to backstab, lie, be two-faced, and be a straight-up opportunist and blackmailer all in one movie." She laughed. "But what's really good is that once she makes it at the end, she meets a young aspiring actress that's willing to do the same things to her. It's a great movie," she said and then sipped some of her drink.

"Sounds like a great movie. I've never seen it," said Elise as she looked around at her girls. "You know, this was a really great idea. I really needed to just have some downtime to relax, and what better way than with my girls. Thanks, guys," said Elise, hugging Lydia and Sherrie, who were both sitting on the floor with drinks and popcorn. Sherrie brought over her famous hummingbird cake and butterscotch ice cream for dessert later.

"I agree," said Sherrie. "This was a good idea. Let's see the next movie," she said as she got up and placed the new movie in the DVD player and hit Play.

*   *   *

When Elise woke up, she was taken by surprise a little to see the girls still there all sleeping in her living room either on the floor or on the couch. They had drank so many Margaritas and watched all the movies until the early morning that they didn't even realize how tired they'd become. The next thing Elise knew, everyone just made a night of it and fell into a deep sleep. Elise was pleased because she didn't want to be alone again last night, so she was grateful that she had her girls there with her. She rubbed her eyes and glanced at the time on the DVD clock and then on the glass clock on her end table that was given to her by a coworker. It was almost 9:30 a.m., and no one was stirring. Elise went into her room and pulled out four separate blankets to cover herself and the girls. She made herself comfortable on the couch again and started to turn over when she heard a click at the door and then someone coming into the front door. She sat up and saw a gorgeous tall figure appear, dressed in a blue-and-white jogging suit and wearing a Cowboys baseball cap. Elise sat there for a moment and stared at the figure and, when she finally realized that she wasn't dreaming, stood up in surprise.

"Quinton?"

CHAPTER 30

SHERRIE

It was the next evening, and Sherrie walked anxiously back and forth across her bedroom floor, wringing her hands. She was very nervous about Brad coming home from his trip to Houston. Brad had called an hour earlier to tell her that his plane had just landed safely and that he'd be home shortly. Sherrie tried desperately to hear in his voice if there was anything different in the way he spoke to her or how he sounded, but he didn't give any signs that anything was wrong. He acted normal, no different than usual, and this was driving Sherrie crazy. For the life of her, she couldn't understand how he could have this information and not be visibly upset with her. She still didn't know what she was going to say to Brad even if he did confront her, but the fact that he hadn't yet confused her even more.

Sherrie wished like hell she could go back in time and change everything, but there was nothing she could do. The affair happened, and although she knew it was wrong and wished to God it never happened, she couldn't regret that her beautiful little girl, Jillian, came out of it. She wondered if her marriage could survive her indiscretion and if Brad could ever find it in his heart to forgive her. But first of all, she had to find out how much he knew and what made him have a paternity test in the first place. Sherrie knew that all of these years, she'd been very careful, and she never did anything to make him suspicious that Jillian was anything other than his daughter. So what exactly gave her away, and when did it happen? She had so many questions and no answers, and the suspense was beginning to drive her insane. Sherrie sat down in her chaise chair, glancing out the bedroom window, and began to reflect on her life and home with Brad and Jillian. They had once talked of having another child, but it hadn't come about, and Sherrie couldn't help but wonder if this information was the reason for Brad's reluctance to expand their family. She laid her head back into the chair and glanced at the newest edition of *O* magazine at the base of the table. If ever she needed a miracle, it was now. She closed her eyes for what seemed a moment and then opened them to see Brad standing in the doorway. Startled, she jumped up from the chaise chair to greet him as he stood there watching her silently.

"Brad, I didn't hear you come in," she said, fixing her hair and regaining her composure.

"I just came in and saw you lying there taking a nap. You looked so peaceful and beautiful, I didn't want to wake you," he said as he came in with a suitcase in his hand.

"How was your trip?" asked Sherrie.

"It was fine, you know, the usual stuff. We got some really good information to take back to the hospital, though.

Sherrie walked over to Brad to hug him and give him a kiss on the lips. He kissed her back and began taking off his traveling clothes. Brad was an extremely handsome man with a beautiful caramel complexion and black wavy hair with a hint of gray in the front, cut close like Sherrie loved it. He was 6'3", had a muscular build, always keeping his physique tight and sexy, just like Sherrie liked it. He was very physically fit.

"Where's Jillian?" he asked.

"She's asleep, and Isabella should be downstairs somewhere."

"Good, because I want to take you out to dinner tonight," said Brad, smiling at her.

Sherrie breathed a sigh of relief. She couldn't remember the last time she and Brad had gone out to dinner together alone. It would be a welcome distraction. Maybe he'd decided not to confront her about Jillian and the affair. Sherrie was hopeful and she was happy.

"How does Blackstone's sound to you? I made a reservation for 7:30 p.m. from the plane," he said smiling.

"Brad, that's perfect!" she said, squealing and clasping her hands together. *A night alone together is exactly what we needed,* she thought to herself. "I'll get changed," she said smiling and heading toward her custom-made walk-in closet.

"You do that. I'll grab a shower, and we can be out of here within the hour, right?"

"You got it," said Sherrie, admiring the deep-purple halter dress she selected from her closet. She'd purchased it a while ago from Neiman Marcus and was waiting for just the right occasion with her husband to wear it. She pulled out a pair of purple Manolo gladiator-strapped pumps to complete her look. Sherrie placed the dress against her and she gazed at herself in the full-length mirror in her closet. She'd all but forgotten about the anxiety she felt before Brad's arrival or the envelope locked away in their bedroom safe with the incriminating evidence of her infidelity. The only thing that mattered was that they were going to spend an evening together, and Sherrie was going to absorb every moment of it.

*   *   *

It had been a wonderful evening for the both of them. Sherrie and Brad laughed together, drank the cabaret Brad ordered for the two of them, and ate their lobster with butter sauce, one of the best entrées on the menu. Blackstone's was one of their favorite spots, although it had been ages since they last dined there together. Sherrie's favorite dish was the salmon, and Brad usually ordered the prime rib, but tonight it was broiled lobster tail all around. It almost felt like a celebration to Sherrie and a renewal of their marriage just to have a moment together alone with her husband. She was happy, and Brad couldn't help but notice the gleam in her eyes and how beautiful she looked tonight. He smiled to himself as he watched her glancing over the dessert menu, which he found a little endearing since Sherrie rarely ordered dessert. He loved the fact that she was very conscious of her weight and the time and care she took in maintaining her appearance. They'd been married for nearly ten years, and while many of his colleague's wives had fallen into the stay-at-home-wife syndrome, neglecting their appearance and avoiding any physical activity past taking care of the home or chasing the kids, he was proud to say that Sherrie had not allowed herself to succumb to such a fate. He took another sip of his cabaret and took Sherrie's hands into his own.

"You look beautiful, you know that?" he said in an adoring tone. Sherrie pulled her long hair behind her right ear and began smiling at him as well. She longed for his attention.

"Brad, it's so wonderful to have this time with you. It's been a long time, you know. We need to make time for each other," she said.

"I agree. That's why this evening isn't going to end with dinner. I have plans for later," he said almost suggestively. "So you might want to conserve your energy."

"I like the sound of that," she said in a giddy tone. "What kind of plans do you have for us?"

"It's a surprise, and I don't want to spoil it," he said.

"Okay, just give me a hint," she said, excited to know what he had in store for their evening while inside hoping it was a night of steamy lovemaking.

"Let's just say, it's something we haven't had together in a long time and something we both need," he said, sipping his wine. Sherrie was excited and intrigued at the same time. When Brad put his mind to it, he was very good at surprises, like the time a couple of years ago when he surprised her when he chartered a jet for a trip to the Cayman Islands or the unexpected trip to Paris. He was very good with doing things in grand fashion when he took the time to do them. She could only wonder what surprises this evening would bring. Maybe a trip to Hawaii for the week or even another trip abroad, this time Rome; the possibilities were limitless, and she was ready for it with all her heart.

"Okay, I'll let it be a surprise because I know how much you love doing that for me," she said as she lifted her wineglass and they clinked them together.

"Good," he said. "Do you know what you want for dessert?"

"The bread pudding looks good. I think I'll have that."

"Great," he said while signaling the waitress over to their table. Their waitress was a very enthusiastic heavyset woman with long dark hair who was very eager to serve them. She came over to the table, and Brad immediately ordered key lime pie for himself and bread pudding for Sherrie. He then watched her hurriedly walk away to place their dessert orders when he turned to Sherrie's awaiting glance.

"Let's make tonight memorable, Brad," she said, smiling with her eyes.

"It will be, sweetheart. I promise it will be," he said to her assuredly as he drank the last bit of wine in his glass.

*   *   *

When Sherrie and Brad reached their bedroom, there was a beautifully wrapped gift box lying on their bed. Sherrie turned and looked at Brad, and he motioned her over to the box to open it.

"What is this?" she said excitedly.

"It's the first part of the surprise for this evening, so open it and find out," he said with a huge grin. Sherrie rushed over to the bed and picked up the box and gave it a little shake. "Well, it's too big for jewelry," she laughed, but Brad wasn't giving any hints and only motioned for her to open the box, which she began doing excitedly. "The wrapping is almost too beautiful to tear," she said while carefully unwrapping the surprise.

Once the gift was unwrapped, she opened the tissue paper inside to reveal a beautiful black laced nightie with matching panties from Victoria's Secret.

"Oh, Brad, it's beautiful."

"It'll be even more beautiful when you put it on, so go in there and put it on," he said, motioning her to their master bathroom."

"Okay," she smiled and ran into the bathroom with the garments. While inside, she placed on the nightie and matching panties and looked at herself in the mirror. She looked stunningly gorgeous, not to mention sexy. Brad was going to flip when she came out. She fixed her hair, pushed up her breasts to reveal more than enough cleavage, and then sprayed herself lightly with Chanel No. 5. Sherrie was going to rock Brad's world tonight. She gave herself one last glance in the mirror, smiled broadly at herself, and opened the door while maintaining a sexy, sensual pose in the doorway, when suddenly she was stopped dead in her tracks. She fully expected to find Brad in their bed nude awaiting her, but instead he was standing in the middle of their bedroom, fully dressed and holding an envelope. An envelope that was all too familiar.

"Brad, what's going on?" she asked, trying to cover her obvious surprise.

"I have something here I want you to see," he said walking, toward her and handing her the envelope. Sherrie was shocked and beyond devastated as she took the envelope nervously. She couldn't believe this was happening.

"What's this?" she said in an attempt to conceal her bewilderment.

"It's the surprise I've been waiting to give you," he said. "Open it," he said, watching her intently. Sherrie slowly and reluctantly began to open the envelope, knowing exactly what the contents were inside. Her entire life with Brad began to flash before her, and the room was beginning to spin while her hands began to tremble. She couldn't open the envelope and allow everything she'd held dear to crumble right before her eyes.

"Brad, I'm not feeling too well," she said, holding her head and trying to hand the envelope back to him. "Why don't we save this for later?" she said as her eyes began to become misty.

"You don't want to see my surprise?" he asked.

"I think I've had enough surprises for tonight. I think I'll take a sedative and just go to bed," she said, still trying to hand him back the envelope, which he refused to take back.

"I think you'll appreciate this surprise, Sherrie. I know I did when I saw it," he said almost sarcastically.

"Brad, I don't want to, I'm not feeling well . . ."

"Open it!" he shouted. She jumped in surprise at his sudden tone of voice and pulled the envelope back and then began to open it and pull out the report.

"Read it, Sherrie," he said angrily. Sherrie pulled the report out, fully knowing what it revealed, and began reading it silently. "Read it out loud!" he shouted again. Sherrie jumped at his raised voice and began reading the report aloud slowly.

"Paternity test for Bradford Marshall in reference to Jillian Marshall, there is a 0 percent probability that Bradford Marshall is the father," she said as she allowed the report to fall from her hands.

"How could you do this to me, Sherrie? How could you do this to our family? You've been lying to me for years!" he shouted.

"Brad, I can explain," she said now crying uncontrollably.

"Oh, you can explain? Well, explain to me how my wife gets pregnant by someone else and passes the child off as mine. Explain to me how this could possibly happen. Explain to me why I shouldn't walk out on you right now!"

Sherrie was mortified at the thought of Brad walking out on her, although she knew she deserved it.

"I didn't mean for any of this to happen, it just did," she said crying.

"Is that all you have to say to me? We've been married for almost ten years, and all you can say is you didn't mean for this to happen? You've been making a fool out of me for years and that's it?"

"I don't know what to say. I'm sorry. I never wanted to hurt you, Brad. I love you."

"You love me?" he shouted. "This is what you do to someone you love? Sherrie, I don't understand. First of all, if I'm not Jillian's father, then who is?" Sherrie began to fidget with her hands as her lips began to quiver. "Sherrie, I swear to God you better answer me, woman," said Brad angrily.

"David McIntyre," she said reluctantly as she waited for Brad's reaction. Brad took a couple of steps backward as if he was just punched in the stomach.

"You've gotta be kidding me. David McIntyre, the prick! Are you kidding me?" he shouted. "You were sleeping with David behind my back?"

Brad's eyes became wide and wild as he grabbed his jacket and began to walk out. Sherrie ran behind him, urging him not to leave.

"Brad, please don't leave. Let's talk about this." Brad jerked around and stared at Sherrie.

"I can't believe this. You know I've had this report for weeks, but I didn't want to confront you about it because it would make all of this real. But there are still some things about all of this that will never change, Sherrie. I don't care what the report says, Jillian will always be my little girl, and regardless of the fact that my wife cheated on me for some loser, I will never turn my back on her."

"What about us?" said Sherrie with tearstained cheeks.

"What about us? Maybe that's something you should have thought about while you were lying up with David." He turned and began walking down the stairs as Sherrie shouted out.

"So you've known all this time and you planned all of this? The dinner, the romantic evening, all so you can dramatically throw this in my face? You said that tonight would be about something we haven't had in a long time, Brad. I thought you meant togetherness and intimacy."

"No, Sherrie. I meant honesty. We haven't had honesty in a long time, and you know what? You don't get to question my motives when you've been lying to me about our daughter for years!" he said, disgusted by the entire scene. "I've got to get out of here before I do something I'll regret," he said, continuing down the stairs.

"Where are you going?" she shouted.

"Anywhere but here with you. I can't stand to be near you right now."

Sherrie grabbed hold of the stairwell banister and fell to her knees. Her worse fears had been realized, and within minutes, her entire life had turned upside down. Brad may have neglected her and at times seemed more committed to his job than to their marriage, but she had committed a much crueler and unforgivable sin with lies and deceit. As Sherrie watched him walk out of the door and slam it behind him, she thought about how he always kept his promises. He promised that the evening would be surprising and unforgettable, and he delivered on his promise as always. For as long as Sherrie and Brad both lived, they would never forget this night.

CHAPTER 31

LYDIA

Lydia took a deep breath before entering the home of Mark and Justine Taylor, two very successful attorneys who owned and operated their own law firm together downtown Atlanta. Justine contacted Lydia's Loft because she wanted to redecorate their outdated '70s style kitchen to a sleeker and more modern space where family and friends could gather around for cooking and conversation. Lydia had a preliminary meeting with the couple two weeks earlier to discuss their wants and needs for the space and, based on their conversation, put together a fabulous presentation for their new kitchen, which she knew they would love. She rang the doorbell, and within a few seconds, Justine Taylor opened the door and greeted her warmly.

"Lydia, so nice to see you again, please come in," she said, motioning her inside the corridor. This was the first time Lydia had been inside their home, and from the first glance, she liked what she saw. The corridor and adjacent dining room and study had obviously been redecorated along with the grand stairway, which was the focal point as visitors walked inside. The kitchen seemed to be their last project, and Justine was anxious to get it under way. As Justine led Lydia into the family room, which was spacious and comfortable and very welcoming, they were joined by Mark, who greeted Lydia and extended his hand.

"Lydia, glad you could come by," he said smiling.

"Thank you both for having me," said Lydia as she sat down on the leather sofa and placed her laptop on the coffee table sitting directly in front of the sofa. "Well, I guess we can get started," said Lydia as her laptop booted up. "When we last met, we talked about what you were looking for in an updated kitchen design, and based on our conversation, I came up with this design, and I think you're going to like it," she said as she came to the first virtual drawing. "As you can see, the existing walls will be torn down to allow more space in this area and to expand the kitchen nook," she said, pointing to the area as Justine and Mark nodded in agreement, liking what they were seeing so far. "This existing area will be removed to allow for an island and to expand your counter space. As you can see, the cabinetry will be expanded as well to allow more storage, and the existing lighting will be completely transformed from what you have now to an updated ceiling light," said Lydia as she glanced at them for their reaction, which immediately concerned her. Instead of having the wow effect she was looking for, they both appeared to be puzzled by the drawing. Lydia stopped for a moment to ask if there was a question.

"Do you have any questions at this point?" asked Lydia. Justine and Mark looked at each other and, with an almost uncomfortable tone, asked Lydia to continue. As Lydia continued her presentation, it became increasingly noticeable that the Taylors seemed to be a little confused by what they were seeing but allowed her to finish. At the end of the presentation, Lydia gave them an estimate of the cost and a timetable for completion, for which the Taylors took a quick glance and laid it down on the coffee table.

"Can I answer any questions about anything?" she asked as the Taylors looked at each other and then at Lydia.

"Lydia, I don't know quite how to tell you this, but we've already seen this exact presentation," said Justine, clearing her throat, awaiting an explanation. Lydia stared at her for a moment, trying to comprehend what was just said.

"I'm sorry, what was that?" said Lydia.

"We saw the same exact presentation just yesterday from another designer," said Mark and then glanced at the drawings and then the estimate."

"But that's impossible," said Lydia. "This is an original design I created. Perhaps there are some similarities, but it couldn't possibly be the same," she said, confused by what she was hearing.

"I'm afraid you're wrong, Lydia. It's exactly the same, with the exception of the price, which was considerably lower," said Justine. Lydia's face began to become flush as she was taking in what the Taylors were saying.

"Can you tell me which designer you're referring to?" she asked.

The Taylors looked at each other, not sure if they should reveal the name of the competitor since they were looking for a great design at a good price. Lydia sensed their reluctance to reveal the information and decided to throw out a name.

"Okay, I understand your hesitance, but can you just tell me if I'm right?" she said. "Was it Helena Designs?" she asked. The Taylors nodded their heads in unison, and Lydia became livid at the thought of Helena stealing her designs. "Mr. and Mrs. Taylor, I can assure you that this design belongs to Lydia's Loft. Can I show you another design I had in mind?"

"We were sold on this design yesterday but wanted to wait to see what you had to offer. I don't know whose design it belongs to, but at this point, we're looking at cost, and like I said, their cost was considerably lower." Lydia couldn't believe this. Not only did Helena steal her design, but she also underbid her to ensure they would get the job. She'd have to come in lower on her own design to get the job.

"Can you tell me what Helena Designs offered?" asked Lydia.

"I don't think we want to get into that, Ms. Brown," said Mark. "Why don't you give us your best offer, and we'll make a decision and let you know." Lydia was floored at being put in this position. Lydia's Loft was a new business, and with the exception of the Edwards account, so far she wasn't pulling in any new business. She couldn't afford to undercut herself at this stage of the game. The design belonged to Lydia's Loft, so why did she have to underbid on her own design? Although this was a matter of principle, this was also a matter of economics. She needed to bring in income for her new business, and with that thought, she picked up her estimate, revised the price, and handed it back to the Taylors.

"This is my final offer. I can't do this job for anything less, and it's very unlikely that anyone else can either without compromising on the materials I've chosen for your kitchen," she said. "Do you have a business card?" she asked the Taylors.

"Yes, of course," said Justine. "Are you looking for our services?"

"Yes. My design has been stolen, and I may need an attorney," she said.

"This may be a conflict of interest for us, but we can refer you to a very good attorney if you choose to pursue this," said Mark, getting up to go over to a cabinet and pull out a business card of one of his colleagues. "Give him a call. He can help you out if that's what you want," he said, handing the card to Lydia.

"Thank you," said Lydia, powering down her laptop and placing it back inside the protective cover. "I hope we'll be in touch, and I apologize for the confusion here," she said, following the Taylors as they walked her out.

"No need to apologize," said Justine. "I hope you can get this all straightened out. We'll be in touch," she said. Lydia shook their hands and walked out to get into her BMW, which was parked in the Taylors' driveway. She was furious but waited until she pulled out of the driveway to release her anger. She screamed as she sped out of the gated community and into traffic. She pushed a button on the screen and exclaimed, "Call work!"

The computerized voice reiterated the command, "Did you say 'Call work'?"

"Yes!" Lydia practically screamed. The telephone rang twice before Jasper picked up.

"Lydia's Loft, this is Jasper, may I help you?" he said in a giddy voice.

"Jasper, you won't believe this shit! I'm leaving the Taylors now," she said exasperated.

"Lydia, what's going on?." asked Jasper.

"It's Helena Designs. That bitch stole my design!" she screamed.

"Wait a minute, hold on, what are you saying?" said Jasper.

"I just gave the presentation, and the Taylors say they saw the exact same presentation yesterday from Helena Designs!"

"What? How is that even possible? Lydia, I don't understand," said Jasper.

"Neither do I. But some way, somehow that witch got a hold of my design, and she's passing it off as her own. She's also underbidding me, which means she probably has my estimates too. I know that greedy heifer, and no way would she price a job like that lower than my estimate. You know my estimate led little room for profit only because I'm trying to build a clientele. I know her ass, and she would have never priced that job lower than what we estimated," said Lydia furiously.

"What do you want to do?" asked Jasper.

"I have to make a quick stop, but I'll be back in the office in a couple of hours, and we can talk about it."

"Okay, Lydia, I'll see you when you get in," he said, quickly thinking about what he'd witnessed after following Helena to that diner and now the revelation of the drawing being stolen. As Jasper hung up the telephone, he knew he would have to come clean about his relationship with Helena although he'd never mentioned it before because he knew they were competitors and feared Lydia wouldn't hire him because of it. He knew

Helena was extremely competitive and could be ruthless at times, but he didn't know she would stoop to stealing designs. He'd always thought of her as being a very talented designer and a shrewd businesswoman. He couldn't understand why she needed to steal designs to compete with Lydia. Jasper also couldn't get out of his mind how and why Helena was meeting with the person he saw her with at the diner, who happened to be his companion, Lionel. He and Lionel had been together off and on for years, and they made it a point to always get together when Jasper visited Atlanta. Later that evening, while they were at dinner at Paschal's, he questioned Lionel about where he'd been all afternoon, and Lionel lied about it, saying that he'd gone to visit his mother for the afternoon. Jasper let it go at the time before questioning him further to wait for more concrete evidence, and now he had a good idea about how Helena was getting her information. He was worried how all of this would look to Lydia, and then a thought popped into his head and hit him like a ton of bricks as he let out a loud gasp. Could he be the leak at Lydia's Loft?

*　　*　　*

Lydia was just leaving a Home Interior office after picking up a couple of rolls of material for window treatments for the Edwards job when she received a call from Elise.

"Hey, girl, what's up?" said Elise cheerfully.

"I'm a little frustrated right now, Elise. You won't believe this, but I think Helena has been stealing my designs," she said. "I just left a potential client who swears they saw the exact presentation I gave them today yesterday, and the designer was Helena. Can you believe that?" she said, placing the rolls in the backseat of her car.

"What?" said Elise. "Oh, that trick is like a bad penny. She just keeps turning up," said Elise, who was suddenly quiet on the end of the phone as if thinking about her next statement.

"Elise, are you still there?" asked Lydia.

"Lydia, I have something to show you. Where are you now?"

"I'm getting ready to leave the parking lot of the Home Interior store," she said.

"Okay, there's a Starbucks on the same block. Meet me there in ten minutes," said Elise.

"Okay, I'll be there, but what's this about?"

"I'll let you see for yourself," said Elise.

When Elise entered the Starbucks, she quickly scanned the tables and located Lydia sitting nearby with two large cups of coffee and two muffins. She walked over to the table as Lydia stood up to give her a hug.

"Hey, girl, I ordered you a coffee and muffin," she said sliding them over to Elise.

"Thanks sweetie," said Elise as she took a slow slip of the piping hot coffee.

"So what's up? What did you want me to see?" asked Lydia.

"Well, do you remember when you first introduced us to Jasper and I told you later that he looked familiar?" asked Elise.

"Yeah, I remember. You thought you'd seen him somewhere before," said Lydia, taking a sip of her coffee.

"Right. It kind of bothered me, you know when you can't place someone? So the other day I was throwing out some old magazines, and I came across this," said Elise as she pulled an old copy of *Interior Design Today* out of her bag and handed it over to Lydia. "Go to page 22, and you'll see what I'm talking about," she said, watching Lydia as she thumbed through the magazine until she reached the page and saw a picture of Helena Barnes pictured with a young man identified as her godson.

"Jasper Pearsall!" said Lydia in disbelief. "Jasper is Helena's godson?" said Lydia as her mouth dropped open.

"Lydia, I think you just found your mole," said Elise as she bit into her blueberry muffin.

"Oh my god, I can't believe this. All this time and he never even mentioned knowing Helena even after we lost a couple of jobs to her."

"That's probably because he's the one who gave her your drawings and estimates. Do you think she planted him with you to steal jobs back, especially after you got the Edwards account back?" asked Elise.

"I don't know. Damn! I feel like such a fool," said Lydia. "I should have known he was too good to be true. But you know what? He's going to explain himself, and then I'll throw him out on his ass after I tell him that I'm suing him and Helena for copyright infringement!" said Lydia angrily.

"Wait a minute, let's not jump to conclusions. Let's catch him in a lie first," said Elise. "That way we'll have even more evidence of how your designs were leaked. Does anyone else have access to your files other than you and Jasper?"

"No," said Lydia, smoldering from the revelation of Jasper's connection with Helena.

"Okay, that's good. Let's set a trap for him. I'll go back to the office with you, and we'll double-team his ass right before you fire him and throw his happy ass out, okay?" said Elise.

*   *   *

When Lydia and Elise returned to the office, Jasper had just finished a call from another potential client. Jasper was a little uneasy about how he was going to approach Lydia about his relationship with Helena, especially now that it looked like Helena had stolen Lydia's designs. He'd thought about how he would approach Lionel and Helena as well and hated that he was in such a predicament. How could he possibly tell his boss that Helena was his godmother and he suspected that his boyfriend was conspiring with her to steal clients? How would she ever believe that he wasn't involved? As he watched the two of them walk into Lydia's office, he couldn't help but notice Elise eyeing him and then slightly rolling her eyes. He decided that the best way to handle this situation was to tell Lydia everything and let the chips fall because if she found out on her own, the situation would only look worse for him. Jasper got up from his desk and knocked on Lydia's office door.

"Come in, Jasper," she said. As he walked in, he could see Lydia's glaring eye and Elise standing near her with her hands on her hips. "I have a question for you Jasper," said Lydia, but Jasper interrupted before she could ask.

"Lydia, I have something I need to tell you, and I want you to hear it from me," he said and then gave out a loud sigh.

"Okay, I'm listening," said Lydia, who was now sitting against her desk with her arms folded.

"Helena Barnes is my godmother. She and my mother were good friends for years, and I've known her practically all of my life. I didn't say anything about her when I first started because I know the design business and how competitive it can be, and I was afraid that you wouldn't hire me if you knew I was connected with her."

"You're damn right about that, man. Do you know the drama that woman has put Lydia through when all she's ever been to her was a great designer? She screwed her over with the Edwards account!" yelled Elise. Jasper was a little taken aback by this information.

"What? You mean the person you've been talking about all this time was Helena?" he said to Lydia. "I didn't know that," he said.

"Sure you didn't," said Elise.

"Yes, Jasper. It was Helena that took the Edwards account from me and gave it to someone who didn't have the skills to draw stick figures, much less a project of its magnitude. I left her firm because of it, and she's apparently had it in for me since. But what I don't understand is why you found it necessary to hide the fact that you know her," said Lydia.

"Would you have hired me if you knew I was her godson?" asked Jasper.

"No, probably not," said Lydia.

"Are you the one giving out Lydia's designs?" snapped Elise.

"No! You have to believe me on this, Lydia. I would never do anything like that. I had no idea that Helena was stealing your designs."

"So how do you think she got them? Only you and I have access to my files, and only you and I have a key to my business," said Lydia accusingly.

"Lydia, I know this looks bad, but please believe me, it wasn't me, but I think I know who it is. You think you know a person and they completely screw you over. He knows how much this job means to me. I can't believe I gave him all that information. I didn't even think about what he could be doing with it."

"What the hell are you talking about?" asked Elise.

"Yeah, Jasper, you're not making any sense," said Lydia.

"His name is Lionel, and he's a friend of mine. I think he and Helena have been planning this together."

"Oh, this just gets better and better. So it's not you, it's a 'friend' of yours with your godmother who's doing all of this, but oddly enough, you have nothing to do with it," said Elise. "Lydia, throw this fool out of here, this is ridiculous," snapped Elise.

"You're right, it does sound suspicious, but I'm telling the truth," said Jasper, pleading for them to believe him.

"Okay, why should I believe you, Jasper?" said Lydia. "You've already made me look like a damn fool, and you've been lying to me and hiding the truth since day one. How did you even find out about my ad to hire an assistant?" she asked. Jasper hesitated to answer and then, looking down, responded.

"Helena told me about the ad. She knows how I get bored and sometimes don't use my time wisely, and she's always telling me that I need to get focused. I came to Atlanta at her request to check on some old businesses my mother left me when she passed and decided I wanted to stay here for a while. She knows that I really enjoy interior design, but I can't work with Auntie Helena although she and my mother were partners for years. So she gave me your ad, and I showed up here, that's the honest truth," he said.

"Bullshit," said Elise. "The favor you did for her was to con your way into my girl's business and be her little mole. I've heard enough, Lydia, let's throw this fool out on his ass," said Elise angrily.

Lydia looked at Jasper intently, and although she was very angry by the events of the day and the last few weeks, she couldn't help but think Jasper was telling the truth.

"Why do you think your friend Lionel is the one giving Helena the information, and how did he get it?" asked Lydia.

"Because I tell him a lot about what's going on. I didn't think he would do anything with it because he's not even into interior design. I didn't think it would do any harm," said Jasper.

"Yeah, you didn't think," said Lydia. "How is he getting into our files? It's all password protected, and we're the only two with that information. Did you tell him that too?"

"No. But I do keep that information in a book at home. Maybe he got it out of my book. I don't know."

"He must have been in here at some point to steal it off of the computer. Have you brought him here?" asked Lydia.

"No. But he knows where I work, of course, and all of that information, the access code to the alarm, and everything is in the same book," said

Jasper, realizing how careless it was to allow the information to be so easily taken.

"Wow, you're not the sharpest pencil in the box, are you?" said Elise.

"Lydia, I'm sorry. I'm really sorry. I realize this is all my fault, but I know I can fix it," said Jasper.

"How?" said Lydia.

"We can catch him in the act, or we can plant false drawings and estimates. We can get them both."

"Why should I trust you now?" asked Lydia.

"Because I'm pissed too. Helena used me to get to you, and I don't appreciate that. I never want to be used like this against my friends, and I do consider you my friend," he said.

"You consider Lydia a friend against your godmother?" said Elise.

"Yes, I do," said Jasper.

"So what do you think we should do?" asked Lydia.

"Here's what I was thinking." Jasper motioned Lydia and Elise over to him to explain what he planned to do. He was extremely upset with Helena and realized that her main reason for bringing him to Atlanta was to get back at Lydia. He didn't like being used by anyone, not even Helena, and he wasn't going to let her ruin what he considered a good thing, not now, not ever.

CHAPTER 32

CHRYSTAL

"**O**h damn, Manuel! Yes, baby, yes!" screamed Chrystal in a passionate frenzy. She lifted her body and pressed it against him over and over again until she reached her highest peak and let out a high-pitched shriek. "Oh god! So good, baby. Oh god!" she yelled as she lifted her body and began rubbing her breasts and licking her lips. Their bodies moved in unison as the rhythmic motions became slower and then to a halt. Chrystal's limp body fell on top of his, her breasts lying against his hard muscular chest, sweaty and exhausted. They kissed each other deeply and then smiled at each other. Manuel hugged Chrystal and allowed his hands to roam onto her tiny waistline and then onto the fullness of her behind. He squeezed it and then gave it a gentle tap. She squirmed, too exhausted to resist his touch as they both lay still together, satisfied after their third lovemaking session.

"That was amazing," said Manuel. "You're too incredible for words," he said, looking deeply into Chrystal's eyes.

"I know, I am pretty amazing," joked Chrystal. "You're not too bad yourself you know," she said, kissing him deeply on his lips.

They had spent the last six days together celebrating Chrystal's promotion, and she couldn't be more pleased with herself. She had a new position at Goldman and Associates that she knew she was going to love and the pay to match. Having Manuel every night was the icing on the cake, and she fully intended to eat every delicious bite. Normally, Chrystal wouldn't get tied down with any one guy, but she decided to make an exception with Manuel, who proved to be very persistent and eager for her affection. After they ran into each other at the club a few weeks ago, he began calling again, and Chrystal decided to let him pursue her. *Why not?* she thought. He's gorgeous and sexy, and those were two combinations in a man that she couldn't easily resist.

"You know, the first time we were together, you didn't remember a thing. You didn't even know my name," he said teasingly.

"I know," she said, embarrassed. "I was totally blasted, but you were so sweet to get me home and into my bed," she stopped and started laughing about how convenient she made it for him that night to get her into bed. "I remember the next morning. I woke up to the smell of bacon, eggs, and pancakes cooking in the kitchen. You were cooking up a storm. I actually thought you were my girl Lydia." She laughed. "You even went shopping to buy the breakfast food because I didn't have a thing in the refrigerator," she said.

"Yes, I remember it was very bare," he said laughing. "I thought, 'This woman has no food in her home. How does she eat?'" He smiled.

"Lydia or Elise usually feed me," said Chrystal, laughing. "If it weren't for my girls, I'd probably starve."

"Well, now you have me to feed you as well," he said, caressing her cheeks. "You know, when I first laid eyes on you that evening at the club, I knew you were special, Chrystal, and so I wanted to do something special for you that morning. In my family, food is not only to nourish your body, but it is also used to keep us connected with the people we love, and I very much wanted to be connected with you," he said, smiling at her.

Chrystal sat up and stared into his eyes. *What is he up to?* she thought. Manuel was very passionate and yet sensitive too. Normally, she would be turned off by the combination since she once thought sensitive men were weak. But there was something different about Manuel that made her know that he was anything but weak. In the short time she'd known him, she looked at him as being strong, kind, full of passion, and sensitive all at the same time, and she didn't know quite how to handle what was developing between them. Chrystal had never experienced anything like this with a man or anything beyond unemotional sex. The girls called her the "man" of their group, with Elise coming in a close second, because she could hang with the best of them. Chrystal didn't know why she was the way she was other than maybe a couple of heartbreaks as a teenager. However, she knew that she never wanted to allow herself to become emotionally available to a man because she didn't want to open herself up for heartache like she'd seen her girls experience. Like Lydia who hadn't dated in over a year because of a bad breakup with a guy she thought she was going to marry, or Sherrie with Brad and Elise with Quinton. The examples against falling in love were endless, and as far as Chrystal was concerned, that wasn't a road she wanted to go down any time soon, if ever. Lydia once told her that opening herself up was the only way to truly love someone, and unfortunately, heartache was a risk everyone took when they fell in love. But Chrystal knew this would never happen to her because she'd resolved to simply never be in love. Now Manuel was talking about being connected to her and knowing she was special, and she wanted to squash all of that mushy talk before it went any further.

"What are you up to?" she asked Manuel almost accusingly.

"What?" he said unfazed by her reaction.

"I know what you're trying to do," said Chrystal as she gathered up the flat sheet from the bed and wrapped it around her nude body to stand up.

"What do you mean, Chrystal?" he said, suddenly amused by her.

"No, no. You're not going to get me to go there with you," she said, heading toward the bathroom.

"Go where, Chrystal? What are you talking about, baby?" He smiled as Chrystal blew a kiss his way and gently closed the bathroom door behind her.

*   *   *

Although Chrystal no longer worked for Dana, their paths crossed regularly at Goldman and Associates, and Dana never pretended that she wanted bygones to be bygones since she used any opportunity to take little digs at her. Chrystal knew that she had spies keeping tabs on her progress as an intern, and she knew that she needed to work very hard to keep Dana at bay since she thought there was no longer any evidence of her affair. Little did she know that Chrystal was always prepared with a plan B, plan C, and even a plan D. Still, Chrystal knew she needed to keep things between her and Dana fairly cordial to avoid any conflicts.

"I trust you're getting along with Will okay," said Dana to Chrystal one morning as they were both pouring their morning coffee in the office kitchen. "He's very good at what he does. I'm sure that even you can pick up a thing or two from him," she said snidely. Chrystal ignored the comment and stared her in the eye. She refused to give Dana what she wanted, which was to steal her joy and to make this experience miserable.

"I am, and thanks for asking. Will's a great teacher and mentor, and I'm learning a lot from him. In fact, I've learned more about this company in the last two weeks than I had in the last two years," said Chrystal, referring to her time under Dana's supervision. They stared each other down, and then Dana decided to ignore Chrystal's comment as well.

"Glad to hear it," she said as she scooped up her coffee cup and gave Chrystal one last once-over before walking off.

"Have a nice day," said Chrystal after her. Chrystal knew she shouldn't play Dana's little game. *But some people just can't let things go*, thought Chrystal, who also noticed that Dana had apparently developed the skill to make her own coffee. Chrystal wouldn't have thought it possible since one of her more urgent morning tasks from Dana was to make the damn coffee. She poured herself another cup, added some cream and Splenda, and then headed out of the kitchen toward her office. One of the perks of being an intern was getting her very own office adjacent to Will Bauer, one of the senior associates who had been assigned to train her for the next six months. Her new office didn't have much of a view, just the employee parking lot, but it was certainly a step up from the desk she had right outside of Dana's plush office. Will was very different from Dana in every way that mattered to Chrystal, and for her, it was a welcome change. He loved to joke around and have fun, and one evening, while they were working late together, she discovered he was a fan of the HBO series *Dexter* just like her. Chrystal was happy to finally find someone who loved the show as much as she did since none of her girls cared for it too much. They just didn't get the brilliance of the writing and the characters like Will did. Chrystal pulled up the morning reports and began inputting the data into a massive spreadsheet just like Will had shown her the previous day. The reports were due to him every Thursday morning, and she wanted to be on top of her game.

"Good morning, Chrystal," said Will, suddenly appearing in her office door.

"Oh hi, Will," said Chrystal, looking up from her computer screen. "I was just finishing up the report for tomorrow," she said as he stepped into her office holding a Redskins coffee mug and taking a sip of coffee.

"That's great. Hey, when you get a moment, I want to go over a couple of databases with you this morning that you'll be using often, so you'll need to get very familiar with them," he said. "How about we meet in my office in about ten minutes?"

"Sure. I'll be there," said Chrystal enthusiastically.

"Good, see you in a few," he said as he turned around and walked swiftly away in the opposite direction of his office. Chrystal finished the last input, saved it to her hard drive, and then logged off her computer. Will was extremely organized and had prepared an entire outline of her training program from the day she began until six months out. Every day there would be a new task, and Chrystal was enjoying being challenged immensely. As she opened her desk drawer to pull out a notepad, she glanced up just in time to see Dana peering at her from across the hall. Chrystal got up from her desk, walked over to the door, and closed it as Dana continued to stare. *Freak*, she thought to herself. Did she really think that her constant stares were going to shake her?

*   *   *

"You're doing very well, Chrystal. I'm really pleased with your progress," said Will as he closed the last of the databases. "So how do you like the work so far?" he asked.

"Oh, thanks. I'm really enjoying it, Will. Thanks so much for taking the time to show me all of this. I think it's really coming together for me."

"Great, that's what we like to hear. Mr. Sanders is going to be asking about you, and I'm going to be happy to tell him how well you're doing," said Will, smiling at Chrystal. "Now tomorrow, we turn in the report, there's a meeting at 2:00 p.m. that I attend every Thursday, and I want you to go with me. When you feel comfortable enough, I'll let you handle the Thursday meeting. How does that sound?"

"That would be great," said Chrystal. Will glanced at his watch and noticed it was already 5:30 p.m. "Well, it's getting late, let's call it a night and we'll pick up tomorrow, okay?"

"I'll be here bright and early," said Chrystal as she gathered her belongings to leave his office. As she walked out, she noticed that many of the employees had already left for the day, with the exception of Will's assistant, who was typing a memo on her computer. Chrystal nodded at her as she left to go into her office, and she waved back at her. Chrystal did one last check of her e-mails and voice mail before picking up the leather briefcase given to her as a promotion gift from Lydia, picked up her purse, and then closed and locked her office door.

"Good night, Chrystal," said a voice across the hall. Chrystal turned slightly and saw it was Will, who had stopped by his assistant's desk for a moment. "Good night, Will, see you tomorrow," she said back. Chrystal opened the front doors to Goldman and headed toward the parking lot. The air was cold and crisp against her face, and the temperature had dropped at least ten degrees from this morning. She and Will worked through lunch, only stopping for a moment to have a little lunch when they ordered out for sandwiches from Arby's. She was a little drained from the day's training session. Unlike her previous job as Dana's assistant, this position required quite a bit of processes and thinking, and so at the end of the day, Chrystal found herself mentally drained, but she liked being and feeling useful. Once she arrived at her car, she opened her purse and fumbled for her car keys. When she finally found them buried at the very bottom of her purse, she quickly pulled them out and then accidentally dropped them on the ground. "Damn," she said as she stooped down to retrieve them. When she stood back up, she was startled to see Dana standing right in front of her.

"Damn! What is wrong with you, woman?" said Chrystal, lurching back a little, for which Dana chuckled.

"You think this is over, don't you?" said Dana, watching Chrystal intently.

"As far as I'm concerned, it is. The fact that you don't want to move on is your problem. Now if you'll excuse me, I have some ravioli at home with my name all over it," said Chrystal, hitting the button on her key ring to unlock the car doors. Chrystal reached over and opened the driver's side door, when Dana stepped in closer and slammed the door back shut. Chrystal jerked back. "What the hell is your problem, Dana?"

"You think you're so smart, don't you? But I wonder what Mr. Sanders would think if he knew how you really got this job? I don't think he'd be happy to know that you blackmailed me into getting you a better position and extorting money," she said.

"Get the hell away from my car," said Chrystal, waiting for Dana to obey her command, but Dana stood firm defying her.

"Or what?" she said finally.

Chrystal rolled her eyes at what she thought was a pitiful excuse for a human being. "You know, Dana, you're so predictable, and you continue to underestimate me. You don't want to go to Mr. Sanders or anyone else for that matter. It wouldn't be in your best interest."

"Why not? I've burned all the tapes. Even if you went to my husband, why would he believe you over me? He wouldn't," she said snidely.

"Yeah, you burned all of *your* tapes, but are you sure I did the same? You see, Dana, hubby doesn't have to believe me because the proof speaks for itself. Now back the hell off," snapped Chrystal. Dana took a moment to consider Chrystal's comment.

"What do you mean?" said Dana fearful of what Chrystal was implying.

"I mean that your best bet is to keep your mouth shut if you want me to do the same. I don't want to break up your happy home, Dana, but you know I will."

"You're bluffing," said Dana uncomfortably.

"Am I? Try me. Now get out of my way," shouted Chrystal. Dana backed away, giving Chrystal just enough room to enter her car. Chrystal jumped into her car, started it up, and pulled away quickly, leaving Dana standing in the same spot paralyzed by what she'd just learned. As Chrystal pulled into traffic and sped down Peachtree Street a little above the speed limit, she started thinking about what she needed to do to shut Dana down before things got out of hand. The first thing she'd have to do when she got home was make more copies of the tape and have them ready for delivery to Mr. Little and Mrs. McKenna if Dana decided to lose her mind. Chrystal needed to show Dana that if she wanted trouble, she could give it to her. If Dana threatened her again about going to Mr. Sanders or anyone else, she would have no choice but to send the copies of the tapes. Dana left her no choice. If she went down for any of this, she would make sure Dana did too. Chrystal sped through several yellow lights and nearly a red one trying to get home as quickly as possible. Her stomach growled loudly because she was so hungry, but unfortunately, the ravioli from Bambinelli's would have to wait.

Chrystal had just finished making several more copies of the tapes and wrapped them individually to be mailed to the homes of McKenna and Little respectively if the time arose. She took the last bite of the ravioli and washed it down with a glass of white wine. She picked up her cell phone and pressed a number in her favorites and waited for a ring. The telephone rang three times before a voice answered.

"Hello," said the voice in a sleepy tone.

Chrystal picked up the original tape, placed it on the receiver, and pressed play.

"Jeff, baby, are you ready for our little San Diego getaway? . . . I know, baby, but we'll be together for three romance-filled days, and I can't wait."

Chrystal pressed stop on the recorder and placed her cell to her mouth.

"Don't mess with me, bitch, or Paul and Mrs. McKenna will get the shock of their lives." She clicked off her cell before the individual could respond and sat back to sip some more of the white wine. Chrystal looked at the original tape and the addresses on the two envelopes. Dana must have thought she was dealing with a fool, and Chrystal was nobody's fool. If Dana didn't know that, she had better ask somebody.

CHAPTER 33

ELISE

The morning Quinton came back to the condo was totally unexpected by Elise. The way they'd left things between them when he walked out and his refusal to return her phone calls made Elise think that it was over, although she tried many times to call and talk to him. The girls were all asleep, each sprawled all over the floor or couch, too hungover to realize that anyone else had entered the house. But Elise was thrilled that he came by. Quinton explained that he needed some time after he left to think things through and to decide if their relationship was worth salvaging. He told Elise that he loved her, but he was tired of her not being able to commit to him fully. Elise explained as best she could that she was used to being on her own and being independent. She loved Quinton as well, but she didn't know if she was ready to be a wife. The only thing she was absolutely sure about was that she loved him. They talked outside on the patio for what seemed like hours, and before they knew it, it was almost noon, and the ladies had all awakened and left to give them privacy. Elise was happy that they each had a chance to tell each other how they felt, but the question that was still lingering in the air was where would they go from there? Elise didn't want to think about not being with Quinton, and he felt the same way about her.

"So where does that leave us?" she asked, holding his hands gently.

"I don't know. I want to be with you, but you need time to think about what you want," he said. "Maybe we need to take a break," he said finally.

"A break? Are we breaking up, Quinton?" she asked, wary of how he would respond.

"We're not breaking up, we're just taking a break. Why don't we each take some time away from each other and think about what we want," he said, trying to reassure her of the arrangement.

"For how long?" she said quietly.

"I think we'll both know after a while. I don't want to put a timetable on it. I just want us both to be free to reassess ourselves," he said.

"Are you going to be dating other people?" Quinton looked at her, a little surprised by the question.

"Are you?" he answered with a question.

Elise sat back in her Florence patio chair with her head down, still holding Quinton's hands. She hated the thought of them breaking up or taking a break or whatever it was they were doing now. Why couldn't things be the way they were a few months ago when he was just hanging out in her condo and she was fussing at him for leaving his dirty underwear on the bathroom floor? It all seemed so simple then, and now she was faced with possibly losing him forever.

"I don't want anyone else, Quinton," she said slowly.

"Neither do I," he said, now touching her cheek gently. "Let's just call it a break, that's all, okay?" he said.

"Can we call each other sometimes?"

"Sure," he said. "Call me whenever you need to. You know where I'll be," he said as he stood up to leave. She stood up as well, and they gave each other a long hard hug followed by an even longer kiss. It was very painful to see him walk out her door once again, and this time, she really didn't know if he'd ever be back.

*   *   *

As the days went on, Elise threw herself into her work and spent as much time as possible with her girls. Keeping herself occupied helped her to not think about Quinton twenty-four hours a day. There were moments when she couldn't help but think about what he was doing, where he was going, and if he was with anyone new. He said he didn't want anyone else, but what would happen if he met someone that appreciated him the way she couldn't bring herself to do? What would happen to them if he met some cute shapely little thing that would say yes to his marriage proposal? Lydia told her she would drive herself insane thinking about the what-ifs and that she should be taking their time apart to truly think about what she wanted. She hated when Lydia was right, but Lydia was right, so Elise decided to get herself together and try a hobby she'd been putting off for some time. She was finally going to take up white-water rafting.

"White-water rafting? Why the hell do you want to do something like that?" asked Chrystal after Elise made her announcement to her and Lydia.

"I don't know. It's something I've always wanted to try, that's all," said Elise, looking through a brochure for classes on white-water rafting, canoeing, and kayaking.

"I always wanted to try a foursome, but that don't mean I'm going to go out and do it," said Chrystal, biting into a spicy hot wing.

"Girl, you know a foursome is old news for you," said Elise laughing.

"Shut up!" said Chrystal, pushing Elise on her shoulder.

"Okay, ladies," said Lydia. "Chrystal, we need to be supportive of Elise and her new hobby," she said, glancing at the brochures. "Maybe we might want to go with her."

"Will you?" squealed Elise excitedly.

"Hell no," said Chrystal. "Lydia, you crazy as hell if you think I'm getting out there."

"Oh, be quiet and try something new," said Lydia. "You never know until you try it. I think it looks like fun," said Lydia, nodding her head at Elise and turning to Chrystal to convince her it would be a fun activity for the gang.

"All right, I'm in if you are, Lyd," said Chrystal, dipping a wing in blue cheese sauce.

"There you go," said Lydia cheerfully. "Elise, sign us all up!"

"I knew I could count on my girls!" shouted Elise, giving them both high fives.

"What about Sherrie?" asked Chrystal. Elise and Lydia looked at each other and then at Chrystal. They didn't know what to say about Sherrie at this time. They were all aware of the disastrous evening Sherrie and Brad had together and what a mess the entire situation had left Sherrie in. In fact, they had all visited her at her home individually to make sure she was okay and took some food over together just the other day.

"I talked to her last night," said Lydia. "She sounded a lot better, but you know she hasn't heard from Brad. She has no idea where he is right now."

"Wow. That is really something," said Chrystal. "Did she tell you guys who her baby daddy is since it's not Brad?"

"Yeah, a colleague of Brad's," said Lydia slowly.

"Damn, is that right?" said Chrystal.

"Yes, and Brad knows who he is now too, which seemed to make things worse. She said he went ballistic when he heard the guy's name," said Elise. The ladies were silent for a moment, feeling helpless about what to do for their friend. They all wanted to be there for Sherrie and show support.

"We have to do something special for Sherrie to help her out now. I'm worried about her being alone in that big house with just Jillian and Isabella," said Lydia. "Maybe we can take her on a spa day or something, you know, anything to get her mind off of Brad and her troubles."

"You know, you are really something else, Lydia," said Elise, smiling. "You're always thinking about everyone else. You know, we still have that matter with Helena to deal with, and I still don't know if I trust Jasper," she said.

"I know, but I think he's telling the truth about Helena. It was careless of him to leave sensitive information lying around for anyone to see, but I think he was as shocked as I was," said Lydia.

"You think so?" asked Chrystal. "You really think that Jasper's little boyfriend got all of that information from pillow talk and he had nothing to do with it?"

"I do. Especially with the plan he came up with to get them. In any case, the truth is going to come out. It always does," said Lydia. "Helena has stooped to a new low, stealing designs to get over."

"Just shows you for sure who had the real talent at her design firm, girl, and it sure ain't Kameron Tyndall," said Elise.

"So how's the new job coming along, Chrystal?," asked Lydia.

"I'm loving it, girl. I'm working under another senior associate, and he's really teaching me a lot so far. I come home every night with my head about to explode because there's so much information to learn and so many decisions to make with clients. It's such a difference from being an assistant, where the biggest decision I had to think about was whether Dana wanted mocha or vanilla coffee in the morning." She laughed as Lydia and Elise laughed with her.

"So how is Dana taking all of this? Does she *miss* you?" asked Elise teasingly.

"We have a mutual understanding with each other, that's all I'm going to say," said Chrystal as Elise and Lydia looked at her, wondering what that meant.

"She should be happy for you, she recommended you for the job, didn't she?" asked Lydia.

"Yeah, but you know how people get all jealous when they see you doing well and moving forward. Maybe she didn't think I would get the job," said Chrystal, secretly ashamed that she was hiding the real truth from her girls.

"I know that's right," said Elise. "It happens all the time. She'll get over it. Has she hired someone in your old position yet?"

"No, not yet. I don't know what she's waiting on because I'm sure as hell not coming back." Chrystal laughed, taking a sip of her diet coke.

"Spa day. You know that's a good idea, Lydia," said Elise, suddenly thinking of Sherrie once again. She pulled her laptop over, which was on the granite counter, and pulled up a few sites for day spas. "I know exactly where we can take her, and we won't take no for an answer. We have to get her away for a few hours and arrange for Isabella to watch Jillian while we're gone. Here we go," she said, pointing to the Buckhead Grand Spa in downtown Atlanta. "They have a package here called 'It's a Girl's Thing' that will be perfect for all of us, because let's face it, we're all having a little drama right now, with the exception of Chrystal," said Elise, surprised by the realization.

"How did you manage to be drama free when we're all swimming in it, girl?" asked Lydia.

"I don't know. Maybe the stars are aligned in my favor for a change," lied Chrystal.

"Well, stars or no stars, this deep pore-cleansing facial and revitalizing scalp treatment is exactly what we all need. I'm giving them a call for this Saturday. Is Saturday good for everyone?" asked Elise.

"It's good for me," said Lydia.

"Me too," said Chrystal.

"Saturday it is for four women who need to forget about real life for about three to four hours," said Elise as she dialed the number on her cell. Deep down inside, she really wished that a facial would be the answer to her problems with Quinton, Lydia's problems with Helena, and Sherrie's marriage with Brad. Oddly enough, the only one in their group at this very moment truly enjoying a blessing was Chrystal, and Elise was really proud of her and happy that she'd found a career she really enjoyed.

"Yes, I'm calling to make an appointment for four on Saturday," said Elise as the receptionist from the day spa answered the call. Elise could only pray that a day spa was the answer they all were looking for. A facial and deep cleansing would certainly help clear their minds and souls, and wouldn't that be a wonderful thing?

CHAPTER 34

SHERRIE

"Mommy, mommy!" yelled Jillian as she ran into her mother's bedroom to find her lying flat on her back in the middle of the king-size bed with a black laced sleeping mask over her face. She'd been asleep for hours after taking a sedative the night before to help her rest. The evening with Brad had turned out to be her worse nightmare, and she was deeply hurt about the way he fooled her into thinking the evening was going to be about romance. But although her feelings were hurt, she couldn't imagine how Brad was feeling at this moment. She had deceived her husband and dishonored her wedding vows with another man, a man who fathered their only child. Sherrie didn't know if Brad would ever forgive her for this transgression, and likewise, she didn't know if she could ever forgive herself. There were still so many questions that were left unanswered even with Brad revealing what he knew about the paternity, but he never mentioned exactly why he had a paternity test done in the first place. Sherrie considered that maybe it didn't matter because the truth was bound to come to light one day, although she'd hoped that it would happen when she and Brad were both on their deathbeds or too old to care. But now, several days had gone by since Brad walked out, and Sherrie hadn't heard a single word from him. She wanted to call his cell but didn't know what to say to make things better even if he should happen to answer. It was a tough situation that she knew only with the help of her girls, Jillian, and prayer could help.

Jillian climbed onto the bed and crawled into her mother's arms. She pulled the mask off Sherrie's face and laughed.

"Mommy, why are you wearing a Zorro mask?" she asked, smiling. Sherrie was amused. No matter what mood she happened to be in, Jillian always brightened her day.

"It's a sleeping mask, sweetie. It makes it dark and soothing to help Mommy sleep."

"Mommy, can Isabella make me chocolate chip pancakes with chocolate milk?" she said, with beautiful wide eyes, curly long hair, and a wide smile.

"Yes, tell Isabella to make you some pancakes, okay? Go ahead and get something to eat," said Sherrie, turning Jillian in the direction of the kitchen.

"Thank you, Mommy," said Jillian, jumping down from the bed and running toward the kitchen yelling for Isabella. Sherrie lay there for a while, trying to remain very still. She hadn't gotten dressed or showered in days, and her hair looked an awful mess. Sherrie sat up in the bed and quickly smelled under her arms. She grimaced at the odor emanating from her underarms and between her legs. Even she had to admit that she'd gone one day too long without showering, so she got up from the bed, took off her nightie, which happened to be the same one she'd worn the night Brad gave it to her as a gift, threw it in the hamper, walked into the bathroom, turned on the shower with four shower heads, and stepped in. She allowed the water to flow down every inch of her body including her hair. She then reached for the Bath & Body Works shower gel and lathered her body down. The water was wonderful, and she was suddenly grateful for such a refreshing and renewing feeling that only a good shower could bring. Once her shower was complete, she stepped out, toweled herself down, dried her hair, and then applied Body Bath lotion to her body and her face. She stepped into her walk-in closet and pulled out a set of matching bra and panties from the built-in dresser drawers and gave herself a little spritz of her Reveal perfume, Halle Berry's latest fragrance. She then selected a comfortable hooded jogging suit and a close-fitted white T-shirt to wear under it. Sherrie brushed her long hair back into a ponytail and allowed it to hang. She felt a sense of accomplishment in just bathing herself since in the last few days, she didn't have the strength or the will to even move from her bed. The only time she did move was when Jillian came in during the day or when the girls each came by to check on her. They even brought over lasagna the other night for dinner for her and Jillian when they knew Isabella would be off for the evening. She didn't know what she'd do without their support. Possibly losing her husband and marriage was the most painful thing Sherrie had ever experienced in her life, and she was grateful to have such great friends who were there for her. Still, Sherrie didn't feel like doing anything else beyond bathing herself, and she knew she would have to come out of her funk at some point, but she didn't want to do it now. Sherrie was mourning in a sense for the loss of trust with her husband, the loss of togetherness, and in a way, the loss of family. Could Brad still look at Jillian as his little girl although he had proof that the blood coursing through her veins wasn't his own? Sherrie was pondering the question and many others for a moment when suddenly her cell phone began to ring. She picked up on the third ring to the sound of Elise's voice.

"Hi, sweetheart. How are you doing today?" asked Elise.

"Hi, Elise. Well, I showered today. That's about all I think I can manage to do today," said Sherrie plainly.

"Well, that's a good start, but you're going to have to push yourself harder because you're going on a spa day with me, Lydia, and Chrystal," said Elise. So get ready, we're picking you up in a few minutes." Sherrie became exhausted with just the thought of leaving her bedroom, much less the house. There was no way she was going to a spa today or anytime soon.

"Elise, I can't go, I really don't feel up to it," said Sherrie, practically pleading her case.

"It's already arranged. Isabella is going to watch Jillian, and we all have reservations for deep tissue massages in an hour, and we're not going without you, so be ready to jet in five minutes," said Elise.

"Oh, Elise, no, please, I can't, it's really too much."

"Sherrie, I saw a bumper sticker on a car the other day, and it said, 'Life is hard, and then you die.' Well, we know life is hard and we're all going to die, but let's have a nice facial first, shall we? Come on, we're right outside now. Don't make us come in there after you," said Elise. Sherrie slumped down on her bed, feeling a bit defeated. She knew how determined all of the girls could be, and they weren't about to go to the spa without her. She didn't know what to do. She was too weak to leave and too weak to resist all three of them. She pondered her options for a moment but couldn't think of anything that would hold water with the girls, and as soon as she thought she'd had the answer, there was a knock on her bedroom door, and before she could answer, Elise, Lydia, and Chrystal appeared in her bedroom door.

"Okay, good you're dressed. Chrystal, you take one arm, and Elise will take the other. I'll grab her purse and off we go," said Lydia, grabbing Sherrie's purse from the dressing table.

"I don't want to go," said Sherrie, protesting being dragged out of her own home.

"You're going so hush up. I tell you, this facial will be exactly what you need. You'll feel like a new woman," said Elise. "At least that's what the brochure said." She laughed.

"Okay, woman, let's get down these stairs," said Chrystal on Sherrie's right side while Elise was on the left. They practically lifted her down the stairs and outside of the door as Lydia followed closely behind with purse in hand.

"Isabella, we're leaving!" shouted Lydia.

"Okay, Ms. Lydia. Have fun!" said Isabella. Jillian was too busy drinking her chocolate milk and watching cartoons to notice the four ladies leaving for the next few hours.

The girls were right. The spa treatment was absolutely wonderful, very relaxing, and soothing, and for a few hours, Sherrie didn't think of paternity, Brad, deceit, nothing but pure relaxation. It was the best she'd felt in days. After the spa, the ladies went out for drinks and a light snack, laughed and talked about any and everything except their individual problems, and just enjoyed each other's company. It was a wonderful day.

Now Sherrie was back at home, relieving Isabella, who was anxious to go visit her grandchildren and getting ready to tuck Jillian into bed after giving her a nice long bath. Sherrie placed baby lotion on Jillian's little body and then a little powder under her arms before she put on new Barbie pajamas. Jillian laughed as Sherrie tickled her after she was finished dressing her.

"Okay, let's get in bed," said Sherrie.

"Mommy, can you read me a story?" asked Jillian as she walked over to her little library of books and selected a princess story, *The Princess and the Frog*, that Sherrie had read to her a million times before.

"Is this the story you want to hear again?"

"Yes, Mommy, I like it because it has princesses in it," said Jillian.

"Okay, hop in bed, and let me read this to you," she said as Jillian climbed into her white canopy bed with a pink-and-white floral-print comforter and pillows. It was a bedroom fit for a princess.

"Mommy, where is daddy?" she asked. Sherrie was hesitant to answer. Would she lie and say he was working, or would she tell the truth and tell her she didn't know where he was?

"Daddy's taking care of some business," said Sherrie slowly.

"When is he coming home?" she asked.

"He'll be home soon, you'll see because he loves his little girl," said Sherrie, smiling because she knew she was speaking the truth. He may not like Sherrie at the moment, but no one was going to keep him from his little girl. So with the relaxing spa treatment, knowing that Jillian would always be Brad's little girl, and reading their little princess her favorite princess story, Sherrie pulled the sedatives out of her robe pocket, took a look at them, and happily put them away. For the first time in days, she could truly sleep well tonight without them.

CHAPTER 35

JASPER

"Lionel, have you seen my USB drive? I'm running so late this morning, Jasper doesn't know which way is up," said Jasper, grabbing his coffee mug and briefcase to head out the door.

"Yeah, it was on your dresser," said Lionel, handing it to Jasper and giving him a nice smile. "So what are you and Lydia up to today?"

"We have several new presentations coming up. We have to start landing some jobs because Lydia's really bugging out. I can't say that I blame her though. She sank a lot of money into her place, so naturally, she wants to see a return. I think we're going to be all right, though, because she's so talented," said Jasper, winking at Lionel. "Well, let me get out of here before I'm too late. Catch you later," he said, blowing a kiss toward Lionel. Lionel smiled and watched him walk out and then pull out of the driveway. Once he saw that Jasper was a safe distance away, he dialed Helena, who had been awaiting his call.

"Helena, yeah, it's me. Yeah, I copied some new drawings and estimates for a couple of new jobs from his USB drive, but there is still no sign of the Edwards job. I think I may have to go to the Loft again to look for it."

"Do you think the drawings are there?" asked Helena.

"They have to be because he doesn't bring them home."

"Lionel, if you find those drawings, there's an extra bonus in it for you," said Helena anxiously.

"Consider it done," said Lionel. "I'll try to do it tonight. I made a copy of the key Jasper left here at home a while back, so he'll never suspect anything."

"Good."

"Oh, one other thing, Lydia is concerned about not having any new jobs right now. Maybe she's feeling the pinch already."

"Good! Before we know it, Lydia's Loft will be no more," said Helena laughing.

"Absolutely!" said Lionel.

"Keep me informed, and be careful."

"I will, don't worry, I will," said Lionel.

*   *   *

Jasper walked into the office with coffee and scones from Starbucks for Lydia and Elise. He was pleased with himself that his plan was coming together and knew they could expect Lionel to make a move this evening. Jasper began putting out the scones and humming a tune to himself when Lydia and Elise walked in.

"Hey, Jasper," said Lydia.

"Hello, ladies," he said to both of them.

"So what's the word?" asked Elise, and she picked up a cup of coffee and a scone.

"Okay, I planted the fake estimates and drawings on my USB flash drive and left it hanging around just like we talked about," he said.

"Do you think he went for it?" asked Lydia, who now also had a cup of coffee in her hand.

"I know he did. I put the drive down, and he couldn't wait for me to get in the shower before he started snooping." Jasper laughed.

"Really? Did you see him do it?" asked Elise.

"You better believe it. I turned on the water and pretended I was already in the shower, and then I peeked out to see him on the laptop with the USB flash drive and copying it onto his hard drive. Lydia, if I can get his laptop before he erases it, we can possibly tie Helena to this too."

"So do you think he'll make a move tonight?" asked Lydia.

"Yup!" said Jasper. "Girl, I think they really want the drawings to the Edwards account because he's been asking a lot of subtle questions about it. If I didn't know what he was up to, I wouldn't think anything of it, and that's what he's counting on."

"So the plan is to lay low tonight and see if he bites, right?" said Elise, excited to be playing detective.

"That's right. We'll leave these fake hard copy drawings of the Edwards account around and catch him in the act," said Jasper.

"Jasper, how do you feel about all of this, because I know you've been with Lionel for a long time," said Lydia with a concerned voice. Jasper took a moment to think about the question, although he knew exactly how he felt.

"One word. Betrayed," he said with a twist of his wrist.

"Well, I heard that," said Elise.

"But we won't dwell on that, let's get ready for tonight," said Jasper as they began to clear away any authentic estimates and drawings and replaced them with the fakes. Jasper didn't want anything to happen to Lionel, but what else could he do? He had been lying and jeopardizing his job for whatever money Helena was giving him. Wasn't their relationship more important to him than that?

It was 10:00 p.m., and Jasper was pretending to be asleep when Lionel, who waited until he thought Jasper was sound asleep, crept out of their bed, slipped into a pair of jeans and a T-shirt, and quietly headed out their bedroom door. Jasper waited until he heard the front door close before contacting Lydia and Elise, who were waiting across the street from Lydia's Loft in Elise's black Lexus SUV for the intruder to enter Lydia's building. The SUV blended in nicely with the darkness of the street, and Lydia and Elise waited patiently for their cue. Suddenly, Lydia's cell rang, and she picked up on the first ring.

"Lydia, it's me. Girl, he just left. Be ready," said Jasper.

"Good, we're in place," said Lydia, turning to Elise and nodding her head. A few minutes went by when suddenly, they observed a silver Cadillac pull up and park in front of the store, and then they saw a tall man get out of the Cadillac and walk over to the door, use the key, and let himself inside.

"Son of a bitch!" said Elise.

"Yeah, it's time to snag his ass," said Lydia, who promptly dialed 911 on a disposable cell phone. "Yes, I need the police. I believe there's a break-in in progress at Lydia's Loft at 204 Wellesley Place. That's right, it's happening now. Thanks." Lydia hung up her cell while she and Elise stayed in place to wait for the police to arrive.

A few minutes later, a patrol car slowly drove up to the front of the store and turned off the lights. The police officers quietly stepped out of the car and crept up to the store and observed a figure inside of the store with a flashlight. One of the police officers was on one side of the front door while the other touched the doorknob, which was still open, and slowly walked in, throwing on the light at the entrance.

"Hold it, police!" they identified themselves as both officers pointed their guns in the direction of the intruder. Lionel, who was busy going through files and too preoccupied to notice anyone at the window, jumped directly up and dropped the files in his hands. He had been caught, and he didn't know what to do except put his hands way up in the air. One of the officers rushed over to him and began patting him down for weapons while the other kept a gun on him. When they verified that he wasn't carrying a weapon, the officer turned him around and asked what he was doing.

"We received a call that a robbery was in progress at this address. Show me some identification," said the officer. "Slowly," he said as Lionel reached into his pocket to pull out his driver's license.

"Lionel Turner," said the officer. "What are you doing in here, Lionel Turner? This isn't your place of business, is it?" Lionel began to stutter.

"No, officer, you have this all wrong. I was picking up some things for a friend of mine who works here. See, I have a key," he said, showing the officer the copied key he used to get in when suddenly, Lydia and Elise walked in. The officers turned and asked who they were.

"I'm Lydia Brown, the owner of this store, and this is my friend Elise," said Lydia. The officers asked for her identification, and she promptly gave them her driver's license. "What's going on, officer? We were just coming from dinner when I saw the lights on in my building and a police car, so I was wondering what was happening," she said.

"Ms. Brown, we received a call that your store was being robbed, and we came here to check it out and found Mr. Turner here. Do you know him? He said something about picking up something for a friend who works here."

"No, I've never seen him before, and the only other employee I have is my assistant. We're the only two people that should have a key to the store," said Lydia, which was the truth.

"Ms. Brown, can you take a look around to see if anything is missing?" asked one of the officers who was now handcuffing Lionel. Lydia began looking around the files where he was caught as Lionel looked totally terrified to find himself in such a predicament. The police officer patted him down again and found a USB drive.

"Ms. Brown, do you want to check this?" he asked.

"Yes, I do," said Lydia, taking the drive and turning on Jasper's computer. Once the computer was up, Lydia placed the USB drive into it and pulled up all of the copied drawings, including the drawings from the Taylor and Mitchell accounts. "These are my drawings, officer. He was stealing my drawings!" she said, trying her best to sound totally shocked by the discovery.

"Okay, let's go," said the officer as he pushed Lionel along and out the door into the waiting police car.

"Ms. Brown, I need to take a statement from you," said the officer.

"I'll be glad to," said Lydia.

"I'll make a statement too, if you need to me to," said Elise.

"Yes, that would be fine," said the officer.

*   *   *

After Lydia and Elise had given their statements and the police hauled Lionel downtown for booking, Lydia contacted Jasper, who had been waiting to find out if everything had gone according to plan.

"He's been arrested, Jasper, so don't be surprised if you get a call in the morning to post bail," said Lydia. "But honestly, thank you. One down and one to go," she said.

"Bail? Oh no, honey, he needs to call Helena to post his bail, but listen here, I'm glad it all worked out. So what did he have on him?"

"He had the drive with all of my drawings copied on it including the Mitchell and the Taylor account," said Lydia.

"Stupid backstabbing fool!" said Jasper. "And I thought I had a good man this time around. Sorry, I just didn't know he was capable of doing anything like this behind my back and for Helena," said Jasper, upset by the betrayal.

"Well, sometimes you don't know," said Lydia trying to make him feel better. "Anyway, they took our statements, so we'll go from there."

"Good. Well, go home and get some rest, and I'll call you in the morning when I hear something," said Jasper.

"Great, and, Jasper, thanks again," said Lydia.

"You're welcome, but we still have another one to go," said Jasper as he hung up.

CHAPTER 36

HELENA

hat is taking Lionel so long to give me a call? thought Helena, sitting in her office on a Saturday afternoon and checking her BlackBerry for the third time. He was supposed to check in with her hours ago about the drawings, but she hadn't heard one thing from him. Whether he was successful in finding the Edwards drawings or not was all she wanted to know. She couldn't believe that several months ago, she'd taken the Edwards account away from Lydia, only for it to end up back with her at her own design company of all things. *Sometimes life just isn't fair*, she thought. She checked her BlackBerry once more and then began to worry if something had gone wrong. As soon as she heard a tap on her door, she was relieved that Lionel was finally there to give her the news. She immediately asked him to come in.

"Come in, Lionel . . . I've been waiting on you." When she saw who walked through the door, she couldn't believe her eyes because it wasn't Lionel at all but, instead, Lydia Brown.

"Hello, Helena. Were you expecting someone else? Maybe Lionel Turner?"

"Well, this is a surprise. Come to ask for your old job back?" she said, wondering in the back of her mind why Lydia was standing in her office and not Lionel.

"Hardly. You do remember that I have my own business now, right? In fact, you crashed my grand opening party." Helena didn't have time to exchange pleasantries with Lydia; she needed to know why she was here so they could get on with it.

"Then why are you here?"

"That's an interesting question coming from you, Helena. Don't you want to know where Lionel is and how I know about him?" asked Lydia looking at Helena, who was now shifting uncomfortably in her chair. How did Lydia know about Lionel? Something was wrong.

"I don't know any Lionel Turner," she lied.

"Oh, I think you do, or at least that's what Lionel is telling the police as we speak." Now Lydia had Helena's full attention. He's talking to the police? That idiot has been arrested and was probably spilling about her involvement in all of this. Helena had to act fast.

"Lionel Turner was caught breaking into my business last night, and we found a USB on him filled with my copyrighted drawings. Now I've always known that you were taking credit for my work, Helena, when I worked for you, but stealing my estimates and drawings? You stole at least three potential clients that I know of by passing off my work as your own. You've hit an all-time low with this one, even for you," said Lydia.

"You don't have any proof that I even know this Lionel Turner person, much less that I had him steal your drawings and estimates, as if I need to take anything from the likes of you. You learned from me! So if I were you, I'd be careful with the accusations," she snapped.

"Oh, but I do have proof, Helena."

"What proof do you have?" she asked sarcastically as she watched Lydia step aside and Jasper walk in. She was shocked to see Jasper standing with Lydia in a united front.

"Auntie Helena, it pains me to see all of this trickery unfold and know that you are the one behind it. I know you know my friend Lionel because I saw the two of you together at the coffee shop. I also scoped out his cell, and he's called you too many times to count. How could you do this? You used me," he said, obviously feeling hurt by her actions.

"Don't be ridiculous, Jasper. You know, you've always been dramatic. Yes, I was at the coffee shop with Lionel having coffee. He asked me to meet him there to talk about you. Apparently, you two were having some issues in your relationship."

"So why did you lie about not knowing him? Helena, Lionel has already told the police why he was breaking into Lydia's business. So you may want to get your story straight before the police comes by to talk to you," said Jasper. At this point Helena was livid. Who did Jasper and Lydia think they were, coming into her office, accusing her of conspiring to steal Lydia's work? They were going to pay for this.

"What the hell is wrong with you? I practically raised you when your mother was alive, and I've watched over you since her passing. I protected her from all of the little stunts you pulled, spending money like crazy, jumping from one job to another, being gone for months on end without any word while she was ill, and I've taken good care of the business although she left you a percentage. This is how you repay me, by standing by this traitor? Both of you can turn around and get the hell out of my office because neither of you have any proof that I stole anything," she said in a huff.

"But we do have proof," said Jasper as he motioned for someone standing outside of the door to come in. Helena was shocked to see the Taylors, Mark and Sheila, walk into her office.

Mark looked at Helena as he and his wife made their way into her office. "Ms. Barnes, as you know, you presented us with drawings for a kitchen renovation a couple of weeks ago, and then Ms. Brown came the very next day with the exact drawings. Ms. Brown has proven to the police and to our satisfaction that the drawings belong to her, and we're both prepared to give statements to the police, who have asked us to speak with them," he said. "And by the way, we've decided to go with Lydia's Loft for the job. Honesty, integrity, and good business ethics mean a lot to us," he said, taking his wife's hand as they both turned to walk out. Lydia turned to Helena and smiled, knowing that Helena couldn't talk her way out of this one, and if she wanted to try, she could do it with the police.

Helena stood up from her desk and gave out a loud sigh. "Well, it looks like you two have got it all worked out, so now you can leave. I've had enough of both of you for one day," she said in a dismissive tone, but Jasper still had business to discuss with her, and he didn't intend to leave until all of the details were ironed out.

"I'm not finished," said Jasper in a commanding tone. "You asked me to come to Atlanta under the guise that you wanted me to check into my mother's old businesses. Well, I did that, and I also checked into Helena Designs."

"So what," said Helena, annoyed that he and Lydia were still standing in her office.

"Well, I pulled the original business venture between you and my mother, and all of these years, you neglected to tell me that my mother owned 60 percent of the business since she put all of her money into it initially."

"Okay, what's your point?" said Helena, a little troubled by where this discovery may lead but attempting to appear unaffected by this revelation.

"My point is that now I have controlling interest in Helena Designs, and as of right now, I am exercising that control. Do you get where I'm coming from?" said Jasper. Helena pounded her fist on the desk.

"Who do you think you are? Helena Designs is my business and my business alone. You'll take control of it over my dead body!" she yelled.

"So be it. I've already consulted an attorney, and I have a copy of the document right here," he said, reaching into his jacket pocket and pulling out the document to hand to Helena. She snatched it away from him, put on her reading glasses, and read through it quickly. When she finished, she threw it back at him in a fury.

"What are you planning to do?" she asked as Kameron Tyndall walked into the office carrying a box of doughnuts and a cup of coffee. She and Helena were supposed to meet this morning to go over the drawings that were supposed to have been delivered by Lionel. She was surprised to see Lydia and Jasper standing before Helena, and the air in the office was tense to say the least.

"What's going on here? Am I interrupting something?" she asked, not sure what to make of this reunion.

"I'm glad you're here, Kameron," said Jasper. "I was just telling Helena that I'm taking control of this company. My mother had controlling interest, and now I do," he said, looking at her then Lydia and then Helena. Lydia had now taken a seat to watch all of this unfold. She loved it when a good plan came together.

"What do you mean you're taking control? Helena owns this business," said Kameron sharply.

"Oh no, baby, she doesn't. I do, and I've decided that since I don't like the business practices Helena has brought here, I'm going to make some immediate changes starting with you. You're fired!" he said as Lydia sat back in her chair, amused by what was happening.

"You can't fire me, I'm the mayor's daughter!" she shouted.

"Honey, your father will be out of office in a month after running that pitiful excuse for a campaign and losing the election by a landslide. So you can just turn around, check the attitude, and go clean out your desk. But wait a second," he said, taking the box of doughnuts out of her hands. "I'll take these because I'm sure you want to keep that figure of yours together, but Jasper don't have to worry about that since Jasper never gains weight.

Bye-bye now," he said, waving her off. Kameron looked at Helena, who didn't offer any support, so she turned around in a huff and stomped off to clear out her desk.

"That was very dramatic," said Helena. 'What do you have in store for me?"

"I'm going to let things take their course with you, Helena. You'll have your own legal issues to deal with after today because my girl Lydia here fully intends to sue you for copyright infringement, and you have the matter of working with Lionel to break into her business to handle as well. In the meantime, I may consider buying you out, but until then, you can clear out of my office and choose a desk out there," he said, motioning to the room outside her office.

Helena was furious, but there was nothing she could do at this point. Jasper's mother did have controlling interest in the business. After his mother passed away, Helena was able to conceal that fact for years since Jasper spent more time gallivanting all over the country than paying attention to the business his mother left him in part. Now it seemed her entire plan to bring him here to help put Lydia out of business had backfired.

Lydia stood up and grabbed her purse. "Well, it looks like what goes around truly does come around," she said. "We'll leave you to be with your thoughts," said Lydia.

"Oh, by the way, you will be repaying Lydia for the jobs that were stolen from her. I'll make sure they come out of your checks, and if you don't go along with that, Lydia will sue you for loss of income as well. And you can tell that lowlife Lionel that when he gets out, his raggedy suitcase will be waiting for him at the door," said Jasper as he motioned for Lydia to walk out of the door first, leaving Helena standing at the desk with her mouth wide open.

As Lydia and Jasper walked confidently out of Helena Designs, Kameron stood up from her desk and swiftly walked into Helena's former office. Helena was still standing with her mouth open, trying to comprehend what had just happened. She glanced at the doorway to see an angry Kameron standing there.

"Are you going to let this happen? Helena Designs is your firm, and you're letting that fairy and two-bit designer Lydia throw you out?"

"Kameron, no one is throwing me out of anywhere, dear. That was simply Jasper grandstanding. I've known him long enough to know that he'll never follow through with his threat. He's never finished anything he's started."

"That's not what it looked like to me. You know, no one fires me. I'm the mayor's daughter, and even if my father will be out of office soon, we still have a lot of pull in this city," she said, cutting her eye toward the front door where the two culprits had just left.

"Now you're grandstanding," said Helena, opening the desk drawer to get a cigarette. "The sign on the door says Helena Designs, and that's exactly how it's going to stay," she said as she lit the cigarette and took a long drag of it.

CHAPTER 37

LYDIA

"You were fantastic, Jasper, you really were," said Lydia, hugging him after they arrived back at the office.

"So were you, Lydia. Did you see the look on Helena's face when I told her I was taking over controlling interest? She could have passed a kidney stone," he said laughing.

"I think she passed two kidney stones during the whole conversation, especially when the Taylors walked in. She knew she was done then," said Lydia, smiling. "You know, it will just be good to be able to get back to doing what I enjoy. All of this drama isn't for me, and it's one of the things I hated about working with Helena. She and Kameron always kept drama going."

"Lydia, you're a great designer, and you're going to do well here in the ATL. We need you here, and Lord knows there are some people out there that can use our services," he said laughing.

"Now that you've taken control of Helena Designs, what are you going to do? I guess I'll have to look for a new assistant."

"Not for a little while, honey. For once, Jasper is going to finish what he starts. Plus, we have the Edwards ribbon cutting coming up soon, and now the Taylors are back on board along with the Thomasina Mitchell account. We have a lot of work to do here, lady, and I want to be here to finish them with you, and then we'll go from there," he said assuredly.

"Are you sure, Jasper?"

"Absolutely. I insist," he said, taking her hands into his.

"You're the best. I knew it when you first walked in here."

"No, you're the best. I found my way back to something I'm really good at and enjoy because of you. Thank you for helping me stay focused."

"You're welcome, and thank you for everything," she said, giving him another hug. Just then, Elise walked into the office smiling and hoping to hear good news.

"Okay, guys, are we good?" she asked.

"We're real good," said Lydia, laughing. "Everything went according to plan, and Jasper here is the new controlling force over at Helena Designs."

"Whoa! Congratulations, Jasper!" said Elise excited.

"Thank you. You know my first order of business is going to be changing that name, Helena Designs. That just doesn't do it for me." He laughed as Elise and Lydia agreed.

"Well, I know that you guys have a lot to do, but I just came by to make sure all is well again. We need to go out and celebrate later," said Elise.

"Great idea, I'll call the girls," said Lydia.

"Okay, call me and we'll meet up wherever," said Elise as she hugged Lydia and gave her a kiss on the cheek, as well as Jasper, whom Elise now considered a close friend and the fifth friend of their group.

Lydia and Jasper both watched Elise as she left and then looked at each other.

"Well, those projects aren't going to get finished by themselves, let's get to it," said Lydia.

"Right on," said Jasper as they both walked into Lydia's office to finish the Edwards project and begin on the Taylors. It had been a good day for them both, and Lydia was proud to still have Jasper as an assistant but, more importantly, as a friend.

CHAPTER 38

CHRYSTAL

*T*he Thursday afternoon meeting was just coming to a close as all of the senior associates and their respective interns got up from the large conference table to either head back to their individual offices or to other meetings or to continue their discussions in smaller groups. Chrystal and Will had planned to go back to his office afterward to finish a presentation for a perspective new client. She was excited and nervous at the same time about giving her very first presentation, but Will assured her that he'd walk her through it, and then in no time, she would be giving presentations like a pro. As the associates all began to disperse, Will stopped for a moment to speak with Mr. Sanders, who was greeting each of the associates as they were leaving, about the report they had just submitted. Chrystal gathered her folders and notes from the conference table and walked over to Will and Mr. Sanders when suddenly, a loud disturbance erupted in the office across the hall. Will and Mr. Sanders immediately raced out of the conference room toward the disturbance and were surprised to find Susan McKenna and Dana in a heated exchange.

"I told you to leave my husband alone, you tramp!" screamed Susan directly in Dana's face.

"I don't know what you're talking about. Get out of my office!" Dana shouted back.

"I'm warning you. You better stop calling my house leaving filthy messages for my family to hear. Don't you have any decency about yourself?" she said, trembling with fury.

Mr. Sanders and Will rushed over to stop the argument just as Susan pulled back her hand to slap Dana across her face, but luckily for Dana, Will caught it in full swing and pulled her away.

"Wait a minute now, what's going on here? Susan, what is the meaning of all of this?" said Mr. Sanders, trying to diffuse the situation. He knew that Dana and Jeff McKenna were once having an affair, and once it was brought to his attention, he placed Dana on a two-week suspension without pay with a warning that if it happened again, she would be terminated immediately. He thought his actions had taken care of this delicate situation, but now Susan was back making the same accusations. The McKennas pulled their account from Goldman's, so as far as Mr. Sanders was concerned, the firm had no further business dealings with them.

Susan pulled away from Will's hold and turned toward Mr. Sanders. "This floozy called my home last night and played a very provocative recording of my husband and her over the phone. My mother answered the phone and was horrified by what she heard."

Chrystal stood by in shock listening to what was being said. Her heart began to pound faster as she stood there watching and trying to understand the events as told by Susan McKenna. As she listened intently, she began to retrace her actions from the night before up to the moment when she placed the call to where she thought was Dana's home. Could she have called the McKennas' home by mistake? She did have a couple of glasses of wine before she made the call. Was it possible that she accidentally dialed the wrong number? Her mind started to race as she thought quickly about how to cover her tracks. She was happy that she used Lydia's disposal cell to make the call, so at least now the number couldn't be traced back to her. As she watched the two women exchanging insults and Mr. Sanders trying to get them both to calm down, the situation looked more volatile by the minute, and she realized that this could blow up in her face. Chrystal needed to be prepared with a good story fast.

"Liar!" screamed Dana. "I never made any calls to your home last night or any other night. You better check your facts before you come charging in here making false accusations," she said fuming. Mr. Sanders stared at Dana and then at Susan. He was sick and tired of refereeing their disputes in his place of business, and he was going to put a stop to it one way or the other. He stepped inside the office and then turned and asked Will to leave and closed the door behind him for privacy. Outside of the door, a few lingering employees began whispering about what they'd just witnessed while Will asked them to break it up and go back to work. Chrystal stood frozen for a moment, her mind and heart racing at a rapid pace. She couldn't believe how careless she'd been by dialing the wrong number and playing that tape, but she had to recover quickly if she still wanted this to work out in her favor.

*   *   *

Inside Dana's office, Mr. Sanders tried to calm down the two hysterical women to get to the bottom of the situation. He sat down and asked Susan and Dana to do the same.

"I'm trying to get my hands around all of this," he said looking at both of them. "We had a situation before with Jeff and Dana, but I thought we took care of it, and now—"

"She's calling my home with taped conversations of my husband and calling my mother a bitch. I would hardly say that this situation has been taken care of," Susan interrupted.

"Let me finish," he said, trying to remain calm although he was clearly annoyed by the interruption. "Dana was suspended without pay, and you and Jeff decided to take your business elsewhere. Now this is a place of business, Susan. The time to discuss your domestic issues is not here." Susan was insulted by his conclusion and decided to see how much business he was willing to lose because of Dana.

"I have very important friends who also do business here, Mr. Sanders. Would you like them to know that Goldman and Associates condones their employees sleeping around with their married clients?" she said in a threatening tone. Mr. Sanders sat back in his chair and cleared his throat. He didn't appreciate Susan's threat.

"Now, Susan, that's not true at all. We took action when you came to us about the situation, but this is different."

"How so? She's still sleeping with Jeff, and she still works with your organization." Mr. Sanders straightened his tie and shifted in his seat, uncomfortable with the allegation, while Dana sat back in her chair with her arms folded.

"I'm not going to sit here and listen to your lies, Susan!" said Dana. "I'm not sleeping with Jeff, but maybe if you did, you wouldn't have to worry about other women," she said snidely.

"How dare you!" shouted Susan. "What goes on between me and my husband is none of your damn business. Maybe if your husband was taking care of business at home, you wouldn't be chasing mine!"

"You leave my husband out of this!" Dana shouted back.

"Dana! You're not helping. Now please, both of you need to calm down," said Mr. Sanders, and then he turned to Susan. "Susan, tell me exactly what happened last night. You said you received a call and your mother answered the phone," he said in an attempt to get the full story.

"Yes, my mother was taking a nap when the phone rang. She answered and said the person on the other end played a recording of Jeff and Dana talking about wearing thongs and nighties on their trip to San Diego. She was disgusted and so am I," she said, looking at Dana.

"If you don't stop lying on me, I'll slap the mess out of you," said Dana, standing up and pointing at Susan.

"Try it and I'll have you on charges. Just give me a reason," Susan shot back.

"Dana, sit down!" said Mr. Sanders, growing impatient with the entire scene. "Please continue," he said to Susan.

"Like I said, the message of Jeff and Dana was discussing a trip to San Diego. After it played a little, my mother said the person turned off the tape and then said, 'Don't mess with me, bitch, or you'll be sorry,' something to that effect. I know it was Dana thinking it was me who answered the phone, but it was my mother instead. Look at her. She enjoys throwing her tawdry affair with Jeff in my face."

Dana rolled her eyes. "For the last time, it wasn't me that called you." Dana sat back in her chair and folded her arms again. She knew she never called Jeff's home, not even when they were seeing each other, and the recording Susan described sounded just like the tape Chrystal was blackmailing her with. She wondered if after their encounter in the parking lot, Chrystal didn't go home and call Susan instead of calling her. It all made sense when she thought about it a little more.

"Dana, if you didn't call her, then who do you think did?" asked Mr. Sanders. Dana thought about how she should answer the question. If she told on Chrystal, she could send a copy of the tape to Paul. If she didn't come up with a logical explanation of what happened, Mr. Sanders may think that she's still involved with Jeff. "Dana, do you know who may have called Susan?" he asked again. Dana sat up in her chair and looked Mr. Sanders in the eyes with Susan watching her intently. "I do know who called Susan, but I can't tell you."

"Why not?"

"Because, she's blackmailing me with the same tape."

*   *   *

Chrystal could barely concentrate on the presentation Will was going over thinking about what was going on in Dana's office. She could kick herself for making such a stupid mistake, calling the wrong house and playing that tape. She knew Dana would put it all together, and she wasn't sure if she would be threatened enough by the tape and not say anything. No wonder Dana's demeanor was the same as any other day when she came into work this morning, because she never got Chrystal's threat. Chrystal got up from her chair and went over to the window to peek out of the closed blinds at the room across the hall. The door was still closed, so she figured they were still in there talking, but were they talking about her, the affair, or the tape? Chrystal's mind was racing a mile a minute when Will snapped her out of it.

"Anything interesting out there?" he asked.

"Sorry, I'm just a little concerned about Dana," she lied. "Do you think everything will be okay?"

"I'm sure Mr. Sanders is going to handle everything just fine. Do you want to take a break? And we can pick up in a half hour. I have a call I need to make anyway."

"Oh sure, that's fine. I'll see you in a few," she said, walking out of the door. She eyed Dana's closed door intently to see if there was any sign of movement, but there wasn't any that she could see. She entered her office and sat down at her desk to start checking e-mails and voice messages. Just then, a thought came to her. What if Dana decided to tell Mr. Sanders everything? Would it be her word against Dana's, or would Mr. Sanders take Dana's side? He seemed to be a fair man. After all, when he found out about the affair between Dana and Jeff McKenna, he suspended her without pay. Maybe he would keep an open mind and hear both sides of the story, giving Chrystal the chance to make one up. Then again, maybe she would lose her job. She couldn't' think straight right now. As Chrystal scanned through several e-mails, she glanced up just in time to see Mr. Sanders escorting Susan McKenna to the front door. She seemed calmer than she was just an hour ago, and Mr. Sanders appeared to be explaining something to her, to which she nodded in agreement. Then she placed her clutch bag under her arm, turned, and walked out the door. Chrystal continued to watch as Mr. Sanders headed back to Dana's office. She clicked on the last of the e-mails and started to read them when she was startled by the sound of her intercom buzzing. She stared at the phone for a moment as it beeped and then cautiously picked up the phone to the sound of Mr. Sander's voice.

"Hello?"

"Chrystal, can you come in Dana's office for a moment?"

"Okay," she said hesitantly. Her stomach began to twist in a knot as she hung up the phone, and her heart was about to pound out of her chest. She stood up for a moment and felt a little light-headed. *Did Dana tell him everything?* she wondered. Then suddenly, she pulled herself together and remembered why she had to take such drastic measures to get this job and how badly she wanted to keep it. For the first time in a while, she was able to pay her rent on time and utilities without the threat of something major being turned off, and she liked it. She didn't have to harass Lydia, Elise, or Sherrie for money to pay her credit cards, and she was enjoying the luxury of cable TV again. It was nice to listen to phone messages in the evening that didn't come from creditors, and now she could even think about buying a decent car instead of driving around in the 1998 Toyota Corolla her mom gave her. She was making good money, and as far as she was concerned, she'd earned it. Dana wasn't going to help her get ahead, so Chrystal just convinced her that it would be in her best interest to do so, that's all. Chrystal fixed her clothes, took a deep breath, and headed toward Dana's office. When she arrived at the door, she stood there for a second and then gave it a gentle tap.

"Come in," she heard the voice of Mr. Sanders say. She opened the door and walked in to see him sitting at Dana's desk and Dana sitting on the sofa nearby. *This doesn't look good*, she told herself, but now she knew what she had to do to provoke an argument with Dana—lie like hell.

"Chrystal, have a seat," he directed her. She sat down and glanced over at Dana, who was now eyeing her with a slight smirk on her face. Chrystal knew what was coming.

"Chrystal, we just had a discussion with Susan McKenna, and Dana has brought some very serious allegations to my attention that involves you."

He calls all of that confusion a discussion? thought Chrystal. It sounded more like a Mike Tyson versus Evander Holyfield boxing match in there, but however he wanted to phrase it was fine with her. "Your discussion involved me?" she said innocently. "What was it about?" Mr. Sanders looked at Dana and continued.

"Well, Dana claims that you have a tape of a conversation between her and Jeff McKenna and that you used this tape against her."

"What? What tape? What is he talking about, Dana?" she asked, turning to Dana.

"Oh, stop it, Chrystal. I've told Mr. Sanders everything. He knows you're blackmailing me with the tape, and I know that you called the McKennas' house last night, probably thinking it was me who answered the phone. I also told him about our conversation in the parking lot, which is why you tried to call me and play the tape," she said plainly.

Chrystal had always admired Angela Bassett and at one time thought about becoming an actress after taking theater one semester in high school. If she was going to get out of this, she would have to put on the performance of her life. *Now what would Angela do in this situation?* she thought to herself quickly. She would have to anger Dana enough to make her lose it in front of Mr. Sanders. Then in an instant, she had it and turned around to look at Mr. Sanders, who was watching her reaction.

"Mr. Sanders, I honestly don't know what Dana is talking about, and I think it's very strange that she's accusing me of blackmailing her with tapes. First of all, I don't know anything about any tapes. I'm at a loss for words because all of this is hitting me out of left field, and I don't know where it's coming from," she said, becoming visibly upset and misty-eyed.

"She's lying!" screamed Dana. "She came to me with the tape and told me if I didn't get her the intern position and a $2,500 bonus, she would send the tape to my husband. That's the only reason I recommended her, because she was going to tell Mark about Jeff and the suspension. She gave me the tape and copies after she got the job and the bonus," Dana let out.

"I don't believe how you can say these things about me, Dana," said Chrystal as tears began to flow down her cheeks. "All I've ever been to you is a good assistant. Mr. Sanders, Dana came to me about the internship. I wasn't even going to apply at first because I thought I wouldn't qualify, but she told me I would be a good candidate and that she would back me and give a good word for me. I accepted the challenge because I'd worked hard for this opportunity. If I'm guilty of anything, it's for not telling you or someone else here what I knew," she said, hanging her head.

"What was that Chrystal? What did you know?" asked Mr. Sanders.

"This is all a flat-out lie," yelled Dana.

"Dana, don't interrupt," he said. "I want to hear her side of the story. Continue, Chrystal."

"But she's a liar, and she extorted money from this company," said Dana.

"Do you want me to tell him what I did for you, Dana? You're calling me a liar, but do you really want me to share with him what really happened?" said Chrystal in a tearful voice.

"Go ahead, Chrystal," said Mr. Sanders, handing her a tissue from the tissue box on Dana's desk.

Chrystal thought to herself, *Now that I have Mr. Sanders hooked, let me reel him in*, as she went on to say, "I know it was wrong, but at the time I was just protecting my job. I knew about Dana and Jeff McKenna for a long time, and I knew that they were meeting in San Diego every time I made travel arrangements for her trips. I even covered for her while she was suspended when Paul came by looking for her. He didn't know that she wasn't going to work every day when she was suspended for two weeks. I did it because Dana found out that I knew about her and Jeff and she threatened to have me fired, and I couldn't afford to lose my job. Then after she came back to work, she approached me about the internship. I was surprised she wanted to help me, but she told me she was grateful about me not telling Paul about her suspension, and that's why she gave me a good recommendation," she said, sniffling and wiping her nose with the tissue. "I didn't have any reason to call the McKenna house or blackmail Dana. In a way, she was blackmailing me into keeping her secret. I'm sorry I didn't come to you, Mr. Sanders, because now I see I made the wrong decision," she said, turning and looking at Dana, who was now so angry she could explode.

"You lying little bitch!" Dana screamed. "I'll kill you!" she said, jumping up from the couch and tackling Chrystal out of the chair onto the floor. Chrystal screamed and tried to get up, but Dana jumped on top of her and held her down on the floor. "Tell the truth about the tapes and the money!" she yelled as Chrystal screamed for her to get off. Mr. Sanders jumped up from the desk and ran over to pull Dana off Chrystal, who was now scurrying for one of her shoes that had been knocked off in the scuffle. Mr. Sanders helped Chrystal up and pushed Dana to the other side of the room.

"Dana, you are totally out of control," he yelled. He turned to ask Chrystal if she was okay when Dana charged at her again, but this time Mr. Sanders jumped between them. "Dana, I'm warning you, don't make me call security to haul you out of here. Pull yourself together," he said, disgusted with her behavior. Dana pulled away and glared at Chrystal while Chrystal attempted to fix her clothing. A button was missing from her blouse, and the front of her stockings had a huge run in them. Mr. Sanders fixed his tie and turned to Dana.

"You said that Chrystal gave you the tapes. Where are they? I want to hear what's on them to see what all of this confusion is about."

"I don't have them anymore," said Dana, breathing heavily and rolling her eyes.

"But you just said she gave you the tapes supposedly after getting the job. Where are they if you don't have them?"

"I burned them because I didn't want them getting out."

"She doesn't have the tapes because they never existed," offered Chrystal. Mr. Sanders turned to look at Dana. Chrystal had a point. So far, Dana had made these serious accusations and didn't have any proof to back them up.

"So you have no evidence of any of this?," said Mr. Sanders.

"Susan McKenna has the evidence. She said a tape played over her phone last night," said Dana.

"Funny how you're the only one that knows anything about these mysterious tapes and Susan came in here saying that you called her home. Mr. Sanders, I resent all of this. I've worked too hard at this firm and I've been loyal, for Dana to accuse me of something like this is beyond insulting. I don't have any tapes, and I don't know about any tapes. I'm going to file charges against her for assault because this is ridiculous," said Chrystal, trying to sound distraught. Mr. Sanders looked at Chrystal and thought she had a good point. None of this made sense, and since Dana had no evidence, there was nothing he could do.

"Chrystal, if you want to file charges, I can't stop you," he said.

"Mr. Sanders, are you going to let this happen?" said Dana. Mr. Sanders turned to Chrystal and asked her to hold off on doing anything for the moment. He then asked her to leave the office so he could talk to Dana alone. Chrystal put her shoe back on, fixed her clothes, and left the office looking very upset about what had just happened but, once on the other side of the door, smiled broadly. She only hoped that her performance and Mr. Sanders witnessing Dana's assault on her was enough for him to make the right decision to get rid of her. *Angela Bassett would be proud,* thought Dana as she hurried back to her office to change into another pair of stockings and refresh her makeup and hair. She also had a quick errand to run, and the post office was on the way.

*　　*　　*

Inside Dana's office, Mr. Sanders was left to deal with Dana in private. He was very disturbed by what had just taken place, and Dana's assault on Chrystal was totally unacceptable. He closed the door and turned back to Dana.

"Dana, once again you've put me and this organization in a very difficult position."

"What do you mean?"

"I mean physically attacking another employee is not only unacceptable behavior, it's criminal. What were you thinking? If Chrystal decides to file assault charges against you, I would be forced to give a statement since I was here and pulled you off of her. You come in here and make accusations about so-called tapes that you can't produce and tales of blackmail, but you don't have any to proof to back anything up. On top of that, a former client's wife barges in here and causes a scene. This is a place of business, Dana. I can't have this type of behavior going on. Now I don't care how you conduct your private life as long as it doesn't interfere with the office, because when it does, you've made it my business, and I don't like it."

"Mr. Sanders, this has nothing to do with my private life, and this is not something I'm making up to cover my own ass. Chrystal had a tape of a conversation between me and Jeff. She blackmailed me into getting the internship and the bonus for her and threatened to send the tapes to Paul if I didn't do it.

"Can you prove any of this?" asked Mr. Sanders plainly.

"No, but she did it, and I know she was the one who called the McKenna house last night, not me."

"Dana, even if you had the tape, it still doesn't prove that Chrystal made it. It would be your word against hers. All of the assistants tape the Monday meetings. For all we know, Susan McKenna could have taped the conversation."

"Oh no, it was Chrystal's tape because she told me. I don't think she meant to tape the conversation on purpose, but for some reason, she had it."

"Well, without anything other than your word, which has been tarnished since your affair with a client, which cost this firm a ton of money by the way, I'm afraid you leave me no choice. I warned you if there were any more incidents what action we would have to take," he said regretfully.

"What are you trying to say?"

Mr. Sanders looked at Dana. "I'm sorry, but you need to clear out your office."

"What do you mean clear my office? Mr. Sanders . . ."

"You're fired, Dana. I want you out of here by the end of the day." He looked at her again, turned, and then walked out of the office shaking his head, leaving Dana to clean up and clear out of the office as he instructed.

Later that afternoon, Dana left the office with a box full of her belongings and headed out of Goldman and Associates for the last time. Chrystal watched Dana leave from her office and wondered if those assault charges would still be necessary after all. She felt a bit of relief and guilt at the same time after leaving Dana's office, but she had to play the act through and be convincing enough to leave Mr. Sanders with doubt about Dana's accusation. Now with Dana out of the way, she could get on with her job, and if Dana ever approached her again or threatened her, she would file those assault charges.

*   *   *

"Paul, I need to talk to you," Dana called out to him after she entered their home. She had been driving around town for hours, thinking about losing her job because of those two bitches Chrystal and Susan, and trying to figure out how she would explain to her husband about it. It was 8:00 p.m., and she was physically and mentally exhausted after such a trying day. When he didn't respond, she went into the family room to find him there sitting in the dark quietly in his favorite chair.

"What are you doing in here in the dark?" Dana asked as she flipped on the light.

"I got an interesting delivery today," he said, holding up a package addressed to him with no return address and a tape that was inside. Dana could have fallen through the floor to see what he was holding in his hand, and from the look on Paul's face, he had clearly listened to what was on it.

Later that evening, Mr. Sanders was working late at the office when he received a call. His assistant was gone for the day, so he answered his own line.

"Hello, may I help you?" he said.

"Mr. Sanders, it's Dana."

"Dana, what are you doing calling, and at this time of the night?" he said turning to the gold clock on his desk, which said that it was now 8:30 p.m.

"Mr. Sanders, I have the proof that a tape exists because my husband received it in the mail today," she said, her voice sounding as if she'd been crying.

"Dana, like I said earlier today, you have no proof other than your word that the tape came from Chrystal. Can you honestly say that the tape wasn't possibly made by Susan McKenna?"

"Yes, because Chrystal sat in my office and threatened me with this tape," she said.

Mr. Sanders sighed a deep sigh. He was exasperated by the day's events and the entire situation with Dana, Jeff, Susan, and now Chrystal. He honestly didn't know if Dana was telling the truth, and at this point, it really didn't matter to him.

"Dana, listen to me very closely. You came to us and gave a wonderful presentation about Chrystal's qualifications for the internship, and I've personally seen her perform when you were suspended, and she's doing a great job with Will. I've heard nothing but great things from you about her when she was your assistant. I don't know what brought on these turn of events, but I do know that we can't have is an employee assaulting another. I think I convinced Chrystal not to press charges against you so you won't have to deal with that as well. So please, just let this go and move on with your life and career. I wish you the best in the future. Good night."

Mr. Sanders hung up the phone before Dana could get in another word. Now all she was listening to was a dial tone on the other end of the phone. She placed the phone back on the receiver as she sat on the side of the queen-size bed at the Marriott Hotel. By the end of this dreadful day, she was without a job, a home, and now a husband, and it was all because of Chrystal. She picked up the remote control to turn on the TV and began to flip through the channels but couldn't think of anything else but how she would get her revenge.

CHAPTER 39

ELISE

*T*here had been so much going on in the last few days with Lydia that Elise had forgotten all about her own problems with Quinton. After they last saw each other and decided to take a break from each other a month ago, she began filling her days with work, the girls, and new hobbies she'd always wanted to try. The girls had all agreed to go horseback riding with her next weekend, and they even talked about trying white water rafting. But when Elise said she wanted to go fly in a hot air balloon for her birthday which was coming up in two weeks, Chrystal told her she was out of her mind, although Elise had decided she was going to do it anyway. She was happy for the distraction that keeping busy brought her because she was missing Quinton terribly, and although they heard from each other on occasion through text messages, it just wasn't the same. She got up from her couch to look out of the window to see that the sky was clear and a beautiful blue and the air was warm and crisp, so she decided it would be a good time to get in a jog. Just as she was putting on her running shoes, she received a call from Quinton. She answered the phone almost too quickly and was excited to hear his voice.

"Hello, Quinton?"

"Yeah, it's me," he said. "Can we meet at Cold Stones for ice cream?." he asked.

"Sure. I'd love some ice cream," she said forgetting all about her jog and imagining herself rubbing a pint of Chocolate mint ice cream all over that magnificent body.

"Okay, I'll see you there in a half hour. Is that good?"

"Perfect, she said. "See you in a few." Elise rushed into her bedroom, picked up the cutest top she could find amongst the thousands of choices in her closet, put on a pair of jeans that accented her figure, brushed her hair, applied just enough make-up, sprayed herself with Chanel No 5, grabbed her purse and was in her Lexus SUV in fifteen minutes flat. She was excited about Quinton's call although she knew when she arrived, she'd have to be cool about the whole thing and not let on. The ball was in his court since he was the one to move out and suggest they take a break. She would just sit back and listen to what he had to say.

*   *   *

It was a nice warm day, and many people had the same idea about going out for ice cream. There were families that were in line waiting to order along with couples just like themselves out together for a nice afternoon. Elise and Quinton sat at a table for two under an umbrella enjoying their ice cream. Elise decided on a Like It Cheesecake Factory in a waffle bowl, and Quinton opted for the That's How I Roll Like It. They were enjoying each other's company too, although since sitting down, they'd barely said anything to each other. Then Quinton broke the silence.

"I'm glad you could meet with me," he said.

"That wasn't hard. You know I love Cold Stone," She smiled.

"Yes, you do. I remember we used to come here all the time, even during the winter months," he said, smiling back at her. "I've had some time to think about us, and I wondered what you would think about us taking it slow and maybe seeing each other a little more."

"Do you mean getting back together?" she said hopefully.

"Well, let's see where it will lead. I want us to go back to dating before we moved in together. What do you think?"

"I think that any time with you would be special to me, and I want to do that because I really miss you," she admitted.

"I miss you too."

They finished up their ice cream and decided to go for a walk together in the park where there was a lake and benches to sit down while watching others walk by. There were young couples and older couples walking around the park, some hand in hand. Elise imagined herself and Quinton much older like some of the couples that were there. How did they keep their relationships going for so long and still be together? She wanted to find the answer to that question with Quinton. It was funny, but now that she had a chance to think about what she wanted and the answer was a life with Quinton, she could see things a lot clearer than before. She didn't want to rush into anything because she knew they had a lifetime together. But she couldn't wait to tell him about the breakthrough she'd made that surprised even her.

"Quinton, I'm really sorry about everything. I didn't handle our relationship right, and I'm sorry about hurting your feelings. You know, you never realize what you have until you no longer have it. The time we've had apart has really let me see how deeply I care about you. I hope you can forgive me," she said, looking into his beautiful light-brown eyes.

"I do forgive you, baby. I want us to start over again but slowly. We know we love each other, so we can build from there," he said, taking her hand.

Elise was a little overwhelmed by this rush of emotion. She'd always been pretty guarded about not letting her feelings show, so this was a huge step for her to take, but she took it gladly, and she knew Quinton would know how difficult this would have been for her a few months ago.

"I have a birthday coming up," she announced.

"I know," said Quinton, smiling at her.

"Do you know what I would like to do for my birthday?"

"No, what would you like to do?"

"Well, I've been taking up some new hobbies recently that I've always wanted to do. The girls and I are going horseback riding next weekend, but for my birthday, I want to go for a ride in a hot-air balloon." She smiled.

"What? What gave you that idea?"

"I don't know. I guess I just want to experience something a little different, and this seemed like it would be fun," she said, watching him. "And do you know what? I want to go with you," she said, hoping that he'd say yes.

Quinton smiled at her as if considering her invitation and then answered. "I would be honored to fly with you in a hot-air balloon." He laughed. "It should be fun."

"Wonderful!" said Elise almost too loudly. She looked around as some more as couples walked hand in hand around the park. "So where do we go from here?" she asked.

"We go forward, baby. No looking back, just straight ahead." They hugged each other, and with a quick kiss on the lips, Elise laid her head on his shoulder, happy to be where she knew she belonged, which was right by his side.

CHAPTER 40

SHERRIE

W hen Sherrie finally heard from Brad after almost three weeks, she had prepared herself for the worst just imagining what he was going to say. The time away from him had been painful, especially the way they left each other, but she filled her days taking care of Jillian and going out with the girls. They had been such a huge support system for her in this time, and Isabella stayed up with her some evenings as well talking to her and assuring her that everything would be fine with Brad.

"Even if you two decide to go your separate ways, you have to trust in yourself and know that you will be okay," she said. But she finished the sentence by saying she was praying for a happier ending. "You are like family to me, and I want my family to be happy," she said.

But it wasn't to be, at least not right away. After a brief conversation with Brad about where he was staying and how she could get in touch with him, Brad informed her that he was filing for legal separation. He said he'd thought about it long and hard but couldn't bring himself to forgive her just yet. When Sherrie asked if he would be willing to go to counseling, he was open to the suggestion but let her know he would be coming home that evening to pick up his things and would be moving out shortly afterward. He wanted to let Sherrie know that his feelings toward Jillian would never change and that he would always be there for her and provide for her. But their marriage was something different, and he needed some time away from her to know if they could survive this storm.

So while Sherrie was going through their mail one afternoon, the doorbell rang, and Isabella walked over to answer it.

"Is Sherrie Marshall at home?" the person asked.

"Yes, she is," said Isabella. "Can I say who's calling?"

"I have a delivery for her," said the person.

"I can sign for her," said Isabella.

"No, it needs to be delivered to her personally," said the delivery person.

"Very well. Ms. Sherrie, there's someone here to see you," she yelled. Sherrie walked to the front door from her personal office to greet the delivery person who looked at her.

"Are you Sherrie Marshall?" he asked.

"Yes, I am," said Sherrie.

"Consider yourself served," he said as he handed her the package and walked swiftly away.

"What is that, Ms. Sherrie?'

"It's a petition. Brad is filing for legal separation," said Sherrie slowly.

"Oh, Ms. Sherrie, I'm so sorry," said Isabella.

"So am I, Isabella, so am I," she said, watching little Jillian in the other room playing with her dolls.

*   *   *

"Brad, have you really thought about this? I mean it seems that I was served with the petition so quickly after we first spoke. You said you would go to counseling, so why do we have to be legally separated?" Brad had come by the house for a quick visit with Jillian and to pick up a few more of his things.

"Because I think it's for the best, and I've had months to think about all of this. I've known that long that Jillian wasn't my biological daughter, I just didn't tell you I knew."

"She will always be your daughter, Brad, I would never take that away. I couldn't take that away from you." Sherrie had always wondered how Brad became suspicious enough about Jillian's paternity to have a test done besides the actual timing of her pregnancy. Did Brad put it together that her pregnancy didn't coincide with their sexual activity?

"Brad, what made you have a paternity test done? Why didn't you think that Jillian was yours?" she finally asked, genuinely interested in his response. Brad looked up from his suitcase while he was packing some of his personal belongings and stared at her for a moment. It was amazing to him how stupid his wife actually thought he was to think that he wouldn't notice that something was off with her pregnancy. He was a doctor, for God's sake, and an educated man who could count, not to mention all of the times she'd disappear for hours at a time and neither he nor Isabella knew where she was.

"I was wondering when you'd get around to asking that question, Sherrie. How stupid do you think I am? I mean, just because I don't say anything, doesn't mean I don't know. I knew almost immediately the baby couldn't have been mine because when you got pregnant, we hadn't had sex in a while. I didn't want to believe it, but facts are facts. Still, deep down inside, I truly wanted to believe that you wouldn't betray me in such a way and you wouldn't go as far as to have a child from that betrayal. But after Jillian was born, you didn't stop. There were still times I would come home a little early and you wouldn't be here. Or I would call the house or your cell phone and couldn't reach you. Yeah, you gave me the old standard answer that you were out with the girls and lost track of time, but you were lying about that too. You told me one night that you were out having dinner with the girls at Paschal's, but the very next day, I ran into Chrystal at the coffee shop and asked her how your dinner went the night before, and she didn't know a thing about any dinner. I just played it off like maybe you meant another night, but I knew that you had been lying to me all along. It didn't take a rocket scientist to figure out you were having an affair, and so I hired a private detective who followed you and gave me a detailed report about where you went and with who. I guess I don't have to tell you that David is in the report along with all your secret sex hideaways," he added with disgust written all over his face. "After the affair was confirmed, I did the hardest thing I ever had to do in my life, and that was to know for sure if my own daughter was mine. That's why I ordered the paternity test. Opening that envelope and reading the results was like taking a bullet," he said as he balled up a pair of socks and threw them into his suitcase.

Sherrie was mortified. She'd read both reports, and just like Brad said, they were very thorough and excruciatingly painful to digest.

"Does David know about Jillian?" asked Brad. The question caught Sherrie by surprise, and she hesitated a moment to answer.

"No," she said finally. "He has no idea."

"I guess that would get really ugly being that he's married too, huh?" said Brad with a little sarcasm in his voice, to which Sherrie became unreasonably angry.

"You know, you act as if you had no part in all of this!" she suddenly shouted. "You were more interested in your job than in me or our marriage."

"Oh, so I guess I drove you into David's arms, is that what you're saying? I guess I also made you lie down with him, spread your legs, and get pregnant too, is that right?" shouted Brad right back. He clenched his teeth and turned away from her and then turned back to stare her in the face. "You don't get to turn this around on me. Yes, I work long hours at the hospital, and yes, I'm devoted to my work. But I'm devoted to my family too, and I work hard for my family to make sure you have a comfortable life. When I met you, you knew I was going to be a surgeon, and you knew what that was going to be about. I was out there working hard for you and Jillian, and you were out there screwing my coworker!"

Sherrie hung her head down in defeat because as much as she wanted Brad to share the responsibility for what had happened to them in their marriage, she was still the one who went outside of their marriage to seek comfort. "I don't know how many ways I can say that I'm sorry, but I am."

"Saying you're sorry isn't going to make things right. Nothing can when it comes to something like this."

"Brad, I'm begging you, please reconsider. Think about our daughter."

"I am thinking about our daughter, which is why I haven't filed for divorce, at least not yet," he said angrily. "I have to go. I'll get the rest of my things later, but you know how to reach me in the meantime." He grabbed his suitcase and hurried downstairs and then out of the house.

As Sherrie watched him pull out of the driveway from her bedroom window, she received a text message from Lydia on her cell inviting her out with the girls for dinner. She texted back that tonight wasn't a good night for her and she would catch up with them later.

"What's wrong?" texted Lydia. Sherrie didn't text back right away, and within seconds, her cell phone rang.

"Lydia, what's up?" said Sherrie, attempting to hide her pain.

"What's going on, Sherrie? Did something happen with Brad? Have you heard from him?" Sherrie was silent on the other end of the phone, trying to decide how to respond. She wasn't sure if she could tell the girls right now since she hadn't had a chance to digest what had happened. But after Lydia pressed her some more, she let it out.

"Brad filed for legal separation. We're separated, Lydia. That's one step closer to divorce." Sherrie began to sob.

"Okay, listen, I'm on my way, okay? Hang tight."

"You don't have to do this. I'll be okay."

"I'm on my way," said Lydia as she hung up the phone.

*   *   *

When Lydia arrived at Sherrie's home about an hour later, she brought reinforcements with her in the way of Elise, Chrystal, and Jasper and a huge bucket of ice cream and pound cake. Sherrie was resistant about having everyone fussing over her, but just like the spa day they forced her into, it was just what she needed to feel a little better. At least she wasn't alone. Isabella had already prepared a fabulous dinner of roast with red potatoes, green beans, and tossed salad with dinner rolls, and the house was filled with the aroma as the girls and Jasper walked in.

"Lord, have mercy, this is some kind of big house, and I can see Lydia's design all over it, honey. Good job," he said to Lydia as he scanned the corridor, dining room, and study. "I absolutely love this house!" he said as Sherrie came out of the kitchen to greet them.

"Come on in, dinner is ready," she said as she hugged and greeted each of them.

"Good because I'm hungry as a mother," said Chrystal.

"Me too," said Elise. "Let's eat." Isabella set the table and food outside on the patio. Since it was such a beautiful day, Sherrie wanted to eat outside with her friends while Jillian was still taking a nap. Sherrie was feeling better already with her girls there, and Jasper was such a character and hilarious too.

"Girl, you should have been there to see the sting operation we planted for Lionel. When Lydia and I walked in, the cops already had his ass, and he was looking like he wanted to pee on himself, didn't he, Lydia?" said Elise.

"He sure did," said Lydia, taking a bite of her salad. "I thought he was going to pass a brick when the police officer found the USB on him. Finding that on him and him inside my place was all we needed to seal the coffin."

"Serves him right for going through my things and stealing my access codes," said Jasper with a glass of red wine in his hand. "Nobody makes a fool of Jasper, you hear?" he said, clinking his glass with Lydia's. "And to think I was feeling guilty about seeing someone else," he said with a wicked smile.

"Someone else already?" asked Elise.

"Yeah, honey, and he's cute too! Jasper don't let no grass grow under his feet." He laughed while taking a bite of his roast.

"I like your thinking," said Chrystal, giving Jasper a wink.

"Oh, but the best part was finally confronting Helena," said Lydia. "I couldn't wait to get to her after everything she'd done."

"You think you know a person for years, and you never know what they're capable of. Do you girls know that all this time I had controlling interest in the business? My mother would roll over in her grave if she knew how Helena had been running the business and me not paying a bit of attention," said Jasper. "But that's all gonna change, baby, because Jasper is back!" he said, giving Lydia and Elise a high five.

"Dana got fired," said Chrystal, suddenly announcing the drama she experienced this week as well. Elise dropped her fork while Sherrie and Lydia looked on.

"Who's Dana?" asked Jasper.

"Chrystal's ex-boss," said Lydia turning to Chrystal. "What? How did she get fired? Spill, spill, girl."

"She's still been sleeping with Jeff McKenna according to his wife. She came stomping into the office and practically cursed Dana out in front of everybody. Mr. Sanders told her that if there was another incident, he would have to fire her, and so he did. He told her to clear out her desk and leave," said Chrystal, conveniently leaving out a huge part of the story. The part where she was actually blackmailing Dana and the truth would have come out if it weren't for her extraordinary acting skills. Chrystal was grateful for dodging that bullet and didn't see the need to tell the girls how she really got the job and screwed over Dana at the same time.

"I know you're happy she's gone, huh?" said Elise, eyeing Chrystal.

"I'm very happy her ass is gone. Now I can really get through this internship without her eyeing me up and down every single day. The woman put in a good word for me and then got mad when I was selected. How messed up is that?" asked Chrystal as she took a sip of her wine.

"I'm so glad those two thorns are out of my girls' lives," said Sherrie. "Does anyone want any more rolls?" she asked, noticing the basket was empty.

"I am stuffed like a pig, honey, but that was delicious, Sherrie," said Jasper.

"Thank you. Don't know what Jillian and I would do without Isabella. She's a wonderful housekeeper and cook," said Sherrie as everyone turned their attention to her. They did come over to lend their support, and they wanted to make sure she was okay although Brad had filed for legal separation.

"How's it going, Sherrie?" asked Elise. "What's going on with Brad?"

"He filed for separation, and I don't know what I'll do without him either," said Sherrie, smiling sadly at her friends.

"Is he willing to go to counseling?" asked Lydia.

"He said he was, and I've been referred to a Dr. Joy Abrams downtown Atlanta by a couple of friends who used her. She's supposed to be very good, and we have our first appointment with her next week."

"At least he is willing to go to counseling, that's a good sign, isn't it?" asked Elise.

"I guess. I just wish he hadn't insisted on a legal separation. I was hoping that we could work out our problems without going that route," said Sherrie, obviously disappointed and hurt.

"These things are hard, but you're going to get through it, and we're going to be there to help you, right, guys?" said Lydia, holding Sherrie's hand.

"You got that right," said Chrystal. "Don't worry, Sherrie, we got you. Brad will come around, give it some time." Sherrie gave the ladies and Jasper, who also looked very supportive, a huge smile. She knew the road ahead wouldn't be an easy one, but she wanted desperately to save her marriage and to keep her family together, so she was willing to do whatever it took to get Brad back.

"Yeah, everything is going to be fine," said Elise. "I need to use the bathroom," she said to Sherrie, heading inside and holding her stomach.

"I'm hopeful, but we'll see what happens. Well, enough of that," said Sherrie, not wanting to bring down their get-together. "Elise has a birthday coming up. Do we know what we want to do for her?"

"The girl is out of her mind. She told me and Lydia that she wanted to go fly in a hot-air balloon. She's crazier than a loon," said Chrystal, biting into a dinner roll.

"A hot-air balloon ride would be fabulous!" said Jasper. "You know a friend of mine did that for his fortieth birthday and had a great time. She'll enjoy it."

"Yeah, I think she will too since she's on this new hobby kick. We're going horseback riding with her next weekend," said Lydia. "You know, there's a great restaurant that just opened that we have to try. It might be a good place to go for Elise's birthday. It's called Jabot, and it has a beautiful view of the city at night from about thirty-one floors up. It has a beautiful revolving dining room too. That might be a nice place, what do you guys think?" asked Lydia as everyone nodded in agreement.

"What about Quinton?" asked Chrystal. "You know they're dating again, but Elise says they're going to take it slow."

"Well, maybe we can all plan to go out together unless they have their own plans," said Sherrie. "We need to ask her what she wants to do when she gets back," she said as everyone nodded in agreement.

"In the meantime, we're having a ribbon cutting for the Edwards project, the luxurious Westmeyer Hotel will be open for business. Jasper and I have been working practically around the clock to get it finished, but now it is!" said Lydia excitedly. "The project is finally done, and I want all of you there."

"No doubt," said Chrystal. "You know I'll be there," she said. They were all laughing and joking about the week's events including Lydia and Jasper's upcoming ribbon cutting, when Elise came back in from the bathroom and sat down slowly. Sherrie noticed her looking a little flushed and asked if she felt okay.

"I'm fine," said Elise as everyone was now aware that she had returned. "I'm also pregnant," she announced. All of the ladies and Jasper gasped with surprise and excitement. It was usually Chrystal who trumped everyone with news about what was going on in her life, but this time it was clearly Elise.

CHAPTER 41

LYDIA

*T*he highly anticipated luxury hotel, the Westmeyer, located in the uptown district of Atlanta, was buzzing with exuberated guests, including VIPs from Atlanta's high society and the new mayor of Atlanta, Kasim Reed, who entered its lavish front doors for the first time. Mr. Reed had just entered the position of mayor after beating out the incumbent, Mayor Tyndall, by a landslide. It was whispered in political circles that the recent controversy surrounding his highly unorthodox budget plan, not to mention the controversy surrounding his daughter, Kameron, in the opening of the Westmeyer Hotel, were said to have led to his defeat.

The champagne was flowing, trays of delicious hors d'oeuvres of tea-smoked chicken, bacon-wrapped pineapple shrimp, and citrus salmon lollipuffs were being served by waiters, and an excitement filled the air. Kyle Edwards and his assistant, Monica, were greeting guests as they came in and escorted them around for a short tour. Lydia looked beautiful in a long black strapless dress with her hair resting comfortably on her shoulders. She smiled brightly as guests were admiring the furnishings and decorations, all of which she and Jasper selected together especially for the Westmeyer. The hotel was one of the biggest and exclusive hotel/restaurants in Buckshead.

It featured six hundred guestrooms, indoor and outdoor swimming pools, a full spa, three restaurants, and catering services for guests to order for events. Lydia was responsible for the decor of the bedrooms, lounges, and interior restaurants. A huge undertaking, which she conquered like the experienced designer she'd grown to be. Kyle was extremely pleased with the results of his hotel. He wanted a premier look for a premier hotel, and Lydia's Loft delivered it. Now the grand opening and ribbon cutting was happening tonight, he was also pleased that they managed to stay within schedule and slightly under budget. Lydia was a wonder with selecting materials that would give a grand space like the Westmeyer a richness that any guest would appreciate. Lydia was greeting guests as they came in and spotted Kyle watching her from across the room. Kyle walked over smiling at her and gave her a kiss on her cheek.

"Lydia, this has turned out to be the most amazing project I've ever been involved with, and I owe a lot of it to you. Thank you so much for helping me pull this all together. Everything looks absolutely beautiful, and I'm getting so many compliments from our guests. I hope you have plenty of business cards with you because you're going to need them." He smiled.

"You're very welcome, Kyle, and likewise. This project has been a labor of love for me from the very beginning. I'm just so happy that I got to finish it and see the finished product, and yes, I have business cards on just about all the tables. My assistant Jasper saw to it." She laughed. "Here he is now," said Lydia as Jasper walked toward them with two glasses of champagne in his hand.

"I noticed you didn't have any champagne, and that will never do," he said to Lydia, laughing.

"Thanks so much, Jasper," she said, taking the glass. "Well, Kyle, you have an absolutely gorgeous hotel here, and Lydia's Loft did an outstanding job with the interior, don't you agree?" said Jasper, smiling and giving Lydia a shameless plug.

"Absolutely! I was just telling Lydia that she's going to have so much business she won't be able to handle it all. I want to thank you to for your part in all of this. I can't tell you how pleased I am with the results."

"My, pleasure. It's been great working on this project, one of the biggest I've ever worked on, and working with Lydia has been a joy," he said, looking at Lydia and smiling. Just then, Monica walked up to the threesome and informed Kyle that the mayor was ready for the ribbon cutting.

"Wonderful! Lydia, Jasper, please join me and Monica," he said, motioning them both with him, to which Jasper turned and looked at Lydia excitedly and held out his arm to escort her over.

Atlanta's new mayor, Kasim Reed, was at the front entrance as guests crowded around and pictures were being taken by the media for the evening news. The mayor said a few words about the hotel being a much anticipated project that would generate revenue for Atlanta and recognized Kyle Edwards as being the owner and operator of the grand venture. Then Monica handed Kyle and the mayor a huge pair of scissors to cut the red ribbon in front of the hotel entryway. They posed with the scissors on the ribbon for a moment to be photographed and then cut it together while the crowd applauded loudly. Lydia and Jasper applauded as well and hugged each other, very proud to be a part of this great moment. Then Kyle Edwards said a few words about the project himself.

"I would like to thank everyone here for attending, Mayor Reed, distinguished guests, ladies and gentlemen. This project has been a dream come true for me, and I would like to thank everyone involved for their unwavering support. To my assistant Monica Reeves, to the JP Construction Company that came in and turned a little motel into what you're seeing tonight, and last but not least, to Lydia Brown and Jasper Pearsall of Lydia's Loft. All of the beautiful interior design you're seeing was done by this young lady right here," he said, pointing in Lydia's direction. "So if you need any work done in the future, Lydia is the person to see," he said smiling as many people in the crowd turned to look at Lydia, admiring her excellent job. Lydia blushed a little but was extremely pleased with the recognition Kyle had just given her. It was a good feeling to have her work appreciated and enjoyed. She turned to Jasper, who was grinning widely and gave her a high five.

"You did it, lady," he said.

"No, we did it," said Lydia, giving Jasper a big hug. Just then, they both noticed Chrystal and Manuel walking toward them, both looking like they'd just stepped out of *Vogue* magazine. Chrystal hugged and kissed Lydia and Jasper while Manuel did the same with a handshake to Jasper.

"Lydia, I can't believe this place. Manuel and I were just inside."

"It is magnificent," said Manuel in a very sexy Spanish accent. "You're very talented as Chrystal has told me."

"Thank you guys so much for coming. Isn't everything great?" said Lydia, who now spotted Elise and Quinton walking up, both looking very sharp as well. They greeted everyone there and commented on how beautiful everything looked.

"Lydia, you've done it again. Look at this place. I know Kyle Edwards has to be pleased," said Elise.

"He is and so are we," said Jasper, almost squealing. Just then, Sherrie walked in, looking gorgeous as usual in a black form-fitted dress with pink accents in the front. Her hair was long and beautiful, and she looked better tonight than ever. She greeted everyone.

"Hey, everyone. Look at us all looking stunning, right?" she said smiling. "This is just beautiful, Lydia. I want to book a room tonight and just stay for the weekend. In fact, I think Jillian and I will stay here this weekend for a mommy-and-daughter weekend," she said laughing.

"That sounds great to me," said Chrystal. "Maybe Manuel and I will join you." They all laughed at the thought of them all spending the opening weekend in a couple of the hotel's luxury suites.

"Well, I can guarantee you that you'll have all the comforts of home and then some," said Lydia, who thought that really wasn't a bad idea at all. The waiters came by with the hors d'oeuvres, and they all picked from the variety of foods along with some champagne, except Elise, who ordered a glass of cranberry juice. Kyle Edwards came over to greet all of Lydia's friends, and Lydia introduced him.

"Everyone, this is Kyle Edwards, the owner of the marvelous hotel. Kyle, this is Sherrie, Chrystal, Manuel, Elise, and Quinton," she said.

"Good meeting all of you. We're having a little after-party in one of the suites this evening, Lydia, and you and your friends are all invited."

"That would be wonderful," she said glancing at the group, who were all nodding in agreement.

"Great, we're going to be in the Grandby Suite at the very top. See you all there," he said, smiling and moving on to speak with some other guests.

"Lydia, the man is fine. Are you interested in him because I think there's a little chemistry going on between you two," said Elise.

"I don't know," she said, blushing a little. "I don't' mix business with pleasure."

"Isn't the project over?" asked Chrystal. "You can have a little pleasure with that gorgeous man now."

Quinton and Manuel looked at each other and shook their heads. They knew this was the dynamic of their group.

"I think they've forgotten we're standing right here," stand Quinton, to which they all laughed.

"Not me, baby. I'll always know you're right here with me," said Elise, turning to kiss him in the mouth.

"Awwww, isn't that sweet?" said Lydia, looking at Jasper.

"Yeah, it is. Makes me wish for—never mind," he said, taking a sip of his champagne as everyone laughed.

*　　*　　*

The Grandby Suite was one of the best suites of the hotel, and Lydia knew it all too well because she decorated it to fit royalty. There were several people in the suite already when their party arrived, and still more were coming. The suite had a wonderful view of the city, and it was a clear night, so the lights of Atlanta were shining brightly throughout. Jasper was busy talking with two men across the room, and the others were getting something to drink at the bar. Lydia scanned the room but didn't see any familiar faces outside of her friends, when Kyle walked up to her.

"Hi, Lydia. Can you believe this room?"

"Yes, because I decorated it," she said laughing.

"Yeah, that's right, you did." He laughed. "It really is gorgeous," he said, looking into her eyes. "Walk with me, Lydia," he said, heading for the balcony. As they reached the balcony, he turned and looked at her for a second before speaking.

"I don't quite know how to say this, but I would like to take you out," he said suddenly.

"Kyle, really?" said Lydia flattered.

"I knew your policy about dating clients, but our business together is over, right? The check has cleared," he said jokingly.

"Yes, you're right, it is over, and the check has cleared. Jasper checked our account this morning." She laughed.

"Well then, what do you say? You and I taking in the sites, having a nice dinner, whatever you would like. You're a beautiful woman, Lydia, and I've been attracted to you from the beginning," he admitted. Lydia was shocked because she didn't realize he looked at her that way. She knew that they respected each other in business, but although Kyle was very handsome and eligible, she somehow didn't think about becoming a couple, but she liked the idea, especially coming from him.

"I say yes," said Lydia. "I would love to go out with you. We both deserve some downtime after the adventure we've had with this project," she said.

"I agree. You know there's a fabulous new restaurant called Jabot that I've been dying to try out. Maybe we can start with dinner there tomorrow night." Lydia smiled to herself about the fact that they had the same taste in restaurants.

"It's a date. I'm looking forward to it," she said as Kyle pulled her toward him and gave her a kiss in the mouth, to which Lydia responded by kissing him back. They stood there on the balcony holding each other and not wanting to let go for the very first time although it seemed they'd been together forever. Lydia was overjoyed with this evening that brought together a new project, a new beginning, and possibly a new man in her life. That's what life gave you when you showed the stuff you're made of, and with this new beginning, she was ready to show Kyle and the world what she was made of.

CHAPTER 42

CHRYSTAL

After Dana was fired from work, the office became a lot less tense for Chrystal as she was able to fully concentrate on work and her training. Her first presentation alone came off great, and Will and Mr. Sanders were pleased that she landed a sizeable account because of it. "I see great things in your future," said Mr. Sanders after the client signed the paperwork. "This is very good work, very good work indeed, and I have my eye on you," he said to her with a wink. Chrystal was pleased that everything was going well for her now. Mr. Sanders had all but forgotten about the unfortunate scene caused by Dana's temper, and she smiled to herself, thinking about how easy it was to manipulate Dana's emotions. For the first time, she felt she was a real contender for greater opportunities in the office. She even decided to go back to school and take some evening courses to get her bachelor's degree under her belt and then maybe even a master's degree, something she never wanted to do before. Her girls were always encouraging her to go back to school, and all of them had their master's degrees, even Sherrie, who was a stay-at-home mom now, had a master's in public relations. Chrystal regretted not finishing school and decided that now that she had the income and the PR firm would help pay for her courses, she would go back and finish what she started. She smiled to herself again as she walked back to her office at the end of the day. It was almost 6:00 p.m., and she needed to get home to get ready for her date with Manuel. They had been spending a lot of time together, and she guessed they were now officially a couple. Manuel was now teaching Chrystal to speak Spanish, and she loved how he wouldn't do anything naughty to her unless she asked for it in Spanish. She had to admit that it was a great learning tool because every time she got something right, a piece of Manuel's clothing came off. She looked at the clock again and began to put her things away and gather her purse to leave for the evening. Many of the associates were already gone for the evening, except for Will, who was usually there later than most, which was one of the reasons he was on the fast track to becoming a partner, and Chrystal was going to hold on to his coattails for him to pull her right along. She turned off her light in the office and locked the door and then went by Will's office to say good night.

"Good night, Will. Have a good weekend." She waved.

"Good night, Chrystal, you do the same, and great work again," he said smiling.

"Thank you," she said as she turned and walked out the front entryway. She pulled out her keys to her brand new black metallic 2011 Hyundai Sonata. She had traded in her old beat-up Toyota for this updated model, and she absolutely loved it. Chrystal wasn't quite ready for the Mercedes that she aspired for or the car payment. But from a distance, her girls told her the Sonata looked very similar to Sherrie's Mercedes, especially since Chrystal got all the amenities included. As she walked closer to the car, she noticed a handwritten note under her windshield wiper and picked it up to read it.

"It's not over. I'll be back and you'll be sorry"

Chrystal balled the note up and angrily threw it in a nearby garbage bin. She knew it was from Dana and could only imagine that Paul had received her package. What did she expect? She shot her mouth off to Mr. Sanders, and so Chrystal retaliated by sending Paul the tape. A deal was a deal, and Dana didn't keep her end of it. She even called Mr. Sanders about Paul receiving the tape in a desperate attempt to get her job back. Little did she know that Chrystal had already anticipated her move and offered all the tapes from the Monday morning meetings to Mr. Sanders for him to review for any recorded telephone conversations that could be used as blackmail material. Of course, he didn't find anything as Chrystal conveniently erased the damaging conversation between Dana and Jeff. Besides, as Mr. Sanders pointed out, all of the assistants recorded the Monday meetings, so the tape could have been easily recorded by a number of individuals, which didn't exactly point the finger directly at Chrystal. He was also weary of the fiasco with Dana, who in his mind appeared to be the only individual in this scenario with questionable morals and ethics. And so in an effort to bring closure to this unfortunate event, Mr. Sanders told Dana that he was very sorry about her marital woes but he couldn't take any further action since it was her word against Chrystal's and then wished her the best in her future endeavors. Chrystal thought for a second about the handwritten note and retrieved it from the garbage bin. She thought that with the help of a handwriting expert, the note may come in handy later in case she needed any more insurance against Dana, and Chrystal couldn't afford any further mistakes dealing with Dana.

Chrystal hit the button on the key ring and unlocked the car doors, got in, and quickly pulled away. She pushed a button to play a CD, and Whitney Houston's voice rang out throughout the car. "I look to you, I look to you," she sang along with Whitney. She tried to put out of her mind the note and the fact that Dana was still out there although no longer working at Goldman and Associates. She wondered how long it would be before she would have to deal with her one-on-one once again, and then she decided to sit back to listen to the music and relax because it was Friday and the weekend, and she was looking forward to her evening and night out with Manuel.

*   *   *

Chrystal put on her new minidress and six-inch heels to complete her look. She and Manuel had decided to check out the new club Whispers downtown Atlanta for dancing and then have dinner later. She looked at her clock and noticed it was almost 8:00 p.m. and knew that Manuel would be ringing the bell any moment now. She checked her makeup and hair one last time and decided that she was a complete knockout. Just then, the doorbell rang, and she answered it without thinking. It was Manuel standing there with a weird look on his face.

"Hey, are you ready to go?" she asked. "What's wrong?"

Manuel walked inside of her apartment and handed her a note.

"I came home and checked my mail, and this note was in it. Read it, Chrystal. It has some very strange things in there about you. I don't know who it's from or why it was sent to me," he said. Chrystal opened the note and began reading it. It was typed and very short.

Do you really know the woman you're sleeping with? Ask your woman how she really got her promotion at Goldman and Associates. It had very little to do with her ability and everything about blackmailing her boss and eventually getting her fired. Some people will do anything for a promotion. Watch your back because you may be next.

Chrystal was furious. *So this is how she wants to play it?* She wondered if she'd ever be rid of Dana, but now her immediate task was to explain to Manuel that this was all a prank. He didn't know the details of her promotion, nor did anyone else, including the girls, and she wanted to keep it that way.

"Chrystal, what does that note mean? I don't understand. You got a promotion because of hard work and you deserved it, right?"

"Of course, baby. This is someone playing a really bad joke. Don't worry, I'll take care of it because I know who it may be."

"Who would send me such a thing?" he asked.

"Someone who just doesn't understand the stuff I'm made of, Manuel, but she will one day, I promise." *Dana doesn't know what I'm capable of doing*, thought Chrystal. She now had a little taste of a better life, and she knew she was going to go a lot further, and she was definitely willing to crush a little insect like Dana to get there.

CHAPTER 43

ELISE

Elise and Lydia were sitting together in the waiting room of the obstetrician's office for her first prenatal examination. After Elise told the ladies she was expecting, they fussed over her like three mother hens and made sure she was eating and drinking all the right things. They were excited about another member of the group having a baby and shocked that it turned out to be Elise. Lydia was there for support since Quinton was unable to come because he was out of town on business. Lydia was flipping through magazines, showing Elise what stage of development the baby was in right now as she was carrying it.

"See, this is the size of the baby, how it looks right now at three months," said Lydia, pointing to an image in the magazine. Elise frowned.

"That doesn't look like much at all, does it? You couldn't tell the way I'm puking my brains out every morning and night."

"That will calm down after your first trimester is over. How do you feel otherwise?"

"I feel good. My breasts are getting really big and feel tender, and I can tell that my jeans are feeling a little tighter in the waist, but otherwise I'm fine."

"We're going to take good care of you while you go through this. Oh wow, I can't wait to be an auntie again. Just think, another baby in the group, that's going to be wonderful," said Lydia beaming. "How did Quinton react when you told him?"

"He was really excited. He thinks the baby is going to pull us together as a family, and I think he's right. It's just really is ironic that I didn't want to get married and now we're having a baby together that we didn't exactly plan."

"That's life, Elise. But you guys are back on track, and maybe later you'll talk about getting married again. You don't have to rush it," said Lydia smiling.

"How did your date go with Kyle? And don't leave out any details," asked Elise, changing the subject.

"It was very romantic, Elise. You know, I haven't been on a date in a minute, so I was a little nervous at first although I've worked with Kyle for almost a year on this project, but this was different."

"Of course it was, because now it's not business but romance, right?"

"Yeah, but it was really nice. We went to that new restaurant I was telling you guys about called Jabot, and the food was excellent. The dining room revolves, and you can see the entire city. It was beautiful. Then we went on a carriage ride around the city, and that was nice. We had a good time. I'm seeing him again tonight," said Lydia.

"Do you think you'll get a little tonight?" said Elise, teasing. "Because, like you said, it's been a while." Lydia nudged her.

"Girl, be quiet. I don't think anything is going to happen tonight. We're going to take things slow and get to know each other better first."

"Boring!" teased Elise. "The best way to get to know that man is in bed, everything else is incidental."

"You're crazy," said Lydia, laughing. "Everything else is incidental, yeah right."

"I'm just trying to school you. You know I'm right," said Elise as they both laughed. Then a nurse came in the waiting room and called Elise's name to go back and see the doctor.

"Do you want me to come with you?" asked Lydia.

"I'll be fine," said Elise, standing up to follow the nurse down the hall.

*   *   *

After the examination was over, Dr. Natalie Louis asked Elise to get dressed, and she would talk to her afterward. Elise put her clothes back on carefully and then sat up on the bed to wait for her return. Suddenly, there was a knock on the door.

"I'm done, come in," said Elise.

"Okay, well, you're looking good so far. I estimate that you're about eleven weeks along. How have you been feeling? Any nausea?"

"Yes, I have a lot of nausea, especially in the morning."

"Well, you can try to have soda crackers or granola bars with you to help with the nausea. You can also try some hard candy for something a little sweet. But be sure to stay hydrated as much as possible, drink water or fruit juices to help with it. Do you have any questions for me?"

"Yes, do I have any restrictions right now as far as exercise? I jog regularly, and I would like to continue if it's okay."

"Well, there is one very important thing you should know . . . you're having twins," said the doctor. "So I want you to take it easy." Elise's eyes widened.

"Did you say I'm having twins?" Elise repeated to make sure she heard correctly.

"That's right," said the doctor, smiling. "You've got two babies in there, so I want to see you again in about a month. We're going to keep a close eye on you. If you have any problems before then, please call and make an appointment."

"Okay, I will," said Elise, still stunned by the news of two babies. She couldn't believe this, and she wondered how Quinton would react since she was barely staying conscious after the news.

"It was nice meeting you. Please see the front desk to make your next appointment," said Dr. Louis as she opened the door to let Elise out. Elise walked to the front desk and was greeted by a nice-looking young woman who scheduled her next appointment for the following month. "Be sure to call this number if you need to see the doctor before your appointment or if you have to reschedule," she said smiling.

"Thank you," said Elise, and as she began to walk back into the waiting room to join Lydia and tell her the latest development before they left, she spotted a familiar face following the same woman who brought her back to the doctor's office, but she couldn't understand why she would be there seeing an obstetrician.

"Sherrie?" said Elise, sounding surprised to see her there.

"Hi, Elise," said Sherrie, looking as if she didn't want to be seen at the doctor's office.

"Girl, what are you doing here?" said Elise, waiting for an explanation.

Sherrie sighed.

"Elise, I'm here because I'm pregnant," said Sherrie. Elise was stunned, but the next question on her mind was, who was Sherrie pregnant by? She'd always talked about her and Brad not having sex; how could she possibly be pregnant?

"Sherrie, is the baby Brad's?" Elise asked quickly. Sherrie looked at her and lowered her head.

"I have to go. I'll talk to you and the girls later," she said as she followed the nurse into the doctor's office. Elise was puzzled, and she hoped for everyone's sake Sherrie was pregnant by Brad. She walked out into the waiting room as Lydia stood up.

"Are you ready?" she asked. "How did everything go?" But Elise was still thinking about her earth-shattering news and now Sherrie.

"Did you see Sherrie, Lydia?"

"Yes, I did," she said.

"Do you know why she's here?"

"Yes, she's pregnant. She told me when we were at her house for dinner the same day you made your announcement," said Lydia.

"Who's the father?"

"She won't tell me, but I don't think it's Brad," said Lydia hesitantly.

"Oh my god," said Elise, covering her mouth. She knew what she was going to do with her twins and where she and Quinton stood in their relationship. But how was Sherrie going to explain another child to Brad? She couldn't because he would divorce her for sure. Elise looked at Lydia, but Lydia didn't have any words to say about Sherrie's predicament. The only thing she knew was that she was getting herself back on track with Quinton and getting prepared to be the best mother she could be to these babies. She would show her baby the stuff she was made of and she'd learned from her mistakes. She hoped for the same thing for her friend Sherrie.

"Well, I guess we should get going. We'll catch up with Sherrie later," said Lydia.

"Okay, let's go," said Elise. "Oh, and by the way, I'm having twins."

CHAPTER 44

SHERRIE

After Sherrie's appointment with the doctor, it was confirmed what she already knew. She was pregnant again. She hadn't told all of the girls because she knew they would think she was out of her mind, especially since she was going to counseling to get her marriage back on track and because this baby wasn't Brad's either. She confided in Lydia, and now Elise knew after seeing her at the doctor's office. Little did she know that their appointments were the same day and with the same obstetrician. Sherrie was very disappointed with herself and couldn't believe that she allowed this to happen to her for a second time. But now that she was trying to get her marriage back on track, she couldn't tell Brad about this child either.

Their first session with Dr. Joy Abrams went very well, although Brad displayed anger that Sherrie had never witnessed before. She guessed that it was better to show that type of emotion in a more controlled environment. He was right to be upset, and if he knew about her current condition, Sherrie knew it would be all over with them for good. Dr. Abrams looked at Sherrie, who appeared to be somewhere else during the session.

"Ms. Marshall, do you have anything you want to say?" she asked. Sherrie came out of her thoughts and rejoined them back in their session.

She was so obsessed with thinking about how she would handle her pregnancy; she hadn't heard a thing Brad had just said.

"I'm sorry, what was that?"

"You weren't listening?" said Brad. "You see, I could talk all day long and she won't hear me," he said to Dr. Abrams.

"I'm sorry, I drifted off for a moment. What were you saying, Brad?"

"I said that I felt betrayed by what you did, Sherrie. Not only did you cheat on me, but you lied to me about our daughter." Sherrie was silent, thinking that she had done it to him again, only this time she would make sure he never found out.

"Do you understand how he would feel betrayed by your actions, Sherrie?" asked Dr. Abrams.

"Yes, of course I do."

"Do you know why you did it?" she asked. "Talk to us about the reasons why you went outside of your marriage."

"There's no excuse for what I did. Brad was working consistently and never at home. I was lonely and feeling neglected. I met someone who made me feel whole, or that's what I thought at the time. I never intended for any of this to cause him so much pain. It just happened, and I wish I could take it back," said Sherrie.

"That's good, Sherrie. Brad, do you have any response to what Sherrie just said?"

"I don't think being lonely is a good enough excuse to do what she did," he said plainly.

"Mr. Marshall, I counsel many couples, and one of the main reasons for infidelity is loneliness. Often people go outside of the marriage to get something they feel they are lacking. It's not an excuse but it's a reason."

"I understand that, I just don't understand why she didn't talk to me about it," he said.

"I tried to talk to you about it all the time, Brad."

"You tried after you'd already had an affair and had a child from it. You never told me how you were feeling before then. And so I just shut down and didn't want to hear anything from you because I knew the truth already."

"Brad, you mentioned that you suspected Sherrie had had an affair and you hired a private detective. What made you suspect?"

"Sometimes when I came home from work early and unexpected, she wouldn't be in, and Isabella, our housekeeper, didn't know where she'd gone. I would call her on her cell, and there would be no answer, and then she would call me back hours later. This was going on for a while and made me wonder. After I found out that she had an affair, I started doing a little math and realized that I couldn't have impregnated my wife. I had been very busy at the hospital and didn't realize it had been a while since we'd made love. I acknowledge that I was busy and didn't take enough time with Sherrie, I realize that now, but once the math didn't add up and neither did her stories about where she'd been, I had a paternity test done on Jillian. Needless to say, I was shocked to know the truth," he said, visibly upset.

Sherrie began to cry. "I'm sorry, Brad, I am so sorry. I never meant to hurt you or do anything that would hurt our family. I don't know what to say. I made a big mistake. The biggest mistake I could ever make."

"Could you say that your mistake would be something that would never happen again, Sherrie?" asked Dr. Abrams. "Because what we're trying to do here is to rebuild trust, and that takes a long time to do. You have to make a commitment to Brad and to yourself to be faithful to your husband and to your marriage vows. On the other hand, Brad, you have to make a commitment to spend more quality time with your wife and family."

They each looked at each other, realizing that Dr. Abrams was trying to show them that this wasn't about placing blame or pointing fingers. They each were responsible for keeping their marriage in a good place.

"Yes, I can promise that this is something that will never happen again," said Sherrie, hating that she was lying to the doctor, to Brad, and to herself.

"How about you, Brad?" He hesitated for a moment and said that he would make real efforts to spend more quality time with his family.

"Excellent!" said Dr. Abrams, looking at her watch. "Our time is up for now, but we will begin again next week where we left off." Sherrie and Brad got up from the couch, said their good-byes, and turned and walked away.

As they walked out together to the parking lot to their individual cars, Sherrie looked at Brad and asked if he really meant what he said in the session.

"Yes, I did. Did you?" he asked Sherrie.

"Yes, I did Brad. I really mean it," she said. They stopped for a moment to discuss when Brad could come by and pick up Jillian for a visit and said good-bye and left.

When Sherrie returned home, there were a lot of things running through her mind like the session with Brad, running into Elise at the doctor's office, and the pregnancy. She didn't know how her marriage would survive another pregnancy that wasn't her husband's. She thought for a moment and then turned on her computer. Sherrie sat down and thought about her options once again and then went to a site she never thought she'd ever consider.

"Abortion clinics," she said to herself as she jotted down the information. Her husband was too well-known in the city to have any procedure done there, so she would select one in another state and be done with it. Her marriage and Jillian were more important to her at this very moment. Sherrie had many regrets about herself, and this may be another one, but she couldn't allow another mistake to ruin her chances of reconciliation with her husband, whom she'd already caused more than enough pain. She found a clinic and dialed the number. The phone rang a few times, and then someone answered.

"Yes, I'd like to speak to someone about having a procedure done as soon as possible," she said. "Yes, I would like to schedule an abortion," she responded. Sherrie never took the time to think about the emotions she would experience in terminating a pregnancy. She never thought about any long-term effects it may have on her body. All she knew was that she wanted to do what she thought was the right thing, and having another baby by another man was not the right thing to do. So she convinced herself that she would rid herself of the child and be done with it. And just like that, it would be over.

CHAPTER 45

ELISE'S BIRTHDAY

*I*t was Elise's birthday, and just as she promised herself, she booked a flight for a hot-air balloon ride, but she wasn't going alone. Quinton, Lydia, Kyle, Chrystal, Manuel, Sherrie, Jasper, and Jasper's new friend, Alonzo, were all going as well, and she couldn't be happier. The brochure offered an hour-long flight that would ascend them to the heavens above while they serenely floated through the air above Atlanta while enjoying breathtaking views. There were several packages including a champagne package, which Elise chose although she wouldn't be drinking any champagne, but her girls and the men could drink all they liked. Elise was very excited, and so were all the girls. It was her first balloon ride on her thirtieth birthday, and she couldn't think of a more special way to spend it than with the people that meant so much to her. Lydia, Kyle, Chrystal, and Manuel arrived first along with Jasper and Alonzo, while Sherrie arrived just as the pilot was giving instructions on what to expect while they were in the air. They were all giddy with excitement at the thought of flying over Atlanta in a huge balloon while drinking champagne and taking lots of pictures to remember the moment.

"How many people is this balloon going to take?" asked Quinton with his arms around Elise.

"This balloon can carry about sixteen people, so another party of eight will be traveling with us," said the pilot.

"Wow, that seems to be a lot of people," said Lydia as Kyle rubbed her shoulders.

"The balloon is huge. You can take a look at it right over there before we take off," said the pilot, for which Lydia and Kyle walked over to check it out. Chrystal and Manuel joined them along with Quinton. Elise stayed back with Sherrie to make sure she was okay. All of the ladies were aware that Sherrie had been pregnant again and that she had gone to Los Angeles to have an abortion. She was gone for a few days, long enough to recuperate and then fly back home to Jillian. Brad was told that she went to Los Angeles to visit her mother for a few days, who wasn't feeling well.

"Are you okay?" asked Elise.

"I'm fine," said Sherrie.

"You're fine with what happened?"

"What's done is done. I have to save my marriage. It was the only way. Don't worry about me, I'll be fine. I'm just excited to be here with you celebrating your birthday in a hot-air balloon. Check us out, right?" said Sherrie excitedly. Elise gave her a hug, and she hugged Elise back. They walked over to the rest of the group who were amazed at the size of the balloon and couldn't wait to go up.

"We have to get lots of pictures up there," said Lydia.

"We will because I need to see the date that Elise got my ass up in a balloon. I can't even think about that," said Chrystal as everyone laughed.

"Oh, baby, it's going to be fun, and then maybe next time we'll take a balloon ride for two, huh?" said Manuel tickling her, as she giggled and yelled.

"Well, I'm looking forward to it because I've never been in one before, so this should be good," said Kyle, hugging Lydia.

Jasper and Alonzo were starting the party early by breaking open a bottle of sparkling champagne and passing around disposable wine glasses. "Is this a party or what? We're getting this party started now, honey, because Jasper don't know what's gonna happen in the air. I just hope Alonzo is there to pick me up when I fall down." He snickered as Alonzo poured the rest of the party some champagne.

"Don't worry, I'll be there," said Alonzo as Jasper clinked glasses with Lydia.

The pilot walked over to the group to inform them that the other party had arrived, although they had six people instead of the eight he originally had written down.

"Are you guys ready to go?" said the pilot.

"Yeah!" they all yelled at the same time.

"Let's go!" he waved them on. As the group all got together to start boarding the balloon, Sherrie heard a voice calling out her name. She turned around to see Brad standing there.

"I heard you guys were going on a balloon ride. Do you have room for one more?" he asked.

Sherrie was gleaming at the sight of him and just the thought that he took time out of his schedule to be with her and her friends for this special occasion.

"We've got plenty of room, Brad, come on!" said Elise, excited to see him. He walked over to Sherrie and gave her a hug, picking her up and twirling her around. The group all looked on, smiling with hopes that they would be together for good real soon.

"I said I would make an effort for more quality time, and I meant it," he said, giving her a kiss on the cheek while the others watched and clapped.

"All aboard!" yelled the pilot, and Sherrie and Brad ran onto the balloon and took their place alongside Lydia and Kyle.

"Okay, is everyone ready?" asked the pilot.

"Ready as we'll ever be, honey!" said Jasper as the others nodded in agreement.

"Well then, let's go!" yelled the pilot. He pulled on the strings, and suddenly, the balloon began to rise into the air, higher and higher until the buildings were as small as toys and cars looked very much like matchbox cars. There was a slight breeze, and the pilot steered toward the wind.

"Oh my god!" yelled Elise. "Look at this!" she shouted. Lydia, Chrystal, Elise, and Sherrie all got together, taking pictures and drinking champagne while Elise drank sparkling cider. Jasper jumped in a couple of the pictures as he hugged Lydia and Elise.

"This is great, isn't it?" asked Elise, looking at Quinton.

"Baby, this is beautiful and a great idea. Let me get some pictures with my baby carrying my babies," he said, snapping more pictures. "Soon we're going to be a foursome," he said with a broad smile. Elise hugged him tightly at the thought of their growing family and what the future would hold for them.

Kyle also got into the spirit by snapping pictures with Lydia and then handed the camera over to the birthday girl, Elise, who took pictures of him with Lydia, Jasper, and Alonzo. "We make a great team, don't we?" he asked. "You better believe it," said Jasper.

Chrystal and Manuel were hugging and looking at the beautiful scenery as the balloon went up higher. "It is a beautiful sight to see," he said. "Si, es muy bonita," said Chrystal. "Muy bien!" said Manuel, laughing. "Very good, sweet cakes, very good!" he said.

This year had been a trying year for all four of the ladies, but in their own individual way, they were able to show the stuff they're made of. Lydia's Loft was doing extremely well and bringing in more business than she had originally imagined, much of it due to the success of hotel. Lydia was now in the process of hiring another assistant and another interior designer. Helena was ordered by the court to pay damages for infringing on Lydia's copyrighted designs, and Lionel received some time for breaking and entering and attempted robbery.

Jasper was now heading up the newly titled Jasper's Den, much to Helena's chagrin. She protested loudly about the change and raised the roof, but in the end, there was nothing she could do about Jasper taking over the business. So instead of staying and playing second fiddle, she allowed Jasper to buy her out of the business. Now Jasper's Den was 100 percent owned and operated by Jasper, and he knew his mother was smiling down on him.

Chrystal was almost done with her internship and doing very well in her college courses. Also, she had not heard another word from Dana, although she would be prepared if she ever showed up again. Mr. Sanders continued to be pleased with her work and expressed on several occasions that Chrystal was on the right track for a senior position in the future.

Elise and Quinton were busy planning for their new twins and had even talked about marriage in the future, and Sherrie and Brad's counseling sessions were really helping them understand each other more. They were beginning to date again, and Brad had decided he no longer wanted a legal separation. He was now back at home while he and Sherrie continued to work on their marriage.

The ladies weren't perfect and never tried to be, but they were friends that were always there for one another no matter what, and at this moment, their lives were going up just like the hot-air balloon, and none of them could complain about that.

"Let's have a toast and a happy birthday for the birthday girl," said Quinton. "Elise, you are beautiful, and you're going to make a wonderful mother to our babies. May you have many, many more special birthdays just like this one."

"Hear, hear!" everyone yelled.

"Okay, one, two, three," said Lydia as everyone sang. "Happy birthday to you, happy birthday to you, happy birthday, dear Elise. Happy birthday to you!" They all screamed and yelled in excitement while Lydia, Chrystal, Elise, and Sherrie clinked their glasses together and hugged, happy to be together as always.

ABOUT THE AUTHOR

Linda D. Whitlock had always enjoyed reading and writing since the seventh grade when she took a journalism class in junior high school. Since that time, it has always been her dream to write a novel, and with the encouragement and support of her husband and family, that dream is now being realized. When Linda isn't writing, she is decorating, reading, and spending time with her family.

10328861R0

Made in the USA
Lexington, KY
14 July 2011